WALLS OF

RUTH WADE

First published in 2018 by Bloodhound Books

www.bloodhoundbooks.com

Print ISBN 978-1-912604-06-7

Also, by Ruth Wade

Ruth Wade also writes the May Keaps series as BK Duncan:

Book 1 Foul Trade

Book 2 Found Drowned

Dedication

For those I love – you know who you are.

Epigraph

It follows from this account that freedom is an ideal which can never be completely realised, and this ideal coincides with that of self-realisation.

All epigraphs taken from
A Manual of Psychology
George F. Stout (1929)

Introduction

EAST SUSSEX, ENGLAND
WINTER SOLSTICE 1927

Voluntary action is to be sharply discriminated from impulsive action, and deliberation from conflict of impulsive tendencies.

He is so close she can smell his cologne. It has the same spicy vegetation fragrance as the rope. The rope that is around her neck, chafing her skin and pulling at the hairs entangled in its braid. The chair beneath her stockinged feet is smooth, the wood unyielding under her heels.

Please don't ask me to do this.

He registers no surprise that she's spoken. Perhaps the words have stuck in her throat. Or perhaps she is dead already and this is one of those end-of-the-tunnel moments she'd read about. Only she can feel the soft breeze on her skin, hear an owl screeching off into the distance. Sense the passing of time. She licks her lips.

Edward, I don't want to. I thought I did, but I don't.

He is stroking her face now, a curved-knuckle slide from cheekbone to chin. It's been such a long time since a man touched her. Will they finally take things further? Consummate the stretched-out longing that had prickled under her skin for decades.

'Self-murder is not an ignoble act, Edith, because it originates from a position of power. Of control. Of choice.'

I no longer choose to do this!

Her voice is like thunder in her ears. His expression remains calm. She could move. Reach out her hand. Feel his flesh beneath his shirt. Show him that is what she craves. That she still loves him despite everything. Always has, and always will. He is too much a part of her not to. Except her arms are like tree trunks at her side. Extensions of the thick branch above her head. The one he's looped the rope around.

'There is no other way; you know that, don't you? Betrayal is the worst of all the sins they left out of the Bible. Could it be that God didn't see fit to mention it because He didn't consider it deadly? But I do. Because of you they'll extinguish my existence without a second thought. A judicial killing. An eye for an eye. And that's hardly fair as I don't consider I've done anything wrong. I'd put in a plea of self-defence if they'd let me. But they won't.

The stars are out already, Edith. Can you see them? I took the trouble once to learn the constellations but many of the patterns and shapes elude me.'

He steps away from under the holm oak's thick canopy, lowers himself onto the snow-covered ground and lies there, his hands behind his head, elbows bent, as if moon-bathing.

'It's as well you don't move for now, so I'll describe those I can remember. There's the three in a line – Orion's Belt – and above that is Gemini, the twins holding hands into eternity, Castor and Pollox as their heads. Which is the girl and which is the boy, I wonder? They've different shapes so they must be one of each … Then if you allow your eye to travel back to Orion, to the left you'll find the bright and showy Sirius commonly known as the Dog Star because it forms part of Canis Major. I've heard it said by fools and madmen that your future is written in the stars. There's a little patch of empty sky directly above the cottage's chimney. I'd like to think of it as reserved especially for you – your light, your essence. Except it will shine brighter than all those around because we are kindred spirits, entwined souls, and when I join you our star will blaze with the power of two lives cut short. Two energies that never lived long enough on this earth to burn themselves out.'

I can save you. Let me save you. I can take the blame. I'll tell them that it was all my doing. That I misled them in my confusion. You'll be free, and they might find it in their hearts to spare me because of… because of… They know the truth now. I've always known, deep down I've always known.

'Do you have any last words for the world at large, Edith? Maybe I should have insisted you leave a note setting out all those things you are so sorry for. People like to be able to wrap things up with a neat apology, and they do say confession is good for the soul. The Papists believe a deathbed repentance the most precious of the lot but I'm of the mind it comes down to trying to get in God's good books at the very last minute. A cowardice of conviction. Or lack thereof. Only none of us can know that for sure, can we? I mean, we get but one stab at shuffling off this mortal coil and no one has ever come back to tell us what fate awaited them on the other side – despite what a fantasist like that duffer Conan Doyle might delude himself with. Nevertheless, you still have time to clear your conscience over the spilling of our secret. For which you are wholly responsible and I should like to hear you admit the fact.'

I'm sorry, Edward. I'm truly, truly sorry. But I wasn't myself, I was ill. They locked me up and gave me drugs. The doctor kept pressing me to tell him things, playing tricks with my mind, and I have no idea what I said. If I did tell them about you then it was an unwilling act under duress. I promise I've never intentionally done anything to harm you. Why would I? How could I? And haven't I been made to suffer enough already for everything that's happened?

She watches him move his long limbs in a languid stretch. Then he gets to his feet, listing slightly as the muscles in his gammy leg take their share of his weight.

'This is for the best, Edith. The best for the both of us. Far neater than any other ending I can imagine – you, too, I expect. Although I don't believe you ever possessed the same breadth of vision I did. See this as a simple matter of returning things from whence they came. Equations have to be balanced and two into one just won't go. That's more your area of expertise than mine but even mathematics-dunces like myself can appreciate the impossibility of splitting certain fractions evenly. We need to keep things whole. The circle cries out to be completed. One shatters perfect harmony at one's peril ...'

She listens to his voice growing softer as he increases the distance between them.

Until we are reunited, my dear Edward.

And she steps off the chair.

PART I

FLETCHING VILLAGE

September 1926

... no one can directly observe what is passing in the mind of another. He can only interpret external signs on the analogy of his own experience. These external signs always consist in some kind of bodily action or attitude.

CHAPTER ONE

The face was ugly in repose. Saliva oozed from the blubbery lips to collect in saggy neck folds; the crumpled-paper skin, leached of colour by the long years of incarceration, had the transparency of a maggot's. The closed eyelids pulsated a little to accompany the old man's internal wanderings. Under the bedclothes the sparse body was outlined like a tomb effigy – a warrior knight perhaps or a benevolent king. But he was neither of those things, not possessing the righteousness of one, nor the compassionate humanity of the other. He'd had a reputation for greatness in his time, this old, old man. But one should not be permitted to live long enough to see achievements turned to dust and ashes, for pathetic glories to come home to roost. It was unnatural. He was a travesty of nature.

Flexing his fingers in the tight leather of his gloves, he breathed in the odour of soiled linen, the metallic tang of medication, and the musty sweetness of decaying flesh. The old man twitched in his sleep, his hand grasping at the blanket as if to pull himself back into consciousness. Good. This was what he wanted: for him to know his fate. But not yet, not quite yet.

Easing the pillow from under the head, he moved around to the side of the bed and bent forward like a hospital visitor eager to be in the line of sight. He pressed down on the barely moving chest. The old man stuttered a breath. His eyes opened. He smiled. Not in recognition, that wasn't possible, but with the unfocused sentiment of a baby.

Slowly, slowly, like trapping a cockroach, he inched the pillow down towards the face that was all trust now, the mind locked behind the features waiting for a gentle act of ministration or comfort.

And then the moment that made every second of his existence worthwhile: a flash of terrible realisation from the rheumy eyes as a spark of intelligence flickered up from some recess of the thought-to-be-atrophied brain. Would he speak? Would either of them speak? But what was there that could be said when both knew the inevitability of what was about to happen?

With a heave of emotion that could only be described as joy, he pressed the pillow down hard, laughing in his release as the old man quivered away his remaining time on this earth.

*

Edith woke with a shudder. This one had possessed more of the quality of a memory than a dream. But that was hardly surprising; she'd been having them on and off for a year now, only the deepening clarity of the sensory details marking the passage of time. The light seeping through the gap in the curtains was milky. It was early, the birds not yet full-throated in their acknowledgment of a new day. She untwisted her nightgown from around her legs before sliding out from under the bedclothes to place her feet on the cold lino. Then she stripped off, being careful to avoid her reflection in the mirror as she turned towards the washstand; try as she might to find solace in believing that a concern with appearance was nothing more than the product of shallow vanity, she didn't like to be confronted by her lack of feminine contours.

Although at thirty-six it no longer mattered as much as it had done, she could still be taken unawares by numbing regret that the fire had destroyed her body's ability to develop normally. The nerve-endings in the scars on her arms and torso prickled with something too mute to be called pain as she dabbed at them with the soap-scummed flannel. Paying the especial attention she reserved for the hot area between her legs, she wondered when it was she'd first heard of the unholy connection between cleanliness and godliness. Not with her mother's milk surely? The lesson must have been inculcated later, in the aftermath, when she was a semi-orphan and the irreparable damage had been done.

Once dressed in her never-varying attire of tweed skirt, plain white blouse, lisle stockings and black lace-up shoes, Edith mentally prepared her shopping list as she walked downstairs. She needed ingredients for the cakes she'd promised Martha Culpert would be her contribution to the church bring-and-buy. When the new vicar had arrived in the village six months ago, it had been patently obvious his young wife needed help and support to cope with the demands of her role – the reverend's head being so high in the clouds he hardly noticed when it was raining – and so Edith had volunteered herself into organising the woman. Before long it was clear that even that wasn't enough and she found herself changing library books for the housebound; ensuring the Sunday School ran on time and was well attended; filling-in for the teacher at the parish school over at Cowden when occasion demanded; and being in-charge of the flower rota.

Accumulating a reputation as a rock in the matter of good works was preferable to her previous one of the stuck-up daughter of a demented old man, but other people's welfare was exhausting. No wonder she always faced the mornings more tired than when she went to bed. Except that hadn't been the case last night. Last night they had been throwing stones at her window again, causing her to wake up slicked with fear-laced sweat. An itchy feeling that something else might have disturbed her sleep this time pricked at the back of her mind. She pushed her arms into the sleeves of her coat as she tried to remember. No, it had definitely been them up to their usual tricks. A firm line needed drawing and today was as good a day as any to let them know that, unlike hapless Martha Culpert, Edith Potter knew how to recognise when the rot was setting in.

CHAPTER TWO

Edith paused to breathe in the scent of her favourite rose bush before pulling the garden gate closed behind her. Dust puffed up from under her feet as she stepped onto the narrow path of crushed chalk that led to the lane. This bottom part of the village was undisturbed at this time of day; the carters had long since rumbled past to the fields, and the only buildings between her cottage and the road snaking into Uckfield were St Margaret's and the rectory. Hadn't there been a reason she'd intended going there later this morning? The headaches that afflicted her on an almost daily basis were developing an alarming tendency to wipe her memory like a damp sponge on slate. Whenever she allowed herself to think of it, the cold conviction that she was going the same way as her father set a tremor of panic coursing through her mind and muscles. She had to know one way or the other. A doctor's opinion couldn't be avoided much longer. If he did confirm her fears then at least she still had enough of her faculties to make preparations; whatever happened she wouldn't wait until it was too late and she lost the ability to choose.

Four ducks were waddling their way to the Moat Pond. She turned and watched their progress towards the green with its centre of water fringed with sharp-edged sedges and frondy reeds. How she wished she had some bread for them, but if she went back inside to check if there was any left from Saturday then she probably wouldn't make it to the shops because feeding the ducks was another thing with the capacity to make her forget everything else. The simple act transported her back to her childhood. To a specific time when a strictly rationed modicum of fresh air was deemed essential for the recovery of a convalescent – she must have been four or five – and after walking around the park, Granny would have to rest on a bench to catch her breath and Edith would be safe to wander away and secretly pull the bread she'd stolen from the kitchen out of her pocket. The power she possessed to make the ducks splash towards her was an exquisite moment to savour, never dimmed by repetition. Even now it made her want to cry.

Edith tucked the handle of the wicker basket further into the crook of her arm and set off for the centre of the village. The lane skirted the common where a breeze high up in the elm trees rustled the leaves like soft damask. She was nearing The Cross when she caught sight of Kitty and Sadie Cousins. Two peas from the same pod, as wide as they were tall and not an ounce of brain between them. Edith lowered her head and increased her stride, but they were having none of it.

'Coo-ee. Coo-ee, Miss Potter. Wait for us.'

'Yes, wait for us.'

They rolled to her side like barrels of flowery crêpe.

'Haricot beans we're needing.'

'Yes, beans. Scrag end stew for tea. Yum, yum.'

'Don't you reckon you should've looked out the window and clocked the sun was shining before you put on that coat?'

'We're allus hot as a boiling kipper, ain't we, Kitty?'

'Even when our feet are cracking puddle-ice …'

They kept her company all the way to Treadwell's grocery shop. The bell tinkled as the first of the sisters pushed open the door. The interior was dark and cave-like with wooden fittings the colour of molasses that sucked in sunlight through the cracks in the varnish. Smells sat in the air with no hope of escape – birdseed and pickling spice; washing soda and paraffin; smoked bacon and hair oil. Edith's eyes adjusted slowly as the Cousins peeled away to inspect the line of white linen sacks full of dried goods. It was safe for her to join the queue.

'Half a pound of best green back was it, Mrs Mountby?'

The grocer had pulled a slab of bacon off the shelf and was holding it up for inspection, a host of translucent rainbows skittering over the surface. Edith wondered what they would feel like on her tongue. Colourful. The red would taste of ripe berries, the green like freshly cut grass, yellow would be full of the sweetness of a clover floret nipped between her teeth; indigo might possess the flavour of the night.

When it was her turn to be served, she was almost sorry; the hubbub of chatter surrounding her had felt calming. A sort of sadness crept over her. That was what you got for spending so much of your life alone. It was amazing how quiet it could sometimes get inside her head. It was probably that stray thought that drew the words from her mouth.

'I was woken by the geese again this morning.'

Ebenezer Crowhurst was beside her and he yanked at his whiskers as if trying to pull forward a memory.

'Allus been honkers in Fletching, leastways you'd know that if you'd come from around here. *Homelings* we call them born and bred in these parts, *comeling* is what you is; there's some still that, buried in the churchyard thirty-five years underground.'

Edith did her best to ignore the childlike hurt at being so slighted, and concentrated on avoiding any contact with Ernest Treadwell as he passed over her butter. She never liked to brush up against his damaged flesh. The grocer had no fingers on either hand. On the right they were cut off at the knuckle, and on the left the stumps barely escaped from his palm. Their pathetic inadequacy made her think too much of her own and she didn't need reminding of that. She looked up and thought she detected the ghost of sympathy in his eyes. So she took a handful of coins from her purse and counted them out with a slow precision she knew would make him want to sweep them up and toss them into the till. This was what life had reduced her to.

Mr Treadwell clicked his false teeth. 'You have to understand, Wilf Drayton thinks of them birds as his family …'

'Happen no one else would have him. You smelt down by his privy of a morning?'

The shop filled with a general howl of laughter at *Sneezer* Crowhurst's wit while Edith pretended she hadn't heard and examined a display of baby clothes on the end of the counter. Her fingers strayed across the soft wool of a tiny jacket on the top of the pile.

'I hear he's got around to clearing that hedge of yours at the back. Not before time.'

'It isn't my hedge, Mr Treadwell. It would never have got into that state if it were.'

Beside her, the butcher's wife shook her head. 'It's a crying shame the churchyard's in such a state these days. Doesn't do your garden justice, what with you being next door an' all. I was only admiring your roses the other day, Miss Potter. Proper healthy they are. I've got black spot on mine summat rotten and even Old Ma Taylor's remedy won't see it off.'

'Well, it wouldn't.'

Despite herself, Edith couldn't resist showing off her superior knowledge. If there was something the whole village should be in awe of her for, it was her ability with roses.

'It's only a scientific approach will work. You can use wettable sulphur but fixed copper sulphate powder is more effective; I get mine sent down from the Royal Horticultural Society to make sure it's absolutely pure. Mrs Culpert inherited some hybrid teas in an awful state and I've been dredging them with it every Sunday after church. I could write out the details if you'd like.'

'What? And where would I get money like that to spend? It's all right for some.' Mrs Gibson shifted her bosom as if some loose change would fall out from under.

Edith turned her back on the lot of them; she should have known better than to think they cared what she thought. The bell jangled overhead as she left the shop, a beribboned fancy blue baby's bonnet nestling in the bottom of her basket.

CHAPTER THREE

'They were out there, I tell you, banging on my window.'

'Now, now, Miss Potter. Don't you go getting yourself all het up. There was a bit of a blow last night; Mrs Billings woke me up and said I was to go and check the tiles on the roof weren't slipping. You women do like to go worrying yourselves over things not worth a ha'penny's fretting. I reckon it was that tree of yours out back.'

'Do you think I can't tell the difference between a branch and children set on mischief.'

PC Billings pulled his watch from his pocket and tapped the glass. This was a delicate matter. He had to choose his words carefully. The churchyard was the latest place the kiddies had taken to running around right enough, passing warm evenings leapfrogging gravestones having more attractions than helping their mothers, but Edith Potter was … what was the most generous way of putting it? She was a tad prone to outbursts of the hysterical variety. Take that business last week over Wilf Drayton's geese. Like as not they were making a racket fit to wake the dead but that didn't give her call to be throwing anything she could lay her hands on at them. Wilf had brought one of the poor birds into the Police House with a gash the size of a tanner on its head. Shat all over the counter, it did. Took him ages to clean it off, even with the help of some of Mrs Billings' Vim. Sometimes he wondered if his job was not so much keeping the peace as simply ensuring that everyone rubbed along well enough – a thankless but never-ending role in itself.

He sighed as he pretended he'd actually been looking at the time, before returning his watch and patting it against his chest. What he wouldn't give not to be stuck indoors with paperwork on such a fine day. Not that he'd bother to write this up. He'd have filled a dozen of his notebooks by now if he took every one of Edith Potter's complaints seriously. But just because she was in and out of his door as regular as clockwork didn't mean she'd worn out his compassion. Who wouldn't be up to building mountains out of molehills when they'd had such a shock fresh on twelve months back, the like of which would've stopped weaker hearts at the sight? Blaming herself was probably at the root of her fancies. She'd been known by all about as only leaving the village when a trip to Uckfield to pick up his medicines was called for. And to come back from one of the same to find her father dead in his bed. Not that she acted grieved at the time, but was doing so now right enough. They never caught up with whoever did the terrible thing. Broke in thinking there was money lying about, like as not. The vicar was coming out of the rectory and had seen a man running over the fields. They'd been left with no conclusion to draw but that it was a Gypsy or tramp long since back on the road when the alarm was raised. But just because such occurrences were as rare as hen's teeth didn't mean the body on the receiving end wouldn't go suffering under the thought of strange noises and the like weren't it happening all over again.

'It's coming up for when I usually pop upstairs for a cup of tea and slice of Mrs Billings' fruit cake, so now's nigh on perfect to come back with you and see if I can't do something about taking a pruning hook to that tree.'

He smiled with what he hoped was reassurance that it would cure the problem once and for all but the only response he received was a deepening of Edith Potter's sour expression.

'And then I'll be seeing it as my duty to be knocking on a few doors to spread the word that the law will be patrolling the churchyard and will be jumping on any child I see playing within a dozen yards of your cottage. No one takes kindly to me appearing on their doorstep with their nipper in tow so they'll be making sure there's no chance of you not being undisturbed – if only to spare giving the neighbours something to gossip about.'

All eventualities covered, Paul Billings placed his helmet on his head and adjusted the chinstrap before holding the Police House door open for Edith Potter to lead the way out onto the street. He was feeling mightily pleased about the way he'd handled what could have been a sticky moment. As ever, all it had taken was the effort of putting himself in the other person's shoes and setting his mind to thinking about how he would see the world if he wasn't fortunate enough to be a policeman, and didn't have such a settling being as Mrs Billings to come home to of an evening.

He locked the door behind him and caught up with Edith Potter at The Cross. She was staring straight ahead as if she could see something in the distance other than the ordinariness of Fletching. And whatever it was, it wasn't going any way to soothing her unquiet mind. His heart squeezed; it couldn't be much of a life to be alone with nothing to look forward to but getting older. His own time to experience one or both of those things would come right enough but he hoped he'd have the wherewithal to make a better fist of holding onto at least a little bit of happiness. Except maybe the truth was that she hadn't ever had any strong enough to stand the test of time. But he was a firm believer in it never being too late to put things to rights and wondered why attending to her father day and night had been replaced with the mixed bag of delights that was dispensing Christian charity in the stead of dithery Mrs Culpert, and quarterly trips to Cowden WI with Mrs Billings.

They kept an uneven pace until they reached her cottage. It was as if she had arrived at it unaccompanied as she pushed open her gate and stalked up the path without a backward glance. PC Billings tussled with his conscience for a moment about whether to insist she let him into her shed in search of a pruning hook for that tree. Only they both knew he'd been fobbing her off – not unkindly, he hoped – and that cutting down a branch or two wouldn't bring a stop to her feared imaginings when her wits were lost in the recollection of strangers intent on murder.

He waited until he heard the front door bolt being rammed home before trudging up Green Lane. His feet had started to swell already. He looked down at his highly polished toecaps. Tight in the heat though they were, he was very proud of these boots. It was wanting a pair of them that made him join up in the first place. He took a shortcut across the common in the hope the soft ground would be a little kinder than pot-holed chalk, and rejoined the lane just before it met the High Street where he came across a gang of children hunkered down around something. They were a mite young to be amongst those haunting the graveyard but it wouldn't hurt for him to invest a little of his flagging energy in ensuring they grew up to be good little citizens all the same.

'What have you gone and found yourselves here, then?'

There wasn't a ripple in their depth of concentration. He crouched down to join them. His knees creaked in a way that made him wonder if he would ever get up again. It was a desiccated frog, perfectly flat, its legs splayed as if it was sunbathing on a lily pad.

'I reckon it was the horse stomping what done for him,' said a boy with a snotty nose.

PC Billings recognised him as William and Betty Shoesmith's youngest.

'You stay in the road much longer and a horse and cart will be running over you, too.'

Paul started to laugh but caught the expression peeking out from behind little Elsie Markham's tangle of fair hair.

'Now don't you go fretting yourself over a little police humour; a nag with only one eye and a blinker would be able to see little nature-lovers like you from the bottom of the rise. But I have a mind that you should be getting yourselves home for a spot of bread and jam to keep your strength up – where I should be, in fact; Mrs Billings is most particular on not leaving the fruit cake out of the tin for too long.' He straightened up. 'Why don't one of you slip this poor victim of a traffic accident into your handkerchief – Freddy, it's not looking like you've been using yours much – and give it a decent burial? Not in the churchyard, mind, or the vicar will be having something to say about it. And while I'm telling you where you're not to be at, stay away from the Moat Pond. I know a little splashing is attractive to kiddies but it's dangerous. Frogs like that one there should stay in the water and not try to walk up the road while you lot,' he wagged a finger at each of them in turn, 'should stick to this end of the village where your ma can keep an eye on you. Now, hop it.'

Paul Billings chuckled at his unintentional joke and walked away with an exaggeratedly heavy tread to remind the little scamps that there was more than one way to squash an excess of misdirected energy.

CHAPTER FOUR

The obscenity Edith found on her path the next morning was an omen. Something to remind her – as if she needed it – of the portentousness of the day ahead. In a few short hours whatever was left of her peace of mind could be destroyed forever. She returned to the cottage to fetch the coal shovel. Her back muscles protested as she bent to scoop the object into her handbag. It was very, very flat. Nothing but a dried husk of its former amphibious self. Tempting though it was to present it as evidence of an escalation in the taunting, she knew she'd only be tolerated, humoured and patronised in turn before the incident was waved away with one snap of the elastic around PC Billing's notebook. He cared nothing about the burdens she had to live with. Witness the fact that he'd totally ignored her request to come and cut down the tree branch. No, she would save this for when she was less tired. When she had more energy than she needed to survive whatever other horrors the day had in store for her.

The dead frog secure in its black leather coffin, Edith walked down to the road to catch the bus into Uckfield.

*

'So, how are you … well … you know, coping?'

Dr Mackie picked up a pencil and started twirling it between his fingers. Edith remembered his clumsiness at attempting conversation from when he'd attended her father. On those occasions the physician had delivered his diagnosis of a chest infection or gastric upset, then dithered in the hall checking the instruments in his bag as he asked how the roses were doing or if she thought the weather was going to brighten up in the near future. This question carried the same connotations of polite necessity. A portly man with red-veined cheeks and receding sandy hair, his diffident manner had never struck her as being one to set the medical world alight but he was a competent general practitioner. And, more importantly, the devil she knew – although up until this moment she'd never had to call on his services on her own behalf. Despite her childhood trauma she'd been blessed with absurdly rude health, and on the rare occasions she'd been unwell had visited the chemist or treated herself with natural remedies. But this malaise was beyond those options. No fancy-packaged bottle of tonic or foul-smelling herb decoction could stave off the slow disintegration of the mind. Let alone cure it. Except, of course, neither could any doctor. Knowing what to expect was the best she could hope for.

'I've already told you about the headaches, insomnia, and memory lapses; in view of them, how do you think?'

She knew she wasn't helping her cause by being so snappy but, try as she might, she couldn't quell her anxiety enough to stop being defensive; she'd been particularly prickly under his interrogation concerning her bowel habits; although she had been spared the worst. On the fifteen-mile journey over, the dread that had been palpable from the moment she'd made the decision and wrenched herself out of bed had deepened until it had wiped out – and replaced – every other thought in her head. That he might insist on conducting a full physical examination. To have to go through the ordeal of explaining how she'd got the scars, and then to be forced to reveal the rest … But, mercifully, he'd contented himself with a look down her throat, in her ears, and a listen to her chest – through her blouse – with his stethoscope. After each procedure he'd pronounced the results satisfactory. So now they both knew there was no malignant germ behind the reason she was sitting in his consulting room. The discovery was apparently causing him a level of discomfort commensurate with her own.

'Yes ... quite ... What I was actually referring to was your emotional state. After your father's mur ... untimely death. Things can't have been easy.'

The tension of waiting for him to stop pussyfooting was becoming unbearable and she thought that if he didn't desist fiddling with his pencil she'd be unable to prevent herself from reaching across the desk to snap it in two. She stared over Dr Mackie's left shoulder at the print of a stag posed majestically on top of a heather-clad mountain as she considered what to say. Caution at revealing any of her failings had become so second nature that it was a struggle to find the right words to express herself. On this occasion she was aware that pride too was playing no little part in her reticence. But hiding the truth wasn't going to get her the accurate prognosis she wanted.

'I find myself somewhat adrift without the routines of caring for him – the days can often seem longer than simply sunrise to sunset. And having the house violated by the entry of a stranger has resulted in a certain amount of jumpiness ...'

'Quite understandably ...'

But it was more than that; she knew it was more than that. Her father's dedicated inquiry had been into why some people survived life's traumas with their minds and personalities intact whilst others were unable to assimilate the experiences and turn them into memories. As far as she knew, he never reached any conclusions, but if he had would she have been forced to concede the same weaknesses in herself? This was a waste of time. She shouldn't have come. She'd ask her one burning question and then leave.

'Could it be I'm suffering from a form of inherited madness?'

Dr Mackie placed the pencil precisely parallel to his notebook and sat back in his chair. He raised his caterpillar eyebrows.

'My dear, Miss Potter, is that at the root of your concern? Why you've elected to see me today? If so, I can knock that notion on the head this minute. Let me remind you that your father was one of the most intelligent and highly respected men in his field; do you think he could have earned his place as a pioneer in the treatment of neurasthenia in combatants with the time bomb of his own mental disease ticking away? Because such a thing must have been in his blood at birth in order for him to, in turn, bequeath it to you. And the evidence shows that couldn't possibly be the case. As he was over twice your current age when he succumbed, his decline was undoubtedly due to senility; a softening of the mind brought about by the advancing years. Although none of us can be certain we might not be similarly afflicted when our life force begins to dwindle, it is not something we should fritter away our middle years worrying over. The time on this earth allotted to us is ours to live, to make the most of ... Tell me, what do you do with yours?'

The change of direction was so unexpected that Edith was wrong-footed; her assumed composure crumbled and she found – to her acute distress – that tears were filling her eyes.

'I ... I keep my garden. Undertake various things on behalf of the vicar's wife ... I read ...'

'What? Romances, detective fiction?'

'I have a subscription to *National Geographic*. And sometimes I take out books from the public library on the history of scientific discoveries; or perhaps a biography.'

'All very worthy but none likely to afford you much in the way of light pleasure, I'd have thought. Is there nothing you partake in for the sheer fun of it? I appreciate in the light of your loss being so relatively recent, that what I am about to say might draw down an accusation of insensitivity, but wasn't there some hobby or pastime that you might take up again? Re-establishing old routines can go a long way in recovering from grief, in fact I'd go so far as to say that they are necessary.'

Edith wanted to be able to make something up, to invent a youth filled with exciting activities she'd simply been waiting for permission to lose herself in once more. But her life had never been any less bleak than it was now. By the look on his face, he knew it too. In the seconds before her gaze dropped, she saw Dr Mackie's understanding slide into pity.

'Too often these days I see women left to face life alone – one of the many terrible consequences of the Great War, I'm afraid. In nearly every case having like-minded souls around to raise the mind above the mundane demands of simple existence can help dispel the introspection of isolation. My diagnosis is as plain and simple as loneliness, Miss Potter.'

Surely she should be feeling relief? But instead a profound humiliation flooded her soul. To be so condemned: on the one hand as utterly ordinary; on the other as someone whose suffering was entirely a product of their own nature. She wanted to put a stop to this by asking for the bill, except her mouth was too dry.

'And I have access to a suitable remedy I'm going to take the liberty of prescribing. There being a reliable bus service into town, I'd like to suggest to my lady wife that she invite you to join her little group. They meet once a fortnight to chat over topics of mutual interest … music, I suspect, art appreciation and the like … intellectual pursuits at any rate. Most certainly generating the type of absorbing and stimulating conversation you'll find just the tonic you need to take you out of yourself. What say you? Shall I make the recommendation?'

Nothing would induce her to become a curiosity to be probed and prodded, and gossiped about the moment she left the room. But she nodded in a way he'd interpret as considered acceptance, before, at long last, bringing up the subject of settling her account.

CHAPTER FIVE

The man at her garden gate could only be described as loitering. If he was a salesman then she would see him off before he stepped foot on her path. Except the doctor's damnation had left her unsure of being able to handle even the most perfunctory of interactions. For a moment she considered hopping over the churchyard wall and letting herself in the back door but decided that such cowardice was not going to help her any. With a determination that was skin-deep at best, she tucked her chin into her chest, lengthened her stride, and fished her key from the bottom of her handbag; she didn't want to be caught fumbling when it mattered most.

'Hello, Edith.'

She had to look up at that.

'I thought it was you sitting at the back of the bus but didn't think it fair to surprise you in the company of strangers. You haven't changed a bit, you know.'

He was only a yard or two away now but the low sun was behind him causing her to squint, and obscuring any detail more refined than his shape.

'Don't you remember me? It's Edward. I must say it's not very flattering to realise the years have treated me so badly.'

Edith dropped her key. He paced the space between them and picked it up.

'Let me deal with that. This must've come as quite a shock. You are going to invite me in, aren't you? I have come a very, very long way.'

Her throat was so tight she couldn't reply. Edward. He had walked down the path and was putting the key in the lock, his broad shoulders familiar at last. Edward.

*

He filled the armchair in the parlour as if it had been made for him, his long legs stretched out in easy relaxation. Edith waited for the tea to brew in the pot and watched him gazing around the room; free to examine his features, she noted that he had been ruthlessly accurate about the passage of time. He'd been twenty-eight when she'd last seen him. His skin, which had tanned so healthily, was now the colour of walnut juice; it made the tattered-edged scar on his temple stand out. A face matured into elegance and with the same laughter lines – only deeper and longer – that had always led you to believe he hugged a secret joke.

He turned his head sharply and brought her scrutiny to a blushing halt. She leaned over the tray on the table in front of her, re-centring the teacups on their saucers.

'It will have to be with milk; I'm afraid I've no lemon.'

'So you haven't forgotten everything about me then?' His voice danced with gentle mockery. 'Can I move now? I mean, there's only so long I can sit like a portrait subject while you take in the changes ...'

Edith felt her cheeks grow even hotter as she fiddled with the sugar cube tongs.

'Why are you here, Edward?'

The question could no longer be avoided; even though she wasn't sure she wanted to know the answer.

'You were the first person who came to mind the moment I stepped off the boat ... Well, to be more honest, I was overwhelmed with the compulsion to see you ... Because, the truth is, my dear Ede, that you've never been out of my thoughts.'

She bristled at his use of her private name: he had no right to assume a re-kindled level of intimacy so soon – perhaps, ever. She stirred the contents of the teapot, cringing at the rattle of china against china as she replaced the lid. If only she could stop from shaking, give the impression of outward composure at least. He must've noticed. But then what did he expect? This was the second time he'd come back into her life unannounced and initially unrecognised. They'd known each other as children. The Head of the Psychology of the Special Senses lab had often consulted with her father over cases of traumatic accidents and Edward had been one of them. His presence in the house had been a welcome change in routine and they'd politely played together. The visits had dwindled until over a decade had gone by without their paths crossing. Then, one day, a handsome stranger had knocked on the door and asked to speak to the skinny girl who lost her temper when defeated at tiddlywinks. Although she hadn't known any other young men to judge him by, his easy humour and obvious interest in getting to know her again had enchanted her over the months that followed. And then the trouble had started …

'You said you came off the boat; have you been away?'

She focused her eyes on his chin as she passed him his cup of tea. His hand hovered in the air for a moment before taking it.

'Virtually the whole time since we said goodbye.'

That explained the unusual nature of his clothes; the jacket was foreign cut – long and loose-fitting with narrow lapels – his trousers were baggy with no turn-ups; both made from a lightweight material of a greenish hue. His hat, which was now resting on the floor beside the chair, was a slightly grubby battered Panama. A traveller then. Had he been running away for eleven years? But that was unfair: not everybody made their choices on the basis of escape.

'Doing what?'

'Oh … this and that.'

Edward drank his tea, tipping his head to one side as he regarded her. If he felt any awkwardness or embarrassment at their meeting again then he wasn't showing it. Why should he? He'd had longer to prepare for the encounter than she had; she'd only been aware he was still alive at the sound of his name.

'How did you find me?'

He gave her his familiar lopsided smile and Edith couldn't help but unbend a little.

'It wasn't difficult. I corresponded with Dr Myers – you remember him, don't you? I learned your father left Cambridge virtually in my footsteps to retire to an out of the way place in Sussex. The newspaper clipping – which was six months out of date when I got it – mentioned the name of the village ... I was so very sorry to read about the terrible manner of his death, Ede. The Lord knows he was never going to be on my Christmas list after the way he treated me but no one should have to leave this earth in such a way.'

She'd never been privy to the details of what had led to Edward's banishment – which he'd conveyed in a note she'd thrown on the fire in anger at his apparent unwillingness to fight for her, and then cried over for days that she hadn't kept. When she'd thought about it since then she had wondered if her father hadn't miscalculated and it had only been the clandestine nature of the relationship that'd made it burn so intensely, and stretch to fill eighteen blissful months.

'Things must have been extremely difficult for you.'

Not quite the doctor's words but close enough to make her wince. She busied herself with dribbling the last of the stewed tea into her cup.

'Yes, thank you. I'll put the kettle on again and make another pot. It won't take a minute.' She shifted her weight forward to rise from the sofa.

'Not for my benefit, please. I've drunk more than enough dishwater in the last week. I'm sorry, that sounded unforgivably rude. What I meant to say was that years of thick black coffee and strong maté have inured my palate to the extent that I can no longer appreciate delicate flavours. There ... have I scrabbled back onto safe ground and regained my beachhead?'

Edith's throat tickled seconds before the laughter burst out. This man – Edward – sitting across the room as if he belonged there was making her happy. She hadn't been expecting it – neither the companionship nor the lightness of mood – but she was glad he'd come. Pleased to have him teasing her out of her over-serious nature and self-preoccupation. She allowed herself to imagine a future full of them taking each other back to the younger, if never entirely carefree, selves they had been. Only she didn't know if now that his curiosity, desire, urge, to see her again was fulfilled he might not simply vanish from her life once more. Her breath fluttered in her chest at the prospect. She lined up the sugar tongs on the tray.

'You never … I mean … are you … married? Have a family waiting for you in a foreign port somewhere?'

Now it was his turn to laugh. A deep rumble that filled the space between them.

'Good heavens, no. A rolling stone, me. Never really settled in one place long enough to put down what you might call roots.'

He crossed and uncrossed his legs.

'In all truth there might have been one or two occasions when the opportunity could have presented itself, if I had been that way inclined. But even if I had been genuinely tempted, it wouldn't have been fair on the young ladies in question. Because there was never any avoiding the truth that I gave my heart a very long time ago.'

Edith met his gaze directly for the first time. When she saw the depth of his seriousness, she flushed. But she didn't look away.

'I carried a picture of you in my wallet. Do you remember? We were standing under the big oak tree and one of the officers your father was treating for shell-shock had taken up photography to help him get over things. There he was intruding on our precious time, insisting we put our heads closer together or place a hand up against the trunk or whatever else it was he wanted for the perfect composition.'

Did he really think she could have forgotten? It had been 14th June 1915. Her father had been attending a medical conference, leaving them free to sneak off for a picnic in celebration of her twenty-fifth birthday. Edward had borrowed a motorbike and she'd never been so exhilarated by anything before – or since. Her blood had still been tingling when he'd parked up and suggested they finish the last bottles of beer sitting in her father's rose garden. He'd picked an unblemished yellow blossom to tuck in her hair.

They'd kissed – sweetly and chastely; if she concentrated she could still recall the tiny bubble of saliva he'd left on her lower lip.

'I was so angry with him at the time for disturbing us, but blessed him for it ever after. Without that snapshot I'd have had to rely on my memory to conjure you up, living with the knowledge that over time it would fail me until, one day, it would let me down completely and I could no longer picture your face in all its perfect detail.'

He reached into his jacket pocket and pulled out a pipe and tobacco pouch which he held up for her inspection.

'May I?'

Edith got up and fetched her father's ashtray from where she'd hidden it away in the sideboard. She placed it on the arm of Edward's chair. He brushed her hand with his as he repositioned the heavy cut glass.

'As I said, you haven't changed a bit. You were, and have remained, a beautiful woman, Edith.'

All those forgotten girlish, bubbling, heady feelings came back in a rush. Edward had been her first – and only – love. Anyone could have predicted that after such a dispassionate and cloistered upbringing when she finally fell, she'd fall hard. And because she'd been sent away at the height of their shared emotions she'd never had to discover whether Edward could accept the realities of her own ravaged body as calmly as he did his. Perhaps she should be grateful to her father for insisting it was her patriotic duty to undertake urgent War Work in London: disillusionment being infinitely more difficult to live with than idealised longing.

As if he were still dictating terms, the old man's clock in the hallway chimed five. Edward stopped packing his pipe and uncurled himself from the chair.

'I'll smoke this whilst waiting for the bus. There's only two a day; how silly of me, of course you know that. I've taken a room in Uckfield – I hope you don't mind me staying in the vicinity but I had entertained the thought that it might mean we could see each other again. I mean, if you want to, that is?'

Edith didn't trust herself to speak, settling for a chin to chest nod instead.

'Grand. I've no pulls on my time and enough wherewithal to indulge myself as a man of leisure, so am available whenever it suits you. Drop me a note care of the Chequers Hotel.'

'Why don't we fix something up now?' The suggestion was out before she realised she was going to make it. 'We could go for a picnic …'

She watched his features grow soft with delight. He held that day precious, too.

'… Sunday, after church. But don't come and pick me up; the people in this village have nothing better to do than mind everybody else's business.'

'Ah, say no more. We wouldn't want to give them anything to gossip about so early in our rekindled relationship, would we, Ede?'

The room filled with his laughter as Edith cursed her newly awakened tendency to flush with emotion.

'The Uckfield bus stops at Tilgate. There's a lovely copse there with a watercress stream. If we said we'd meet on the road by the entrance to the trees at around one o'clock then whoever's bus is there first shouldn't have to wait too long for the other to arrive. I'll take care of the food.'

'Then consider my contribution to supply the drink. And I'm sure the hotel can spare a couple of rugs. I've a pair of binoculars we can use for bird watching. It'll be just like the old days, won't it?'

It wouldn't, she knew that. But it would be close enough not to matter. Edward leaned forward, and for one heart-stopping moment she thought he was going to kiss her. Instead he picked up the ashtray, placed it safely on the table, and held out his hand. Edith felt her fingers enveloped in his warm, firm grip.

'Until the day after tomorrow then. I'll see my own way out.'

And he was gone.

CHAPTER SIX

Edith couldn't remember the last time she'd been blessed with such a good night's sleep. The lack of nightmares had left her deeply rested, which was just as well as she had so much to do today. She turned to a fresh page in her housekeeping notebook and jotted down the order in which she needed to do things. First, get the range blazing so she could heat up enough water – she should do that prior to leaving for the shops. Then, when she got back, launder her best skirt and the blouse with the lace around the neck. The flat iron would need heating up too.

She'd reached task number fifteen when she was seized by the realisation that she needed to do something about herself; not in the looks department, she'd already thought of everything she could possibly achieve in that regard, but how she could be transformed into a stimulating companion. Someone he could conceivably spend an entire afternoon with without being bored. The answer wasn't long in coming: there was a pile of *National Geographic* in the front room. All she had to do was sit down and cram; at the Ministry she'd been the best at picking up the salient points in the daily briefing reports and remembering topological facts couldn't be nearly as hard as assimilating codes and ciphers. Armed with a little knowledge, she'd be able to get Edward to talk about his exploits. It would entertain them both and – this was the real beauty of the idea – allow them to share in the years that'd separated them. She wrote *become interesting* in large capitals at the bottom of the page, underlining it twice.

*

The shopping for the picnic didn't get off to the best start. The blackboard above Mr Gibson's head showed what the butcher had to offer – and the prices. The lamb cutlets she'd been hoping to cook and serve cold were out of the question. It would have to be sausages instead. Her next decision concerned how small a piece of beef she could roast for the sandwiches. Which reminded her that she should get to the bakery whilst there was still a choice between a split tin or bloomer; the former could be sliced thinner but perhaps Edward liked thick crusts? There was so much about his tastes she didn't know. What if he'd picked up some sort of digestive disorder on his travels and could only stomach fruit and vegetables? Just in case, she'd pick some apples from the rectory trees; some Victoria plums, too, if there were any the birds hadn't pecked.

All her dithering – and Gibson's inability to move faster than a snail's pace – meant it was over two hours before Edith had bought all the food on her list. She was standing opposite the Police House when Martha Culpert careered around the corner looking hot and flustered.

'You'll burst a blood vessel if you don't slow down.'

'Miss Potter.'

'Edith, I've told you before, just call me Edith; anything else makes me feel about a hundred.'

Martha tried a wobbly smile as she danced on the spot like a skittish racehorse.

'I've had bad news and it's thrown me somewhat. My sister's been taken poorly. In fact she's never been right since being delivered of the baby, only this time the doctor says there's nothing they can do but operate. She's to go into hospital and I'm scared she won't come out again.'

'Seeing something in its worst light isn't like you, Martha, you usually think things will always work out for the best.'

'Well, yes, I suppose so. But her husband upped sticks and left a month back saying she was impossible to live with and I'm to go to Bath on Monday to look after the children. Except I can't help fretting that if anything does happen then they'll either have to come here, or I'll need to persuade the vicar to petition for a living in that city and we've only just settled into village life.'

Edith could see the tears getting ready to fall and decided that brisk practicality was the only way to save Martha the embarrassment of breaking down in the street and having the church full tomorrow with those wanting to gossip over the cause.

'I'll cover your slots on the flower rota and organise Mrs Halstead with the cards for the confirmation classes – she can give them out at next week's Sunday School. The collection of clothes for the poor can wait until the end of the month and I'll fit that in when I do the library rounds.'

'Everyone is being so terribly kind. I was going to cancel the bring-and-buy but Mrs Shoesmith said she'd take over the running.'

'Which is what she should've done in the first place if you ask me. Anyway, is there anything else?'

'The refurbishment of the hassocks by Lewes Embroidery Guild; it'll be our first Christmas here and I'd hate for there to be anything about St Margaret's that wasn't absolutely perfect.'

'One way or another you'll be back in Fletching way before then. And if not you can write me a letter with the details and I'll see all the necessary is in hand. Now, I think it best if you take a deep breath and get on with things … and stop worrying.'

Martha's face contorted with the effort of regaining control before bustling off up Five Mile Hill, her head bowed and her legs moving like pistons. Edith continued on her own journey until she drew level with the haberdashery shop where something in the window caught her attention. Would her purse stretch if she put off paying the milk bill until she'd drawn some money out of the post office in Uckfield? She leaned forward to read the price labels on the packets. In the moments it took for her eyes to refocus, she caught sight of her reflection in the glass.

It was the smile making her look even younger than Martha Culpert that made Edith push open the door to purchase a pair of the best stockings Fletching had to offer.

CHAPTER SEVEN

Edward was waiting for her – just as she knew he would be. No one else had got off the bus, but still she lingered by the stop until it disappeared over the brow of the hill. The wicker basket was heavy in the crook of her arm and she was aware of listing slightly as she crossed the road. The macadam, baked by the sun, smelled of coal tar; there wasn't a cloud in the sky. Late-summer days didn't come any more perfect than this. He was leaning against a tree watching her approach, a bundle of tartan rugs over one arm and a small crate of beer hanging from the other hand. She felt as though they were about to embark on an adventure together – an expedition, perhaps, like the ones she'd stayed up half the night studying; Tilgate Wood was hardly the jungles of Borneo but, right now, it held just as much promise.

'Have you been waiting long?'

'Eleven years to be precise …'

She laughed. Edward handed the rugs over before taking charge of the basket.

'You lead the way; your territory after all.'

'Not really. I know of the stream and that there's a hop-pickers' camp way over the fields beyond; other than that this place is new to me as well.'

Which was, of course, why she'd chosen it: she'd wanted the day to be fresh for both of them. Nevertheless she walked on ahead, picking up a narrow trail that came in from the right and snaked onward into the woodland. Above her head, magpies bickered. Edith smiled: *two for joy*. The sunlight filtering through the canopy cast a haze of soft green shadows and made her think she was floating in water. She felt buoyed along by happiness.

The ground sloped down, brambles and bracken began appearing; small animals scurried away at their approach. Edward had fallen back and was puffing a little under the weight of the beer crate and basket of food.

The trees thinned out to reveal a clearing of grass dotted with dandelion clocks, fuzzy-headed thistles, and thousands of daisies with centres like freshly polished brass buttons. Insects hummed and darted in the air, gauzy clouds of them swirling above the ribbon of slow-flowing stream.

'Will this do?'

'Perfect. Simply perfect. I can't tell you how much I've missed the English countryside; I'd take this any day over miles and miles of scorched *pampa*.'

He placed his burdens on the ground then turned and held out his hands. She gave him the rugs which he unfurled before crawling across them on his hands and knees, squashing down the lumps and bumps. Once they had settled themselves, Edith started to unpack the basket while Edward pulled an opener from his pocket and prised off the caps of two Pale Ales. He handed a bottle to her.

'Cheers.' He took a long pull. 'Boy, I needed that; if I'd have known we'd have to walk so far I'd have worn a lighter jacket, or even donned shorts like a bona fide hiker.'

She smiled. Some intrepid explorer he was, he'd probably had a retinue of porters to carry his belongings on his travels. The beer was soft and fruity. The combination of alcohol and sunshine made her brain buzz. Resting the bottle against the basket, she unwrapped the packages. The cooked sausages were scummed with grease but the sandwiches hadn't suffered too badly, the bread still plump and uncurled.

They ate and drank with only an odd word exchanged to point out a butterfly, or bird alighting on the opposite bank. It wasn't until they were on to the scrumped fruit – and their second beer – that Edith felt time slipping away.

'Tell me about yourself, Edward. You said you went abroad, where exactly?'

'South America.'

'Why there?'

'I decided it was as good a place as any. My father's business was all-but ruined before the War so I knew it wouldn't provide a living. And when you add in what little else remained available to me it was patently clear I no longer had a future in this country ...'

The look he gave her from under lowered brows made Edith fiddle with the empty squares of greaseproof paper, folding them over and over before tucking them into the basket. She was going to ruin this if she didn't relax. With an effort to appear unconcerned, she unfolded her legs from under her and stretched them out until her ankles were prickled through her gossamer-fine stockings by the grass beyond the rug. Edward mirrored her mood by unlocking his elbows to lie back, his hands behind his head.

'After I discovered your father had salted you away out of the reach of my clutches ... I don't suppose you know it was that sneak Cooke told him about us – the one who set up camp at the bottom of Dr Myers' garden. When I didn't hear from you I sought him out amongst the rhododendrons and he confessed he'd revealed our secret meetings a fortnight before. Anyway, Cooke regretted his big mouth and put me in touch with his brother who was using the opportunity of a lull in Atlantic U-boat activity to seek his fortune in rubber. The upshot being I went with him. On August 21st 1916 we sailed from Liverpool – and that was quite a journey, I can tell you, seasickness almost from start to finish. By the time we were in the middle of the ocean, I wanted to die.'

He raised himself up on one elbow to reach for his beer. He drained it and placed the bottle in the crate. Edith wondered if he was going to crack open another pair. She would have to refuse hers if she wasn't to succumb to a sleep-inducing lethargy; to miss even a moment of his company would be such a waste. But he was flat on his back again now, his face soaking up the warmth.

'Your turn, Ede, I'm talking myself dry again here. What have you been doing with yourself?'

How to select what to tell him? Condense things, fashion amusing or interesting anecdotes out of what had seemed at the time – and still did – as a stretch to be endured or made the best of? It came to her that she resented having to recount any of it; if he had been there then not only would this struggle to reinvent or embroider be unnecessary, almost all of it would never have happened.

'Was it ever explained to you why I had to leave so suddenly?'

Why had she elected to start way back then? Now she'd be forced to walk the fine line between honesty and not revealing too much.

'Of course not. Dr Potter would've chased me off the premises with a shotgun if I'd had the temerity to ask. I had hoped you might enlighten me yourself though.'

'I tried writing a few times but always tore the letters up. I ... I was scared of making you feel ...'

She'd thought the pain long gone, but here it was bubbling in her chest like a kettle about to boil over. She tugged at some blades of grass, letting them fall one by one through her hot and sticky fingers.

'I thought, in the end, that the kind thing would be to set you free. To find someone else who could give you everything I couldn't ...'

She had been about to say: *give you the children I never could.* But their relationship had never got that far and if he hadn't known about her state of barrenness then, what would it profit either of them to have it revealed in a flurry of reminiscences now?

'It was you I wanted to be with, Ede. You I loved ...'

He'd never said that before. They'd never said it to each other. The thrill his words gave her wasn't as all consuming as it would've been aged twenty-five, but it was there. The thrill was still there.

'It was probably a day or so after you say Cooke told him about us when my father summoned me to his study. I was informed the professor engaged to tutor me in mathematics had taken up a position in Whitehall and wanted me by his side. It was made abundantly clear that I couldn't refuse such an honour. Not that I was actually given an opportunity to do so as the next minute I was presented with a ticket to London and instructed to catch the milk-train. So, you see, I really had no choice in the matter.'

She risked a glance. He turned his head and met her eye.

'You might have chosen to post one of those letters … Although I was gone myself within the month without a forwarding address. So let's take it as read that you're forgiven.'

He removed one of his hands from behind his head to wave fingers in her direction.

'Carry on …'

Was he teasing her? Or adopting a dismissive demeanour to cover up his disappointment in her younger self? But at least he'd made it obvious he didn't want to dwell on that subject, for which she was grateful.

'It was long hours and boring work in the main but most of the other girls were friendly and we managed to have some sort of a social life.'

'Cocktails at the Café de Paris?'

Edith laughed. 'Hardly. A plate of pie and mash at a chop house was about our limit, but we did get to see a few shows when the theatres were open …'

Now she was grateful to Edward for another reason: in the private stitching together of her history, she'd neglected to include the good times. There might not have been many, but they were as real in her memory as everything else. What was the tall fair-haired northern girl's name? She thought they might have been preparing to share a flat together. Just before the little world she'd built for herself blew up in her face.

'Not long after the Armistice, Mr Cartwright stood beside my desk and told me I was surplus to requirements. Only he didn't quite put it like that. The hostilities ending didn't mean the work wouldn't still continue but, according to him, positions could no longer be filled by women now all the brave young soldiers were returning home.'

Edith swallowed the lump in her throat. Should she ask Edward for another beer? A fly was buzzing above his nose and he hadn't moved to swat it away; had he fallen asleep? No matter, after all she was telling her story for herself as much as for him.

'Well, there didn't seem to be so many men to me – certainly nothing like the numbers I'd seen queuing outside Victoria Station for embarkation – and none of them was knocking on the door for the job of being shut in an airless basement cross-referencing files of classified documents and aerial photographs.'

'It still upsets you, doesn't it?'

His voice had made her jump. She watched the shadows of the trees creep over the bank on the opposite side of the stream until they quenched the sparkles on top of the water.

'So there I was with barely enough money to pay the rent and, having been educated in things other than secretarial skills, precious little prospect of finding myself alternative employment. Then I received a letter …'

'Ah, the letters sent and not sent, eh? I've no doubt a book could be written on that subject. Who was this one from, a lovesick boyfriend you'd kept waiting in the wings?'

Now he was being thoroughly disagreeable on purpose. Was he intent on punishing her, despite his protestation of forgiveness? Or was it that she was being over-sensitive and that it had been a joke. It was inevitable she'd have forgotten how to appreciate a sense of humour. Besides, in her experience it was always safest to assume she was the one at fault.

'It was from the vicar of a place I didn't recognise who spelt out, in no uncertain terms, that my father was in the grip of advanced senility, and Christian duty, filial obligation – and everything else he could lay at my door – decreed I come and care for him. All of which was news to me because in the two and a half years I'd been at the Ministry I'd had no contact from my father except one Christmas card in 1916 saying he'd moved but not where to. So, you see, most of my life has been dictated by circumstances beyond my control.'

'Isn't that the same for everyone?'

'Maybe. Except perhaps someone stronger than myself might have stood their ground occasionally.'

'And if you had done then we wouldn't be here now. Together again.'

He had sat up and was hugging his knees to his chest, staring at her with a look she couldn't interpret but was disturbing in its intensity. She shivered.

'Don't torture yourself over what might have been, Ede. Much better to save your energies for doing what you can to shape the future …'

His face assumed a wistful expression before he turned his gaze away and began retying his shoelace.

'… it's all we've got.'

The sun was dipping behind the trees and a malevolent breeze had started up, bringing with it the coolness of the water. Goosebumps sprang up on Edith's bare wrists. But she didn't want to suggest they leave just yet.

'It was rubber, wasn't it, that led you to South America? I take it you must have been successful to have stayed so long.'

'I got there at the height of the final boom, then left just at the right time when the industry was on its last legs. I worked for a German as his overseer, travelling for days or weeks at a time to survey areas of the forest to be cleared to plant more rubber trees. Journeying by canoe and picking up a horse at the nearest *barraca* was the only way to get to some of the places he'd marked for speculation. And you can forget about maps; Indian local knowledge was all I had to go by, and more often than not it was unreliable – directions being easy to pay for but impossible to verify until you got there – or they would deliberately mislead in an attempt to preserve old hunting grounds or some such.'

'You spoke the language?'

'Picked up enough to get by, but I always let my guide do the actual negotiations over provisions and all the other important stuff. My skin was the wrong colour, you see, which was a major factor if one of the tribes turned out to be cannibals. Except escaping their cooking pot wasn't the end of things because if they didn't eat you, then there were plenty of other things that would. Clouds of mosquitoes so thick it appeared to be night-time; jaguars unafraid to stalk through a tent-flap; snakes fatter than these tree trunks ready to squeeze out the life before swallowing you whole; crocodiles haunting the river banks only pretending to be half asleep ...'

He was really enjoying himself and Edith was, too; this was exactly the sort of romantic impression of his travels she'd hoped he'd share with her.

'But the forest wasn't only home to the stuff of nightmares. There were parrots and macaws, and butterflies so big their outstretched wings wouldn't fit on a dinner plate. I had a pet monkey for a while. Chatty little thing it was. I called it Norman after that pilot who'd follow us into the pub babbling gibberish – remember?'

Edith laughed before she could catch herself; one of her father's cases, the poor man's shell-shock had manifested itself in the need to constantly make a sound to prove he was still alive. It was an unkind comparison, but perhaps it was only someone who understood how easily life could change in an instant who could mock the afflicted with no cruelty intended. Then Edward did something totally unexpected: he stretched out his hand to grab hers. She could feel the bones of her fingers grate.

'Can you keep a secret, Ede?'

She tried to re-inject the mirth into her voice: 'I think if the military top brass can trust me with all those *For Your Eyes Only* documents then I'd say you can consider anything safe with me ...'

What on earth was it that had suddenly gripped him with such urgency? His eyes were wide and shining. He shuffled closer.

'I discovered something whilst I was out there. And this time there is a map – one verified as accurate by a Dutch prospector on his deathbed. It pinpoints a source of untold riches ...'

'Eldorado, you mean?'

'You don't believe me.'

'I do, Edward, I do …'

'More than enough to keep us in comfort for the rest of our lives.'

Us. He'd said *us*.

'A ruined city – I've been there, seen it with my own eyes. Stumbled across it, truth be told. We'd abandoned our horses and were on foot, making slow progress through the curtains of lianas. The first clue was the unnaturally straight line of an overgrown wall. The guide told me the Indians had always known of the place, and it was one of the things they'd been hoping the jungle would continue to protect. When I was back in La Paz, I got talking about it to some men in a bar and found out the Dutch prospector had identified it as a possible site of one of the lost silver mines the Portuguese had been desperate to claim.'

He shuffled again to stretch his damaged leg in front of him, lying back on one elbow in order not to increase the space between them.

'So the next morning I tracked him down; he was dying, as I said – of malaria as it happens – and was anxious for someone to continue the quest in his name. He gave me the map on the understanding I pass on a portion of whatever I might find to his relatives back in Holland. It wasn't difficult to agree. Only I didn't have enough capital to mount the sort of expedition it would take, which is one of the reasons I'm here.'

For a moment she'd been swept away with his account. But she got the picture now: he was looking for someone to finance his Rider Haggard fantasy. It was unlikely her name was first to spring to mind but once he'd learned she was a spinster with no dependants and the title deeds to a property …

Edward let go of her hand at precisely the same time as she snatched it free. He didn't seem to notice as he stood and began shaking out his stiff joints.

'Shall we pack up? I don't want to miss the bus because I need to catch the train to London. The man I'm hoping will sponsor me has agreed to a meeting first thing tomorrow. I really shouldn't say any more about his possible collaboration at this stage but he's been involved with one or two similar speculations, and was very enthusiastic in response to my telegram.'

He started to gather up and fold the rug he'd been lazing on.

'I've had a wonderful time – here, with you – and I'm counting on us having lots more like it. I'll be gone for a few days I expect. Then if I get the green light I'll be sailing again in the spring. Until then there'll be a lot of things to get lined-up but I can do much of it from Uckfield with only the occasional trip up to town. Which should work out perfectly because, not only will I draw less attention from any rival fortune-hunters by being based out in the sticks, I'll have the very great pleasure of being able to see you as well. Although, to be honest, I do have an ulterior motive in that regard ...'

He'd placed the rug on top of the beer crate and was reaching for the basket. Edith hadn't moved. She wanted to be still sitting down when he told her he'd need the money from the sale of her cottage as his sponsor's proof of commitment.

'... you were always so good at organising things – how you arranged Dr Potter's diary so you could get away to meet me for one – and I was sort of relying on being able to get your opinion on the feasibility of the logistics as I draw up the plans.'

He looked across at her, his expression full of the bashfulness of a scholar caught skimping on his homework.

'The fact is, Ede, maybe our lives worked out the way they did only in order to arrive at this moment when I tell you I'd be – quite literally – lost without you.'

In return, Edith realised that love, true love free from the chains of duty and obligation, was about being wanted and needed in equal measure. From now on, there wasn't anything she wouldn't do for Edward.

CHAPTER EIGHT

The oil lamp gave off coils of smutty black smoke as the flame licked the wick into submission. The air in St Margaret's was always chill and Edith wished she'd put her coat on over her cardigan. She retreated to the back of the nave and slid into her usual pew. She often came into the church when she couldn't sleep. When the dreams remained as vivid with her eyes open as when she'd been asleep. Here she could take refuge in things outside herself – beyond herself. She was free to just be.

The moonlight barely penetrated the jammy hues of the stained-glass windows and she couldn't see much not directly in the path of the lamp's yellowish glow but she didn't need to. She already knew the freshness of the flowers she'd arranged that morning to replace the ones that'd looked so woeful they'd distracted her throughout yesterday's service. Mrs Mountby had no eye or appreciation for shape or form – who could ever have thought baggy-headed white chrysanthemums would go with delphiniums? She, on the other hand, had sacrificed the most intense of her blood-red roses. Of course they'd have dropped their petals by next Sunday and no one but the Reverend Culpert, and the verger when he came in to polish the silverware, would see them at their best but beauty existed for its own sake not for admiration.

Edith ran through the familiar lines of the Lord's Prayer, her lips moving in a ritual pattern rather than in outline of the words. They had never meant anything anyway, contained no message of any relevance to her life. Except the bit about daily bread. That had made her tremble as a child because she'd wonder if God knew about her underhandedness in the matter of feeding the ducks. But she'd grown out of that quickly enough when she'd noticed how He chose to ignore so many other – far greater – transgressions. Was there anything she should be asking forgiveness for? Her too-quick judgements about people perhaps. That attitude of superiority would have to change if she didn't want Edward to think her snooty. Because he, of course, was the reason for her inability to sleep; his reappearance had flooded her with too many exciting possibilities to let her rest.

The realisation that her future would no longer be one devoid of anything other than a bleak hopelessness was exhilarating. It was almost overwhelming. When Edward had completed his expedition and returned a wealthy man, they'd start a new life together in London. Or Buenos Aires. She didn't really care where as long as there weren't any geese to ruin her garden. But she'd be sad to leave her rose bushes behind – her father had acquired some rarities. Maybe she could have those dug up to transplant wherever they settled. Would roses survive in the South American climate? It was one of the many things she'd have to investigate. As for the cottage, they'd have enough money not to have to bother selling it and she could let it rot. Along with the memories it contained. And the ghost of her former self.

Which made her wonder if, as a parting gesture, she shouldn't replace the wooden cross marking her father's final resting place with a headstone. If so, what would she want it to say? Not *much mourned* or *forever missed* or any of the other empty sentiments people appeared compelled to have the stonemason carve. And over her own dead body would she have the lie: *rest in peace*. Hadn't she done all she could to ensure that wouldn't be the case? Like insisting he not be buried where the vicar had wanted him rubbing decaying shoulders with the one other village notable, but at the back of the churchyard; shoehorned between the crumbling mausoleum dedicated to a long-extinct line of landowners, and the unconsecrated ground reserved for suicides. They'd thought her selection a product of shock at his unlawful killing. Equally wrong had been their assumption that the cutting she'd planted and assiduously tended had been a rose. It had been nothing of the sort, as would be apparent to anyone who ventured into that part of the graveyard. A thick vine of the rampant clematis, traveller's joy, now grew above – and was fed by – Dr Potter's rotting flesh. A fastidious man in life, he would have wanted to be respectably tidy in death and if there was any such thing as an afterlife she hoped he loathed what he was forced to look down upon.

Words tickled the back of her throat. She wanted to let them out. To leave them behind with all the other things she'd no longer have a need for. Because they belonged to the old Edith, the Edith she no longer wanted to be. The weight of them would hold her down and prevent her escape if she didn't release them into a cold dark church where they would be resurrected to live on whenever voices echoed in prayer.

'I've been wanting to tell you this for the longest time. I'm only sorry that it had to wait until you were dead, I'd have so much rather seen the look of shock on your face at me breaking a near-lifetime of silence towards you. But I have every faith in my ability to imagine it. You see, I did use to do that sometimes – imagine how you'd react if I told you this. I used to play the game over and over when I was shut up in my room and you thought I was doing calculus. When I didn't know any better and thought everybody lived in a cold and distant household; before I learned you equated the showing of emotion with mental exhaustion and neurosis; before you condemned me to being a critic of every one of my thoughts and a distant observer of every one of my feelings. And later, when I was engaged in all that work for the Ministry that I couldn't tell anyone about, it got so that the strain of being plagued by burdensome secrets became too much and made me want to scream them all for the world to hear. But I never did. I never told a soul. But something has happened and I want to now. It's too late for it to make any difference but I need you to know …'

Edith shifted in her seat and her shadow writhed up the wall.

'I hate you. I've always hated you. Ever since I was old enough to remember feeling anything, I've hated you. And because I know how much store you always set by evidence, I'm going to be precise about the reasons why …'

She stretched out her cramped fingers to count on.

'For having me educated beyond any fulfilment I could ever expect as a woman; for making me live a façade of a childhood shut up with that witch of a grandmother; for never showing me unconditional love; for treating me like a puppy to abandon when I was no longer of interest. I hate you for not caring enough to accept the responsibility of everything you didn't do to make things any better … But most of all I hate you for condemning me to live every day with the conviction that I didn't deserve to be your daughter.'

CHAPTER NINE

The boy had been on the lookout and so, with his quicker wits and reactions, had dropped his stolen booty and run full-pelt, hurdling the low wall with only a small adjustment to his stride. He, on the other hand, had been expecting to meet no one on his gentle stroll around the garden and could only stutter a few yards before the graveyard swallowed the figure up. The would-be thief was probably hugging himself with glee amongst the gravestones, bent double as he caught his breath. But his triumph wouldn't last long. If there was one thing his life experiences had taught him it was that patience was always rewarded. Everything, in the end, came to those who wait.

He perched on the window ledge, tracing the lines of the book's cover with his fingers in a meditation to still his mind and sharpen his senses. It was something most people weren't capable of doing. They lacked the discipline, often because they had no conception of how deep you had to go to recognise the things that were at the core of being. It was a cardinal error to think it was the ability to hold abstract beliefs that separated man from the beasts of the earth. There was no difference. Only a lazy arrogance that refused to allow the body to perform the duties it was designed for. He closed his eyes, directing his energy and attention to his fingertips. The leather under them radiated thin veils of warmth, the mountains and valleys of the pores a magnification of his own skin's make-up. If he hovered his fingers he could intuit where the embossed lines and swags were by the minute changes in the cushion of air.

He was nearly ready. Almost distilled down to nothing but a bundle of nerve-endings sparking electricity into the night.

He lifted his lids just enough that the top of his vision was lash-fringed. It took him a while to train the controlling muscles. Once he'd locked them into an un-fluttering squint he dropped his chin to bring the ground to the right of his outstretched legs into view. The moon silvered the patches of scabby grass. A black beetle wove between the blades like a ship cresting waves. Worm-cast spirals made the pattern of music, little minims dotted on staves. His lips buzzed as he hummed each one, maintaining perfect pitch. He opened his eyes fully now. Training his gaze on the indigo shadows sprawling out from the churchyard yews he mapped the length and angle of the branches by the texture and density of the darkness beneath.

The sound of childish laughter was the sign. It was thin, and the direction impossible to discern by anyone not prepared enough. Without undue straining, he heard a yelp, followed immediately by the splat of a body hitting water. A girl's gulped sobbing: 'I'll tell my da on you. He'll give you what-for, Alfie Thresher …'

He spun the book through the open sash into the room behind. Like a predator with the sweet scent of tender young prey in its nostrils, he glided out of the garden and onto the green. Nestled in the gap between the oak tree and the wall he tracked the progress of three figures – one dripping wet and crying, the others alternating between telling her to hush her row and speculating if she could hide her soiled clothes in the privy and sneak into the house unseen. The victim's escalating sobs made it clear that wasn't an option. Clearly the boy wouldn't be the only one who would be punished for a misdemeanour tonight.

The ragged procession disappeared up the lane and the gentler noises of the night came back into focus. Small creatures snuffled in the undergrowth. He could've heard the fluttering of a moth's wings and taste the trail of glistening powder it left behind. A fox padded past, so close he might have reached out and plucked a hair from the end of its brush.

His back had begun to stiffen before he heard a bicycle spitting stones from under its tyres; then the rhythmic whoosh of reed fronds against spokes. A dozen paces out of his hiding place and he could see his target racing around the pond. Legs pumping the pedals, his arse clear of the saddle. But he wouldn't show his hand here where there were too many opportunities for evasion. If a rat couldn't be cornered then the next best thing was to intercept it on the way back to its nest. A child of his nature would be unable to resist the temptation of riding home across the common: he knew because if ever he'd been granted the magnificent gifts of lust and liberty, he'd have done exactly the same.

*

He positioned himself between the banked ditch on his left, and the elms flanking the lane. The steady whirr of wheels reached him. Loose links clacking against one another as the chain bounced in the sprockets. Coming closer. The stone felt made for the shape of his hand. The flint smooth against his thumb as he rubbed it up to the sharp edge and back again. The anticipation was everything. Almost better than the moment itself. Almost. Laboured breaths panting out lungfuls of vapour into the surrounding air. His … and his … synchronised into togetherness.

He'd told himself he'd need only count to twenty-five. He liked the patterns numbers made in his head, the way they could be made to fit. To stretch, but conversely condense, the distance between the waymarks on any journey to a named desire. He tasted the words as he whispered his voice out into the night … fifteen … eighteen … twenty … He'd estimated correctly. The shape of the hurtling figure was discernible now … Twenty-four …

He stepped into the path of the bicycle. The machine wobbled before crashing sideways, spilling the boy to the ground. He heard the gasp … saw the stricken look … felt the flint grow in his hand … all in the seconds before he tasted the sweetness of retribution.

CHAPTER TEN

Edith closed the church door behind her. Her vigil had left her purged but also feeling invigorated with an energy that would make going back to bed straightaway a pointless exercise. A turn or two around the churchyard perimeter should settle her down enough to sleep. Her moonlit shadow seemed to tease her onward; vanishing when she was under the trees, then skipping ahead as if waiting for her to catch up. Something white was glowing between the tombstones up ahead. A barn owl spreading its wings prior to flying off with a meal perhaps? Except it wasn't moving. She hoped such a beautiful bird hadn't become entangled in wire or eaten poison intended for buzzards. She crept onto the grass verge towards it. A hunched shape like a giant puffball.

Another few paces and the white was clearly a piece of cloth. She stopped treading lightly; it was probably something that'd blown off Wilf Drayton's washing line – except she wouldn't have expected it to be so clean. A yard further brought a halt to speculation: it was the body of a boy, sprawled face down across an ivy-covered grave.

'Edith …'

The voice was so unexpected it felt as though it was in her head. Edward emerged from behind the figure of an angel, its right arm – which should have been pointing heavenward – severed at the elbow. The front of his jacket was splodged with dark stains; long smears tracked down the sleeves. He had a twisted expression, caught halfway between guilt and terror.

'What have you done to him?'

'Nothing … it was an accident …'

'Why aren't you in London?'

Questions kept popping into her head; stupid pointless questions that she didn't need to know the answers to because whatever he said wouldn't change the appalling nature of the scene at her feet. She couldn't stop staring at the pathetic bundle of clothes and flesh. The skin on his bare legs was a bluish-grey and lacerated from thigh to ankle as if he'd been dragged through a bramble thicket; one shoulder had been dislocated, the scapula protruding sideways in the area where the child's ribs should've been rising and falling with his breath. A large patch of hair on the back of his head was glued to his skull with blood. The small defenceless wrists protruding from his shirt cuffs were ringed with black bruises.

'I came back … wanted to tell you … Edith … all my dreams, my dreams for our future … There is to be no sponsorship … He wasn't interested in the expedition, only curious to meet someone who was as big a fool as the old Dutch prospector … I'll be a laughing stock; he'll have queered my pitch with everyone of influence …'

'Edward, what have you done?'

'Nothing, I told you … He tripped and fell, hit his head. I gave chase when I saw him climbing out of your study window …'

Edward loosened his arms from his sides, raising them palms upward as if in supplication to the stonehearted angel. 'I did it for you … to protect you.'

'We have to go to the police. You can explain, they'll understand.'

'I can't … they won't …'

'Of course they will. PC Billings knows they've been hanging around my cottage, he'll see it was only a question of time before one of them tried to break in. You weren't to know I wasn't inside; as you've said, you were protecting me.'

'I did … I was …'

Edward was pacing around in broken circles. Sparks of agitation flew off him, filling the air between them with electricity. Edith felt the soft hairs on her arms stand to attention; she knew how easily the simple fact of being in the wrong place at the wrong time could result in nightmarish consequences. If her mother hadn't laid her down for a nap when she did …

'Come on, the Police House is up at The Cross; let's get this over with.'

'He had something of yours … I had to stop him …'

'And if you repeat all that without leaving anything out then even that halfwit of a constable can't fail to see that you were simply attempting to apprehend a thief.'

She kept her voice deliberately even, hoping the analytical tone would rub off on Edward. If he didn't get a grip on himself then he almost certainly would find fingers of suspicion pointed his way. For a man so supposedly inured to the life and death nature of the jungle, he was bordering on the hysterical. She tried to think of any arguments she could marshal on his behalf.

'I'll tell them the truth: that you knew Dr Potter from childhood, have just returned to this country, was horrified to learn the circumstances of his death. Add all that to the shock of seeing someone running from my cottage and it's no wonder you would assume the perpetrator had returned.'

'Do you have a cigarette on you, Ede?'

'I don't smoke. And I'd rather you didn't call me that in the circumstances.'

'What circumstances?'

'There's a boy lying here dead, Edward! Or have you conveniently put that out of your mind?'

'Of course not … Only I can't keep my thoughts going in the same direction for long. I got so far as dragging him here to give me time to develop a plan, but it isn't working … I admit I'm in a bit of a panic. I was going to leave him here and go to the cottage to ask you what I should do …'

'I've already told you: go to the police.'

'No … no, that's out of the question. I'm not as sure of myself as you, and I know that under interrogation I'll get confused and end up saying something foolish.'

'Can't you think of anyone but yourself?'

'Who else ever really matters when the chips are down?'

'Me … I thought you cared about me.'

Edith was ashamed to hear how feeble her voice sounded; how it trembled with the wound of a heart hurt by a casual betrayal.

Edward ran his fingers through his hair. 'I do … of course I do. We can't let this misadventure ruin everything we have together, everything we've ever meant to each other … This untimely death will serve to remind us of how much of our own time we've lost, wasted … what little there is left in which to make amends.'

She couldn't stop herself from glancing once more at the body. A stab of self-loathing went through her as she thought that, whether Edward's prospects of riches were scuppered or not, she'd have to leave the village right away. This hadn't been her fault, but to be the unwitting cause would be enough for the parents to blame her. Was his mother even now wondering why he was still out so late at night? Or had she left him safely tucked up in bed and he'd sneaked out for a bit of moonlit adventure? Edith shut her imagination down before she ended up in the same state as Edward. One of them had to resist giving in to their emotions. Except it wasn't that easy.

'But, Edward … couldn't you tell he was just a boy?'

'The places I've been, the things I've seen … you act first and think later. And my concern was only for you. Your safety … the privacy I know you'd do anything to preserve … I did it for you. I read somewhere – a very long time ago – that the person who loves the most is the weakest and must suffer … And that's me, Edith. So pity me, please. I'm not as strong as you … as sure … But I'll do anything to keep you from harm; that is my burden, willingly carried for your sake …'

His voice had begun to assume a whining quality that set Edith's teeth on edge. Her sympathy had started to drain away the moment it dawned on her what was behind the words he was babbling. He was trying to exonerate himself by laying the responsibility for everything that had happened firmly at her door.

It was her fault he'd travelled back to England in the first place, come to Fletching, rushed down from London to tell her how his proposal had been received. Her cottage he'd witnessed burgled; he'd acted for her sake, been her gallant knight. So she didn't have to wait for the villagers' condemnation after all: the man who'd said he'd always loved her had got in first. The easy charm that had beguiled her less than thirty-six hours ago now looked to be a close cousin of the childish desire to evade accountability.

'Our future together rests on me finding another means of securing funding for my project. Only I need to know that everything here has been taken care of or I won't be able to concentrate … Can't you come up with something? … Tell me what I can do with the body. Somewhere it won't be found for a long time – if ever. Then there's his bicycle, it's back there. If we can get rid of both then there'll be no questions to ask. Our secret will be safe. Please, Ede, please … We've been parted twice; it'll be against all odds for us to survive a third time. Now I've found you again I can't lose you, I can't lose you …'

Gone was the beseeching tone: in its place a low, harsh urgency. Edith couldn't think of anything beyond his desperate need of her. And the depth of her need to be loved.

'Use the sexton's wheelbarrow – he'll think the children have stolen it again to ride in. There's an abandoned chalk quarry a third of the way along the ridge between here and Tilgate. Follow the hedge that curves around to a line of trees and keep going up until you cross the old drovers' track. Head east. After you've … done what you have to … stay on the path. It skirts the edge of Cowden. The road to Uckfield is beyond the dairy.'

Edward held out his arms and made a move as if to hug her but she plunged through the tombstones and headed for the cottage to change into her gardening clothes.

CHAPTER ELEVEN

Edith got off the bus and waited for it to pull away. The street was full of traffic and the noise – both inside and outside her head – was disorientating. She walked down the main road for a hundred yards or so and then plunged into the welcoming peace and quiet of a side street. After a series of twists and turns she arrived at the square, in the corner occupied by the police station. The bright light from the low September sun glared off the shop windows and she had to look down at her shoes to stop her eyeballs being stabbed with hot needles. She careered into a string of shoulders as she darted into the nearest strip of shade.

Once her head had stopped throbbing, she glanced around to get her bearings. It was market day and the space was thronged. She was tempted to take the succour offered by the blue lamp above her head at face value and ask the desk sergeant for a glass of water but, sorely in need of refreshment though she was, there was something else she needed more: to talk to Edward.

She braved the sunshine to cut the corner of the square. Once on the north side it was a question of darting between a vegetable stall and a group of young men wheeling bicycles to reach the Chequers' protruding entrance porch. The air in the doorway smelt of furniture polish and fried bacon. It was cool inside. An official in a bowler hat was standing at the end of the reception counter tapping with his pencil on a clipboard whilst the hotel clerk was shuffling through a boxful of index cards.

'Excuse me, do you happen to know if Mr Rochester is on the premises?'

'I'll be with you in a moment, madam, only I have to find the details wanted by his nibs over there or it'll be me travelling from pillar to post with no fixed abode.'

'If you give me his room number then I can go up and check for myself – it is rather pressing.'

'Just give me a minute and I'll deal with your request in full … Ah, here it is.'

He walked away, placed the card on the official's clipboard, and returned to reoccupy the space in front of Edith.

'Now, madam, what was it you were after?'

'Mr Rochester. He's been staying with you for a few days.'

The clerk flicked over the pages in the register.

'No one here of that name.'

'Are you sure?'

'Perfectly.'

And then it came to her that perhaps Edward had assumed a different identity; more than once he'd mentioned having to keep his quest – in fact even his very presence in the country – secret from those who would want to keep him from the fortune he sought. Behind her a dog started barking; the clerk pointed an accusatory finger.

'Tie him up outside. It was disgusting what he did all over the sofa in the residents' lounge.'

'But I only want a drink.'

'Not in here with him, you don't.'

'Spike will be as good as gold; yesterday was on account of something he ate but it's free of his system now.'

'The cleaner who had to clear it up knows that well enough –'

'Would it help if I described him to you?' Edith could feel her focus sliding; she had to see Edward, talk to him. It was important – urgent. Would it help to win the clerk's undivided attention if she told him it was a matter of life and death?

'Madam, I came on duty this morning, having been brought in especially for market day and already I've seen more faces than a barber's on a Saturday. Look … Oy! You take one more step over that threshold and I'll have the both of you slung out … I'm sorry

I can't help you. There are one or two other decent hotels in the town and you could consider checking with them in case you got the establishment wrong.'

She hadn't. Edward had crossed this carpet, was possibly walking above her head at this very moment. But although she couldn't demand to search the premises, neither could she stand here all day on the off-chance he came down the stairs. Edith rubbed at her temple which had begun to throb with the tension headache behind it. The action was both soothing and seemed to release a stuck memory; Edward wasn't at this or any other hotel in Uckfield: Edward was up in London. If only she'd remembered the fact before she'd left home then she wouldn't now be having to put up with the racket caused by the clerk and the man in the doorway playing at tug-of-war over an over-excited collie.

Back in the sunshine, Edith zigzagged from the shelter of one stall's awning to another, absentmindedly weighing down her pockets with pilfered trinkets as she went. Her progress was slow as all around her people were haggling over prices, catching up on gossip, shoving and getting in her way. Flocks of young children ran in circles around their mothers and shouted at the tops of their voices. It was too much. Edith lowered her head like a bull about to charge, and pushed and stumbled her way to the nearest exit from the square. When she looked up again she was at the mouth of the road she knew led down to the sanctuary of the library. The panic in her stomach subsided to the sort of queasiness she often got prior to a bout of indigestion. She continued walking until she came to the chemist's. As she paused to consider whether it was worth going inside for some chalk tablets, she caught a flash of her reflection in the plate glass. It was distorted by the rows of coloured jars and bottles but it was clear that her features were pinched and she looked about a hundred years old. She didn't need Dr Mackie's medical qualifications to know that whatever was upsetting her constitution wasn't going to be cured by even a basketful of patent medicines. Something much stronger was called for.

*

The Rising Sun was surprisingly clean and, it being just after opening time, mercifully empty. Edith stood at the half-moon bar with its high shelf and two small etched-glass panels at either end. She purchased her malt whisky and took it over to a table by the fireplace where she sat beside a strip of wallpaper recoiling from a badly executed painting of a hunting scene that was all trees and few hounds. Rattling around in her head were recollections of a life so distant she felt as though she was observing herself through the wrong end of a telescope. Or, rather, a kaleidoscope where the images were fractured colours requiring contemplation to make sense of. She sipped at her drink and, as the first slick of peaty smoothness slid over her tongue, she thought of golden fires and a house decorated with candles and streams of coloured paper, and a large Christmas tree in the corner like the one her father had shown her in Trafalgar Square. He'd been to a meeting at the Institute and had taken her with him. She must have been about six or seven – she remembered the chafing of her woollen tights against the still-tender scars. She'd been allowed to sit at the back of the room with a jigsaw puzzle on her lap. But she couldn't do it without risking the pieces falling on the floor and she'd known how disappointed he would have been if she hadn't been able to keep more still and more quiet than any ordinary child would have done. She'd been grateful at the time for the trouble he was taking, for the attention. Only much later did she see through it to the warped ego of a selfish man.

The glass felt light in her hand as she let the last few drops touch her lips. She hadn't realised that she'd drunk it all quite so quickly. There was a movement beside her and the landlord was standing at her table holding another whisky.

'On the house.' He put it down in front of her. 'We don't get nearly enough of your sort in here. Add a touch of class, you do.'

She felt a desire to laugh in his face. Her sort? Did he have any conception of what that was? How could he, when she barely knew herself. She accepted the drink, then reached up and loosened her mackintosh collar; she was getting hot and, as there was nowhere else she had to be until it was time to catch the bus back, she had better make herself comfortable. She took a sip from her glass and let the liquid glide down her throat and quieten the remnants of her headache, already the insistent throb in her temples had gone. She could think more clearly without it.

In whisky-fuelled weakness, she clicked the kaleidoscope around once more. The image stared dully back at her in shades of grey. She was sitting on the edge of her bed, dry-eyed, tearing up the pages of her diary into confetti-sized pieces. Her grandmother had removed it from under Edith's pillow and placed the slim volume on the counterpane, where she'd found it after her bath. It had contained nothing but comments on the weather, the lessons she'd undertaken that day, or what she'd had to eat, but the lack of childish secrets to mock didn't make the humiliation of its discovery any less searing. It came to Edith that there were some memories that were impossible to inhabit without wondering why she'd selected them as worthy of being laid down in the first place. Because nobody could possibly salt away the detail of every moment or they would be too preoccupied to experience anything new and would forever be running to catch up with themselves. A particular problem if cursed with a tendency to over-analyse. Had that started in childhood? She couldn't answer that now, and she certainly couldn't have then: you never can make objective judgements about yourself when you've nothing to measure against. There could never be any conception of what you could have been had someone given you a different set of rules to live by, a brand-new box of pieces to fit together. If they had, would she have done the sky first or the edges? What if no one had ever shown her the picture, would she still know what it was supposed to be? Could she finish it if someone had jumbled up the puzzle with another one or would she have ended up with something so mystifying that the frustration outweighed any challenge the extra complication might pose? A little like her life.

The walk to the bar was a short one and she only stumbled slightly on the way back. The pub had got busy without her noticing. Some commercial travellers were sitting with their cases by their chairs as they wrote notes in fat books held together with rubber bands; small clusters of market traders compared business with one another over glasses of beer.

Her father had never been much of a one for drinking, a sherry at Christmas or a bottle of stout on the rare occasions he had to take to his bed with a cold or a touch of something he called *phlegmatic melancholia*. However, whatever his temporary incapacity, he would still go through her calculus and attempts at solving algebraic equations and give her the number of crosses she had to write up on the chart on the wall in the drawing room. Never the ticks – maybe they were too infrequent to be worth mentioning – but always the faults. Her faults. Her shortcomings. Her inability to be who he wanted her to be.

It really was getting awfully hot now. She could feel the flush on her face and the unpleasant way her blouse was sticking to her skin. As she shrugged her arms out of the sleeves of her coat she banged her elbow on the table. A slick of whisky lurched out of the glass. She dipped her finger in and licked it. Her gaze caught the feet of a group of men dripping little pools of water on the floor.

Was it raining outside? When had that happened? She tried to look up to see out of the window but her head felt too heavy. She picked up her drink and swirled the ice around. Things had changed. It was no longer cuboid in shape; no longer transparent either, it now had a misty graininess at the centre. Most of the structure had broken down and it could realistically no longer be called ice. What must it feel like to drip and drain away like that? To become something other than what you started out to be, other than what everyone thought you were? She giggled when she realised the illogicality of the questions. How could ice know? Where were its nerve-endings and brainstem and capacity to feel? She giggled again loudly causing someone nearby to aim a comment at her. She stared rudely back.

But then she felt it. She felt cold and wet and disintegrating. She felt herself melting. Diminishing. She knew she was becoming no more. She sensed the edges of her being flooding out from where she sat and wanted to do nothing to stop it. It felt good. She was loose and free and a part of everything around her.

She was drunk.

CHAPTER TWELVE

PC Billings had been diverted from his business of last Thursday by a bit of bother over a missing cat. Then his time had got itself taken up with an appearance at Lewes Crown Court over an arrest for badger-baiting he'd made five months back, and enough paperwork to make his brain boil. But with the new week stretching out before him he could at last take up the cudgel again of having that word with the parents of the latest crop of rascals. It didn't seem like the blink of a gnat's eye since he'd been doing the same when the grown-ups were themselves no more than nippers. It made him feel old right enough. Like one of the oak trees at the back of *Giblets* Gibson's slaughterhouse. But it made him feel good too. Fletching may be a no-account place to those passing on the London road but it was his little world to keep on the straight and narrow.

He stopped at the pump for a drink before checking his notebook. Six down, only Alfie Thresher to go. He'd been keeping him until last. He wouldn't put it past him for there to be a grain of truth behind Edith Potter's imaginings of stones on windows if the boy was involved in the churchyard hauntings. Made from different stuff to the others he was. A proper little ringleader – but also not afraid to go out on pranks of his own. Like the time he set a bucket of what could've been anything from ditch water to horse's piss over the haberdashery's back door when the sun was shining strong enough to need such things left open. Ada Wicklow had come into the Police House dripping and smelling like nothing you'd want in a place with such small windows, screaming that all the kiddies – and some of the regulars down the Barley Mow come to that – should be birched or, better still, hanged. He'd had to work hard not to smile. It was common knowledge that Ma Wicklow had a taste for cuffing small boys around the head for no cause anyone could see, and marching them down here to the pump for a good dousing if she had a mind. Sometimes, despite the uniform, he couldn't help reckoning that justice was best served by those who were doing scant more than repaying.

However, all that aside, if the boy had been tormenting a sad and lonely spinster for no other reason than she was a bit odd then it was an entirely different kettle of fish. He didn't hold with that sort of thing at all. Didn't bode well for the future, see. Scallywags grew up into toerags and he had to nip this in the bud before the tyke started getting up to the sort of mischief that would have him turning up in front of the magistrates on a regular basis. A man of the law – even one who believed in smoothing over rather than firing up – would then have far more on his hands than a little monkeying around the Potter place.

But the Threshers lived right up at the top of Five Mile Hill. Like as not they wouldn't be in anyway; the father was a carter on the run into Lewes, and Florence … well, she was oft times visiting her mother over at Cowden – although he suspected blood wasn't nearly so thick as a shared taste for gin in that arrangement. Perhaps he could save his boot leather and pay a visit to Treadwell instead. Alfie worked there as a delivery boy of a Saturday and maybe the threat of the holding back of a tanner or two for upsetting a valued customer would go further than a half-baked dressing down by parents who shouldn't be allowed to raise chickens, let alone a headstrong boy.

*

Ernest Treadwell slammed the till drawer shut. 'Afternoon, Paul. What can I do you for? I'm fresh out of cheese if that's what you're wanting. I know you're partial. Delivery tomorrow.'

PC Billings flicked off his chinstrap and placed his helmet on the counter. 'No need to be putting some by, thanks all the same.

Mrs Billings has gone into Uckfield and will pick some up there. I'll tell you what though. I couldn't half do with a mustard soak. Boots pinching me summat rotten. Worst torture known to man, sore feet.'

'I've a kettle on. Come on through. I'll have a bowl and a pinch of Colman's ready by the time you've undone your laces. Just don't go telling everyone or I'll have nought in here but the walking wounded.'

He held up his incomplete hands and Paul flashed back the expected response.

He was still smiling when he was sitting on a chair in the back room pulling his socks off.

'You're looking more like your old self, Ern, been a bit peaky of late if you don't mind me saying. I ain't hardly seen you looking happier than you do now since they took sugar off the ration. Business picking up is it?' He lowered his feet into the steaming water. At the tinkling of the shop bell, Ernest Treadwell left him and went to see to his customer. When he returned, he put the kettle back on the range and pulled a couple of cups off the hooks under the shelf beside the mantelpiece.

'Fancy a cuppa? I'll not be offering summat stronger because it's early yet and we've both still a job to do, but if you're out doing your rounds come suppertime then pop in and I'll have a drop for you. Traveller left me a bottle of good brandy the other week on account of me taking some unwanted goods off his hands.'

A wavelet of water lapped over the edge of the bowl as Paul Billings came to life and sat up.

'I hope you ain't going to tell me summat you shouldn't: once a policeman, always a policeman, even without the boots on.'

Ernest Treadwell flushed and Paul felt a little guilty. Mrs Billings was always telling him that he shouldn't be forever seeing the criminal in everyone, but he was of a mind that it was his habit of doing just that kept the villagers of Fletching on their toes. Unlike him. Right now he'd swap his feet for Ern's stumpy hands any day of the week.

He watched the grocer fill the pot with boiling water, then tuck the top of the newly opened packet of leaves over on itself.

'Here, take this,' he said as he pushed it across the table, 'best quality. The champagne of teas – from Formosa – can't get it around here for neither love nor money. From my own special supplier; I'll not see you go short.'

Paul accepted the gift with a nod. Ernest stirred the pot, brought it over and poured them both a pale amber cupful. He splashed the milk in then spooned out heaps of sugar.

'I know you ain't just come in for my company – you being a busy man an' all – don't tell me someone's been mouthing off about the quality of my merchandise. Because they won't get better anywhere else.' He slurped at his tea.

'Come on, Ern, you know I ain't one to be wasting my time listening to tittle-tattle over a stone in a sack of spuds. No, I'm on the lookout for sorting something that's likely to be causing an awful lot more trouble if it's left to run its course. There's some in this village who see it as their business to go scaring others out of their wits and that ain't right – however thin the hold in the first place.'

'So what do you be wanting from me, then?'

'Just keep your eyes skinned for anything that Alfie Thresher might be getting up to. And maybe put a stop to his delivering to those folks down by the church. It's him I reckon at the bottom of causing Miss Potter to be in and out of the Police House like a whipped top. I don't want you going taking the law into your own hands mind – no offence, Ern – but that'd be like me taking it on myself to re-stack all your shelves. And Mrs Billings won't even let me loose in the larder.'

He laughed to make sure the message was taken as meant: from one responsible citizen to another. He picked up the towel beside the bowl and began to dry his feet. Ernest Treadwell sucked on his ill-fitting false teeth.

'I'll be telling him when he's next in that I'll have him on the bacon if he can't be trusted to be out there on shop errands without getting up to no good.'

Paul paused in the lacing of his boots. Ernest Treadwell had been terrifying two generations of village nippers into nightmares with how he'd lost his fingers when he used to have the slicer in the back room and had got himself distracted for a moment, he loved to see their faces sicken and their mouths open as he waved his stumps at them. The truth was that it'd been his bad luck to be given a faulty Mills bomb grenade during army training. There was no accounting for the depth of black in some people.

'You be putting the word out if you will that he's to know we're watching him. No more than that.' He stood up. 'Wilf still got the vicar paying him as sexton?'

'Ain't got the push yet as I know of, even though anyone with his head not in the Bible can see he can't be relied on to dig a grave in the right place.'

'Then I'll be off to be telling him to pull down any tree camps or the like might have been built in the churchyard; children can't be skulking where they shouldn't be if there's nowhere to hide. Be seeing you, Ern. Thanks for the tea – wet and dry.'

He chortled at yet another of his spontaneous jokes and set the bell above the shop door tinkling.

*

Wilf Drayton wasn't in when he called. PC Billings knew that straight off because the man's geese were making their usual racket out back and there was no evidence of his evil – and lingering – pipe tobacco. He'd a good mind to tell him that smoking that stuff was illegal and he knew for a fact that he stole Miss Potter's rose petals to mix with it. Blamed it on the geese, right enough, but he'd seen him do it with his own eyes.

Paul looked across at the garden next door. It was unusually dishevelled with only one bed half-dug and the rest nests of weeds. Miss Potter normally kept a good length and it was achingly sad to see it in such a state. Her bedroom curtains were drawn. He had just decided that he'd leave her in peace – though how she could sleep with all that honking – and come back another day, when the front door was thrown open and Edith Potter, in a saggy baggy cardigan all buttoned-up skew-whiff, staggered out of her cottage and down the path.

'I've been robbed!'

PC Billings jumped over the hedge and took her by the arm before she fell down.

'Officer, I've been robbed, arrest them, arrest them.'

'Now who exactly would that be?'

Paul spoke quietly with the calm voice that he knew distressed persons liked to hear.

'The man who did it, of course.'

Her hysteria was mounting and Paul had to work hard to remind himself that Miss Potter could not be made to snap out of it sharply like one of the Barley Mow regulars when they were on about some imagined slight over a game of darts.

'You just be telling me from the beginning what is missing and where from.'

'My money. They've stolen my money. I went for a little rest and when I came downstairs my mackintosh was on the floor and I knew someone had been through my pockets.'

For the first time, Paul Billings caught the tang of something stale and unpleasant. Had she perhaps been at the drinks cabinet and taken a medicinal drop too many?

'Ten shillings. I had a ten-shilling note on me this morning and now it's gone.'

'Do you think maybe it could be lying dropped somewhere?'

'I haven't been out of the house.'

But that couldn't be right. Paul had seen her sitting at the back of the Uckfield bus when he'd been waving Mrs Billings off. Maybe whatever Edith Potter was afflicted with was causing her such upsetment that she was forgetting what she'd been about. He'd make it his business to pop by tomorrow and call up the doctor for her if she wasn't out and about and lambasting Wilf Drayton over something and nothing.

'Well, there ain't a lot I can be doing to look into where he's got to now; I can't be whistling and eating flour at the same time, and I'm up to my neck after having a word about the knockings you say you've been hearing in the night. Although it must be said that I'm still not altogether sure it weren't that tree of yours playing tricks.'

Edith Potter pulled herself up straight and wrenched her arm free. 'If you won't do anything about finding the thief then it's about time this village had a policeman who will. I shall be writing to the Commissioner concerning your gross dereliction of duty in this matter. And while I'm at it I'll make sure he knows about all the other heinous crimes that have been perpetrated right under your nose.'

She took a tentative step back towards her front door.

'Including the public disorder caused by those diabolical geese. I've a raging headache and thanks to your neglect it's getting worse by the second; why don't you just take a shotgun and shoot the whole fucking lot of them?'

Paul Billings couldn't have been more shocked if he'd heard the vicar blaspheme. Perhaps her affliction was a touch more than a gippy tummy after all.

CHAPTER THIRTEEN

Saturday came around much sooner than Edith expected. Any sense of time passing had been lost in a blur of sleeping and waking but the oblivion must've done her good because she felt very rested. Quite like her old self in fact. So much so that she was seized by the urge to sort out her life. She'd make a start on tackling the piles of things that were perching everywhere. It was as if she came into the cottage and left whatever she was carrying on the first available surface. Just when she'd managed to acquire such a slovenly habit she couldn't say. Neither could she explain why she hadn't noticed the chaos before. But, no matter, it had been brought to her attention now and would be rectified forthwith.

At the top of the stairs, she stepped over a cushion that had somehow ended up on the landing. Only her room would need attention because she never went in the other one. She'd locked it the minute they'd taken the body away and put the key in a place she was pleased to have forgotten. There were some benefits in having a mind too full to contain the trivial.

Her bed was strewn with books and *National Geographic* magazines. She gathered them up and placed them on the dresser. Newspapers littered the floor. Three trips out to the dustbin at the back and they were gone. She'd been shocked to see that the earliest was dated over a year ago; what good had she thought it'd do to hold onto it? All the events of those days were long gone. Dead and buried, you might say. A second cushion was wedged between the washstand and the wall; she suspected she had brought it up so she could sit and read in bed. Underneath was a box of men's handkerchiefs. They couldn't be her father's, surely? His name had been Gerald and these were monogrammed with the letter *M*. It was one mystery amongst the many others in this house and didn't warrant any more thought than where it was to go. She picked the box up and slipped it into her pinafore pocket. A quick look around the room, a tweak of the counterpane and then, with her arms full of stray cushions, Edith made her way downstairs to face the far more daunting task of clearing the accumulation of unwanted and displaced possessions from the parlour.

It was lunchtime before she allowed herself a break. She needed a cup of tea. The dust and fluff that seemed to have come out of nowhere had irritated her nose and set off a number of sneezing fits that had in turn aggravated her sinuses. She filled the kettle and slid it over the hotplate on the range. Lighting the fire was the first thing she'd done on waking and it only needed a quick prod with the poker and a smattering of fresh coke for it to begin to burn strongly. There wouldn't be too long to wait.

She sat at the kitchen table and lifted her feet up onto the chair opposite, sighing as her calf muscles relaxed and flattened themselves against the cool wood. The kettle began to whistle softly and she rested her eyes for a moment.

*

Edith awoke to wreaths of steam from the fiercely bubbling water. Her neck was stiff, and her throat raw from breathing in through her mouth. She staggered to her feet and leaned across to push the kettle away from the heat but as she bent forward, her pinafore caught on the handle of the range and ripped. One entire side of the pocket was torn off and the contents tumbled onto the floor. She hadn't been aware of carrying anything around with her; she must have gathered them up as she'd gone along with the intention of finding a home for them eventually.

She stooped and picked them up. They were an odd assortment: the handkerchiefs – she could remember those – a baby's shawl, a blue knitted bonnet, a wrapped tablet of soap, and a pair of knitting needles. Where had they been hiding and how had they got there? A headache pushed at her temples as she tried to think. When it got too much, she opened the cupboard door above the range and stuffed the strange collection inside; she would come back and sort it later.

But it worried her. She drank her tea and took her slippers off to massage her feet and still it worried her. Because accumulating unexplained possessions couldn't be considered normal. Be defined as the pastime of a rational person. She struggled to think when she'd first come across the concept of kleptomania. Probably in the notes she typed for her father on shell-shock. Yes, she seemed to remember that a previously well-behaved man perpetrating petty crimes was one of the signs of an approaching breakdown the Regimental Medical Officers were trained to spot. Had Dr Mackie been right in his bumbling way: that what had happened, here in this house, had affected her more deeply than she was willing to admit? Just because she didn't mourn the old man didn't mean the manner of his death might not have become twisted in her mind into the need to acquire things as overcompensation for what had been snatched away. A behaviour aberration unwittingly acquired could be dissected, understood, and rectified but first she had to scope the problem by gleaning every last piece of evidence.

*

The basket at her feet was full by the time she sat at her father's desk in the study. She'd found things everywhere. The strange, the incongruous, and the unnecessary. None of which she'd ever seen before. She supposed that she should begin to catalogue them but she was too tired. She'd add them to her kitchen cupboard hoard and do the whole lot later.

Edith yawned as she pulled open the desk drawer. Five – no, six – cards of buttons winked up at her, glad to be out in the daylight. Sharp-cut jet like shiny blackberries, a pair enamelled with deep blue irises, sugar-almond coloured Bakelite, and a mourning set decorated with delicate silver filigree. She lifted them out and dropped them into the basket. Her fingers slid back into the drawer in the expectation of finding something else that had slipped her mind.

*

She sat in the study as the afternoon sun slid behind the churchyard trees, the journal on the desk in front of her. It had a green leather cover tooled in gold with a pattern of swags and curls. It was altogether too romantic and florid for a man like her father but she recognised it from when it would sit on the corner of his desk in the Cambridge house. She remembered it because she'd never seen anything like it before or since. Edith stroked the spine for a moment and then laid the book down and flipped open the cover with the nail of her index finger. The front page was foxed with little brown splodges like drops of long-ago dried blood, the edges nibbled into uneven waves. It was not written on. Neither were the next half a dozen. The first thing she came across was a list of dates – each followed by a sort of shorthand or code. Edith shivered as a breeze spun in through the open window. She flicked through the following pages. They were covered in writing peppered with blotches and crossings out. It only took her another few minutes to see that the remainder of the first half of the book was all like that.

But then something changed. The script was more legible and the style less frenetic. The pages just past the middle had been written in a state of reflection. These were the words of an older, and possibly wiser, man. They certainly had something about them that was wearier but at the same time more cautious. Had he meant this part of the book to be read by eyes other than his own? Not hers, surely? He'd never have wanted to commit himself in any way to her.

Then she saw it. Her name. Her name wrapped up in a thought that made her teeth chatter and the band around her head squeeze so tight she thought her eyes would pop out. Her father … writing that … about her …

Edith picked the book up and flung it with a force she didn't know she possessed against the wall. It bounced off the plaster and lay sprawled on the floor like a wanton harlot, the leery scrawl daring her to pick it up and indulge in a little more depravity. Her eyes were dancing with sparks as she staggered over to the shelves and began pulling off volume after volume. When she had made a space large enough, she retrieved the leather journal and stuffed it in its new hiding place before replacing the books in front.

There: out of sight, out of mind.

She had forgotten it already.

CHAPTER FOURTEEN

Red Admiral and fritillary butterflies fought each other delicately for the last drops of sweetness from the flat heads of the ice plant. Edith kicked at the grey fleshy leaves as she passed. They reminded her of dead men's fingers. She'd always feared them. There was little else in Wilfred Drayton's garden – the geese had seen to that – but she hadn't pushed her way through the hedge to finish their work. She had business to do.

She picked her way over to the small coffin-like box balancing on three oak stumps in the middle of the muddy grass. A faint buzzing disturbed her concentration for a second. She shook her head and pretended it had gone away then squatted down to peer into one of the rat-sized grubby windows in the side of the box. There was nothing. She tapped at the glass and stretched her arm out to reach for the next one, only to recoil when an angry rumble of protest started to swirl out. She hadn't announced herself properly.

'I'm sorry to disturb you. I am Edith Potter. I live next door.'

A handful of bees flew out of the slit in the far end.

'You might have seen me from time to time pruning my roses. The centifolias have a nice smell, don't you think? It's a shame they only bloom once but the portlands are almost as good and they flower throughout the summer. But of course you'd know that.'

One of the insects settled briefly on the pink ribbon threaded through the front of her nightdress and waggled a little dance before flying off again.

'Oh.' Her lip trembled. 'I forgot to bring my door key to tap on your little house with. Is that why you don't want to stay and talk to me?' Her bare feet shuffled forward. 'Is it true that I have to tell you about a death? I know that's what they believe around here,' she lowered her voice until it blended with the hum of the hive, 'but they're pig ignorant. You've more brains in your furry little bodies than all of them put together.'

Her fingers began to beat a light tattoo on the box lid.

'Because there has been one, you know. But I want it to be our secret. I don't want you to go spreading it around or, who knows, another might happen.'

She brought the flat of her hand down hard. When she lifted it again the body of a worker bee lay twitching in its last throes.

'Just like that.'

CHAPTER FIFTEEN

Inside the Barley Mow, Rodney Davies was making a big show of polishing a couple of clean glasses and keeping his back turned to the cluster of drunken strangers standing at the bar.

'You might as well push off because you ain't getting served here.'

'What's the matter, our money not good enough for you, that it?'

'Them's who've had a skinful then stroll on in here at closing time ain't going to be adding a monkey's spit to my takings. So clear off.'

'Who you calling a monkey? I'll bleeding have you for that.'

PC Billings – off-duty or not – decided it was time to walk the slippery path between civility and the law.

'C'mon, boys. There ain't no call to be taking on so. Leave peaceful like, and we'll say no more about it.'

Sneezer Crowhurst looked up from his dominoes and poked the air with his pipe stem.

'He don't have to serve 'em, do he?'

'No, he ain't obliged. But he'd do well to treat visitors respectful all the same.'

'I don't have to serve 'em, do I?'

Paul sighed and raised his voice to that of small-time crowd control. 'No, Rodney, you don't have to serve them but you'll be aware like as not that getting a reputation for speaking to customers worse than you would to your dog ain't a good thing; come next week's fair you'll be expecting some trade.'

'I'd sooner be seeing meat rotting on the slab than have cooty pickers in my shop.'

Giblets Gibson drained his tankard. Then he wiped his mouth with his fingers and flicked the foamy residue towards the strangers' boots.

'I wouldn't piss on their likes if they was on fire.' Sneezer Crowhurst sniffed. 'Fill these up again, Rodney.'

A heavy hand slammed onto the counter and set the line of newly washed glasses rattling. Paul could sense this was getting out of hand already. These were probably East End dockers down to join their families in the hop fields at Nutley for the weekend. And they weren't the only ones in the pub who'd had too much drink for their own good.

He could taste the villagers spoiling for a fight, never being ones to extend the warmth of companionship to rag-tag passer-throughs at the best of times. And now was a long chalk short of being one of those because yesterday Florence Thresher had come into the Police House to report her son missing. Seems he'd been gone five nights although there was nothing fresh in that – the boy had often done a runner over to his gran's at Cowden to avoid his father's strap and this time it seemed there'd been a row over missing rent money – but Florence had trudged over that morning to find Alfie hadn't been near there in weeks. Given the cunning nature of the little tyke, there was no call to make things official with the Lewes force as yet; holing up after he'd been caught up to no good and watching his parents stew in guilt was a favourite trick of his. Only not everyone in Fletching was blessed with the same sense of proportion and rumours had been flying his disappearance was the work of the Gypsies turning up for the Taro Fair. Abduction and the like. Paul had done his best to quash whatever came to his ears by pointing out it would take less brains than those possessed by one of their worn-out nags to steal a child from the village they were camped in, but the rabble-rousers were having none of it. How much they believed their own talk and how much was down to working the fields too long in the unseasonable sun, he couldn't say. But the result was the hotheads were even more keen to land a fist than normal.

So, all in all, what was brewing in front of his eyes didn't look set to end happily. He wiped his upper lip clean of beer foam, took a deep breath, and walked up to the more approachable-looking of the strangers.

'Like to take a moment of your time to introduce myself. Constable Billings is the name – with or without the uniform. So let's be hearing your feet moving. I don't want to be having to go against my better nature and be locking you four up. A charge of loitering ought to do it.'

He watched the sort of shared look he didn't warm to flick between the burly men. Then, with one last thump on the counter for good measure, they stomped towards the door. He followed them out. Then turned to face the handful of regulars that'd tagged along behind.

'Be setting about making yourself scarce, you lot. Shout at the wife, kick the cat or whatever you do of an evening, but be making it summat I won't be having to have you up in front of the magistrate for. I'm going to escort our visitors here as far as the Moat, and I don't expect to see any of you here when I get back.'

He'd allowed a little more edge to creep into his voice than he'd intended; he didn't like having to throw his weight around at the best of times and especially not when he had a street full of beer-soaked would-be brawlers in front of him. It didn't look like he'd be tucking up with Mrs Billings and a cup of cocoa anytime soon …

Mrs Billings. Bloody hell. She was over in Splayne's Green attending a lecture with slide show in the village hall on missionaries in Africa, or lampshade making or some such. He'd said he would meet her off the bus. For a moment, she'd slipped from his consciousness and he knew enough about modern thinking to know that displacing your loved one from your mind was not a comforting thing to do. He'd send one of the more sober-looking youngsters to fetch her.

'Donald. Go and get my bicycle and wobble down to the Tilgate stop – the ride should sharpen your wits a tad. Be telling

Mrs Billings that I was held up by summat I could hardly help, and walk her back.'

Sneezer Crowhurst sniggered. 'I wouldn't like to be taking a try-on of his shoes when she finds out he forgot her.'

Donald Loader scurried off. Paul was watching him turn the corner out of Baker's Lane when he caught sight of a handful of horseshit flying through the air. It hit Sneezer on the shoulder.

'Let's see just how much you can swallow with that bleeding big gob of yours, carrot-cruncher.'

A glass then hurtled in the other direction and exploded on the wall of the forge. The air was full of threats and curses. Paul tried to shout above it all but he was like a puppy in the middle of a dogfight. One of the dockers had taken his jacket off and thrown it on the ground, his shirtsleeves now pushed up to his elbows. Another snatched up a fallen branch. Giblets Gibson had unsheathed the knife he always carried for skinning rabbits. Paul wondered if he had time to run back to the Police House to fetch his truncheon.

The only thing that stopped things escalating into an all-out bloodbath was the sight and sound of Edith Potter dressed only in her flannel nightie, her hair sticking out like a storybook witch, weaving right and left, hammering on doors and screaming *Merry Christmas!* at the top of her voice.

*

By the time he'd read the riot act, threatened imprisonment, seen the hop-pickers off with the assurance that he'd recognise their faces in they ever came to Fletching again, and told sleepy wives that their men could all do with their heads dousing in buckets of water, Edith Potter had been wrapped in a blanket hastily gathered from Mrs Billings' spare bed. She had refused to step into the calming atmosphere of the Police House so Paul had thought it best to take her back to the familiar surroundings of her cottage. There had been more than enough unpredictable goings-on in the streets of a small village for one night.

He locked her elbow under his as they walked. They made erratic progress, partly due to the increasing darkness the further they walked from the lamps glowing in a smattering of windows, and partly because of the woman's stubborn resistance to being helped.

'I am perfectly capable.'

Paul turned his face away from the rush of whisky fumes. 'No one is saying otherwise.' He smiled in the hope it would give his voice added sweetness. 'But I always think it's a fine thing to have a companion when you're travelling; it makes the journey a pleasure of its own making. Many's the time I wished they'd issued me a tandem so I could take Mrs Billings when I have to fetch up in Lewes on police business; it's a long way to pedal with only your own thoughts for company.'

Edith Potter seemed to accept this and stopped trying to pull away and thwart his gentle – but insistent – propulsion. After a while she started singing softly, each word drifting out as she planted one foot, heel-to-toe, in front of the other.

'One … man … went … to … mow …'

After that things got progressively slower until Paul was forced to a complete halt a third of the way along Green Lane. There was still about the same distance to go again until they reached her cottage. He wondered if he should scoop her up and carry her; except the last thing he wanted was for her to go thinking she was being kidnapped or suchlike. A woman in her state couldn't be relied on not to be leading bodies to be thinking all sorts of goings-on were, in fact, going on. Besides, Kitty and Sadie Cousins lived down aways and they were the type of onlooker no police constable needed in the more delicate aspects of the pursuance of his duty. He waited until he thought Miss Potter might have got her breath back and then moved off again, almost teasing her along with him.

'Last time I took to checking the calendar on the wall, it said it was still September. I've the young'uns to deal with over their bonfires and throwing bangers before we get anywhere near Christmas.'

He looked across at her as she picked her way along with doll-sized steps. She was swaying so much she shivered like an ear of barley in the breeze.

'I am as aware of the passage of time as the next man …' and she broke up into howls of laughter.

Then the howls turned into whimpers, then sobs that shuddered the blanket from around her shoulders. She seemed to be shrivelling before his eyes. Paul took her in his arms in the hope the contact would still her into quiet. But the poor soul couldn't – or wouldn't – stop crying.

'Please, Miss Potter, please don't be distressing so much. You'll be making yourself sick.'

She pulled free, wailed once long and loud, then flung her hand up to her mouth and clamped it tightly shut. He didn't think it possible for a person to have so much of the hard stuff inside them and still be standing.

'I'm … going … to … get … a … new … bicycle,' she began chanting in a childish voice, 'what … about … you?'

Paul felt as though he was having one of those nightmares after too much cheese for supper. He picked up the blanket and wrapped it back around her shoulders. Then he pushed her gently forward until they were once more walking towards the church.

'Nearly there now, Miss Potter. Soon have you in the warm and you can tuck yourself up in bed once more. You'll feel right as rain once it's worn off in the morning. I wouldn't go trying to dig over your rose beds though; I reckon your tummy might be complaining a mite if you do. Take my advice and have yourself a pot or two of sweet tea before you go doing anything more than getting washed and dressed.'

They were standing on the path outside her cottage at last. She raised a ghostly white finger and wagged it at him.

'No kisses goodnight. Father will be watching at the window and won't like it. He's very much against me having man-friends. He wouldn't have been so beastly to Edward if he wasn't. And if he doesn't consider someone with breeding and education good enough for me then he certainly wouldn't approve of a common little public servant with his brains up his arse.'

In the time it took Edith Potter to turn away from him and push open the gate, Paul no longer saw a confused and disorientated villager needing his care and protection but only a spiteful and crazy woman who drank too much and cared too little.

For her part, as she stepped over the threshold and felt the pain receding into the hollows of her body where it had rested for so long, Edith Potter became more convinced than ever that she drank too little and cared too much.

In the end, it was only a matter of temperament.

CHAPTER SIXTEEN

Old Sophie accompanied Paul down through the village. He'd made it his business to be knocking on her caravan door at sun-up to ask if she had a potion for overindulgence ready made up. It being the Christian charitable thing to do, especially on a Sunday. He'd not thought it kind to be seeking out Ern Treadwell at such an hour and asking for the loan of a tin of liver salts and having the reason for the urgency gossiped around the village – particularly if it was thought to be on account of Mrs Billings' plum duff. The Gypsy had heard him out then insisted on tramping into the copse to pick herbs she said would help beyond the first shock of getting reacquainted with the world. Privately, Paul thought it would take more greenery than there was in an undertaker's wreath to be getting anywhere near curing what was at the root of Edith Potter's ills; if she was drinking far too much than was good for her then she had a deeper reason for it than wanting to loosen her grip on the present. But the Gypsy had been drawing up every September since he'd been in Fletching – and nigh on twenty years before that – and was said to be able to work miracles; he could name dozens of others he wouldn't be trusting as much.

They were halfway down Church End when he heard it. Squawks accompanied by splashing and flapping and a series of reverberating cries that didn't sound like anything he could put a name to. Old Sophie started her flesh wobbling in a run at the exact moment Paul set his boots pounding on the chalk. Even as he whipped off his helmet to give his head room to breathe he thought what an odd sight the two of them must be making to those twitching their curtains to see what it was curdling their breakfast milk. He reached the green just as his lungs were telling him he needed to be getting his weight down if he was to be attempting the hundred yards' dash any more often.

Beside the Moat Pond two mallards were lying on their backs with their necks severed, their blood turning the grass a slippery magenta; another was hobbling in anguished circles, one wing clearly broken and the other a tangled pile of matted feathers floating on the water. From over by the church, skin-tingling sounds of agony came nearer and nearer until one of Wilf Drayton's geese bolted out of the bushes honking in one long cry of distress, a slash of red from beak to breast. Close behind was Edith Potter swinging a woodcutter's axe and howling like a dog with its leg caught in a gin-trap.

Old Sophie grabbed the wounded duck and moved her practised hands to wring its neck as Paul threw himself at the goose and tried to prevent it from flapping its way towards the houses. All the while, Edith Potter ran in circles, her lust for mayhem seemingly not yet having had its fill.

The axe was high above her head and beginning its descent when Old Sophie stepped into her path. The chapter headings of the police manual flashed through Paul's brain: there wasn't one came anywhere near close covering this eventuality. All he knew was he had to keep calm and not make matters worse; Old Sophie had long years horse-breaking and would do whatever it was came naturally.

'You have no need of that now. Give it to me. The work is done.'

Paul prepared himself to see the edge of the blade disappear into the Gypsy's ample flesh. But it didn't happen. Something in what was left of Edith Potter's senses seemed to become aware it wasn't poultry standing in front of her and her body gave the sort of shudder you see when a to-be-slaughtered beast is stunned, then she dropped to her knees. The yowling she was making turned into the squealing of a hound-cornered leveret.

PC Billings walked over and gently released her grip on the axe as Old Sophie knelt beside the frightened woman, gathered her into her arms, and hugged her close.

CHAPTER SEVENTEEN

The warm water in the tin bath swirled around her and the sensation was so pleasant that Edith didn't even object to having strange hands lathering her hair with soap. It was cosy in the bedroom with the fire lit and the curtains drawn, and it reminded her of being ill and having to stay in bed with soup and maybe a boiled egg and toast soldiers. Then, if she was lucky her father would come up and read to her … but of course that was stupid. The great Dr Gerald Potter would never have done that, she must have imagined it.

The water from her wet hair dribbled down her back and made her spine feel tingly. She hadn't liked it the way the gyppo had made her drink that vile-tasting stuff. She'd said she didn't want any more but she'd been made to finish the lot – she'd had her nose held – and then she was so sick that she thought her stomach would come up as well. But she didn't mind so much. She could feel that the filthy-dressed creature meant well, and anyway, Edith felt sorry for her.

That was enough now, she wanted to come out.

Give me the towel.

Why didn't the fat cow do as she was asked? It's very rude to ignore someone.

I'm cold and I want to get out; pass me the towel please.

There, she'd been polite this time; maybe that was it, maybe like Granny she was going to pretend she hadn't heard until she'd said the magic word. Funny how she should think of that after all this time. She'd never liked Granny. She'd a face that sunk in on itself and one leg too short made her walk with a stick. And she smelt. What was it she sometimes used to call her? Not *Edith*, she used another name that always sounded strange when it came out of her squashed face. She always felt like she was someone else with Granny.

Edith shivered. There were other things dripping from her memory like the water off her skin. Granny would tuck her in every night and rap her over the knuckles with her cane if she put her hands under the bedclothes. Said it was unhygienic. But her hands got cold in the winter and sometimes she wouldn't even know they'd snuggled under the blankets and were nestling in the clammy warmth. But Granny would always know and she'd come in and make her get up and walk around the bed – even if Edith was so tired she was still sleeping – and shout things at her. Sometimes she would have to keep it up until her legs crumpled, and the witch would make her get up and back into bed and tell her that if she transgressed again she would die in the night but without the love of Jesus. She hadn't cared about that, you could keep love, it wasn't anything very special anyway; what she'd wanted was sleep.

'Have you not had enough yet? You are shivering and it is not good for you to get cold after what I gave you.'

Are you completely stupid? I asked to come out ages ago.

'I put a towel to warm in front of the stove in the kitchen; I will only be a moment.'

Get a move on then or I'll be frozen.

'Stay in the water until I get back. I will be quick. It will not help you to feel your blood has turned to ice.'

She can't hear me, that's the problem. Deaf as well as daft. But she can hear the man downstairs. I heard her talking to him. Granny never spoke to Father. I know because I was outside the door when she was ill and he was telling the doctor. He said that she had never forgiven him for what he did and that I'd grow up to hate him too.

What was it that dirty gyppo gave me? It's like I am dreaming stories I knew before … or maybe it's the water flushing them out. If she doesn't come back soon then I'm getting out anyway, I don't care if I catch pneumonia.

'There you are. Just stand up now and I will wrap it around you.'

Edith did as she was asked and was swaddled up tight.

'Can't you speak, or have you no reason to? Silence can in itself be healing but only if it is from choice. But I'll make no demands on you to satisfy my need to know. I will keep talking and you can nod if you want something or shake your head if you don't. There's no need to tire yourself; I will see the smallest movement.'

Edith started to cry.

*

The parlour was crowded with the three of them in there. PC Billings had stoked up the fire until it was in danger of setting off a chimney blaze.

He sat and watched as the Gypsy handed Edith a cup of tea. The poor woman clutched the edge of the saucer as if she didn't know what it was for but didn't want to be dropping it anyway. She looked all shrivelled inside her clothes and he reckoned that Old Sophie had been a mite thoughtless to be dressing her in dark wool; it made her look even more like she should be inside a coffin than she had before. Happen she had caught a sight of herself reflected and it was that which was distressing her so. He put his own cup on the floor beside him and gripped his hands between his knees.

'You've … been … ill.'

'She is choosing not to speak, she can hear well enough and will not do so any better just because you shout. Her mind is not her own at present; talk to her slowly as you would to a child in a fever and she will come back to us in time.'

'I'm away to be fetching the doctor but first I have to know if you were doing anything else with that axe before we found you.'

Old Sophie reached out, took Edith's cup and saucer away, and then began to rub her hands in hers.

Paul could hear sandpaper rasping. 'I'm not saying as you've done anything wrong – I don't blame you going after them geese after what they've put you through, what with the sleepless nights and the state of your garden – but I have to be ready if someone comes knocking on the Police House door full of tales of chopped down trees or broken windows. I'll be knowing right enough which of them will be trying to lay the blame elsewhere for things they done themselves but a policeman has to have the full facts of the matter before he goes accusing.'

Edith Potter's eyes remained focused on the far wall and her breathing continued shallow and fast.

Old Sophie turned her head to him. 'Such questions will keep for a later time. For now, I need to understand what it was that happened in the moment before she felt driven to put her anger outside herself. When the doctor comes he will give her something to make it impossible for her to remember and, if I am to help her, I must do it now.'

She continued rubbing Edith's hands while the fire spat and a yellowy spout of smoke curled out from one of the lumps of burning coal. Then she slid off her chair and knelt on the floor. Paul shivered with embarrassment at the thought that she might start praying.

'Tell me what it is that caused you to hurt so deeply. You must give it a voice or it will destroy you.'

Paul heard the chair legs scrape a blink before he saw Edith Potter pitch forward and fall onto the Gypsy's lap. Then Edith's whole body started twitching as if a bolt of lightning had shot through her. Her lips stretched back over her teeth and her mouth spewed foam. He leapt up and helped Old Sophie lay the stricken woman flat and loosen the neck of her dress. Her heels were thrumming on the floorboards.

'There's a telephone at the vicarage. I'll be telling the doctor it's an emergency.'

'He could fly here on wings and he would be able to do no good for her now. She has faced her truth and wants no more of it. Her moment of pain is over. She will feel no more.'

Paul wasn't so sure. With the conviction that every second wasted would be one too many, he ran out of the cottage faster than if it'd been his own life at stake.

PART II

LEWES

January 1927

[The psychologist] is concerned with the experiences which make up the life-history of the individual mind.

CHAPTER EIGHTEEN

Lewes County Lunatic Asylum was visible for miles around with its high walls enclosing a thicket of evergreen trees like a hilltop cemetery; the only building with greater prominence in the Ouse Valley being the prison straddling the chalk escarpment: the town planners had known precisely what they were doing.

Dr Stephen Maynard tossed his briefcase from one hand to the other and stretched out his blood-starved fingers. His breath huffed out in dragon puffs and he hunched down further into his scarf to keep the gobs of icy rain from chilling his neck. Winter had come heavily and viciously this year.

When he reached the large iron gate he tugged on the chain above the grimy plaque that had *visitors* engraved on it. There was the creak of rust breaking its hold as the bell began to swing stiffly and clang out into the quiet morning.

These sorts of days always made him despondent. When the sun was shining it was so much easier to face the thought of spending an hour or two locked away from the world because there would always be something life-affirming to come out to – birdsong; the smell of the soil baking in the heat; roadside verges laced with cow parsley; the bright confusion of poppy-studded cornfields. The institutions he visited were usually surrounded by the most calming scenery imaginable and he considered it such a shame those deemed to be too mad to let loose in society were denied the simple and soothing hand of nature.

He curled his frozen toes inside his shoes. The long trudge from the station had set his muscles tingling and produced enough of a light sweat to stick his shirt to his back but his internal warmth was evaporating rapidly in the biting wind. Although he undoubtedly looked like a drowned rat, he was sure he would create the impression he desired – professional, authoritative, gifted. Four years ago, on the back of his work with the shell-shocked, he had secured a position at London's Maudsley Hospital in the clinic for the treatment and study of insanity; however, with his fortieth birthday rapidly approaching time was running out for him to achieve his ambition of being the youngest in his field to be awarded a professorship. His trip to this godforsaken place was part of his attempt to speed the process a little: he was intent on finding a cure for the rare but intensely disabling condition of catatonia.

Someone was coming at last. The man was so bundled up in coats and scarves and a blanket over his shoulders that it was impossible to tell whether he was an attendant or inmate. No matter. Stephen was prepared to be escorted through the grounds by an axe murderer if it got him into the warm and dry. Despite the weather and the dull ache in his feet, the journey through the grounds was not unpleasant; a double row of cypresses beside the path, lawns and flowerbeds, and a small formal garden with sundial and birdbath. Even in the driving rain it held a promise of better days. It cheered him up a bit.

But once in the entrance hall of the main building, his optimism vanished. It was much more depressingly bleak than he had imagined. Paint and plaster were peeling off everywhere and no effort had been made to make the place any less repressively institutional than the Bedlam he'd learned about in the early days of his studies. He was only grateful that his first visit was likely to be a short one. His clinic having been notified by the asylum trustees that they had a case of catatonia, all he had to do was ascertain that the patient was still in their care and that she was suitable for his study.

He was relieved of his sodden outer garments and shown into a small and untidy office just down the corridor from the entrance hall. The nameplate on the door read *Dr Victor Johns*. Stephen sat on the grubby and battered armchair beside the enormous radiator and watched his turn-ups begin to steam.

After a few minutes, a man in a white coat with a grey moustache and a vacant air stumbled into the room. Stephen introduced himself before embarking on his customary introductory speech.

'... and your co-operation would help us greatly with our knowledge of this condition.'

A thought flicked across Stephen's mind that he hadn't checked that this man was, in fact, the Institute Director at all. He could do without discovering he was explaining all this to one of the patients. But of course he had to be; only someone with the weight of this place firmly on his shoulders could look so haggard.

'And what exactly is it you want with her?' Dr Johns rubbed his red-rimmed eyes. 'This is a lunatic asylum, not a teaching hospital.'

Stephen smiled with a mixture of sympathy and understanding. He'd met many doctors like the one in front of him, some more dedicated than others but all overworked and unappreciated. He wouldn't wish his job on anyone.

'My requirements are simply to spend some time with her; to sit and observe and maybe undertake a few routine clinical tests.'

Dr Johns was still looking as though it would all be more trouble than it was worth. But Stephen couldn't do anything without his permission.

'Why should you? What's she to you?'

'In, and of, herself nothing. But deeply catatonic patients don't come along very often and it would make all the difference to my work if you would give me the opportunity to study her ...' he slid the asylum director a sideways glance '... and there might be something in it for you as well.'

Stephen trusted he had judged it correctly and that the man's desperation to lessen some his burden of responsibility would overcome his inertia.

'As well as the work for the clinic, I'm undertaking some research of my own on the lengths to which the mind will go to defend a secret – be it actual in the sense of something the individual has done, or fabricated out of an emotion such as shame or disgust leading to self-hatred. It's my belief that someone in your patient's state has induced her catatonia to prevent any probing or prying into that thing which she feels she needs to hide at all costs. Any breakthrough I may make as a result of working with her would, of course, draw attention to your institution and perhaps the trustees could be persuaded to give you an assistant.'

Dr Johns looked as though he was beginning to soften. His shoulders dropped slightly and his jaw relaxed. Stephen gave him a moment to contemplate an easier future, and then pushed on.

'You have my word that I won't in any way interfere with the running of the asylum, or in the long-term treatment of the patient. All I want is to have the chance to try to understand what could be going on in her mind.'

Stephen coughed to cover the lie. Of course he intended treatment. The paucity of suitable subjects meant that he had to grab every opportunity that came his way. His theories were solid, but, as yet, untested. He had become convinced by the empirical work he had undertaken so far that by applying Jung's principles of psychological analysis, he could peel away the protective layers and get the individual to confront their need to withdraw. Yes, there was a risk – under deep hypnosis the rational mind could, in itself, become the part that was repressed and that would lead to profound and irrevocable insanity – but it was one he felt he had no choice but to take. None of his colleagues seemed prepared to sacrifice their free time in the pursuit of healing such deeply disturbed minds. The fact that it might make his reputation was a bonus; his inability to do anything meaningful for soldiers hospitalised during the Great War with shell-shock – or *war neurotics* as Freud so unfeelingly termed them – haunted him and was the force behind his passion. He would not let scientific ignorance dictate the marginalisation of the misunderstood.

Dr Johns offered Stephen a cigarette, and when he refused, took one for himself and lit it. As he inhaled, he began to gather some papers from the over-crowded shelves in front of him and make an unstable pile on the corner of the desk. Stephen pulled out a pad and pen from his briefcase.

'If you could just tell me what you know about her?'

'Actually very little, I'm afraid.'

Dr Johns picked over the loose files in his wire tray then selected a thin one, opened it and skimmed the contents. 'It seems she came to us after being committed by a psychiatrist called in by the hospital her general practitioner had sent her to following a complete nervous collapse. It says here that she has some pretty horrific scars on her arms, legs, and torso; you'd be surprised just how many we get who've at some point or another set themselves alight – intentionally or otherwise – with a candle applied to a flannel nightgown. I really can tell you nothing more than that.'

Stephen scribbled a few notes. 'Is anything being done to try to ameliorate her condition?'

Dr Johns sighed. 'You must understand that this is not a hospital but an asylum: a place of containment – no more, no less. None of these people will ever get better mentally, and as for physically, we don't even waste our time conducting examinations or looking for any organic problems because there is nothing we can do about them. If they have a fatal disease or infirmity they will die, if not, they won't. Take the case you're interested in for instance; the fact that she has scars forms part of our records so that any member of her family can't turn up at a later date and claim she received them here. We have no idea – or interest in – what caused them. I'm sorry to sound so callous but there it is.' He threw out a thin smile of regret. 'I determine the level of sanity present and that's my job done, and as long as those deemed to be unstable are safely locked away with no danger of being released on an unsuspecting public, no one requires that we do anything further. All I can say is that she doesn't possess any of the normal physical indicators: deformed ears, misshapen palate, receding or prominent chin or brow, an abnormal skull, misshapen limbs, webbed or supernumerary fingers or toes. I can't judge if she is easily distracted or can entertain concepts or has a poor memory, but I can say that while she has been here she has not demonstrated emotional instability of the kind that manifests itself in impulsive outbursts of violence or screaming.'

'Can you only tell me what she is not?' Stephen's disappointment leaked out in the sharpness of his tone.

'I am not a bloody miracle worker, Dr Maynard. I have over two hundred lunatics on the main wards alone. I do my best to keep them from killing themselves and each other, and that degree of attention is more than some have ever had lavished on them in their lives before. To continue: she is not an Idiot, an Imbecile or a Feeble-minded Person and, as her father was a prominent neurologist, I have to assume her insanity is not inherited. She could be a Moral Imbecile of normal intelligence or have contracted mental illness due to extreme shock or fright or exposure to danger.'

Dr Johns looked up at the clock on the wall. 'I have to go. Look, you do something for me and save me the time and the trouble of conducting a full assessment into the extent of her condition – flesh out these notes a bit – and I'll arrange for you to have access whenever and however often you like.' He brushed the pile of papers off his desk and into his arms. 'It'll be one less for me to worry about.'

Stephen was reeling too much from the doctor's remark about the woman's father to be grateful. 'Who was he?'

'Who?'

'Her father.'

Dr Johns seemed to be having some trouble remembering. 'He studied under Wundt in Leipzig … his ideas on neurasthenia were very influential.' Johns swept out of the room.

Stephen's hand was trembling as he held the pen. A drop of ink dripped from the nib. Dr Potter. He had to mean Dr Gerald Potter, the man who had been – along with William McDougall and W.H.R. Rivers – a pioneer in the field of shell-shock, and one of the inspirations behind Stephen's current hypothesis. He'd followed his career via the psychological journals, including reading about his murder at the hand of a person, or persons, unknown. He couldn't believe his luck to be given the opportunity to include Potter's daughter in his research. This was undoubtedly the case that would be the making of him. He felt a bolt of excitement electrify his nerve-endings as he leapt across the room and stuck his head through the doorway and out into the empty corridor.

'What's she like?'

His voice bounced off the walls. The distant sound of a metal door swinging open accompanied Dr Johns' disembodied words: 'A bloody zombie; if you get anything useful out of her, it'll be a bloody miracle.'

CHAPTER NINETEEN

The key being turned in the lock unnerved Stephen for a moment. He didn't think it was ever a thing he could get used to. Eventually, after a wait long enough for his trouser legs to spawn patches of dryness, a man with bedraggled greasy locks and an air of transparency had arrived at the door of Dr John's office and beckoned him to follow. He was led through a series of narrow and dimly lit corridors. Each one began and ended with a barred gate – not unlike those on lion cages in a zoo – and the man went through a lengthy ritual at each one, selecting the right key from the giant ring he had hanging from a chain around his waist and then locking the door again behind them.

To say Stephen was over-stimulated didn't even begin to capture his feelings; he was perturbed, curious, anxious, and excited all at the same time. What would she be like? Would he be able to get anything useful for his research? Was the secret her mind was concealing something to do with her eminent father or was it something else she was protecting by refusing to communicate with the world around her?

He couldn't begin to say how much he hoped that her father was at the bottom of it. Just imagine if his research uncovered something about the background motivations of the obsessively private Dr Potter? Or his death: perhaps he'd been ritually slain by a patient who blamed him in some way for his worsening condition. Insight into either of those things would be enough to elicit a coveted invitation to join the British Psychological Society – a requisite step on the route to being granted a professorship – and if he was also able to gain proof of the validity of his hypothesis concerning the treatment for catatonia, then he would indeed be on his way to the top. It all depended on how co-operative Edith Potter would turn out to be. He faltered as his nostrils caught the first whiff of the wards. His whole future depended on the lucidity of a woman whose mind had elected to remove itself from the world. The thought was not a comforting one.

His escort having abandoned him on the other side of the last door, Stephen walked down the final few yards of the corridor before turning the corner to where, from his knowledge of the layout of other asylums, he assumed the ward office would be. His way was blocked by a ragged clot of patients dressed in the standard shapeless and colourless institutional uniform – over-washed and much-repaired shifts, or trousers and strange baggy shirts. Shaven-headed to ward off lice, dead-eyed and expressionless, both male and female looked alike. He tried to reach the one nearest him with a smile but the young man refused to look at him and continued to bang his body against the wall, his back echoing out a hollow thump with each contact. Stephen wanted to hold onto him and smother him into stopping.

'Don't mind 'em. They don't mean nothing. Don't even know you're here, most of 'em.'

An attendant had appeared in the doorway of a room off to Stephen's right. He had hollow cheeks and a sagging stomach and only his weathered skin and the better cut of his clothes distinguished his appearance from those around him. He raised his voice suddenly: 'Fuck off back to your wards. You'll get tea when I'm good and ready to give it to you and not before.'

Stephen flinched as the man grabbed his elbow and pulled him into the room as a sailor might rescue a drowning man. The office was little more than a broom cupboard furnished with a chair and a gas ring. A red electric bell push glowered at him. There was no natural light – the only window being the one in the corridor wall – a sickly sulphur yellow glow from the bare bulb making it feel as if he was standing under a dying sun.

'Firm but fair; it's the only language they understand; treat 'em like the children they are and you can't go wrong. Now, what can I do for you?'

Stephen longed to be let out and find the nearest pub for a stiff drink but he clutched his briefcase to his chest and explained his agreement with Dr Johns.

'You talked with him you say?' The attendant looked doubtful. 'Didn't know he was in. Can't say I'd recognise him to look at if I had've done. Doesn't visit this ward often. Nobody comes here unless they have to. I'm off myself tomorrow, you're lucky to catch me. A couple of months is about all any of us want to spend with this lot.'

The attendant reached his hand out and slapped his palm on the mucus-streaked glass that separated Stephen from the despair and smells of the corridor. He watched as the young man stopped banging himself against the wall long enough to spit a gob of phlegm towards the sound, then turn and start using his forehead to batter the brickwork. The attendant didn't even seem to register the brutal change in tone of the impact.

'Come and go as you like. I can't give you a key, mind. This is the worst ward of the lot. Disturbed. Only place we got bigger loonies is the padded cells but I don't expect you'll want to be going there.'

Stephen resisted responding with the expected shudder even though the implied threat brought back his childhood fear of the dark. He fingered the stethoscope in his pocket for comfort. 'Were you here when they brought her in?'

The attendant looked blankly at him. 'Who? … Oh, number thirty-two. Wouldn't know, they all look the same to me. No, wait a minute, I couldn't have been. I remember she was lying there like a useless lump when I got here.'

'What about the wardress who admitted Edith Potter, can I have a word with her?'

'Not here. Anyone who can get a better job is off quicker than a rat up a drainpipe. If I had any sense I'd be gone myself but then this is the only place that'll have me.'

Stephen didn't think he was joking. He hesitated for a moment before taking a cigarette from the packet the attendant had thrust his way; now seemed as good a time as any to reacquaint himself with the habit. He inhaled a long drag and held the smoke in his lungs for as long as he could to kill the musty traces of decay that had settled around him like a fog. He felt equally drenched in hopelessness. 'Who takes care of her?'

'She gets a tube stuffed down her throat and gruel poured in her regular like them suffragettes they had banged-up. Then there's a loony from one of the other wards who comes in and wipes her down with a wet sponge from time to time. And that just about does it. After all, there ain't nothing else she needs doing; it's not like she's going anywhere.' The attendant laughed through his nostrils. 'Only way out of here for her is feet first in a box.'

Stephen didn't know whether it was the buzz from the Capstan Full Strength or the cruel truth of the words, but he felt queasy and wanted nothing more to do with this oaf who was now pulling faces through the window's square of grimy glass. Stephen pushed his half-smoked cigarette into the bucket of sand that was being used as a doorstop and adopted the coldest manner he could.

'I just need a few answers from you and then I'll go and see the patient – '

'Inmates, we call 'em. Inmates or loonies. *Patients* sounds as if they might get better and that really would be leading 'em up the garden path, wouldn't it?'

'Is she always insensible?'

'Don't know. Can't tell. Her eyes are closed all the time.'

'Has she ever complained of headaches, vomiting, seizures?'

'Never complained of nothing. Never says a dicky bird in fact.' The attendant yawned and stretched. 'Right, got to go. Love you and leave you with this lot. Ring the bell if any give you trouble. I'll be back when I've seen to the men … hold on, though … wait a minute … Rumour is she was brought in after a fit. Only thing

I do know about her, she's a thrasher when she wants to be.' He farted loudly and padded from the room.

*

The female ward for the disturbed had as many beds as the cottage hospital where Stephen had done his clinical practice. Twenty-four on either side under barred sash windows that might once have been painted white but were now nicotine yellow. The walls were a dark green laced with scabby patches of flaking plaster up to waist height and, above that, a dirty cream that reminded him of unwashed bandages. Three central lights hardly gave enough illumination to cut through the hanging veils of cigarette smoke, and the air was cold. The stench of unwashed and uncared-for bodies was almost overwhelming.

Stephen kept his gaze focused on the prostrate form down the end in bed number thirty-two and forced himself to walk slowly and naturally past the women lying, sitting, standing by, or in one case strapped onto, their beds. He couldn't bear to think of them as someone's daughters. The word *pity* didn't contain enough. He could almost see his way to understanding – if not forgiving – the harsh cruelty of the attendant; the distance of disgust or ridicule would be as much for his own self-protection as anything else.

A new smell assaulted him as he drew level with a pale young woman cradling a pillow in her arms as though it were a baby. The sickly sweetness of blood. He allowed his eyes to drop for a second and glimpsed a shocking pool of red spreading out to kiss her toes. He only hoped it was menstrual. She certainly didn't seem to be in pain, and it wasn't restricting her movements as she shuffled in an erratic pattern that streaked the already stained floorboards. He would find a way of alerting Dr Johns about her when it was time to leave.

He arrived at the designated bed and could at last concentrate his mind on the task in hand. The woman was about forty years old with a spiky re-growth of hair sprouting from her scalp. Her skin looked clammy and there was dried saliva crusted in the corners of her thin lips. Her breathing was slow and regular, and stayed that way even when he bent over to introduce himself. From the lack of response he knew she'd be unlikely to give either help or hindrance in his assessment. On balance, he was probably relieved about that. The rise and fall of her chest and the tiny bubble of spit oscillating between her lips were the only signs of life.

Stephen placed his notes on the end of the bed and started his neurological examination, being careful to explain everything he was doing in a low, steady voice: just because she was choosing not to speak didn't make her an imbecile. He was sure Dr Johns had been quite right about that. He traced his finger in a line from her forearm into her palm. Then he took a pin from his lapel and stabbed the fleshy part of her thumb twice. He listened to her chest with his stethoscope. He lifted the heavy head and felt for any rigidity or stiffness in the neck, and then slipped his fingers around to find the carotid pulse. He ran his hands over her scalp feeling for lesions or unusual bumps, and finished the head examination by gently lifting each eyelid in turn and checking the status and reaction of the pupils.

For a blissful few minutes, Stephen had been lost in his clinical observations, but once he had paused to jot down a few remarks, his surroundings battered in on him again. He was disgusted to realise that he saw the locked door to the ward as symbolising release for him, rather than imprisonment for them. Where had all his medical detachment gone? He couldn't allow himself to be so affected by it all; he had a job to do and he had to get on with it even if his natural inclination was to pick up his briefcase and flee. Luckily, only one more test remained. He pulled up the corner of the bedclothes and ran the tip of his sharpened pencil over the sole of one of her grey-skinned feet, observed the muscular response, and then replaced the blanket. Now he could go. He would write his notes up on the train back to London.

Stephen looked up as one of the lunatics came level with the end of the bed then lifted her shift to expose thighs as classically shaped and creamy as a statue's, and pudenda. Then she squatted and urinated.

He counted every step as he walked briskly to the ward office and the bell that would undoubtedly be the sweetest sound he'd heard all day.

★★★★★★★★★★★★★★★★★★★★★★★★★★★★★

Medical notes

EDITH POTTER

The patient was not alert or responsive. Waxy skin. Could not or would not speak. Half-closed eyelids.

Unable to test for memory, orientation, intelligence or psychological disturbances. Next time?

PRELIMINARY OBSERVATIONS

- Non-cortical sensory system – insensitivity to pain. No response on peripheral nerves.
- Decreased muscle tone – Hypotonia; exacerbated by lying in bed or was she like this before? Muscle strength not tested.
- Corneal and conjunctival reflexes okay. Pupils are normal size and reactive to light. Eye movements conjugate.
- Plantar reflex – big toe flexion, no evidence of Babinski sign.
- No undue stiffness in neck. No meningeal inflammation?
- Automatic nervous system seems to be functioning. No trophic changes in skin or nails; skin temp. seemed normal (though so bloody cold, what's normal?).
- No grip reflex.
- No respiratory distress observed. Lungs clear.
- Pulse shallow but normal.

Theories?
Easier to say what it is not – no evidence of encephalitis. No lymphadenopathy or thyroid enlargement. No definitive signs of epilepsy. No evidence of spinal shock (check if she fell violently in her seizure).

Catatonia?? Can't be sure without further tests – and she has to speak to me. Will she?
Is this the best she has been or the worst since the noted decline? Can't rely on observations in my absence. Might have to try some medical intervention. Spk Dr Johns.

★★★★★★★★★★★★★★★★★★★★★★★★★★★★★

CHAPTER TWENTY

Stephen had measured every day working in the clinic as either one further away from the smells of the asylum that seemed to be permanently seared into his nostrils, or one day closer to his next visit to purgatory. And, inevitably, the following Tuesday came around sooner than he would've wished.

His first shock was that Edith Potter was no longer there. Something catastrophic had obviously happened in his absence. The minute he'd seen the empty bed he'd had to steel himself from shouting out in panic and running after the attendant to ask if she had met some accident – or worse; there wasn't one person in the asylum he wouldn't suspect of a soundless suffocation with a pillow or a firm grip on a vulnerable carotid artery. And the staff had more reason than most.

His second surprise was that when he finally located the asylum director in a tatty common room just off the airing court, he was with a policeman.

'Ah, here he is now.' Dr Johns waved Stephen in with a fistful of papers. 'I'll leave you to do the necessary.' He left in a flurry of white coat and cigarette ash.

Stephen felt as though he'd got to the end of a book only to find half the pages missing. The story couldn't possibly have ended so soon. He felt confused and disorientated and not a little frightened. This must be what it was like to be in Edith Potter's head; the thought didn't even count as an insight. He introduced himself and shook the constable's hand.

'You're looking like you've seen a ghost. It's the uniform that does it – even to those with no call to have their heart thumping at the sight – never known anyone not to start thinking they're a wrong 'un when they get to seeing a man in blue.' PC Billings laughed. 'Dr Johns has been telling me we're fetched up here to see the same soul. She was in my village before. Fletching. And just because a body's no longer sleeping in their cottage of a night, doesn't mean my taking care of any business surrounding them comes to an end.'

Stephen began to feel a little sick. What had happened to Edith Potter?

'Come up here regular I do when County Court's sitting. A tramp having away a sheep. Bit of summat and nothing – should've let him go but he'd made it worse for himself by sitting in the field bold as brass grilling a pan full of chops. What can you do? It's like some people are just asking to have their collar felt. I thought it would be a kindness to be getting her away from here.'

Stephen had to remind himself to take one or two deep breaths; he was finding reality as difficult to hold onto as a snowflake. A thought almost as bad as her demise struck him.

'Edith Potter can't have just got up and walked out; she's in a withdrawn stupor with a limited awareness of the world around her and anyway, she's been certified and would be classed as an escaped lunatic. If you know where she is then you have to tell me before it's too late.'

PC Billings pulled at his whiskers. 'She ain't gone far, like. And I'm not sure there's much as can happen between here and there but as I'm acquainted with the depth of her disliking of unexplained noises and people coming up on her unawares, I reckoned she'd feel more at home having a room of her own. When I learned she was here I spoke up right off to the asylum guardians – Dr Potter for a father likely to be having some sway in these matters – but a place in the shell-shock wing has only just become vacant. I'll be doing my part on behalf of any in need of receiving from the Police Benevolent Fund in return.'

Stephen could've kissed him. Instead he started to pace up and down the small room. The adrenaline spiking his blood made his fingers itch and he rubbed them together until his hands were sticky but his thoughts calmer. He didn't want to go through a scare like that again. But it wasn't the policeman's fault, it was his. He wasn't detached enough, was investing too much – nothing less than his future career in fact – in a middle-aged woman with a fragile mind and an unknown capacity for self-destruction. He had to remember where he was: a lunatic asylum was a place where the incarcerated rarely, if ever, lived up to others' expectations.

He stopped in front of the window and looked out into the courtyard with its high grey walls, rows of closed and barred windows staring bleakly down. He watched as the more ambulatory and physically aware inmates shuffled around in the freezing cold, some with little more than a threadbare blanket falling off their bony shoulders. It was a particularly dispiriting approximation of exercise. A sadness at the hopelessness of their lives scratched at the back of his throat. He would do what he could to change that for at least one of them. If he was right. If she could, and would, let him in.

He turned back, his pulse now something close to normal. Free from his fear that Edith Potter had been lost to him forever, Stephen's need to find out as much as he could about her background took over; it was not beyond the bounds of possibility that he might not get an opportunity like this again. But he had to broach the subject carefully. PC Billings was evidently a protective type who saw it as his duty to shield a vulnerable ex-villager from any undue unpleasantness, and probing of a highly personal nature – albeit from a medical professional – might well fall into that category.

'Do you know anything of the world of psychoanalysis?'

PC Billings grinned. 'I suppose you could be saying that. I've been doing a bit of reading up on it from the library – that's another thing I'm getting around to doing when I'm here in Lewes. Slave to human nature in and out of work-time, my Mrs Billings says.'

'Then I needn't tell you the lengths a mind can go when it needs to conceal what it wants to remain hidden. In some cases the mere fact that a secret exists – particularly if it's one from a deeply buried past – can tip a person right over the edge of sanity.'

'You're not talking about Miss Potter now, are you? She was a tad odd in her ways with people but as full as a shilling as you or me.'

Stephen studied the grubby mark at the bottom of the door where it had been kicked – maybe in a fit of temper – once too often.

'I doubt that very much. In fact I'd hazard a guess that she's been battling with whatever it is that has caused her condition for a very long time. Maybe since the day she was born. Is there anything you can tell me about her father?'

'No, there ain't nothing I can say I knew about him when he was alive. Not much after he was dead neither. Although the manner of his passing weren't what you'd be wanting for your nearest and dearest – and for an enforcer of the law, most unwelcome. Except it did come to my attention about the terrible fire.'

'When was that? Where? How did it start? Was it a long time ago? If so, do you think there is anyone still alive who remembers? Would the police have any record?'

'Whoa up … whoa.'

Stephen had opened his briefcase and was scrabbling for his pad and pen. He sat down in one of the grubby and cigarette-burned armchairs. He had to remember that not everyone was as desperate to get to the heart of this case as he was. He busied himself writing the information PC Billings had given him so far on a blank sheet. It wasn't much, but it was more than he'd known before – the name of the village for example – and he was about to be treated to what could turn out to be crucial to his understanding of what lay behind Edith Potter's self-imposed retreat from the world. He looked up and smiled to show he was ready.

'It was my wife had the idea. We was saying when we was counting our blessings at Christmas as to how sad Miss Potter's life had been and wondering if she'd had any pleasantness come her way. Mrs Billings had remembered they'd both gone to a lantern talk and Miss Potter going all poetical about the stained-glass windows in Ely Cathedral. Upshot of which Mrs Billings suggested we should pay a visit on my next weekend off, kind of a holiday seeing as I never take her anywhere. So we borrowed my brother-in-law's little runabout. We got to Cambridge and it was then Mrs Billings said that was where they'd lived before and as we should find out what we could about Miss Potter's past in case it might help her future, like. We went to the library and struck lucky right off because the woman behind the counter told us she knew the old lady – that's Dr Potter's mother – before they fetched up to live with her. She'd heard nothing from him while he'd been abroad but then one day he returns with a suitcase, a box of papers from the university, and a scrap of a daughter about five years old. The blaze took their home and everything in it. The mother died saving the little mite.'

'And?'

'That's it.' He picked up his helmet from the low table and made a move towards the door. 'When you see her be telling her I was here, will you? I've to get along or Mrs Billings will be thinking my bicycle chain's fallen off again and I don't like her to be worrying when there ain't no cause.'

Stephen felt a glow that wasn't only down to the feeling that maybe he'd just been granted the key to unlocking Edith Potter's silence; who wouldn't collapse eventually after a lifetime of guilt arising from a dead mother's sacrifice? No, it was the policeman's unabashed kindness that warmed him. It was touching too, the way he thought she would even realise he had ever visited her. There wasn't the remotest chance that was the case of course. But then the odds hadn't been much better on him finding out the details of the fire, come to that. He waved a sort of salute as PC Billings left the common room, and chewed at the inside of his cheek as he mulled over the exchange. It was all tied up together – he knew that much – her secret and the fire and her father and her catatonia. And it was up to him to unpeel the layers and get to the truth.

But it would mean him going out on a limb – as all the things worth achieving in life did – because there was a possibility that she might not be a suitable subject and her psychosis might deepen to the point of total disintegration. Then he would have lost his chance because she would continue closing down all her rational functions one by one, and before long there would be no way of ever helping her divest herself of the burdensome secret she had buried in the depths of her mind. No way of reaching her ever again.

The thought of what lay ahead for the both of them made Stephen clench every orifice he could. It wasn't only Edith Potter's sanity that depended on her ability to co-operate.

*

Stephen walked across the grounds to where the surly attendant in the hallway had told him the shell-shock wing was located. He paused for a moment and watched the asylum cat playing on the terrace with her kittens. He continued down the front path and then veered off to his right.

A squat white building was set back beside a stand of trees. He let himself in – no locked doors here – and headed down the corridor until he got to the room with her name on a card in a brass holder. He knocked and went in.

'Hello, Miss Potter. You might not remember me. My name is Stephen Maynard. I've come to try to find out what we can do for you, if I may.'

He walked over to the chair under the window.

'I'll just sit here quietly if it's all right with you; it's a bright clear day and you've such a nice view. If you want me to go away at any point all you have to do is tap your finger on the blanket, and I'll leave you in peace.'

He sat back, slowly crossing and uncrossing his legs every few minutes. So much of psychoanalysis was a waiting game.

'I do hope you can sleep in here, some people find being on their own too quiet after the pandemonium of the ward. Do you think you might feel like talking to me a little later on?'

He looked out of the window again. One of the kittens must've followed him; it was bouncing around as if stalking every blade of grass. The contrast in energy between cat and woman was heart-rending. It was obvious that it was too soon to try to get through to her. Maybe the best thing was to complete the remaining clinical observations and leave. He walked over to the bed.

'I'm sorry to subject you to this,' he said gently, 'but I have to conduct a few more tests. I'll be as quick as I can.'

He started to run through the familiar routine of looking for symptoms and portents of increased sensibility. And he did find some; maybe the transfer into kinder surroundings was helping her to unbend a little. For his final examination, he picked up her arm and, cradling the elbow in one hand and holding the wrist in the other, he pushed her forearm away from him. Edith Potter resisted the movement with remarkable strength. It was a promising sign. A shiver of excitement rustled through him; he would ask Dr Johns if he would institute a short course of electric shock therapy to see if that would increase her sentience further. If it did, then Stephen could start the hypnosis. He tucked her arm back under the bedclothes.

'I've some chocolate I bought at the station kiosk, would you like some? I'm going to.'

He reached into the pocket of his jacket, pulled out a thick slab of Fry's, then broke off a piece and slipped it between his lips. He sucked on it noisily. In a while he snapped off another and ate that too.

Edith Potter's nostrils widened slightly; her fingers twitched on the blanket.

'I have to go now. Thank you for allowing me to sit with you. I'll leave the rest of the chocolate here if I may.'

He unwrapped the bar completely and placed it within her reach on the bedside cabinet.

'Too much can make you sick and I spend more than enough of my time in hospitals as it is.'

He thought he detected the semblance of a smile but it was too fleeting to be sure. But even the possibility that there had been one was cause for hope. The next time he came down to see her there was every chance she would let him in.

★★★★★★★★★★★★★★★★★★★★★★★★★★★★★★

Medical notes

EDITH POTTER

Patient is a little more responsive. She is either less in a catatonic state OR is choosing to repress less. One is conscious, the other subconscious: but which one?

She has been moved to the shell-shock wing. More relaxed, quieter – less distractions.

Observations

- No speech so dysphonia, dysarthria, dysphasia and aphasia not tested. Abnormalities unlikely as policeman confirmed she had speech before.
- Nothing appears to be organically wrong with her mental processes.
- Grip reflex returned.
- Positive response to pain.
- Waxy flexibility – held posture for 5 mins.
- Increased muscle tone with cogwheeling.
- Oral intake must have improved although still probably minimal.

Theories?

Her immobility has been induced by severe mental shock. Resulting in profound anguish as though she wants to escape something she has done or something inside herself, or both. She is undoubtedly blocking and repressing memories:

Silence	= cannot / will not express unpleasant memories
Immobility	= holding back reactions to memories
Stupor	= deadening painful memories

Her catatonia is a way of channelling her increasingly strong emotions into resistance. What emotions?

In infants the two most likely to cause convulsions through an excess of them are FEAR and ANGER!! Is this the same for Edith? Is that why she is reverting to being a child and shutting out reality?

Hypnosis might allow her to let go of her control over her facility of speech and, as a state of abstraction, might assist in the recovery of her repressed memories.

NOTE: Go gently. Her strength of will to eliminate all traces of herself is formidable.

★★★★★★★★★★★★★★★★★★★★★★★★★★★★★★

CHAPTER TWENTY-ONE

For the next ten days, Stephen was able to get someone to cover his afternoon appointments and was at the asylum from three until lights out at seven-thirty. On every visit, Edith seemed a little brighter. Admittedly he had precious little to base it on other than feeling she was able to sense his presence on an instinctual level. Physically, she must've begun feeding herself – or be willing to be spoon-fed by another – because she had lost the signs of incipient malnutrition. Although she was still criminally thin.

He'd found a note from the asylum director on his third trip down. Dr Johns had made an exception to his rule of non-intervention and had been administering the electric shock therapy Stephen had asked for. It would have helped bridge some of the connections in her brain and nerve-endings but that was a very different thing to re-establishing consciousness. And that was the delicate task ahead of him now she had been forced into relating – however tangentially – to the world again.

All he required was patience. And her co-operation.

*

'Are you feeling any better today, Edith? I do hope you don't mind me using your first name but Miss Potter sounds excessively formal when one of us is wearing nightclothes. I must say that you do look a little more rested. I'll just sit here and take in the view for a while. Except it's raining so the grounds can't be said to be looking their best.'

Stephen felt the weight of the tin of sardines in his pocket as he took his jacket off in the overheated room and draped it over the back of the chair. He'd brought it for the kittens but, not surprisingly, they hadn't been out playing in the wet. He stole a glance at the bed. Edith had turned her head slightly to look at him. He had to work hard to pretend he hadn't noticed. He didn't want to scare her by appearing too eager. Everything had to be done in her time.

'I haven't any more chocolate I'm afraid but I suspect you're the sort of woman who'd distrust someone who always came bearing gifts. And quite right too, we doctors can be a sly old lot; I'm sure you've heard the proverb: *feasting is the physician's harvest.*'

Stephen rested his pad on his knee and began to make a few notes. Every now and then he glanced up and tried to look for any evidence of real awareness in the eyes that he felt had never once flickered in their gaze. He had to start probing the state of her mental capacities; while she was still without speech it would be difficult but, he hoped, not impossible. He had a hunch that a direct approach would elicit the best results.

'Can you hear me, Edith? You've been ill and I want to help you. I believe I can find what is at the root of your trouble and then, once it is out in the open, we can work together to overcome it and make you well again. Get you out of here.'

The offer of a complete recovery was undoubtedly a promise too far, but if what was left of her rational mind didn't at least have something to clutch onto then there'd be no incentive for her to drop some of her defences. He watched as her body shifted; not so much in terms of movement but in attitude as if thin strands of energy had started to seep through the reserve and make her weak attention more focused. Stephen began to feel he was making a difference. He leaned forward in his chair, his elbows resting on his knees and his hands flopping.

'I'd like you to indulge me and consider the logic of this. I believe something went very wrong for you in your past and that you never really had a chance to confront the truth of whatever it was that happened. Now circumstances have forced you into a position where things are equally out of your control and your mind knows only one way to cope: to shut down; to stop thinking; to stop feeling; and to react again like a ten-month-old baby.'

He tried to meld his gaze with hers.

'I can help you, Edith. I can facilitate the unlocking of those memories and that, in turn, may assist you in finding a way to come to terms with your situation.' He straightened up. 'If my intuition is right then, like me, you believe that it's always better to learn the truth – whatever the consequences.'

An energy rippled through Edith's body. It was a tiny movement but one he'd been trained to spot. It was signal enough that she was ready to let him in a little. A short session of deep hypnosis would test how much further she was prepared to go.

'All you need do is relax and let yourself drift; be prepared to let your mind wander where it will. You're in control at all times, Edith. Think of your memories as being shut tightly in a closed room. It's one you've built yourself and for which only you have the key. No one can force you there and no one else can get in unless you allow them to. My job is to help you to walk as far inside that room as you want, as you need. I'll always be here at your side, and you can turn around and walk out again at any time.'

Stephen stood up and pulled the curtains; it had stopped raining and a slick of winter sunlight from where they didn't meet in the middle fell across the bed and suffused Edith's features with a soft glow. He walked over and arranged her pillows so that one was supporting her head, and the other two at her sides for her arms to rest on. Stephen re-positioned the chair so that he could sit beside, and a little behind, her head. The air in the room was heavy and conducive to sleep. Her breathing slowed as her eyelids flickered shut.

'I want you to do some small things for me, Edith. I want you to use all the power you have to scrunch up every muscle in your feet; to feel every bone and sinew pulling and jumping to dance you out of bed. I know you can do this. You only have to want to hard enough and you'll remember how.'

Her face was impassive, but under the bedclothes her body twitched.

'Good. Now I want you to feel all the strength drain out of them again. Ask your mind to make it happen …

'… your feet are heavy as though you're pulling them out of mud and now you couldn't move them again even if you wanted. They are blocks of stone …

'… I want you to do the same with your legs. Feel the muscles as tight as if you were going to leap up in the air – way, way up until you can touch the ceiling …

'… now come down and feel the touch of your shift on them; the texture of the material. Press down with your back and feel it on your spine and across your shoulders …

'… let the edges of your flesh melt away until you can feel nothing but the cloth, and you can no longer tell where you end, and it begins.'

The skin over Edith Potter's cheekbones tightened as her face relaxed and her jaw dropped open. The rise and fall of her chest didn't break rhythm as Stephen picked up her wrist and gently let it flop back down onto the pillow. All resistance had gone.

'I want you to imagine yourself on the terrace of a large house, Edith. It's a hot sunny day and you can smell the warmth of the bricks, and you want to kick your shoes off so you can feel the heat rise up through your feet. Do it. Do it, Edith. Kick off those shoes.'

He watched as the bedclothes ruffled.

'Now walk down the steps and stretch your hand out to touch some of the lavender growing there. Hear the bees as they buzz around you – but they won't sting you, Edith, you are safe from harm …

'… crush some of the flowers in your fingers and take some deep, deep breaths …

… one … two … three …

'… the smell makes you drowsy. You see a daybed under the big cedar on the lawn. Walk over to it, Edith. Feel the grass tickle. It makes you want to laugh but you're too tired. You need to sleep …

'... you reach the cool shade where you can smell the spice of the wood. Now you can't keep your eyes open any longer, so you sit down on the cushions and feel yourself drifting off into a slumber so deep and calming that you may never want to wake up.'

Her head sunk further into the pillow.

'What do you feel, Edith? Tell me, what do you feel?'

The voice, when it finally came, was croaky through lack of use: 'Relieved everyone's leaving me alone. I know no one can find me because I am invisible with the sunlight blinding the windows of the house. I'm weary but I'm not tired. I don't want to sleep but I am getting a headache.'

Stephen dipped forward and spoke softly so that his words would be little more than a rush of air in her ear. 'I can show you how to let go of those things that are hurting you, Edith. All you have to do is to tell me what they are. Let them escape out of your mouth.'

He sensed a rigidity returning to her jaw and he thought that maybe he had pushed too early in his desire to get through these initial stages; every patient responded differently to the process, and he suspected Edith Potter had no intention of making things easy for him. He sat and picked at a piece of skin at the side of his thumbnail until it became sore.

'My thoughts are crowded as though there are too many people ... there is an intruder here. I can sense a presence and it makes me afraid.'

The first skirmish in her internal battle was over.

'Nothing can happen to you, Edith. You are safely here with me. No one will harm you.'

'How can you say that?'

Her voice had gone up an octave, and Stephen could feel the anger encased in the inexorable will the poor woman was fighting with. For. Against.

'... How can you possibly understand? Everything I believe in has its basis in empirical fact, irrefutable evidence; I have lived my life by the rules of logic and it is too late for me to abandon them now...'

But Stephen wasn't going to let her give up after she had made such a phenomenal effort. He needed to appeal to both the conscious and subconscious parts of her mind, and to do so in a way that allowed her to convince herself to let go for him. Such an approach was a calculated gamble; she was the only person in a position to undermine her defences but those protective barriers once thoroughly dismantled would be almost impossible to re-erect. If his treatment resulted in a cure then such momentary discomfort would be worth it but if not … if not … she could be left with her emotional vulnerability shockingly exposed. But it was the only route to progress and he felt he owed it to her trust in him to try.

'You are lying under the tree, Edith, and you see a bird fly above you and perch on one of the branches. You think it's funny because you can see it clearly but you know that your eyes are closed. You wonder if your sight has gained magical powers or if the bird is inside your head but then you realise that it hardly matters. The bird is there and you can see it. You let your eyes discern the feathers and the outline of the beak, and you're no longer afraid that you're going mad because you know the bird is real.'

Once again her breathing had slowed to match that of his as if she were trying to subsume her physical presence in another; she had a long way to go before she would come out of hiding. She may be co-operating, but she was still catatonic.

'We had a canary once. Granny did. Horrible, smelly thing it was. Used to pluck its feathers, and its skin was purple and puffy underneath, and you could see its guts like a nest of tiny snakes. Granny used to make me clean it out and I knew … I knew that all I had to do was take it in my hand and squeeze it and squeeze it until I heard the bones crack, and then I wouldn't have to clean it out anymore. It made me feel so good just knowing that. Power over another life is a very precious and dangerous thing but it is a defect, a mental defect, which has its roots in the wish to destroy and be destroyed.'

Her voice had shifted in tone once more.

'One day I did put my hand in the cage and I pulled the bird out and held it tight and stared at its ugliness until I couldn't stand the sight of it any longer. I took it to my room then – and every day after that – and I started to teach it and teach it until it could hop on and off a rubber ball and push a grain of rice with its beak and fly from the top of the wardrobe onto my head. In time, as I knew it would, the bird stopped plucking at itself and the feathers grew back until it was beautiful and bright and happy. Then, one day, after it had performed all its tricks and was flying back to land on my shoulder, I opened the window and it flew out and over the trees …

'... I found it dead the next morning.'

'How did that make you feel, Edith? Tell me, how did that make you feel?'

He could see a ripple of pain convulse through the facial muscles lying just under her skin.

'I was heartbroken and bitter with myself for what I had done … but, late at night, when I was in bed and outlining the map of my scars like I always did when I couldn't sleep, I was happy. I was glad I'd done it. I was pleased it was dead …

'... and I wished it were me.'

CHAPTER TWENTY-TWO

The London train up from Brighton was late. Stephen had to stand on the platform for over half an hour. There was a Waiting Room with a paupers' fire burning in the grate but it was full of men coughing, sneezing, and smoking. He needed space and air to help clear his thoughts. A beer when he got into Victoria would be nice to look forward to but he had to return to the clinic; there would be no patients to see but there would be paperwork. Always paperwork. And, in addition, he had to write up his private notes on what had happened with Edith under hypnosis. Try to draw some conclusions. Or speculations at least. It had gone well in terms of how she had been able to retrieve early memories. But he hadn't anticipated such a depth of desperation. And he should have done. With his experience of Olive, he should have done.

He watched the train get larger as it puffed up the line. A bell on the wall clanged. On cue, the stationmaster bustled out of his office and put his head in both the Waiting Room and the Ladies' Room to announce the arrival. Stephen walked up the platform away from the emerging mothers admonishing their children for whining about the cold, and a gaggle of young women screeching in their excitement over window-shopping in the West End. A couple in evening dress huddled together. En masse, people were such herd animals, standing shoulder to shoulder as if to ward off the invading train. On the whole he thought he didn't like them much. People, that is. Individuals were fine; individuals he could relate to. Disturbed individuals he could treat. But a society that colluded in believing it could bury the collective memory of the Great War in Selfridges, or dinner and a show, was unfathomable.

With the tang of coal tar smoke in his lungs, Stephen stepped up into the carriage. It was one without a connecting corridor, and he hoped that by choosing to be so close to the guard's van he would have it to himself. He sat with his briefcase on his lap, ready to leap out and swap at the last minute. He relaxed as he heard the wheels squeal on the rails and the deep bellow of the engine as it began to chug away. It wasn't particularly warm in the compartment but he took off his overcoat anyway and bundled it into the luggage net above the seat opposite; hadn't his mother always told him he wouldn't feel the benefit of winter clothes if he wore them indoors? He'd never understood that particular concept. A coat's ability to function effectively was defined by its material, thickness, construction, and fit; not by some innate capacity to suck up cold that diminished if it was worn too often or in inappropriate places. Two tangled thoughts pushed their way into his consciousness: had Edith Potter's mother had time to pass on any wisdom – spurious or not – to her daughter? And cold, like pain, was relative so maybe the coat thing wasn't such nonsense after all.

Pain and Edith. Edith in pain. Because she was. Under that cocoon of indifference to her existence she was hurting very profoundly indeed. Was he being cruel in forcing her to bring it to the surface? And were his motives to do so rooted in selfishness? He had known the risks involved in taking her back to a childhood in which a major tragedy had occurred, and from which she still – literally in the physical sense – bore the scars more than thirty years later. He had felt at the time that he was weighing them up appropriately, but how much was his decision to press on influenced by his ambition? His hunger to prove himself. His need to gather irrefutable evidence on the efficacy of hypnosis in acute cases of catatonia.

He stared out of the window. The South Downs were rolling away to reveal a river and marshy fields. The silver-grey of a heron spiked up from a clump of mace rushes. Cows scattered as the engine breathily puffed past. Ever since he'd been a small boy he'd loved train journeys. The trips down to the coast at Bexhill or Hastings had been such rare treats that he'd sit with his nose pressed to the window trying to memorise every inch of the way in case each one was to be his last. Then, as he'd got older, he'd begun to appreciate the anonymity of being somewhere in time but nowhere in space; of being blindingly in the present with the past left behind on a station platform, and the future waiting for him at a point down the line. Of being between expectations. How he wished he could recapture that freedom now. But even as he sat there, Edith's future weighed heavily in the briefcase on his lap. But not only there.

Because he'd got it wrong once before. Terribly, terribly wrong. Olive hadn't been catatonic but she had been severely and deeply depressed. Her face had been more sad and tormented in its sorrow than any other he'd come across. He'd treated her for a period of months and had thought she was getting better. She had responded readily to hypnosis and had seemed to enjoy their sessions. He'd even been thinking of seeing if he could arrange for her to spend some time out of the hospital to lodge with his landlady at the weekends – a sort of test to see how she coped in ordinary life with ordinary people. He was going to take her to Forest Hill. She would've liked that and he would've loved to see her smiling, her face wiped clean of worry. He hadn't thought her capable of suicide. Refused to believe that she was so unreachable.

What if he could cure Edith's catatonia with hypnosis, what then? Might she have to live the rest of her life like Olive, wrapped in impenetrable misery? But the whole point about Olive was that she hadn't wanted to live with herself. What if, once confronted with it, Edith found her own reality too much to bear? In theory, patients in a lunatic asylum should be safe from themselves but he thought her capable of achieving anything she set her mind to – however self-destructive.

But he couldn't abandon her now out of fear. Out of not wanting the responsibility. His interference with the asylum's laissez-faire approach to treatment had already altered her; had made her withdrawal less complete. He had no way of knowing at this stage whether the chink in her defensive armour he had opened would warp into a gaping hole she'd be unable to plug with anything except despair. Only by continuing was there a chance he could forestall the need of ever having to find out.

He took his pad and pen from his briefcase and began roughing out a diagram of the interactions between the human conscious and subconscious: the workings of the mind. Every now and then he glanced out of the window before scribbling down another word. He kept at it until they plunged into the netherworld of Balcombe tunnel on the other side of Haywards Heath. He rubbed his sore eyes and waited until they were in the daylight again before studying what he had come up with. He underlined the key concepts: *repression*; *conflict*; *dissociation*; *rationalisation*; *self-perception; adaptation*. The order within the pattern sprang out. It took him down a different line as neatly as the throwing of the points' switch would on the track.

Olive's problem had been that she had never been able to reconcile and live with the conflicts her life threw up; she was always raw and in pain and every day was a constant reminder of her failure to adapt to who she was. Edith, on the other hand, could well be suffering from the opposite problem. What if she was actually unaware that there was any conflict? Could anyone's repression be so great? He was beginning to think so. If he accepted that the conscious and subconscious were actually fighting for control then it wasn't too much of a leap to imagine that one was gagging – starving – the other into submission: as good a definition as any of catatonia. And if such an extreme form of repression and splitting was what was going on in Edith Potter's mind, then the danger of pushing her faster and further than she wanted to go was negligible compared with that of doing nothing. He had to pull her back from where she had already been allowed to remain for too long or she would, indeed, destroy herself. Without his intervention, she would continue the internal battle until withdrawal no longer became a defensive position of choice, but one of necessity. She would spend the rest of her days in a permanent coma.

CHAPTER TWENTY-THREE

Stephen made the train journey in reverse on the following Sunday. In the intervening week he'd managed a couple of snatched telephone conversations with a harassed, but increasingly intrigued, Dr Johns. The asylum director had reported an astonishing improvement in Edith Potter's condition and had begun to institute a programme of cold baths in addition to the electric shock therapy. There had been more than a note of pride in his voice when he'd announced that she had begun talking. Stephen let him believe that any progress was down to physical intervention, although he remained convinced it was his clandestine hypnosis that had been the key.

He brushed away the last remaining cobwebs of a late night on emergency call at the clinic, and let himself into Edith's room.

'The good doctor tells me you're speaking to us at last. He says you complained about the state of the electrotherapy room. Bravo. They say that nature, time, and patience are the three great physicians but I'm all in favour of a little spunk from the patient myself. A blood-rousing altercation never did anyone any harm – but you'd better not tell anyone I told you that; it's not quite a textbook thing for a psychoanalyst to say.'

He sat down and settled into the familiar routine of pulling his papers from his briefcase and sifting through them in an exaggeratedly slow way in order to give Edith time to get used to his presence. He stole glances at her but not once did her gaze waver from a spot on the ceiling above the door. He wondered if this was the trade-off her conflicted personality had decided upon: a loosening in control over speech in exchange for no eye contact. He fished out Jung's *Association Method* from his other papers and put it on the bedside cabinet before stuffing all his other notes back in the briefcase.

'How would you feel about conducting a simple word game? Nothing too strenuous, but I do believe it would help us get to the bottom of your condition.'

His proposal received a timid nod. Edith Potter may have been talking but she wasn't giving anything away. He picked up his pen again and intoned the introductory sentence as Jung had written it: 'I will read you one hundred words and I want you to answer as quickly as possible with the first word that occurs to your mind.'

He cleared his throat and began.

'Head …'

'Neck.'

The sound was faint but distinct: she would co-operate.

'Green …'

There was a longer pause. Stephen wondered if this was going to be the first indicator. He counted the seconds of silence.

'Skirt.'

'Lamp …'

'Burn.'

Her voice had quavered a little. He made a note of it.

'To sing …'

'Canary.'

'Dead …'

'Canary.'

That was hardly a surprise.

Stephen read through the next fifteen words slowly and clearly, giving Edith at least ten seconds to respond before he started to count the length of the pauses and annotate his notes.

'White … '

'Paper.'

'Tree …'

'Paper.'

'Book …'

'Filthy lies.'

Stephen continued with the rest of the test. When it was over he had a page full of notes and a slightly clearer idea of what he was working with. It was extremely promising. He slid the results back into his briefcase and allowed himself a self-congratulatory smile. He probably should leave it there but he was too excited to stop; she would be tired with the strain of having to think after so many months of silence but when this was all over she would have long years in which to rest.

'There are just one or two other things I want to ask you before I go. I promise I'll make this as brief as I can but I need to know if you can remember any physical symptoms in the weeks or months leading up to finding yourself in hospital. I'll tell you why.'

He'd decided he would try out the beginnings of his diagnosis of her, on her. He still had no real idea how much she could comprehend but he was convinced that being spoken to – even if she didn't understand what was being said – was the best way for her rational, conscious mind to know it was being championed.

'I'm convinced your catatonic state is as a result of repression. Now there's nothing new in that because we've known the connection from the neurasthenics in the military hospitals during the Great War – much of the work carried out by your father, in fact.'

A shudder rippled through Edith's body but she didn't shift her gaze from the spot over the door, or alter her expression. Stephen felt the beginnings of a current of resistance in the air between them. He thought to make a note of it in his observations and carried on.

'Then there are Pierre Janet's findings that the conflict between the repressing and the repressed forces produces mental and emotional exhaustion; however, I think your mind has taken that one stage further and moved into the physical realm as well.'

Edith's eyes had closed. Her breathing was growing shallow. Stephen knew he might lose her if he pushed too hard; her mind was fighting him – as well as itself – in its efforts not to reveal what it wanted to keep so firmly hidden. He would have no choice but to leave the rest of his tentative conclusions until another time and finish his questioning before she cut him off completely.

'Just tap your finger on the bedclothes if you've felt any of the following. Can you do that for me, Edith?'

A bony finger shivered in the air for a second and then fell back down to rest with the others on top of the blanket. Stephen focused all his attention on her scrawny hand.

'Thank you. Remember, I'll notice even the slightest of movements so you don't have to worry about the effort involved.' He hoped his reassurances were reaching her subconscious. 'Any pains about the body, particularly the back?'

A long pause and then a shaky affirmation.

'Weakness in the eyes?'

Nothing.

'Headaches? These might've felt like there was a weight around your neck or a metal band tightening across your forehead. Is that something you recognise?'

She waggled her finger.

'These next may be a little more difficult to identify but I want you to think hard. Any restlessness and difficulties in sleeping?'

No reaction.

'An inability to concentrate?'

Again, nothing.

'An overall feeling of malaise or depression?'

When there was still no reaction, Stephen began to wonder if she had fallen asleep. He decided that he would risk one last symptom and then leave.

'An increase or diminution of the sex impulse?'

He felt like a schoolboy as he caught himself blushing.

'No.'

The word had been forced out between tight lips with all the explosion of a gas grenade.

★★★★★★★★★★★★★★★★★★★★★★★★★★★★★★

Medical notes

EDITH POTTER Page 1

Some speech but limited communication. Where is she inside that body? Still no indications of why she is doing this. Much clearer picture of how – her repressed tendencies are cut off from the rest of her personality. Wholly subconscious. Obscures the conflict behind it. A very thorough approach to dissociation – to be expected from someone of her mental capacities. What, if anything triggered it? She could have been – and probably was – repressing for years so why the collapse when she did?

Word Association Test Results

- Unable to read much into length of time to answer. Catatonia too masking.
- Majority of responses fall into opposite or association categories. No surprises.
- Some definitions on luck; behaviour; to choose; pamphlet. Symptom of her scientific training or refusal to co-operate and follow the instructions given? Unclear.
- Predicate responses significant. Correlation between words expressing emotions and her emotional judgements. Indicates deep problems with feelings. Classic repression:

WORD	*RESPONSE*
Despise	'too complicated to explain'
Ridicule	are the ones who are stupid'
Anxiety	worry; forget'
To Fear	fear itself'
Foolish	foolish. What's foolish?'
Sad	won't cry'
Angry	won't cry'l know what you want' (laughter)

Most interesting but for which I am unable to draw a conclusion as to the significance:

women; pride; behaviour; child; lie; pure; false; to abuse; to prick

She <u>REFUSED TO ANSWER.</u>

Notes:

<u>Supplements</u> – too many words – symptom of negativism (catatonia) or reinforced object-libido (Freud)? More likely former; her persona and scientific background do not lend themselves to excess of enthusiasm but she does display an inner void or dissatisfaction. <u>Repetitions</u> – sign of impeded adaptation to me and world around her. Could also be testing me. Display of assumed superiority?

★★★★★★★★★★★★★★★★★★★★★★★★★★★★★★

★★★★★★★★★★★★★★★★★★★★★★★★★★★★★

Medical notes

EDITH POTTER Page 2

Theories:

Dissociation terminates conflict but repression merely obscures the conflict from the consciousness. Repression is often a gradual process but dissociation is likely to be sudden.
Amnesia – most common form of dissociation. Does Edith have it? OR
Is she experiencing dissociation to such a degree that she is splitting?

Consider: as part of her disintegration, her sentiments are divided into two conflicting systems (conflict = repression = dissociation = catatonia). Each part would have its own memories and be distinct and discontinuous with the other part of the personality. Remember she said it was crowded in her head – did she mean literally?

Evidence? Not conclusive but the groups of words to which she gave predicate responses and those she refused to answer must have some – differing – connections. These connections – not just the words – are of significance to her.

What does she get from her catatonia, her flight into incapacity? There must be some purpose in it. She is trying (successfully) to hide something. Is this the meaning of the functional disorder or is there something deeper?

Jung – "The patient has a story that isn't told and which no one knows of. It is the secret, the rock against which he is shattered." Does not even Edith know her secret?

Sexual repression – too Freudian or accurate? Would she ever be able to tell me? Dare I ask again?

Whatever the cause, Edith is in deep conflict; incompatible motives compelling her towards incompatible goals. With someone like her, they would go unrecognised because of years of rationalisation to explain and excuse the stirrings of unease.

If I can expose the conflict and reduce the opportunities for rationalisation (under hypnosis) and get her to acknowledge it, then the need for repression might vanish.

Action:
Need to be able to conduct more sessions of deep hypnosis. There remain signs of resistance –toward me or a symptom of her inner conflict?

Consider discussing her case with her as a way of appealing to her scientific judgement and eliciting co-operation. From the test results, logic and reason still form a large part of her personality (but for how long?)

★★★★★★★★★★★★★★★★★★★★★★★★★★★★★

CHAPTER TWENTY-FOUR

Stephen pulled for a third time on the rusty bell. Why were they taking so long to come and let him in? It had been a month since he'd been able to return to the asylum. The frustration had nearly driven him crazy. It was as if everything was conspiring against him. First, he had succumbed to the influenza that had been doing the rounds of the hospital and then, when he had returned to his duties in the clinic, he'd found his caseload increased because so many of the other doctors were off sick. But he was here now. And impatient to find out what progress, if any, his patient had been making in his absence.

*

A vase of early daffodils was on her beside cabinet. He wondered what kind soul had thought of that. Edith would be sure to have noticed the additional colour in her room; every stimulation of her senses at this time was helping towards making her more conscious of her environment.

'You're certainly looking brighter this morning. A bloom of colour on your cheeks.'

This wasn't bedside flattery; she really did have a flush of liveliness about her that he hadn't seen before.

'I'm sorry I've neglected you for so long, but I see that they're taking good care of you. How are you on the talking front? Do you feel like indulging me a little today?'

He dragged the chair over to her bedside and got himself comfortable in the usual manner.

'Hasn't anyone told you how irritating that is?'

Her voice was strong and clear but her face was turned, as before, to the ceiling. It was etched with lines but no emotion.

'Why don't you be the first? After all you've already had some practice with Dr Johns; come on, do me the honour of letting me be the next recipient of your astute criticism. I'm sure I could do with it.'

'All that crossing and uncrossing your legs.'

This was far more than he'd hoped for. Not only was she talking voluntarily but she was expressing a reaction to his presence. She was acknowledging a feeling. And in addition, she was demonstrating she was capable of processing and evaluating information. Maybe his weeks away had been good for her after all; her mind had used the time to unlock and unbend a little.

'*Physician, heal thyself* – that sort of thing?'

She grunted.

'It's a point well made, Edith. Maybe we should swap places – bearing in mind of course that doctors make the worse patients – but I'm willing to give it a go if you are.'

'Swap places.'

'Yes, we can do that in a moment but first I'd like us to discuss one or two of the more interesting aspects of your own case.'

'Swap places.'

Stephen flicked a swift glance her way but Edith's face was blank. He swallowed a tinge of apprehension and ploughed on with his plan of making her a partner in her own therapy: her willing compliance from this point on was critical.

'I promise we will. But for now I want to ask your opinion on how I'm doing. I'm sure with all this rest and relaxation you're getting you must've thought once or twice about my progress with you. Be as critical as you like, I can take it.' He wiped his palms on his trousers.

Silence.

'In that case, I'll start with a few of my own views if I may. Let me say now that I'll tell you the truth as I see it but to tell you everything would be misleading; however, I promise you it's only my ill-formed and tentative conclusions I'll leave out. What do you think of my proposition?'

Edith blinked once or twice rapidly but said nothing.

Stephen forced himself to breathe slowly and wait. He had to learn patience; he'd tried the chocolate and the jokes, and that was the only thing left according to what had been the late Dr Maudsley's favourite proverb: *the best physicians are Dr Diet, Dr Quiet, and Dr Merryman.* He would hold his tongue for the entire session if he had to.

The answer, when it came, was not the one he wanted to hear.

'Swap places.'

He wanted to roll on the floor and scream. She was exhibiting another of the most common symptoms of catatonia: echolalia. Such parrot-like repetition was not a good sign; it showed she was still not responding to him on a fully conscious level, and clinically speaking, it was often indicative of profound resistance. Whatever the conscious – or subconscious – message Edith wanted to give in adopting this approach, he would be unable to break it down. The irony of her causing him frustration because of her frustration wasn't lost on him but he was hardly able to continue, let alone smile. But continue he must because having made a promise to be open with her, it would be unethical – and potentially destructive to their tenuous relationship – not to keep it.

'To start with the basics first: a neurosis is a product of a failure to adapt. The adaptation may be to people or the environment or any given situation but the effects are always the same: a lack of inner harmony. It's as though the framework we use to organise our perceptions has broken down and we no longer know who we are. Am I making myself clear, Edith? I want you to follow this because it'll become very important when I move on to what I think may be happening with you.'

'Swap places.'

There was nothing behind the words. They were empty of thought and feeling.

'One of the reasons such disturbances cause us so much distress is that they tend to bypass our reason and intellect and affect our instinct, our emotions. And that's especially difficult for someone like you who's used to being able to think their way out of a problem because, with only a portion of your faculties available, it can only ever be guesswork. There are so few clues for your rational mind to work on. Without outside intervention, that is.'

He stood up and walked over to the window. The lawn outside was fresh and green, and cobwebs still danced with last night's dew. He wished he had some way of gauging how she was responding to all this. Was her rational side compelling her into the role of an interested observer, or was her emotional side getting angry at the picture of disintegration he was painting? It would make a difference.

'Everybody, every single one of us, has a secret. Some of us have more than one.'

His breath frosted the cold glass until he could no longer see out but he didn't want to turn around. He wasn't ready yet.

'And all our secrets have their roots in the past; it may be the recent past or, as Freud would have us believe, from our childhood.'

'Swap places.'

Her voice had an edge to it, a harshness that hadn't been there before. He had to return to his seat and observe or he might miss one of the crucial stages of her decline or release. He felt a shiver of distaste at his clinical thoroughness; at this pivotal juncture, he was aware that Edith wasn't the only one accessing and acknowledging habitually repressed feelings. In him, the man and the doctor were waging their own war, too.

'When something happens to us it marks its passage through our experience. It may be only fleeting or it may be of such significance that it blows our whole world apart, but it changes us irrevocably; it helps make who we are about to become. And this next point is important, Edith. There are no value judgements on whether the changes are good or bad: they are just as they are. They are valid because they exist and we have to accept them as such. The reason this is so crucial is because the mind can't allow an experience to remain unassimilated for any length of time. If – for whatever reason – a part of ourselves refuses to accept or take responsibility for what has happened then it will lock the experience away where it can no longer be reached. That can lead to conflict and repression and ultimately dissociation – the splitting off of parts of ourselves. And that's where I think you are, Edith.'

Just for a second, her gaze slipped over his face but it was so vapid he was unable to pick up anything of her state of mind. He thought she was co-operating the best she could but it wouldn't be enough to enter into hypnosis this time. Her resistance was too great. The childlike, frightened part of her seemed to be growing stronger each time they met. A knot of compassion lodged in his throat. He coughed. He had been worried for the last few days about whether to pursue this line and now the moment had come, he really didn't know if he could go ahead. The responsibility of distressing her further was almost too much. He felt a flush rush up from under his collar, took a deep breath and gabbled it out before he could change his mind:

'Recently published research by Sir Frederick Mott and his pupils shows that in many cases of dementia praecox there is evidence of maldevelopment of the sex glands. You'll understand why I can't ignore this as a possibility when we take your physical damage from the fire into account. There are forms of catatonia with hormonal connections and that ...'

He was perspiring now and his jacket was uncomfortably heavy.

'You've never been married have you, Edith? Not that there's anything intrinsically unhealthy in that but any failure in the sex instinct may be linked to biochemical changes in the brain and that would give me an entirely different avenue of exploration.'

When the silence finally became too oppressive, Stephen left.

CHAPTER TWENTY-FIVE

'I want to take you further back now, Edith. I want you to imagine that I have a long, long piece of string in my hands and on it is a series of knots. You tied them for me. I am going to give the string to you and I want you to run it through your fingers. Feel the weight of it. Feel the thickness of it.'

Edith Potter's fingers trembled. Stephen leaned forward on the chair until he was just inches from her face and could taste the mustiness of her exhaled air. It had taken him a long time to get her into the hypnotic trance but now she was there he wanted to take her as deep as she would allow him to go. It was even more imperative than ever that he broke through her reserve as quickly as possible. Last Thursday an announcement had appeared on the clinic notice board detailing the British Psychological Society's next meeting. As usual they were calling for papers and he'd put his name forward only to spend a sleepless night pacing around his room, pulling his research to pieces and regretting his temerity. The hypothesis still stood up – he was pretty sure about that – but without any evidence of practical application it remained interesting, but not startling. He needed proof.

A blackbird outside the window was calling out its song and Stephen thanked providence for giving Edith such a gentle reminder that the world was still out there softly waiting: she might very soon need that reassurance. He found some comfort in it himself.

'Pull the string through your hands and feel where the knots are.'

Her thin hand clasped and unclasped rhythmically.

'Now I want you to see if you can sense when one is coming up before your fingers get there. When you can intuit every single knot and its order on the string, I want you to pick one for me.'

He paused for a moment or two.

'Pick one for me and hold it between your thumb and finger.'

Edith performed the pincer-like movement. Her face was relaxed and her breathing steady.

'Tell me what it represents. Can you do that for me, Edith? I will be patient until you are ready. Could you start to do that for me?'

The notes of the blackbird's song and the soft hush of some slippered footfalls in the corridor outside were the only sounds.

'I am in a room …'

'Where is the room, Edith?' He was almost whispering.

'I don't know because it is dark …'

'How old are you?'

'I don't know because it is dark …'

As he'd had to in their last session together, Stephen worked hard to crush his disappointment. This could be a sign of verbigeration: seemingly meaningless responses for her to hide behind. If her mind's need for catatonic symptoms was so great that it was inducing them even in her trance-like state, then he had misjudged badly. He ran his hand over his forehead and felt his hot skin rasp. He had to stay focused.

'I keep calling and calling but no one comes, and I don't know where anyone is …'

This was better.

'What do you feel, Edith? Tell me what you can feel.'

'Something is pressing and pressing on me and making my skin scream.'

Her voice was shaking and growing higher with every word. He reached forward and touched her wrist.

'Keep hold of the string, Edith. Remember that it is your contact with me and I am not about to let you go. While you have one end and I have the other, you're perfectly safe. Tell me what else you can about what is happening around you now.'

'There is a burning right in the centre of me and I can't seem to make it go away and I can't remember it not ever being there.

There is not an inch of me that doesn't hurt inside and out, and my eyes are sore from crying.'

Her whole body emanated an aura of pain; Stephen's chest tightened in sympathy.

'Find one word, Edith. Find one word for how you feel.'

'Alone.'

'Get right in the knot and tell me what it is like on the inside …

'… take yourself in as far as you can go. I have the rest of the string here, tight in my hand; you can pull yourself back. If it is too much, you can come right back. I want you to know that there is nothing holding you there; it is only a knot and you can unravel it and find your way out any time you want.'

Would this be the push too far?

'Cold … Sterile … Confusing …'

He'd helped her access the rational side of her mind again. However, she was still talking about feelings. Logic and emotion were becoming reunited: it could be the beginning of the crucial stage.

'… I can't stop the swirling inside my head … it's like patterns in a kaleidoscope … I don't want to be here, I want to be … somewhere else … someone else. I look on the inside and there is nothing … I am like an empty shell …'

'Now try very hard to stop thinking. Switch the adult off, and show me the child. Find the child you still are deep within that knot you tied so tightly around yourself, and tell me what is happening to you.'

A long expanse of nothingness. Then a shudder like the slamming of a door. A second later, all muscle tension vanished. Her chest was barely rising and falling, her breath little more than a flutter from her lungs. Edith's mind had willed her into unconsciousness.

Stephen leapt from the chair to prise her mouth open and stop her swallowing her tongue. He knew – and was aware that a desperate part of her did too – that they were getting uncomfortably near the truth.

CHAPTER TWENTY-SIX

Stephen had stayed with Edith until her pulse had become strong and steady, and then had sought out Dr Johns to ask him to arrange for her to be checked up on at regular intervals. He'd been pleasantly surprised at how readily the asylum director had agreed; obviously he wasn't the only one who thought Edith Potter worth saving.

*

Another interminable week in the clinic, and he was back. He let himself quietly into the room. One of the kittens had followed him and he pushed its furry body gently outside again with his foot.

'How are you feeling today, Edith? Any better?'

The face turned to the wall was hostile and fringed with fury. He could only say that in her position, he'd be exactly the same.

'I can understand your blaming me for what you're going through, for the turmoil you must be experiencing, but we're so very nearly there.'

Maybe he should have let the cat stay. It would undoubtedly be more welcome than he was. He picked up the chair and moved it to the side of the bed where he would be within range of those hooded eyes should they wish to show him any forgiveness.

'You have trusted me this far, Edith, stay with me a little longer. Please. I promise you that at the end of this, you'll feel freer than you've ever done in your life before. You will be back in touch with your true self.'

Her fingers busied themselves obsessively gathering and pleating the strip of sheet under her hand. Stephen saw that it was grey and greasy. It was another catatonic symptom: stereotypy. He thought that probably the next stage would be for her to go back around the loop into stupor and withdrawal again. Beyond the reach of hypnosis – possibly beyond the reach of them all. The thought that he might very well be about to hasten her descent down that path made him feel queasy. He looked up as a light spattering of rain started to flick onto the window.

'Can we do the same as we did before, Edith? Will you allow me to take you back to your childhood again so you can show me what went on then? I'm convinced the answer to your psychosis lies in something in your past. I can't promise that it won't cause you any pain, but I can say that it can do no more damage than you are doing to yourself; your mind is refusing to accept what it knows and it's destroying you. I need you to exercise your will and help me to reach the truth before your mind causes more disintegration than I can ever hope to repair. It's the truth that will save you, Edith; as it's only ever the truth that will save us all.'

He couldn't bring himself to tell her his truth: that he was now deep into unknown territory and he had no idea which way it would go. He watched as the pleating of the sheet continued; the muscles over Edith's jaw began to tense and ripple as her fingers started to pluck more and more fervently. The counterpoint of the ping of the rain on the glass. Then the compulsive movements gradually became smoother until they faded into the background. Finally they stopped altogether. Something inside Edith had resolved itself.

The moment he had been almost dreading had come. He stood up and arranged the pillows under her neck and arms, drew the curtains, and then shifted his chair to its usual place just behind the bed head.

Now she had decided to co-operate, Stephen was able to get her into a trance with such ease that he felt like a fraud; it was as if she was doing it to herself. When he was convinced she was receptive, he started the process of taking her deeper than he had ever attempted with any patient before.

'This time what I want you to do for me is to think of yourself as a field mouse as small as small can be. You are curled up warm and cosy in your little burrow, free from harm in your nest of dry grass. You start to run your little paw over your ears to clean yourself. Your fur is soft …'

He watched for the telltale signs of compliance in the softening of the muscles in her face.

'Now you grow a little – just a little – and you are a kitten sleeping with its mother in a basket in front of the fire.'

Her neck lifted off the pillow for a second, then she relaxed and a soft smile crept around her mouth.

'You can taste her milk on the inside of your lips and smell her very special scent of love, and you know that she smells that way only for you. Smell it, Edith. Wrap yourself up in it because it makes you feel safe and secure and lazy as you stretch out to sleep some more.'

He waited while the room filled with the energy of Edith's happiness. She was feeling the emotions with everything at her disposal.

'While you have been asleep you have grown again. This time into a baby. You are still feeling safe and warm and lazy but now you can feel a little more around you. The sheet resting over you is cool and smooth. The pillow under your head is soft as it squashes up around your ears. The mattress cradles you and lets you kick out in your sleep when you want to. Kick out now for me, Edith.'

The bedclothes rippled under the assault of a flurry of weak jabs.

'Very good. It's time for you to wake up now, Edith. You have slept as much as you want, and you are refreshed and happy and excited about seeing your mother again. You know she will come in to you as soon as she realises you are awake so you grab hold of one of the bars of your cot and shake it just as hard as you can.'

Edith's hands on the pillows transformed into two fists that lifted slightly into the air and trembled in weak imitation of violent movement.

'Your mother comes in and she picks you up and holds you close, and you feel safe and special and as though nothing bad can ever happen to you. She starts to dress you. What do you wear, Edith? What is she putting on you?'

'A vest.' Her voice was high and thin. 'It itches. It's not soft like it used to be. It smells of soap. And my blue jacket. My favourite. It has ribbons around the neck that Mummy ties for me and if I pull my hands up I can make them disappear inside my sleeves. And now she's pushing my feet into my shoes.'

'Are you sure you are still a baby, Edith? You sound a little older to me. You sound very grown up indeed … How old are you, Edith?'

A pinprick of laughter bubbled out from between her smiling lips. She suddenly flung her arms across the bed and hugged herself.

'We are going for a walk. I love walking out with Mummy, she is so pretty and everyone looks at her, and I know that they all love me too because I am a part of her. We're off to the park where I can play on the swings but she won't let me go very high. She says that although I'm strong and brave, I'll have to wait until I'm older.'

Two tears slid out from under Edith's closed eyelids.

'I never did go any higher.'

He waited until her breathing sounded calm and measured once more. A part of her was observing the process, not yet fully immersed. He had to help her get beyond this. He leaned forward and began to whisper in her ear in a voice that was softly pitched and smoother than his own: 'Can you be brave for me once more and tell me what happened the last time I tried to keep you safe?'

Nothing for the longest of times. Then: 'Mummy?'

'Yes.'

'What do you want me to talk about?'

'The night of the fire. Tell me what you remember.'

'It is dark … I'm hot … I am all wrapped in the sheet … There is a funny smell …'

Her voice was rattling from somewhere deep inside her chest.

'It tickles my face, and I cough and cough …'

Her tone had become frantic.

'… I start to cry and the door opens and there you are … the air is getting hotter and hotter and I can't breathe and the inside of my mouth stings but I can't close it … and you're holding me tight, and we're running and running out of the room and down the stairs … then I'm flying and it's like when I'm on the swings only much, much higher and faster, and I want to laugh and shout for you to watch me but I can't see you anymore … then I fall from the sky, and the ground is hard and hot and everything is orange and red and there is a sound in my ears. The blanket is getting tighter and tighter and hotter, and I can't move and it sticks me down and there is a smell that won't go away, and I can't hear you and the middle of me is empty, and it hurts and hurts and hurts … I want you to make it go away …'

Her sobs contained all the torment of a lifetime of forgotten pain. When the last echoes had died away and Stephen could once more hear the rain slashing on the window, he took a handkerchief from his pocket and gently dried Edith's face. Her eyes remained shut but he could see her lids shimmer with movement and knew that she was still – but only just – in her hypnotic trance. He guessed that he wouldn't have long.

'Where are you now, Edith? Tell me what you can see.'

'A green wall.'

'What can you hear, Edith?'

'Walking. Lots and lots and lots of walking.'

'What else?'

'Laughing.'

'Who is laughing?'

'I don't know.'

'What else?'

'Crying.'

'Who is it who is crying?'

'Me.'

'What can you smell, Edith?'

'Soap. And prickles. And a hot smell that never goes away.'

'What is in your mouth?'

'Nothing … a taste …'

'What do you feel?'

'Sad …'

'Is that why you cry?'

'Yes … no … I hurt … that's why I cry.'

'Where?'

'All over.'

'I want you to think deep inside yourself, Edith. I want you to stay where you are in the hospital after the fire, but I want you to go deeper and take a look at what it is that is causing you so much pain. You don't have to touch it but I want you to move it with your mind into a big box that you wrap up with string, nice and tight. Now I want you to pick up the box and carry it out for me.'

'No.'

'Yes, Edith. Bring it out for me and put the box on the floor by the window where a warm ray of sunshine can reach into every corner. I'll undo the string for you … There, it's open now. I want you to look and tell me what you see. Whatever it is, it's in the box and is no longer a part of you and can do you no more harm.'

'It is.'

'It is what?'

'It is a part of me.'

'What is it, Edith? Tell me what you see in the box.'

She didn't answer.

'You can hold it away from you as far as you want but you must take it out for me.'

Silence.

'Bring it clear from the box and put it down on the floor. Then come back and stand beside me and tell me what you see.'

Her breathing became snatched and punctuated by fluttery wheezes. Stephen took a moment to lay his fingers on her neck and check her pulse. At the contact, Edith's eyes sprang open.

'Father …'

'He's not here, Edith, I am.'

'Dead … he wants me …'

Stephen jerked his head up as the door to the room was thrust open and the light from the corridor streamed in. Edith screamed.

'GET OUT! GET OUT, MAN!'

'I didn't know she'd be having company; I thought as she'd be on her own …'

The door clicked shut behind a red-faced PC Billings but before Stephen could steady his breathing once more Edith Potter's body had become rigid and he knew her mind had finally taken refuge in a place where she could never be hurt again.

*

Once he was sure she was physically stable, Stephen stepped out of the room. As he suspected, the off-duty constable was waiting for him.

'I left explicit instructions that I was never – in any circumstances – to be disturbed whilst I was working with her.'

'I'm sorry, Dr Maynard, truly I am, but I've only a minute or two this visit as we're on our way to pay a call on Mrs Billings' mother and I didn't want to go wasting time reporting to the office in the main building. There wasn't any way for me to be knowing you was here.'

'Do you have any idea of what you've just done?'

He leaned wearily against the wall then rubbed his palm across his face. He had been so close. Only a short while longer and he would've been able to release Edith from her self-imposed prison. But there was no chance now that she would ever allow herself to make contact again. The thin thread of free will her mind had stubbornly clung onto had vanished under the overwhelming need to protect her secret. Her catatonia was at last complete. And permanent. His one chance had been and gone.

Stephen accepted a cigarette.

He was stubbing out the remnants of a second before he trusted his voice enough to speak his thoughts.

'Edith Potter is free from distress now. Whatever it was she was so desperate to keep locked inside has won. She wanted no one else to know it, she herself had no conscious awareness of what it was until the second you barged into the room. Then, when she faced it, she knew it so terrible she'd rather lose her mind than accept it. There's nothing more I can do.'

'That's as maybe but I'll be keeping her cottage ticking over as before all the same. You don't know Miss Potter like I do; I'll be wagering my best boots that she ain't given up and she'll be back to see to her roses before too long.'

Stephen wished he could share in even a little of the man's blind faith. He patted the constable briefly on the arm then walked down the corridor towards the door.

PART III
LONDON
September 1927

The play of motives passes through all kinds of vicissitudes as the alternative courses of action and their consequences are more fully apprehended to the self.

CHAPTER TWENTY-SEVEN

Stephen took a moment to pause in front of the window. It was childish and vain, it was true, but he knew the soft sunshine gave his hair an interesting depth and colour. The pretty young student certainly seemed to think so; she was gazing at him with the same rapture with which she hung on his every word. He allowed himself a smile as he looked down at his notes. Another year of this and on the back of his triumph with the British Psychological Society, he would be sure to be offered the post of Head of Clinical Practice – a guarantee of being awarded a professorship. In preparation he'd grown a beard to give him gravitas and match his status as a ground-breaking psychoanalyst. He was ready to receive every honour they wished to bestow.

'Well, if there aren't any questions,' he raised an eyebrow in the direction of the female student, 'then I suggest we move on to the next case. But before you write up your treatment plans for this one, I urge you to read my piece on the similarities between the repression of war experience and catatonia when it comes out in next month's *Journal of Psychology*.'

He was inordinately proud of the way he'd said that: authoritative but dismissingly casual as if having his work published was an everyday occurrence. The gaggle around him began to glide towards the door to the private room just down the corridor. A voice stopped him as he made to join them.

'Dr Maynard. A telephone call.'

'I'm in the middle of rounds. Get them to leave a message.'

'I tried that but he says it's important.'

Stephen sighed and waved his students on with his sheaf of notes. 'I'll be with you in a second. Try your hand at observation while you're waiting and see what you can ascertain as to' he checked the next name on his list, 'Mr Black's state of mind. No asking him any questions though, that would be cheating. Can I trust you?'

The shining faces and solemn nods he received confirmed – as if he didn't know it already – that he really was a very good mentor.

*

'Hello. Can I help you?'

'Dr Maynard? Dr Stephen Maynard?'

'Speaking.'

'Victor Johns here.'

The smell of the place came back to him first.

'No instant recall? Can't say that I blame you, we'd all put Lewes Asylum out of our heads as quickly as possible if we could.'

That he hadn't been able to accomplish – much as he wanted to – but he had managed to lock the memories away under the pressure of hard work. Except now the image of Edith Potter lying there dead to the world loomed up, large and menacing. He tugged at the hairs fringing his bottom lip. It was a habit he'd acquired in times of stress; he'd have to learn to resist the impulse or else start shaving again if he didn't want to look as if he had the mange.

'Dr Johns … yes … yes, of course. How are you? I'm sorry but you'll have to make this quick, I've a room full of students staring at a patient like cats eyeing up a goldfish in a bowl.'

Stephen could hear him taking a long draw on a cigarette.

'In that case I'll jump the pleasantries and cut to the chase. Edith Potter. We've had a bit of a breakthrough with her.'

'What do you mean *a breakthrough*?'

'Well …' Another puff on the cigarette. 'I read the conclusions you drew very thoroughly and decided that your insights about the parallels with shell-shock were spot on. So I continued with the cold baths and electric therapy, and added a dietary regime of my own devising, and she's come back to us.'

'What?'

Stephen winced and looked down to see a clutch of wiry brown beard hairs rooted to his fingertips.

'She's been out of her stupor for almost eight weeks now. I wanted to wait until I was sure she wouldn't relapse before ringing you. But …'

Stephen could hear him smiling.

'I think that, between us, we've effected a cure.'

'Are you out of your senses, man?'

Stephen was aware his voice was bouncing around the tight little office but he couldn't seem to control it.

'There *is* no cure for the root of her psychosis. The catatonia was merely the symptom. Now you've gone and removed that, the poor woman's mind will be plunged into a veritable living hell. How could you have been so bloody … bloody … irresponsible?'

He could feel the sharp intake of breath travelling down the wire; this was the last reaction the man had expected. But he'd had it coming to him; Dr Johns may be the director of a lunatic asylum but he wasn't a trained psychoanalyst, wasn't even experienced as a practitioner in the field of dissociation and concomitant catatonia.

Stephen felt the heat of hypocrisy flare in his cheeks as he remembered how incompetently green he'd been himself when he'd first walked through the asylum gates nine months ago. But that was as maybe, he'd become something of an expert since then and he knew as surely as he could feel the constriction in his lungs, that the man's meddling amounted to an almost criminal act. A spasm of heartburn forced a trickle of bile into the back of Stephen's throat as Edith's admission that her father had wished her dead reverberated in his head with all the clarity of a fire alarm.

'I'm sorry, Dr Johns, but there seems to be some sort of commotion going on that needs my attention.' He dropped the receiver back into its cradle.

*

Stephen's room was right under the eaves at the top of the house. It was little more than a poky attic with the light barely feeling its way through the grimy windows. In it there was a bed, a small wardrobe, a washstand, some bookshelves, and a desk and chair. He may be on his way up to the top of his profession but that didn't mean he could afford anything better in the heart of London; and he had to be within walking distance of the clinic in case one of his patients had a psychotic episode in the night and he was wanted in an emergency.

Tonight the telephone downstairs in the hall had been mercifully silent but that hadn't meant he'd had any uninterrupted sleep. He'd been tossing and turning for hours, and when he finally gave in and wrenched his eyelids open, his pyjamas were stuck to his skin with sweat.

His hand groped on the floor beside the bed for the alarm clock. He picked it up and squinted at the luminous face. Three-thirty. Dead slap bang in the middle of the mournful hour when his blood sugar would be at its lowest and his bodily processes merely ticking over. He didn't need this. What he needed was some quality sleep so he would be refreshed and alert to face the full day of patients he had ahead of him. Maybe a snort of whisky would help quiet his racing mind and loosen the tension in his muscles. He disentangled his legs from the sheet and shuffled across the room to the wardrobe. The linoleum was cold and clammy under his bare feet and he involuntarily thought of corpses. He shuddered. Wasn't that what he'd been dreaming about?

He'd been locked in a room somewhere – a sun-filled high-ceilinged room with a crystal chandelier, and a grand piano in one corner. And there'd been an armchair. Its high back was facing him and he was walking towards it … no, he'd been dancing towards it. Waltzing to something by Strauss being played on the piano. Except there was no one at the keyboard. But that didn't bother him. The music was clear and precise and played with such feeling he wanted nothing more than to have a partner draped in his arms. And she was over there. He imagined her face as she sat patiently, a delicious smile stretching her ruby lips as she anticipated his hand being held out to her, then being pulled up to become as weightless as he was. It was the young student. Margaret was her name, but he'd call her Maggie. The top of her head would graze his clavicle and she'd nestle in the crook of his arm so sweetly. And he raised himself onto the balls of his feet and whirled lightly once more. The girl's hair looked silky in the sunlight, the lowest curls bobbing on her shoulders. One last pirouette and he was standing in front of her, his arm stretched out to wrap her in his embrace.

But it was Edith Potter waiting for him. Edith Potter with her cadaverous face and empty eyes. She'd grinned and exposed green furry teeth; fat black bluebottles zipped out from behind them and buzzed around his face. He'd screamed. He'd screamed and begged her to leave him alone. And then he'd woken up.

God, how he wished he hadn't been able to recall it all so vividly. His hand was shaking as he wrenched open the wardrobe door and fumbled inside for the bottle nestling behind his pair of Sunday-best black shoes. His fingers closed around the smooth neck and he scurried back to bed, not even bothering to search for the glass he knew was somewhere amongst the books and papers on his desk. He prised out the stopper and took a swig. The top of the bottle clinked painfully against his teeth. He wiped his lips with the back of his hand as he waited for the burning sensation to dull in his throat, and the edges of his consciousness to be softened by the drug.

Why couldn't Dr Johns have left well alone? Left her in blessed ignorance. And why had the asylum director felt the need to ring up the clinic to tell him about it? Perhaps he'd had what they jokingly called on the wards, a *Jesus-raising-Lazarus* moment? Stephen supposed he could understand the man's excitement and need to boast about his success to someone, but why in God's name had he chosen him of all people? Couldn't he have confined himself to walking down the corridors of his dreadful place shouting *hallelujah*? But he was being unjust, unkind, and unfair. Every doctor worth his salt would be proud of an achievement so momentous as bringing someone out of a catatonic stupor – after all, he'd nearly accomplished it and had poured all his self-congratulation into a paper that had astounded his peers with the unambiguous nature of its conclusions.

Only Dr Johns hadn't known the truth. But now Edith Potter did. And it was because of him and his need to prove to himself that he'd been right about how no secret was too terrible for a mind not to be forced to face it. If he'd bothered to employ a little imagination instead of being so hell-bent on achieving his goal he might've realised Dr Potter would blame the child for his wife's death. Then, when her father had been murdered, how her mind would have regarded that as a symbolic act of revengeful patricide – leaving her with a double burden of guilt. That was what she now had to live with. Thanks to the great Dr Stephen Maynard. His ambition. Compounded by his negligence. And, lastly – and this was the most damning of all – his abandoning of her once he'd had all he needed and could turn her into the case study that had established his reputation and kick-started his rise to eminence.

Stephen wrapped the eiderdown around his shoulders and waited for his teeth to stop chattering. And for the dawn to come and release him.

CHAPTER TWENTY-EIGHT

Stephen felt the familiar prickle on the back of his neck; it had been seven years since he'd worked his apprenticeship at the Tavistock Clinic under Dr Crichton-Miller but, back here again, he could feel the great man looking over his shoulder and telling him that he wasn't quite coming up to scratch. The talk this evening was *The Resurfacing of Latent Trauma and its Guises.* He hadn't recognised the name of the speaker when he'd seen the details pinned to the notice-board but it was a topic that had been skirting the edges of his mind ever since Dr Johns' telephone call. The room was hot and airless. If the man hadn't made any startling revelations about the research he'd been engaged in by now, then he wasn't going to and this was a waste of valuable drinking time.

He exhaled in an effort to make himself smaller and, in a simian hunch, slid out of his seat and along the row as inconspicuously as he could. A minefield of briefcases and outstretched legs later, and he was walking down the centre aisle, the speaker's admonishing throat-clearing punctuating his progress. At the back of the room was relief – and not just in the shape of the brass-handled door: a friendly face. Peter Hargreaves. He hadn't seen him in ages. He was looking as individualistic as ever in a threadbare corduroy suit and moth-eaten trilby. Stephen put his hand to his face and mimed a yawn before raising an imaginary glass. He received an enthusiastic nod.

*

It was only a short stroll across the squares of Bloomsbury to the Lamb and Flag in Lamb's Conduit Street. They had come here many a time – he, Peter, and Helen – when they'd been fledgling doctors full of ideals and enough energy to want to spend their evenings stretching their minds in earnest debate. The pub was dark inside, the mahogany panelling sucking in the greenish glow from the shaded lamps. They had no difficulty finding seats and Stephen went up to the bar. Peter was wreathed in a grey-blue spicy pall of pipe smoke by the time he returned with the beer. He placed the glasses on the table and sat down.

'Don't know how you can drink mild and bitter, haven't you any taste buds?'

'I'll have you know that my palate's as refined as they come.' Peter blew out a cloud of pipe smoke as if to emphasise the point. 'Honed on fruit and hedgerow wine these days. Helen and I have amassed quite a good cellar of the stuff. Developed a taste for it in France where they manage to turn the most amazing things into alcohol. Pure alchemy. Astonishing really, seeing as we barely had enough to eat most of the time. Still, that's all over and done with now.' He raised his glass. 'Good to see you again, old son. Here's mud in your eye.'

Stephen took a gulp of beer and felt the knot at hearing Helen's name dissolve in his stomach.

'So, what are you up to now? I didn't expect to see you there tonight; dabbling in the black art of psychoanalysis now are you?'

Peter unfurled his soft smile. 'More like dipping my toe. I run a place in the country – a home from home, you might say – for veterans from the War. It's near Lewes. Beddingham Hall.' He snorted a laugh. 'The men call it *Bloody Hell Hole*; a sense of humour's a wonderfully healing thing. You should come down and visit sometime. A walk on the South Downs would do you the world of good – you're looking paler, and an awful lot thinner, since I last clapped eyes on you.'

Stephen was barely able to acknowledge the invitation. Lewes. Did the whole world have to lead back to that accursed asylum and the unexploded shell that waited for him there?

'Can't say the same for you.' He injected as much lightness into his voice as he could. 'I'd say you had the beginnings of middle-aged spread if I didn't know we're about the same age and I'm not ready to see myself as an old man quite yet.'

Peter patted his stomach where it pushed against the edge of the table. 'That's what the love of a good woman does for you – and her legendary steak and kidney puddings.' He tamped down the tobacco in his pipe with the end of his penknife. 'Why don't you try it? I assume you've not taken the plunge or she wouldn't have let you grow that dreadful face fungus.'

Stephen stroked his cheek. 'I see you haven't lost your knack for not sparing anyone's feelings unnecessarily. But I'll have you know that some women find a beard irresistible.'

'What do you mean; blind, like Braille?'

'Her name's Maggie. She's got the most beautiful mouth and radiant smile – and she happens to love my beard. We're what I suppose you married types would probably call *going steady*.'

'Bring her with you when you come and see us then; the more the merrier. Same again?' Peter picked up both glasses and walked towards the bar without waiting for a reply.

As Stephen watched him go, his irritation switched from the arrogant assurance of his companion back to himself. Why did he always resort to lying about the facts of his life in the hope of impressing Peter Hargreaves? He'd got into that pattern early on but there really was no need for it now: they were both doctors; both apparently successful in their chosen fields; both intelligent, reasonably handsome and personable ... but he knew why. One of them had Helen. And it wasn't him. He had to change the subject or risk making a complete bloody idiot of himself.

'Tell me more about your work,' he said when Peter had returned. 'Have you been doing it ever since you got your ticket home?'

'Not exactly. When hostilities ceased, I moved into general medicine for a bit – one can see a little too much of man's innards to make for restful sleep – and I thought a country practice would be just the ticket. But, needless to say, I got pretty bored treating in-growing toenails and farmer's lung so I leapt at the chance of Beddingham Hall when they offered it to me.'

'Who did?'

'The army, Ministry of Defence, government; whoever. Seems I had established some sort of reputation for myself in the clearing station at Etaples, and they wanted me to set this thing up. Sip your beer with reverence, old son, because, according to the powers that be, you're in the company of a medical pioneer.'

Stephen gave a mock salute with his glass; Peter's worst fault – if it could be called that – was an overdose of humility and if he was making a self-deprecating joke then he must be engaged in some very remarkable enterprise indeed. Stephen squashed a bubble of envy; his own work could hardly be called pedestrian.

'Hospitals and treatment centres already existed for amputees and those who were so seriously wounded that they needed constant medical attention.'

Peter took his pipe from between his lips and refilled it. He didn't resume speaking until he'd added significantly to the veil of smoke hanging just below the nicotine-yellow ceiling.

'But these men needed something more specialised; a place they could call their own where they wouldn't be persecuted with jeers or spat at – or worse.'

'Who on earth would do that to someone who gave almost everything they had for their country?'

'The man in the street … the young woman with a babe in arms she wanted to protect from horror above everything else … oh, you'd be surprised at the instinctive and elemental reaction of the human animal at times. Just wait until you come and visit and then you'll see what I mean. They are dreadfully – and I use that word in the literal sense of arousing fear and disgust – disfigured. Predominantly facially. So much so that they can't exist in what we laughingly label normal society. It's funny, but there's something about people's faces that has the capacity to make us either intensely love or intensely hate the person behind the mask. Maybe it's because it acts as a mirror for us to see our own selves, who we really are in the deep dark recesses of our being. That bit that we keep so closed and airtight that we sometimes barely know what form it takes ourselves.'

Stephen shuddered. Edith Potter, again.

'Isn't it an onerous task, rehabilitating men like that?'

'Oh, I don't rehabilitate them, only the greatest miracle the world has ever seen could do that by making every single one of us non-judgmental, tolerant, accepting, and guilt-free overnight …'

Stephen knew that the loaded pause was so that he could consider just where he was on the spectrum of sainthood. But he didn't need it; recent events were bringing it to mind all the time.

'… and we both know that's never going to happen, so what we work on is helping the men adjust to their tragically new-found circumstances and identity.'

His voice was thick with compassion. Not a trace of the anger Stephen knew he'd feel if he were responsible for the mental robustness of the men in Beddingham Hall. It gave him the courage to broach the subject that had been haunting him all week.

'I've been enjoying a modicum of success myself lately. I wrote a paper that got me accepted into the British Psychological Society; all about catatonia. Broke new ground.'

'Here's to you then.' Peter raised his glass.

'Thanks. I'm very proud of my work but …' he reached up and pulled at his beard '… I seem to have got myself into a bit of a predicament. With a patient.'

'You haven't, have you?'

'What?'

'Compromised yourself – sexually, I mean.'

Stephen's cheeks burned. 'Of course not! How could you think that?'

'I was wondering if this thing you've got going is with a young student. After all, it's not an unheard-of occurrence; up on our pedestals not many of us get opportunities to form attachments outside our profession. I'm a case in point; no one else would have me but a fellow quack.'

They were getting sidetracked and it wasn't a route Stephen wanted to go down; he'd sidestepped Helen once already. He took a long swig of his beer. 'I can't tell you in any depth about the case – for obvious reasons – but I'm faced with a situation I've never encountered before and I'm in two minds what to do about it.'

Peter laughed. 'A most appropriate turn of phrase for a man in your line of work, if I may say so. What this is all leading up to is that you want to pick your Uncle Peter's brains, eh? Why don't you feel free to tell me all and I'll do my best to dredge up some opinion or other.'

Did he really have to make things worse? Stephen felt his vulnerability exposed enough as it was without Peter seemingly enjoying humiliating him further.

'I … I … Why don't you drink up and I'll get us both another one in? We've got time before you have to catch a train, haven't we?'

Peter drained the last quarter of his glass and handed it over. 'But let's make this the last; I'd forgotten how swiftly you can put them away and Helen'll have my guts for garters if I don't have a clear head tomorrow.'

Stephen joined the, now obviously drunk, students at the bar. He could smell the inviting oblivion of whisky. Maybe he should buy a bottle to take back to his room – sleep would elude him tonight for sure. But he resisted the temptation and wove his way back to the table, carrying the glasses above head-height to avoid any elbow knocks.

He sat and started on his beer while Peter regarded him in silence. Stephen thought he'd make a very good psychoanalyst with his natural knack of waiting patiently until the other person's need to talk became overwhelming. Lubricated by alcohol, and a desperate need to unburden himself, he slipped into the void.

'She – this woman – was in a catatonic stupor that seemed to all intents and purposes to be profound, and permanent. I'd been treating her with hypnosis and we'd been making excellent progress until she remembered something and took refuge in deepening her alienation from the world. Well, that's what I thought anyway. But the director of the asylum telephoned on Monday to tell me that she's lucid again.'

'That's good news, isn't it? Shows that you must have given her something of life to hang onto, deep down. You should mark it up as another wounded soul saved.'

His sincerity was so palpable that Stephen had to fight not to lash out in his shame and confusion.

'However, before she did – and I must say in my defence that no one else was bothering with her – I skipped a few of the landing stages in the plumbing of her mind's depths and as a consequence she's left with a part of her consciousness being able to recognise the shape and texture of the appalling truth it wanted to hide from itself, but with no safety net strategies of how to live with it.'

'Is that what you're worried about?' Peter was sucking on his pipe again. 'That you might have unwittingly pushed her into a suicide situation? But she's in an asylum, isn't she? They would never allow her access to the means.'

'But don't you see how that makes it worse?' He couldn't stop his voice from rising in pitch and volume. 'I can't think of anything more terrible than wanting to put yourself out of abject misery, and not be able to.'

'You don't mean that, surely? It's in the marrow of your bones to want to preserve life; besides, what you think she may be contemplating is the most grievous of sins.'

'Don't go all Holy Joe on me now, Peter, please; I can't argue against your religious convictions as well as everything else. The thing is … I don't know what to do.'

He thought that Peter would leap in with something about his moral duty and the Hippocratic Oath, but he did the silence trick again. And it's exactly what he'd have done. He sighed.

'I know I should go and see her, but I don't want to. I know I should continue her treatment and see if I can help her to reach some accommodation with her *tragically new-found circumstances and identity*, as you so succinctly put it, but I don't know if I can.' He felt his throat constrict. 'I've never felt so inadequate in all my life.'

'It would do you more good to examine just what gives you the bloody right to indulge in such childishly self-serving pity. Where are your guts, man? Not spilled in the Flanders' trenches or shackled to the diseased mind of a defenceless woman, that's for sure. You said she'd have stayed safely locked away from the world in the first place if it weren't for you, and so now you have no choice but to finish what you started. Remember how we used to discuss the philosophical question: if you save someone from drowning are you responsible for that person forever? The truth is that what all of us in the medical game indulge in is playing God and, for that privilege, we must carry the accountability that goes with interfering in another's existence. You owe her, Stephen.'

Peter sank the rest of his beer and stood up. 'I didn't have you down as a quitter or a coward. This bullet's got your name on it, old son, and you'd better not dodge it or you'll never put yourself in the firing line again. And it would be a great shame for the profession to lose one of its brightest talents just when this crazy world needs you the most.'

He leaned forward and rested his hand on Stephen's shoulder. 'Believe me I have enough faith in your abilities for the two of us. I was only pretending not to know about that paper of yours; I read it and was astonished by your insights. We're very proud to be your friends, Helen and I. Now it's up to you to do something you know will make you proud of yourself.'

Stephen wanted to stand up and hug him in the hope of breathing in some of his certainty. Instead, he just allowed himself a weak smile and kept his eyes on Peter's back as he walked across the pub and out of the door.

CHAPTER TWENTY-NINE

Stephen stood in Dr Johns' doorway.

'I thought you said she was out of her stupor? I was with her for a full ten minutes and she didn't even give any sign that we'd met before.'

'And good morning to you, too, Dr Maynard.' The cigarette wedged in the corner of Victor Johns' mouth bobbed up and down. 'Want one?' He held out the packet. 'Nicotine's the only thing keeps me going – that and endless cups of coffee. But I'm sure you've got your own vices to contend with. Now, you're talking about Edith Potter I assume?'

'Of course I bloody well am. Who else?'

Stephen entered the room and slumped into the battered armchair. The days and nights of trepidation at what reception he could expect from her had led to a build up of so much adrenaline that the anticlimax of her passivity had left him punchy, but exhausted.

'Sorry. It's only that it wasn't easy to free myself up enough to get down here and then to find that I had a wasted journey.' Stephen was gratified to hear his voice contained just the right amount of disappointment. Of course it was relief he felt more than anything. A profound appreciation that, having been stung into this visit by Peter's accusation of moral cowardice, he had, in the end, been let off the hook: Edith Potter remained oblivious to the terrible – and intractable – cause of her condition.

'I think you'll be pleasantly surprised when I dig out the details.' Dr Johns pulled a file from the middle of the pile on his desk, almost causing the whole edifice to topple over. 'She's come and gone a few times but I can assure you that for the best part of the summer she's been with us for good.'

He pulled the cigarette off his bottom lip and added the ash to a messy pile on his blotter. When he looked back at Stephen he was smiling benignly.

'Contrary to what you eminent members of the British Psychological Society might think, we humble lunatic asylum directors do know a catatonic stupor when we see one – even if we are denied the resources to do anything about the condition. Only, as I said, I made an exception in her case. You weren't the only one to grasp at the opportunity to probe the mental capacities of someone with such an illustrious father and I gave up my free time to see what could be done. By the way, Dr Potter would have a bone to pick with you over the conclusions you extrapolated in your paper; undoubtedly dismissing them as a tad broad to be based on only one case.'

'But she was – is – the most profound. And I did make reference to others – '

'In passing.'

'Can you tell me then, if you're so certain you know the difference between the superficial consciousness sometimes manifested by patients in a catatonic state and those levels of awareness that can only be said to be present in one who is truly sentient, why Edith Potter regarded me as a perfect stranger just now despite the fact that my identity would be lodged within her subconscious? My ability to repeatedly hypnotise her over all those months proves that fact.'

'Maybe because of your beard. I nearly didn't recognise you myself when I saw you walking through the grounds.'

'Are you always this facetious?'

'Not intentionally. But you must admit that you do look remarkably different. Did you speak to her?'

'I said hello and asked her how she was feeling.'

'What did she say?'

'She mumbled something pretty indistinct, and then closed her eyes again.'

'Ah, she was sleeping.'

'No, she wasn't bloody sleeping. Aren't I getting through to you at all? Edith Potter is back wrapped in her protective catatonia.'

'If you won't take my word for it then I'll read you a little from the notes I asked the orderlies to keep – behaviour, state of mind, noteworthy mood swings; things like that.'

Stephen surreptitiously slid up the cuff of his jacket and glanced at his watch. If this didn't take too long then he could catch the 1.15 back to Victoria. Maybe reach the clinic in time to catch Maggie and ask her out for that drink. But Dr Johns was saying something so far outside what he'd expected he found himself leaning forward in his seat, straining to make sense of it.

'... and then on the first Thursday of last month was when she had a row about the quality of the food and ended up throwing a bowl of rice pudding at the orderly. After that it seems she became increasingly belligerent with everyone. I'll find you a direct quotation: *She was in the corridor doing her nut screaming blue murder at one of the shell-shockers. Accusing him of all sorts. Half-inching her clothes so she couldn't leave being the least of it.*'

He looked across and shrugged.

'You'll have to forgive the informal language, I'm afraid; I'm having to interpret some of the spelling as it is. And she's taken to wandering the grounds at all hours. It's not down here,' he tapped the file, 'but I was leaving one evening just as it was getting dark and came across her pulling up the flowers; she said they were in danger of strangling the roses. Odd behaviour, granted, but not that of someone experiencing profound catatonia, as I'm sure you'll agree.'

Stephen didn't know what to say. His bluff had been called. Why hadn't he just popped his head around the office door to say his farewells as he'd intended? He pulled at his beard.

'I feel as though you're showing me a picture of a cat and swearing blind it's a dog.'

'Are you implying the staff in this asylum are liars or that I am fabricating for my own amusement?' The smile was long gone.

'No, of course not. But I can't understand how it's possible that Edith Potter could've gone from a person of such volatility to the half-dead woman I saw just now.'

He really didn't want to continue this conversation but his professional integrity was being called into question.

'When did you say the most recent incident was?'

'The last recorded one?' Dr Johns ran his finger down the page. 'Monday morning. We had a new orderly starting and he was late with her tea.'

Stephen wanted to hit his head against the wall for being so stupid. Drugs. They were lacing her intake with drugs.

'What exactly have you started giving her, Dr Johns?' His tone was icy. He abhorred the routine stupefying of those in the grip of psychosis; it confused any attempts at reaching a meaningful diagnosis. It certainly seemed to have fooled him on this occasion.

'Oh, the usual; croton oil to act as a purgative – '

'Good God, man, the woman's constitution will never take that.'

'– and daily doses of bromide.'

'To keep her docile.'

'To help her to sleep, and to dampen any disquiet or distress she might be feeling. I seem to recall telling you when we first met that this is a place of containment, not a hospital and, as such, it is our duty under the law to ensure that the inmates cause no harm to themselves or others. Edith Potter has, left to her own devices, exhibited signs of possessing the capacity to do both. I really have no choice. Had she remained in the catatonic stupor in which she arrived, then, as she posed no danger, these steps wouldn't have been necessary. As it is ...'

He held out his hands, palms upwards. Stephen got the message.

'So it's all my fault, is it? I'm the one ramming that stuff down her throat night and morning?'

'I can assure you there's no coercion involved and she takes her medication of her own volition.'

'How on earth can she be exercising any free will at all when she has no earthly idea of who she is and what she wants? If she truly is in some way in touch with her conscious self again ...'

'Why do you persist in maintaining your disbelief? If I didn't know any better then I'd say that you have some reason for wanting her to be catatonic again; it's what you lot call *projection* isn't it?'

Stephen felt the heat of a flush stealing up his neck. He stood up and leaned forward with his knuckles on the edge of Dr Johns' desk.

'By dint of my research paper I drew attention to this appallingly archaic, barbaric, Victorian-valued medical institution – '

'Lunatic asylum, Dr Maynard. This is a lunatic asylum.'

'– and in the process brought you an increase in funds which I now realise you will probably only use to buy enough bromide to dose up every patient to the eyeballs the minute they set foot through the door.'

'The fame and fortune you seem to think you've bestowed on us wouldn't even go to buying everyone here a fresh egg for breakfast. Have you any idea how truly thinly the money stretches between two hundred inmates? Most of them requiring even more care and attention than Edith Potter.'

'Care? You call this bloody care?' He was shouting directly into his face but Dr Johns hardly blinked.

'We contain. Alleviate as many of the symptoms of distress as we can. At the very least we protect them from a world where many people have medieval minds and would burn someone as odd as Edith Potter for being a witch if they thought they could get away with it.'

'Now you're treating me like one of your imbeciles. Do you think I'm not aware of the facts of life as they affect those teetering on the edge of sanity? Except in my clinic we attempt to entice them back to normality, not poison their bodies into the same state as their minds.'

'Are you trying to tell me that your methods unfailingly result in success?'

'Of course not, that would be presumptuous and arrogant.'

'And far be it from me to accuse you of that.'

'Why is it that everyone seems to have it in for psychoanalysts?'

'Who said I was making a generalisation?'

'At least we try.'

'Not in this case. All you did was regard her as a condition, pick over a diseased mind for what it might profit.'

'For the benefit of scientific research. I could hardly embark on anything else; the woman was bloody catatonic, for Christ's sake.'

'You used her for the glorification of your career, and you're even more self-delusional than our Napoleonic lunatics if you refuse to admit otherwise.'

'So, I'm a selfish bastard and you're … what? A lickspittle to the Asylum Board of Governors who want a tidy ship full of zombies incapable of disgracing themselves when the inspectors come calling?'

'It's a good job we're here in my office where personal insults are an everyday occurrence; in any other circumstances you wouldn't find me nearly as tolerant.'

Stephen rocked back on his heels as Dr Johns thrust the file at his chest.

'As it's patently obvious that you think you could do better, be my guest. Prove the brave new world of psychoanalysis has all the answers and can work miracles. Come on, take it …'

Stephen did so to prevent the papers falling to the floor. Dr Johns made a show of washing his hands.

'I'll arrange for the forms to be sent. You need only get them signed and witnessed to assume full legal custody for her ongoing treatment in some much more conducive environment of your choosing. I'll wager that in no time at all you'll be able to effect a magnificent recovery with only the aid of a shiny black couch, and, I may add, without the need for a white coat to protect yourself from getting covered in blood or vomit. God, how the other half lives.'

'That is a ridiculously childish suggestion and you know it; she's not some parcel of neuroses to be bundled up and passed on for a bet.'

'Go on, I dare you. What are you afraid of? The worst that can happen is that you fail as spectacularly with her as you seem to think I'm doing.'

Stephen took a few deep breaths. 'Of course I'll fail. There is no cure for that woman.'

'Alleviation of symptoms, remember, that's all I've ever set out to do here. You could accomplish that at least, surely?'

'The lowest possible denominator in psychiatry? Of course I could achieve that but what real good would it do?'

'Edith Potter would be happier.'

'She'd still be torturing herself.'

'She'd get more personal attention that I can give her here.'

'To what end? What is wrong with her won't ever go away, I tell you. The best she can hope for is to make an adjustment to accommodate the root of her psychosis.'

'Well, do that for her then.'

'I can't.'

'And neither can I. So what are we to do, leave her here to rot out her days full of larger and larger doses of sedatives until her body can't take it any longer? Or would you have me be cruel and cease the doses so that she can become reacquainted with whatever misery it was that brought her to our doors in the first place? Damned if I do, and damned if I don't: welcome to the world of an asylum director.'

Dr Johns crumpled into his chair. He sat with his head bowed for a moment and then began drawing patterns in the ash on the blotter. 'Please tell me how I can possibly do anything better than contain? This institution is everything you say it is but, for my sins, I'm the one in charge. I'm the one who has to try to do something with these poor souls the rest of society doesn't want. The men and women going about their business on the streets of Lewes right now would be more than content if I just set some explosives and blew this whole bloody place up.'

Stephen felt as if he'd been picking on the runt in school – the skinny one with the broken glasses and no defences. He walked over and stood in front of the bookshelves. He stared at the battered spines with their gold lettering and obfuscatory titles. Testaments, all, to a professional vanity that he knew was at the root of his own aspirations. Dr Johns had ruthlessly exposed that with the scalpel-precision of a surgeon and there was nowhere left to sidestep. It was Stephen's selfish ambition that had propelled Edith Potter into her present state: whatever hell she was in was of his making. She was his responsibility. And his alone.

But what was he to do with her? Maudsley Hospital wouldn't have her as a patient on a long-term basis; besides, it would damage his career irreparably if anyone got a sight of the case notes and thought to ask why he'd taken an interest in her again after letting her languish in the asylum. What he needed was a residential institution where no one was going to pump her full of drugs the moment the going got rough. Because, given what doctor and patient both knew, there was no doubt that it would.

He returned to stand in front of the desk. Dr Johns was lighting another cigarette. Stephen smiled at him with even more compassion than he felt for Edith Potter.

'Forgive me, please? My friends tell me I can be an insensitive prick at times.'

He received a firm handshake in reply – which was more than he would've been able to muster if the boot had been on the other foot.

'You don't know how sorry I am that there's nothing I can do to make anything easier for you here, except maybe to tell you that I think you're a very altruistic man, Dr Johns. And just to show you that everything you've said hasn't simply gone in one ear and out the other; I'll lighten your load a little so that you only have 199 charges to worry about from now on. God help me if I'm making the biggest mistake of my life, but I'll take on Edith Potter. Only I'll need to square a few things before I can make it official. Can I use your telephone?'

'Be my guest.'

'Do you have the number for Beddingham Hall?'

'The *Hear no Evil, Speak no Evil* place?'

Stephen couldn't help pulling a face. Victor Johns laughed.

'That's what we all call it around here. Don't tell me you didn't know there's a hierarchy even amongst the institutions for the permanently maladjusted? Saints alive, you've got a lot to learn.'

He grabbed a bundle of files from his desk and walked towards the door. 'It's in the book. Let me know when you have everything organised and I'll set the wheels in motion. And give my kind regards to Edith Potter when she's back to her old self again.'

Stephen felt a cat walk down his spine as he wondered exactly when that would be – and quite what they would both have to endure in their unlikely partnership before then.

CHAPTER THIRTY

From his perch on the seat of the cart, Stephen could just see Beddingham Hall's chimneys in a distant dip of the South Downs. He'd been lucky in managing to hitch a lift with a local farmer because he'd have had a devil of a job finding the place unaided.

It had been almost three weeks since Edith Potter had been transferred but Peter had been adamant she'd need all that time to acclimatise and adjust before being subjected to any reminders of her past life. And that, of course, had included his presence. He'd received the royal summons yesterday and so this morning had gone to her Fletching cottage and, with the help of an old Gypsy he'd found cleaning the place, got together the things he'd been instructed to collect.

The journey was turning out to be a pleasant one. The sun was low in the sky, a gentle breeze licking the skin of his face and carrying with it the smell of baking chalk. His companion was not given much to talking and Stephen was left to admire the countryside. The high hawthorn and hazel hedgerows of the lane were broken at irregular intervals by five-bar gates affording views of meadows dotted with fat sheep and yellow flowers. He wished it were a bottle of beer and a packet of sandwiches in the basket at his feet; it was the perfect day for a picnic. Maybe, when he felt he'd made enough headway with Edith for him to be able to spend his free time on more leisurely pursuits, he'd provide himself with just that and come out here again with nothing more on his mind than indulging in a lazy Sunday. But there could be snow on the ground by then for all he knew.

*

Half an hour later and the farmer left Stephen at the edge of the fringe of trees with directions of how to continue on foot. He gave his thanks and started hiking across the grass. The clopping of the horse was soon replaced by nothing but the soft rustle of leaves. A fence snaked down into the dip on his left. Beyond it were some grazing cows clinging to the slope, the perspective making them look as if they had no legs. He tracked beside the fence until he came to a gate. He guessed he was approaching the Hall from the back – through a farm by the look of it. He wondered if this was something Peter had instituted as a means of occupational therapy.

Past a cow-byre, an open-sided barn, and a well-tended allotment, and Stephen was at the house at last. The building was large but unimpressive. A wing on either side embraced a flagstone semi-courtyard but the architecture was flat and had something of the back elevation of St Bart's about it. He hoped the façade was more inspiring. If only for the sake of the men who lived here; a sweeping marble staircase or some crenellations would at least make them feel as if it wasn't a sanatorium. The terrace around the east wing was fringed with low box hedges.

When he reached the limit of the stone paving, he could see a handful of scattered cottages linked by narrow tracks cut into the chalk. Wider paths meandered up to the main house. The ground in front of him sloped away and he walked down it for a dozen or so yards before turning to get his first proper look at the place. He set the basket at his feet and let out a low whistle. He was glad now for his trek across the fields; this way the surprise had remained intact until the very last minute.

There was no flight of marble steps but the front door was enveloped by a Norman arch of proportions that wouldn't disgrace a cathedral. And there was a turret with thin latticed windows graduating to larger squarer ones near the top; it was capped by the sort of roof normally seen on a dovecote – except with lichen-dappled tiles instead of wooden shingles. The castellations were there, with tiny dormer windows peeking over them like small children trying to hide behind a wall. The whole building was in a warm red Sussex brick and it glowed proudly in the clear autumn sunlight.

The contrast with Lewes Lunatic Asylum couldn't have been starker and, as he picked up the basket and strolled towards the front door, Stephen hoped that Edith Potter was able to take some comfort in the fact. Peter had told him on the telephone that one of the evening delivery vans would take him back to Lewes; that gave him the perfect amount of time to get reacquainted with her, and then to join Peter and Helen for a drink or two. There was no reason why his Sunday should have to be entirely devoted to duty.

The hallway was panelled in the mock-Tudor manner, a vaulted ceiling high above evidently once painted with crests or flags now scabby and flaking. A wide wooden staircase led to a landing where two narrower staircases branched off to feed the wings. It exuded an air of shabby neglect only partially lifted by the scent of lavender polish. No one had come when he'd rung the bell but he could hear a buzz of conversation from somewhere above. Unwilling to intrude on what was probably the highlight of the day – toast, crumpets, and cocoa; the standard teatime fare of any well-run institution – he opened the door of the room on his immediate left and walked inside. It was almost clinically bright from the large window and white-painted walls. A chess set was laid out on a low table, magazines and books strewn over the chairs and couch, a half-finished jigsaw puzzle on the hearthrug, a billiards table at the far end with a green glass lampshade hanging low over the centre. The room smelt of stale cigarettes and over-boiled coffee.

Someone grunted from the doorway. He turned to introduce himself but the words he was going to say transformed into a gasp. He dropped the basket. It creaked obscenely as it hit the floor, listing onto one side like a sinking ship. There, standing in front of him, was a thin man in a white collarless shirt, and dark serge trousers belted tightly around a girlish waist. Stephen barely glanced at the flapping sleeve where the man's lower arm should've been. He screamed. He screamed long and loud. The horror had a mouth gaping where his throat should've been, and an eye – one skin-stretched eye – in the middle of a soft and boneless forehead. Stephen shuddered and sweated. Then there were more. Filling the doorway. Men with no faces. Or too much face spread over heads like a squashed toad. One of the creatures was coming towards him. A snake's hiss escaped from Stephen's lips as he staggered backwards.

'Stephen! Stephen, for pity's sake get a hold of yourself, you bloody fool.'

And then the world went black.

*

His neck was stiff and his head throbbed. He was lying on the couch, Peter standing above him pouring a finger of brandy.

'Here, drink this.' He held the glass out with undisguised contempt.

Stephen had to lick his lips before he could swallow. The alcohol burned his throat, but set his pulse racing again.

'I'm sorry … it was the shock,' he muttered the words as they came to him, '… I didn't expect … come across them like that … unprepared …'

'And do you think they were prepared for it when a shell fell out of the sky and blew them to bits? What the hell came over you, Stephen? I thought you had more bloody common sense – let alone clinical training – to react like that.'

'Broken minds, not bodies. The things you can't see are my forte, remember.'

Peter's brusque tone and lack of sympathy were beginning to make Stephen defensive. It was preferable to the sick shame he'd felt when he'd first come around.

'Didn't have you down for the type to be prone to a touch of the vapours either.'

He wasn't being forgiven exactly, but Stephen knew a half-joke at his expense was the best he could expect. He formed his mouth into a smile. 'Want me to go and apologise?'

'That would only make things worse. They're used to it anyway; why d'you think they've taken to calling this place home from home?'

Bloody Hell Hole. He remembered that's what they really called it. He held his glass out for another snort of brandy. Peter was right; he had to get a grip.

'Helen said she'll be sorry she missed you. She's gone into Haywards Heath to spend some time with an old friend before lecturing there first thing in the morning at the teaching hospital. Next time, eh?'

Stephen felt his cheeks flush and hoped Peter would think it the brandy. He couldn't have borne if it she'd witnessed that appalling scene. He offered up a silent prayer for that kindness, at least.

'Now, what have you got in your basket, Little Red Riding Hood? Not a freshly baked apple pie for Grandma, I assume?'

Stephen swallowed the jibe along with the last dregs of brandy. He placed the glass on the floor and reached out for the offending basket.

'The clothes you asked for and a few bits and pieces I thought Edith might like to have around her.'

Peter clapped his hands. 'Right, even I'm getting bored poking fun at you. Down to business. We don't have many rules here, but we do have some. And, despite you being on the side of the ministering angels, I expect you to adhere to them along with everyone else. Nothing is to be brought in that might cause distress – mirrors especially. Neither do we welcome anything with which the more fragile could cause themselves harm.'

'Christ, Peter, I spend my entire waking life in clinics for the depressed and suicidal, and institutions for the insane; do you think I don't know that?' A thought came to him. 'But what about the farm; you've scythes and pitchforks and whatnot there, surely?'

'Please don't blaspheme. Only those who've been here for a minimum of a year have access to those, by which time they will have grown into acceptance of their lot. Desperate but not despairing is how I'd label the vast majority if I had to. But we don't do that here, either. No one is a condition, or a walking mass of healed wounds and scar tissue. They are merely men who went to do their duty and came back changed beyond recognition: literally, in many cases. It is refuge from society they seek, not refuge from themselves or from life itself.'

'I'm not sure I can say the same for Edith Potter.'

'Not now, maybe, but you will in time. If anyone can cure her, you can; once you apply yourself to something you can be impressively single-minded.'

Stephen couldn't stop a shudder rippling through his muscles. 'Trust me; she will never be released from what's tormenting her.'

'Resigned to herself then, like the other residents here. She's made remarkable progress settling in with us, so much so that we decided to move her into one of the cottages. Peace and quiet is exactly what she needs right now; a healing strategy much underrated by you interventionists.'

Stephen nodded. Peter wasn't trying to score points.

'To maintain her equilibrium, I want you to be especially careful about what you leave with her. We don't operate a watch system here and unless there is a behavioural crisis of some sort we will maintain her privacy as much as we can. There aren't any kitchens in the cottages so the residents eat here in the Hall or we have food taken down to them. So far, Edith has preferred to dine alone. Maybe that will change and the two of you will eat together. How often will you be coming to see her?'

'Every Sunday. A whole weekend when I'm not on the clinic rota.'

'Perfect. If you need to stop over you can stay upstairs in the flat with us. Helen will love having someone with more discerning taste buds than mine to cook for. She blames smoking a pipe for my being unable to tell the difference between one of our own veal cutlets and the butcher's cheapest stewing steak.'

Stephen busied himself turning out the contents of the basket onto the floor. He didn't want to think of sleeping in the next room to Helen. Not yet anyway. Peter bent down and picked out the *National Geographic* magazines and books, and the brightly coloured scarf the old Gypsy had donated.

'I'll keep these back for a while if you don't mind. She might get a little over-stimulated to be reminded of her past all at once ...'

'But I specifically wanted her to engage in some of her old habits such as reading.'

'I've been doing my best to explain to you how different it will be for her here; a residential situation is nothing like an asylum or a hospital, and I find that the most productive way to soothe acute anxiety is undertake something physical ...'

'Acute anxiety? Have you got any idea what's the matter with the woman?'

'Are you going to tell me?'

'No.'

'Well then. You can hardly blame me for stumbling around in the dark. I know our methods are alien to someone wedded to the *talking cure* but they are effective, Stephen. And if you want us to take care of her here then you have to do what I say and avoid causing her a degree of agitation that we just won't be able to cope with. Otherwise, she'll have to go back to Dr Johns.'

'He wouldn't have her. He made that quite clear.'

'Another lunatic asylum then – there are plenty of those around.'

Stephen breathed deeply and backed down. 'Is she off the bromide?'

'Clean as a whistle.'

'No side effects?'

'Only the usual but she's evidently sleeping better; that's one thing I'm sure you'll agree we've managed to do for her in our amateur way.'

'Please don't get me wrong, Peter, I'm very grateful to you, really. I want Edith Potter to receive the best possible care and treatment, and I know that, between the two of us, she'll get it here.'

'Then hightail it down to the last cottage on the right and make a start. Leave the scarf though, eh?' He mimed tying a knot around his throat and strangling himself. 'You, not her.'

Stephen only just stopped from asking if he could take the bottle of brandy.

CHAPTER THIRTY-ONE

Stephen stood outside the cottage door, unsure if he should peek in the window to observe her manner as she waited for him. But Peter had made a point – one of many, and they all rankled – about respecting the residents' privacy. Resident. It would take an enormous shift for him to regard Edith Potter as anything other than a patient but he supposed the choice of nomenclature was important; after all, hadn't he been more than a little frosty when the asylum attendant had insisted on calling her a loony?

He decided to opt for the conventional approach of knocking just as any other normal visitor would when paying a pre-arranged call. But still he didn't put down either the basket or his briefcase in order to do so. Stephen's hesitation was to buy time as much as anything else. He didn't know what to expect on the other side of the door. She might be huddled in a corner trying to create the confines of the shell-shock wing of the asylum for all he knew – perhaps he should snatch a glance to check. Being in an institution did strange things to people and from his limited experience of those tasting life again beyond high walls, being let out was often difficult to adjust to. However, he had to trust the Hargreaves' judgement that Edith Potter wasn't exhibiting any signs of trauma or they would have kept her under observation up at the Hall. Although he hadn't been fooled for one moment when Peter had said they didn't institute a watch system here; it wasn't a coincidence that someone was paying especial attention to trimming the grass with a pair of shears in front of one of the far cottages, and no doubt would continue his rounds to the others in due course. It was more subtle than pressing a face up against the hatched window in the ward doors but it would be just as effective – the Hargreaves obviously took their duty of care very seriously, even if it was with a somewhat unorthodox approach.

There was no sound from inside. Perhaps she was asleep? Stephen allowed himself a thin smile; he had to stop behaving like a nervous schoolboy summoned to the headmaster's office. He knocked and received a surprisingly strong 'come in'. If he could only focus on which of them had more to dread from this encounter.

*

'So, Edith, do you remember me now?'

He was sitting on a small over-stuffed armchair by the fireplace. She was perched on the edge of a high-backed chair, legs uncrossed, her hands folded in her lap. She exuded an aura of suppressed agitation – or distrust. It was impossible to gauge which until she gave a little more of herself away. As he'd settled into his seat, he'd observed the physical changes she'd undergone since the last time they'd met. He could hardly believe she was the same woman; without the bromide and croton oil flooding her system she looked almost well. The muscles of her face were no longer immobile but neither did they work to portray any distinct expressions, rather moving around her jaw to maintain a distant neutrality. She appeared to have put on a little weight although his assessment was based on only ever seeing the outline of her body beneath bedclothes. At last her hair had been allowed to grow. The light brown crop gave some definition to her features and she no longer resembled a diseased pauper. She was wearing tartan slippers that were too small and scrunched her toes, beneath a calf-length flowery cotton frock with a rampaging pattern that dwarfed her frame. He occupied the silence by trying to decide if the yellow splashes were supposed to be buttercups or impressionistic rosebuds.

A flush crawled up Edith's neck as she registered that he was staring.

'Helen made it for me. From some old curtains or a tablecloth no doubt. Ugly isn't it? But, I think we can both agree, a distinct improvement on my previous garb. Are those my clothes?'

Stephen handed over the basket. She was verbally dextrous and obviously alert to her surroundings. But she still hadn't displayed any emotion towards him.

'You're Dr Maynard.'

'So you recognise me then? Even with the beard.'

'Peter Hargreaves told me who you were and that you'd be coming today. I expected you earlier.'

This was better; mild annoyance was something he could work with – indifference wasn't.

'I'm sorry but I had to go to your place first to fetch these. I'm pleased to tell you it is being well looked after.'

'Nobody does something for nothing these days so I expect they've one eye on moving in themselves.'

So she did realise she wouldn't be resuming her life in Fletching any time soon. Her acceptance of the need to be at Beddingham Hall would make life – for the both of them – easier.

'You know why you're here, don't you?'

'Again, he told me. Do you think I'm simple or something? Well, I'm not.' She tapped her head. 'My marbles are all here.'

Stephen took a moment to compose his reply. It was essential that he start where Edith was in her understanding of her reality and not pitch her into an exploration of her psychosis until her mind was ready to face it squarely. This first session was to get her to accept him again, and to ascertain how much she was able – or willing – to remember about what had gone on between them. Only then could he decide on the appropriate course any treatment should take. Because there was no doubt that her mind would latch back onto its protective strategy of choice, catatonia, if he got it wrong. Staying on this side of intrusion for the time being would eventually allow familiarity to breach the more outlying of her defensive barriers. That's what he was banking on anyway.

'Why don't you go and change into some of your own things? I'm sure it'll make you feel much more comfortable.'

He'd only just stopped himself from saying: *more like your old self.* He clenched his hands together in an effort to stay rooted in the positive.

'I'm feeling fine as it happens, but yes, if you say so.'

'It's just a suggestion, Edith, not an order. No one here is going to try to make you do anything against your will.'

'I've no idea what you're talking about.' She stood up. 'I'll be back in a minute. Don't steal the silver.'

She didn't smile. Stephen watched her disappear around the curve of the narrow stairs before taking the opportunity to appraise Edith Potter's surroundings. The cottage would've been built for one of the Hall's retainers; only this room downstairs – with presumably a simple bathroom in what would have been the scullery – and a bedroom above. He wondered how she would manage for heating in the winter; there was a hearth but he thought it unlikely Peter would allow fires in the cottages. A wise precaution in Edith Potter's case, given what licking flames must symbolise. However there was electric light so perhaps they would provide her with a heater of some sort. He hoped so because it would be a very long and bleak winter indeed if she had to spend it in bed fully dressed and wrapped in blankets. He pushed the image out of his mind and forced himself to return to the present. What he had to concentrate on was establishing a relationship with her again. But he could only do that if she would allow him to, and, so far, she was exhibiting precious little sign of that.

She came back down into the room wearing the men's slippers Stephen had found under her kitchen table, a baggy grey cardigan, and a skirt and blouse that had once probably fitted but now hung off her bones. She had the appearance of any middle-aged spinster prone to self-neglect. The external trappings of normality never failed to cloak and deceive.

'So, how are you finding it here?'

She regarded him for a moment as if she'd been startled by his presence. He hoped he wouldn't have to introduce himself once more. It really was a waste of precious time to keep re-tracing ground with her. On the other hand, perhaps it was inevitable given that only a few months ago she'd been in a stupor from which he'd never thought she would emerge. Maybe she still hadn't entirely because there were different degrees of withdrawal, some less debilitating than others but all rooted in the same need to escape. He could only begin to judge how many layers remained in place by encouraging her to share any thoughts she had on her current situation. The exercise would be instructive and a benchmark against which to measure progress; comparing the state of mind of the Edith Potter sitting before him with the asylum inmate she had been would be less than useless: no longer being a zombie was not a sign of recovered sanity. He decided, after all, to start again.

'Edith, I am Dr Stephen Maynard. I treated you for a while.'

'What for, rheumatism?'

'No ...' he glanced at her expression and relaxed a little '... you're teasing me, aren't you?'

'There isn't much else to find amusing around here.'

'Ah, you've met some of the other residents then.'

'I go for a walk some mornings. They're often about. Look nothing like nature intended. You should do some of your doctoring on them.'

He felt sure he should deliver one of Peter's lectures on the nature and ethos of the place but adopting the role of an authority figure might only serve to remind her of how thoroughly she'd been rejected at the hands of her earliest. And they were nowhere near ready to confront her revelation that her father had wished her dead.

'I'm not that sort of a doctor, Edith. I'm a psychoanalyst. I work with the mind, not the body.'

'Well, they have to be crazy to walk around with faces like that. Any self-respecting person with an ounce of dignity left would wear a mask.'

'Would you, Edith?'

'What?'

'Wear a mask.'

'Don't we all anyway?'

This was the opening he'd been waiting for. 'That's very astute of you.'

He had to stop himself from wincing at his automatic adoption of a jollying-along tone. Edith was displaying signs of being as bright as any patient he'd ever had, and cut-throat sharp; she'd surgically dissect him if he gave her cause. Being patronised probably headed her list of transgressions deserving punishment.

'You could say that's what I deal in; the personas the mind adopts to protect itself.'

'So which one have you got on?'

'Sorry?'

'Which mask are you wearing for me now?'

'None that I'm aware of, Edith; I've nothing to hide.'

'Oh, I think you have.'

Stephen's hand reached up to his chin to pull at his beard. Edith wandered over to the window and looked out.

'My father, Dr Gerald Potter, was an eminent neurologist – perhaps you've heard of him? I used to assist in the editing of his academic papers on shell-shock, so I'm not totally ignorant about all this.'

'I never said you were.'

'But you're implying it in your very manner towards me.'

'I'm sorry if I gave that impression; I certainly didn't mean to.'

'No you didn't, did you?' She turned to face him. 'And that's the mask you've got on: that of trying to be reasonable when all you really want to do is snap your fingers at me with irritation.'

Stephen forced himself to hold her gaze. It was as if she were outmanoeuvring him with every change of her demeanour. One minute she was acting as though she was confused and disorientated, the next … the next as if she was trying to trick him into being provoked. Who was the real Edith Potter? Not the woman he'd encountered in the asylum, certainly. That was a phase in her evolution. He wished he'd asked how she'd conducted herself in the village when he'd been there; subjective opinions had their uses, particularly in the absence of any of his own.

'Will you agree to my coming to see you every Sunday to talk together as we're doing now, and maybe exploring some ways in which I can help you? Because you're not happy in yourself, Edith, are you?'

'No.'

A little-girl voice full of uncertainty, quite unlike the aggressive tone she'd begun to adopt.

'If I refuse, will you send me back there?'

So she did remember the asylum.

'Whether you want to co-operate or not will have no bearing on where you live for the foreseeable future.'

It was a lie, but what else could he say? She was unbending towards him a little at last.

'I suppose I might as well then, as I've nothing better to do'

She smiled. There wasn't any merriment in it but it was a start.

He stood up. 'I'll see you next week then. I'll telephone Dr Hargreaves when I've sorted out my travel arrangements and he'll let you know what time to expect me.'

'And if I'm not here then I'll be in a box up at the church; that's all any of us here have to look forward to.'

It made his heart shrink to see she wasn't joking.

CHAPTER THIRTY-TWO

Edith woke to the smell of porridge. She was surprised to feel a lightness in her limbs. Her back wasn't aching either. Perhaps the drugs were working; she'd eat everything they had put on the tray if they were going to make her feel this good. Besides, she was ravenous. She looked across at the pile of clothes on the chair. Where had they come from? Hadn't she always worn long-sleeved dresses made of soft and floaty material that wouldn't press too heavily on her skin? The blouses looked to be passable – gleaming white at least – but the matronly skirts were another matter altogether. When she'd done as she'd been told and put one on yesterday she'd felt as though she'd been auditioning for a part in amateur dramatics. He'd seemed pleased with her though. That she'd been willing to join in. Although he hadn't demonstrated nearly as much effort and had obviously not gone to her London flat at all but picked this lot up in a tat shop. She'd put some of them on today in case he was watching her; the rest would need to be thoroughly boiled.

After she'd had a cat-lick wash, changed, and eaten her breakfast, Edith set out on her mission to find the laundry. And whilst her mind had been on cleaning she'd decided that the poky bathroom could do with the application of a little soap and bleach. It wasn't as if she was incapable of looking after herself, just that they hadn't supplied her with the wherewithal. The moment she had determined how she was going to spend her day she'd known that the only trouble with her was that she was under-occupied; idle hands and all that …

*

Edith walked up the path that meandered over the expanse of green towards the Hall. A blue van sat with its motor purring on the driveway near the tower; her journey from the world outside was fresh enough in her memory to make her glad she wasn't sitting in the passenger seat. One of the frog-faced men waved at her. He was carrying a sack somewhere. She waved back. Before they'd let her move down to the cottage she'd hated to be paid any attention and had probably been quite rude. But once she'd realised her every interaction was being assessed by the Hargreaves and they would make judgements about her based on how well she socialised, she began to make an effort to be less cold.

The rewards weren't long in coming: Helen clearly appreciated having another woman living on the premises and began seeking her out for advice and support; they went to Firle Place to look at which upholstery fabrics the men should use on the chairs they were repairing; the next week visiting three local churches to see if it would be worthwhile offering a specialist service cleaning tapestries. Edith had no expertise to offer in either case but she had an eye for detail, and was able to calculate costs and profit margins in the time it took for Helen to finish discussing the niceties of colour-matching. A contract from Firle Place for re-springing and re-covering a half a dozen chaises longues resulted in her being invited for celebratory tea and cake in the Hargreaves' flat. From then on she found herself thinking of Helen as an ally in the triumvirate of doctors who held her future in their hands. A flourishing of warmth which surprised her. She discovered qualities in some of the uglies as well which made them tolerable company; silence was one of the attributes she valued most. Although she'd made the mistake of allowing herself to be collared by one or two who'd talked as if delivering a wireless broadcast, but as that required her to give nothing in return she hadn't minded so much. Besides, a modicum of social interaction would help pass the time until she was ready to pick up her old life again.

Except would she ever get the chance to do so if someone was manoeuvring to take over her flat? It'd been the only thing that had stuck with her out of the encounter with Dr Maynard yesterday – apart from these terrible clothes – primarily because it had made her cross and the drugs didn't allow for many fluctuations of mood. It wasn't the biggest in the block but it did have the view across the park. Perhaps it was the flighty number who lived on the other side of the corridor, she'd always made of point of commenting on how nice it must be to look out on trees whenever she came to borrow – but never return or repay – milk, writing paper, her maroon leather belt, a cup of sugar. No doubt the brazen hussy would have made plans to throw out that beautiful rug she'd bought from the Oriental Bazaar in Theberton Street to make the place look homely. Perhaps she should manufacture a reason for Dr Maynard to go back there and whilst he was at it to have a word with the landlady about boxing up her things. She thought she had some books she'd like to rescue. And hadn't she had a journal as a birthday present from the ginger-headed clerk so she could record her impressions of wartime London? It would be interesting to read that again.

A gong sounded from up at the house. They'd be serving morning tea in fifteen minutes. Maybe she should stay up there after she'd finished her business with the laundry and have a cup; the cottage had been closing in on her lately with its poky rooms and dirty corners. A change is as good as a rest, so they say, and as that was what the doctor had ordered for her – why she was here convalescing – then she'd hasten her recovery by a dose of different surroundings. She increased her stride up the incline to join the cripples. The other cripples.

*

The house was buzzing with men's voices. Edith stood in the hallway for a moment as she tried to remember her way to the kitchen. She'd been shown around when she'd first arrived but that seemed like years ago and her sense of direction hadn't been particularly acute then. In fact none of her senses had. She was glad she'd left that phase behind; it was much more satisfying to have an awareness of time and space. To have an awareness of herself. She climbed the stairs. The lingering smell of cooked bacon led her to the large dining room on the first floor. Rows of tables were already laid for the midday meal with plates and cutlery – forks and spoons, no knives – and snowy-white napkins. She assumed they must get through an awful lot of those given the strange-shaped holes that passed for many of the men's mouths.

She retraced her steps and, once in the hallway, walked down to the far end. A passageway was secreted under the stairs with a short flight of stone steps leading into a semi-basement. A mangle with rollers the size of tree trunks stood in one corner, a pile of firewood in another. Sheets hung over a line rigged between two of the ceiling's supporting pillars. A man was stirring a large copper with a sturdy pole. He was stripped to the waist, his back muscles gleaming with sweat. Edith almost wanted to stroke them; they looked as if they had enough power stored in their fibres to charge her like a battery. If she did then she'd be out of here tomorrow. But she didn't want him to turn around and for his torn face to spoil the illusion of masculine perfection. The room was hot and steamy. On a bench under the open window sat pristine blocks of yellow soap. If she could help herself and leave then maybe the man would never notice her presence.

She had crept halfway across the room when he reached to his side for something. He looked straight at her. Edith didn't know which one of them was the more startled. His face was beautiful in its symmetry. She felt the heat in her cheeks intensify. Mumbling something about extra washing, she dropped the clothes on the nearest pile and darted back towards the door. But not before she'd tucked a block of soap into her skirt pocket.

That glimpse of the unexpected had unsettled her and she sidled into the recreation room as she had done in the early days, taking her tea and crumpet from the trolley without looking at anyone. Never at ease with the thought of being caught with butter dribbling down her chin, she kept her head bent low over her lap as she ate, scrubbing at her mouth with the back of her hand when she'd finished. With the hollowness in her stomach taken care of, Edith slipped out of the armchair intending to make a start on the cleaning but a one-armed Cyclops thrust a white pawn into her hand and began pulling at her cardigan sleeve.

It was pity rather than his insistence that made her sit at the chessboard; he rarely had anything other than an imaginary opponent because of his habit of wandering away mid-move. He would return eventually but then another eternity would have to pass before he would release his hold on the piece. Helen had told her his behaviour came from being scared to commit to anything in case he made the same mistake as he did in the trenches. A cast-iron logic Edith found impossible to fault. They'd played twice before and she'd enjoyed pitting her tactical wits against his. On this occasion, the game lasted for an hour and a half until the moment of her inevitable resignation came and she left to return to her cottage.

The enforced concentration had exhausted her and she went upstairs for a lie down. But her mind refused to settle enough to doze off. Snippets of memories kept forcing their way in until up popped, with bright clarity, the day she'd bought her first wireless set. She saw herself fidgeting at her desk in the basement of the Ministry, rushing through the last of the files in order to be able to leave on time. Barely civil to the soldier on duty as he ticked his list of persons exiting the building, she had to run to catch the bus to Holborn. Gamages had always been her favourite department store and she knew the maze of rooms, steps, passages, and ramps well enough to take the side entrance in Leather Lane. Past the sporting goods, and camping equipment, and at last she was standing in front of a Ward & Goldstone Atlantic spark-transmitter unit. It was a month's wages but such a thing of beauty she would've paid twice as much to have one. She began to tap the Morse key while she waited for the salesman to come over and show her the wireless catalogue.

And then things warped a little. The message she remembered spelling out so precisely changed from:

Hello. I'm writing this, Edith.

To:

Hello. I'm watching you. Edward.

Perhaps this hadn't been a memory at all but a dream. Except it couldn't be because she could feel the tufted pattern of the bedspread under her calves, and hear the frantic buzzing of a bluebottle as it flew repeatedly up against the window. So she wasn't awake, and she wasn't asleep. What other states were there?

*

By the time her evening meal arrived, she had decided that her body was acclimatising to the drugs and the effects weren't lasting as long. For example, her eyes had begun bothering her at about three o'clock each afternoon with everything changing shape whenever she tried to focus too hard. Drugs were the only explanation. She looked at the plate of egg and cheese salad and wondered where they were. The beetroot was the most likely in its pool of juice resembling blood. She turned her head away.

'What's the matter, aren't you hungry? I'll leave the cloth over it and you can eat later. Why don't we take the chairs and sit outside for a bit? It's a lovely evening; far too nice to waste indoors.'

Edith watched as Helen took the two high-backed chairs and positioned them beside the front door where they would catch the last rays of the setting sun. Then Helen sat, her face raised to the sky and her eyes closed. Edith felt a spurt of annoyance at the way Dr Hargreaves, even in a moment of relaxation, couldn't drop her profession's habit of making you make the decision for yourself about whether or not to join in. She much preferred being ordered around as she had been by the warder in the other place because it removed so many possibilities of misjudgement. Of misreading. Of letting her guard down – always a dangerous option, and never more so than when surrounded by psychiatrists. But Helen didn't look as if she was about to make the effort to winkle out secrets, so Edith tried to stop acting like someone in the grip of paranoia and pretend to act like someone for whom seeing out the day's end in pleasant company came naturally.

They sat in silence for what seemed like hours. But the slinking shadows hadn't reached them yet so she knew it was her mind distorting reality again. She really shouldn't be wishing her time away like that. What had happened to all those minutes, hours and days when they said she'd been insensible to the world? Were they stored up somewhere for her to spend wisely on something pleasurable? What could possibly come under that category in this life she now had to call her own? Sitting here, probably. So she had to make it count. To engage in conversation. Except she hadn't a thought in her head worth saying. It was easy when they were talking over furnishing materials and costs per unit. But she'd never been one for idle chit-chat; being brought up in a house filled with near-silence had made her appreciate the value of not wasting words. The downside of which was not knowing how to go about talking meaningfully about nothing. If she found something to do then maybe the strain would lessen and a topic would come to her. She started tracing the patterns the closed-head daisies made in the grass.

'Do you like it here, Edith?'

A flutter of apprehension disturbed her concentration. How could she answer such a question truthfully without appearing ungrateful for the concern in Helen's voice? It was somewhere to be … and then somewhere to leave. The same as everywhere else. It occurred to Edith that maybe it wasn't, maybe it was different. If the ridiculous saying, *home is where the heart is*, meant anything at all then perhaps this was home. Temporarily. Reluctantly. There was nowhere else she belonged any more or less, no one but the woman sitting beside her whose feelings she cared about enough not to hurt. Back to the tricky problem of choosing the right words. Except Helen wasn't waiting for them, she was chattering away dreamily as if she'd never expected a response.

'... it's funny, isn't it, how it always ends up being such a small world? I mean about Stephen. Him arranging for you to come here. Keeping up your treatment. I never thought to see him again, that our paths would re-cross. We went to medical school together – him, me, and Peter. The three of us were inseparable back then.'

'What was he like?'

This wasn't so difficult after all. Mainly because she didn't have to feign interest; Edith genuinely wanted to know what made the man tick. A case of know thine enemy perhaps; because Dr Maynard certainly didn't – however often he kept saying his only aim was to help her – come into the category of friend.

'Oh, God, if I met any of our younger selves now I'd want to stick our heads in a bucket of water. We were so full of ourselves. Thought we knew everything. Took the whole world so seriously because we didn't know how to view certain aspects of life as a sick joke. That changed after the War, of course. Well, it did for us, and I'm assuming the same for Stephen. I hope so because he always found it almost physically painful to laugh at himself; it made him such an easy target to tease, and Peter was forever sharpening his wit in those days. Stephen would respond with such a bewildered puppy openness that I always took his side … I probably shouldn't tell you this but at one time I thought he might be the one I ended up marrying.'

Edith looked up from her study of the daisies. Helen hadn't moved from the languid pose she'd adopted when she'd first sat down. It was the longest Edith had ever seen her maintain an attitude of motionlessness. Normally Helen was fiddling with her hair or reaching out to touch something; she was a mass of restless energy. Edith could imagine someone as buttoned-up as Dr Maynard being attracted to her. For all her fidgety ways – which would've had Granny bringing her cane down hard on her knuckles – there was a calmness about her, a surety of purpose that was beguiling. But she couldn't for the life of her see what would've made such an exceptional woman succumb to even a second's temptation to settle for him. Perhaps copious amounts of alcohol had been involved.

'Have you ever had too much of a good thing, Edith?'

'Potential husbands?'

'I was thinking more about choice.'

'Sometimes I'm not sure I ever had any – even when I thought I did I knew there was always someone in the background pulling the strings. You see, there was someone once. He put a stop to it of course.'

'The man?'

'My father.'

'Ah. Were you very young?'

'Naïve, sheltered, unworldly perhaps but not young. I don't think I was ever that.'

'You must've had a very difficult childhood.'

The airing of every psychoanalyst's pet subject felt like a betrayal of the confidence. Helen turned and squinted at her.

'You were staring, I could feel it. At this?' She raised her hand to flutter around the scar puckering her forehead. 'This didn't come from something nasty in my own youth, if that's what you're thinking. It happened in a front-line casualty station in Flanders. It was my own fault, everyone always said that this red hair of mine would act like a beacon to draw enemy fire, and, wouldn't you know, I was washing it outside the tent one day when a shell blew a hole in the mud the size of a double-decker bus.'

'You should cover it up.'

'Grow a fringe, you mean? What would be the point? I'd still know it was there and so would everyone else who'd ever seen it. And it would hardly be a good advertisement for the work we do here, would it? Some of the men ended up with us as a direct result of misguided attempts to do just that. I don't suppose you've heard of the Tin Noses Shop?'

Edith hadn't. She wanted to laugh at the image it threw up in her mind but didn't think it appropriate. She opted for silence instead.

'That's what the Tommies called it anyway, the Masks for Facial Disfigurements Department was the official title at the

3rd London General Hospital. Because that's what they did, they made the men masks to hide behind. They could only do it for those whose relatives could supply a photograph to work from and the process was slow and painful. But it gave them hope that they would be accepted as a human being again. It restored self-respect. The masks were made from thin electroplate tinted with oil paints to match as closely as possible the remaining flesh. But however talented the artists, it never fooled anyone. And they did nothing for the psychological damage. For some of the men, the very act of wearing of a mask created an even deeper level of disturbance because they realised the main purpose of doing so was to not *shock the horses*. After all, they themselves knew what was underneath; they took them off every night; they knew they would never again be acceptable for what they were. The horrors they had become. There was no pretence in their own minds, and there is none here.'

'Why do you do it?'

'Because someone has to. Beddingham Hall had been requisitioned as a convalescent home in 1916, and the next year the elderly owner died leaving no heirs but having expressed a wish that the place should continue to be useful. So then the powers that be decided a home was required for returning veterans who needed the safety and security of somewhere they could be unobtrusively cared for, and lead useful lives.'

'But not normal.'

'No, Edith, not normal; it would be pointlessly heartbreaking for any of us to believe that would be possible. But they can pick up some of the skills and trades they had before, and learn the new ones we need to keep the place going. It's a never-ending battle to maintain our heads above water but it's the least we can do in view of the tremendous sacrifices these men made for this country.'

Edith had to breathe against a tightness in her chest that was threatening to overwhelm her. Helen was leaning back in her chair again and had begun tracing her scar with her fingertip.

'I suspect that the world would be a better place if all of us wore our damage proudly on the outside, but we'll never know, will we? Life makes us who we are, Edith – deformities and all – and how we react to the cards we're dealt is what makes us unique individuals. In the end, it is our differences that define our humanity.'

No it wasn't: it was humanity that defined the deformities. The insight tugged forward what had been pressing at the edge of Edith's mind …

It was the spring of 1917 and she was placing the last of the files in the box to be picked up by the courier and delivered to the War Office. Her work on interpreting the patterns in the aerial photographs was monotonous but she took pride in always worrying at the anomalies. And it invariably yielded results. She was the best at her job. Everyone knew it. They regarded her as odd – *a queer fish* she'd overheard the Section Head call her – but respected her dogged determination to identify the ammunition dump that no one else had been able to pinpoint, or the suspiciously shaped hill that Intelligence would later confirm was an attempt to disguise the formation of a new German artillery position or a fuel supply depot.

It had been a frustrating day and she was looking forward to getting back to her flat and putting her feet up with a book and the remains of yesterday's stew. She was setting the seal when the man walked in. At first she'd assumed he was the courier but he wasn't in uniform and didn't have the frantic air that spoke of a motorbike ride through the London traffic against an immovable deadline. Her initial instinct was to telephone the soldier on the front desk to demand to know how an unauthorised civilian had been able to enter the building and to tell him to come and escort him away. But something about the distracted way the man was scanning the room stopped her from lifting the receiver. It was almost as if he didn't know where he was or how he had got there. He looked like a hospital patient. But there was no sign of any battle wound. The more she studied him in silence, the more the signs of shell-shock jumped out at her: the trembling hands hanging limply by his sides; a tipping of his head as if he was listening to something just out of range; feet planted solidly against being bowled over by some unexpected force.

She'd finished twisting the wire ends of the seal and was about to suggest they walk out into the street together when he reached into his jacket pocket, pulled out a cut-throat razor, and swept it in an arc from under one ear to the other. He stood and looked at her for the longest moment of her life before the blood started spurting. It covered her, and a patch of the wall, in seconds. A ghastly gurgling filled the room as he tried to say something. What? *I'm sorry … this could just as well have happened in any other office … it's nothing personal … please tell my mother …* What? His final words on this earth were lost forever in the sob and suck of bloody air. But what could they have possibly mattered anyway? And in the chasm of time between his legs buckling and her starting to scream, she was aware of feeling nothing but a surge of pure envy.

She prised her eyes open. Helen was standing in front of her, chafing her hands in hers.

'Breathe slowly and deeply, Edith. That's it … come back to me … you're quite safe … it's September 1927 and we're outside your cottage in Beddingham Hall. Take a look around you. Can you see the turret and the trees? They're real, Edith. Listen to the rooks roosting in the copse … if you really concentrate hard you can smell the cows in the milking parlour. Take a moment to absorb these things. When you're ready, give me a nod and I'll help you back inside.'

The picture in Edith's head faded as her surroundings came back into focus. She tried to stand, but her legs refused to hold her weight. An arm snaked around her and lifted her up again. Every step to the door felt as though it would be the one to drain her bones. She almost collapsed on the climb up the stairs but eventually she was lying on her bed with the eiderdown tucked tightly around her.

'Go to sleep now. If you wake up later, you can get undressed properly but for now just close your eyes and rest. I'll pop back in the morning as usual with your breakfast.'

The last thing Edith saw was the figure of a flame-haired angel sitting on the end of the bed, her hands fluttering restlessly in the air around her.

CHAPTER THIRTY-THREE

Stephen leaned back on the chair. 'So, how do you feel, Edith?'

'How do you expect me to feel?'

'I don't expect anything; it would just be helpful to know.'

'Helpful to whom?'

'To the both of us. If we're going to be able to make any progress together then I need to have some idea of what's in your head.'

'Nothing.'

'What?'

'There's nothing in my head. How could there be when I'm on release from a lunatic asylum?'

This was promising. It showed some recognition of why she was here. Unless of course it was merely another example of the Hargreaves' approach of treating their charges as equals; he would really have to ask them to make an exception in Edith Potter's case, otherwise how could he tell what she remembered and what was regurgitated information?

'Let me start by reassuring you that you are a long way from being clinically insane. What you're experiencing is the problem the mind has in accepting what it is having trouble accommodating. It happens to all of us to a greater or lesser extent; in your case, because you are an intelligent woman and it has been going on for a long time, your conscious self has devised elaborate layers to cloak what lies beneath. It is my job to explore how you can get under those layers, and eventually discard them completely.'

But now he was the one being evasive. He had been worrying all week about the most appropriate approach to take with her. After ruling out all the other options as likely to provoke an explosive reaction he might not be able to handle, he'd come to the conclusion that the one likely to yield the best results was for him to probe and unravel the symptoms of her distress without directly addressing the fundamental cause until she was ready to do so. It wasn't skirting the issue exactly, more allowing a certain amount of mental healing to take place in order that she would be strong enough to face the truth and find a way to live with it. But by no stretch of the imagination could that ever include abandoning all of her subconscious protections; to do that probably would drive her insane. The path had to be prepared, and then trodden softly.

'Do you remember how, when I hypnotised you, I told you everything I was doing every step of the way?'

'No.'

'I made a point of doing it to engage your rationality. I would like to do the same with you again but this time without the induced trance. If there's anything you don't understand or don't see the point of, let me know and I'll go through some of the underlying theories. I think it will help speed the process if you are able to do a little psychoanalysing of yourself in-between my visits.'

'Do you out of a job you mean?'

'Not exactly. But I'll be more than delighted if that proves to be the case.'

'They'll have to pay me then.'

'Who's *they*?'

'Helen and the man she chose above all others to be her husband.'

'That's rather a convoluted way of describing their relationship.'

'But accurate: she told me so herself. When we were discussing the concept of regrets.'

'Were you? When?'

'I'm sure she'll report back to you any content of our recent conversations deemed of relevance to my case.'

'I thought you understood that the Hargreaves have kindly agreed to take care of your immediate needs but have nothing to do with your treatment. It's me who carries the sole responsibility for that, and to which end I willingly donate my Sundays.'

He attempted a laugh but turned it into a cough when he saw she wasn't smiling.

'I rather suspect you do so because you've got a guilty conscience.'

His hand reached up to pull at his beard. 'And why do you think I should have one of those?' He could feel the prickle of sweat under his collar.

'For locking me up in that other place.'

'I didn't send you there, Edith; you were committed at the time for your own protection. You had some sort of a fit – a fugue is the medical term for it. After that incident, you were in a state of withdrawal for months.'

'Was I? How nice for me.'

Her mind had abandoned using a catatonic stupor to act as her gatekeeper to reality but only so that it could be replaced with the tactic of extreme denial. He pulled a sheaf of papers from his briefcase to have something to occupy him in the heavy silence. The top sheet bore the results of Edith's word association test. If he did it with her again maybe her responses would give him some clues. Although, of course, he would be interacting with another persona: a woman unreachable except via deep hypnosis could hardly be said to have the same mental processes as the one regarding him coldly now. But it was worth a try.

'Edith, in order for me to gauge the best way forward, I'd like to conduct a simple experiment with you. We've done it once before, in fact. There are no right answers and no question of failing. It is just an established method I use to afford me some indications as to my patients' state of mind.'

'We're residents here.'

'Yes, sorry.'

She glanced over at the door. 'As if a change in terminology makes any difference. Go ahead, doctor, I'm ready.'

Could he trust her not to play games? He thought so.

'After I say each word, I'll be expecting you to respond as quickly as possible with the first thing you think of.'

She nodded and closed her eyes as if to aid her concentration. He took that to mean she would take it seriously.

'Blue.'

'Van.'

'House.'

'Work.'

'To dance.'

She opened her eyes and looked around a little. 'To the beat of a different drum.'

'Birds.'

'Wrung necks.'

'Circle.'

'Wholeness.'

'Twin.'

'Doppelganger.'

'Anxiety.'

'Your face.'

He looked up and saw her smiling.

'If there were any mirrors in this place I'd tell you to go and take a peek at yourself. Then tell me if I'm not right.'

Stephen forced his muscles to relax by breathing slowly and deeply. She wasn't being antagonistic, merely making an observation.

'Okay, Edith, point made. I confess I'm somewhat apprehensive about how this session will go; we didn't exactly get off to a flying start, did we? And you squeezing the life out of that cushion isn't doing very much to reassure me that you're entirely comfortable with all this.'

'You disturb me no more than most, and a lot less than coming face to face with some of the horrors living here. But look, cushion down, see?'

'Edith, your hands. I've only just noticed how red and chapped they are. Do you have a history of psoriasis?'

'The only thing I have is a lot of scars that will never flake off. I've been cleaning up a little, that's all. You'd be surprised how filthy I found it was once I got started. Do you think you could get them to let me have some Vim, and a little bleach – if I promise not to drink it?'

Stephen squashed the impulse to raise an eyebrow. Instead, he wrote the request on his pad. 'I'll ask Peter and Helen when I drop in on them up at the Hall.'

'It's not that complicated is it?'

'What?'

'My shopping list.'

He shrugged. 'No, but my memory isn't infallible at the best of times and I don't want to let you down by forgetting.'

'That's another thing we agree on then: how frustratingly tedious it can be to everyone concerned when the mind can no longer be relied upon.'

'And the other?'

'That you're very bad at hiding your feelings, whereas I'm very good at it.'

'So you admit you have some.'

'Of course.'

'Do you want to enlighten me?'

'What, and squander my momentary advantage?'

Now she was playing games.

'Why don't we get back to the word association test? What comes into your head when I say *lie*?'

'A withholding or perversion of the truth.'

'Book.'

'Acute absence of.'

'I did bring some actually. They're up at the Hall with Peter. I'll ask him to give them to you.'

'Very kind and thoughtful. I hope you chose them well. It will be interesting to see if by some miracle you've been able to come anywhere near my reading tastes. I'll have to revise my opinion about your perceptiveness if you have.'

'I did my best.'

'Well, that's all any of us can ever do, isn't it.'

'True enough. Only another four to go. *Women*.'

'Deemed surplus to requirements.'

'To die.'

'A blessed relief, given the alternative.'

'Which is? …'

'To endure decrepitude.'

'Angry.'

Silence.

'Come on, Edith, give me your first reaction; you've done very well up to now.'

'Don't patronise me.'

'Was I?'

'That's my answer.'

'Child.'

With a burst of energy he hadn't thought her capable of harbouring, she rose from the armchair and pushed her face to within a foot of his. It took all his willpower not to flinch.

'This is a trick. A cheap, filthy, disgusting trick. You know, don't you? You pretend not to with your around about ways and your false sincerity about wanting to help me. And you think you're so clever trying to get Edith Potter to trip up … but you're not …'

She raised her hands, and for one sickening moment, Stephen thought she was going to fasten them around his neck.

'Now, if you will excuse me, I have to go and wash. You can't always see deceit but it leaves a tidemark all the same – inside and out.'

She turned and stalked towards the bathroom. Stephen thought better of still being in her firing line when she returned, and let himself out of the front door. The entire encounter had given him more than enough to chew over until the next time they met.

CHAPTER THIRTY-FOUR

The Hargreaves' flat was at the top of the turret. Stephen had got out of breath climbing the steep stone staircase that snaked up relentlessly in a disorientating anticlockwise direction. He wanted to elicit his friends' opinions but to do so would require a great deal of circumspection; Edith was his official patient and therefore had every right to expect a high degree of confidentiality. He was duty-bound to share anything about her current state of mind that might impinge on the Hargreaves' pastoral care of her, but her anger at him could hardly be said to fall into that category. Except he had unwittingly awakened a deep-seated aggression; he would leave her request for bleach for another time.

He allowed himself to sink into the soft couch and rest his neck on the back. His gaze fell on a watercolour in smoky greys and greens. A church took up most of the foreground, its tower and roof unfinished. The land it sat on was an impressionistic smudge. He thought of the summer he'd spent exploring the priory on Holy Island. This painting captured perfectly the emotions he'd had at the time: awe at the effort required to build monumental edifices in the middle of nowhere; envy at the simplicity of having a single-minded purpose; melancholy at the reality of impermanence and mortality.

Peter handed him a glass of whisky. 'Helen's having a bath. She'll join us in a little while. I see you're admiring my painting.'

'You did it?'

'It isn't quite how it was, but the conditions weren't ideal. In fact, it was pouring with rain that day; if you press your nose up to the glass you can see where the water made the colours bleed.'

'It's very good all the same; where were you? It has something of the North Country about it.'

'Mons. There'd been a heavy bombardment and we'd been operating all night. I remember thinking that if I had to sever one more limb or sew up some poor blighter's abdomen knowing that he wouldn't live to see the daylight hours, I'd throw myself on the bloody sawdust and howl. So I took out my watercolour box. The church had received a direct hit. Fifty of the villagers were inside praying. None survived. It turns out I walked away from one scene of death and carnage to find solace in painting another. Ironic, don't you think?'

Stephen didn't know what to say. He sipped his drink, the painting now totally transformed from a romantic study to yet another vivid reminder of the Great War. He forced his gaze away from the broken promise of peace and sanctuary. The thought, inevitably, brought him back to Edith.

'Whilst I'm here, have you got any journals covering the latest theories on personality changes resulting from repression? If not I'll have to wheedle my way into Prof Inkman's library and be forced to endure stories of his fishing trips.'

'Of course, old son. Why?'

'I've a few things buzzing around in my brain and I thought having a quick look at them might help me sort out my thinking. I'm concerned with the long-term effects of being unable to adequately release deep and profound anger in order to readjust to normal life.'

'Then I wouldn't waste your time ploughing through a load of dry papers on the subject because Helen's the one to ask about that. How it's manifested in shell-shock cases is by way of being a bit of a specialism of hers. Ellie, darling,' he called, 'are you about to grace us with your presence any time soon? Our esteemed guest has a philosophical question or two for you on the meaning of life after near-death.'

And then she was in the room with them. Stephen felt the air as charged as in the aftermath of a lightning strike. Tall, and as slender as she'd always been, her body was wrapped in a black and purple silk kimono. Her alabaster skin was luminous in contrast. He flushed to notice the outline of her breasts as she came towards him. Clumsily, he stood up to greet her. She was smiling broadly, her arms open. As the light hit her, he saw the scar. An impertinent gash on her beautiful face. His stomach flipped at the pain of realising there was something about her he had no knowledge of, no part in her acquiring; that she'd had a life outside his heart and thoughts; that it had been Peter who'd watched her imperfection fade year after year, who would've woken up every morning and traced it with his fingertip or kissed the ragged outline softly to show her that it made no difference to his love. And he experienced a flash of murderous jealousy because it should've been he who'd done those things. Who'd been grateful for the fact that she'd been stricken as it meant he could share it with her.

All that in the time it took for her to fold her arms tightly around his shoulders and place a kiss on his cheek. He didn't dare return the hug because he thought that if he did he'd be in danger of never letting go. Once free of her embrace, he slumped back on the couch. Peter handed her a glass of whisky and then crossed the room to top up Stephen's.

'You'll stay for dinner, won't you?'

Her voice was exactly as he remembered.

'No … thank you … I really have to get back to London at a reasonable time; I've a full clinic tomorrow.'

It wasn't true but he didn't think he could stand a whole evening of feeling this self-conscious.

'Another time then.'

She perched on the arm of Peter's chair and playfully snatched away his tobacco jar as he tried to fill his pipe.

'Right, so what was it this inarticulate husband of mine was saying about philosophy? I have to warn you that my days of being able to pontificate at will are long gone. But then I suspect the arrogant certainty of youth has left us all for good.'

Her expression clouded and Stephen longed to be able to say something that would cause her to unleash the beauty of her smile again. However, as any witticism eluded him, he'd have to settle for impressing her with his insightful intelligence.

'Do you agree that anger is fundamentally a frustration at not being able to sublimate feelings of inadequacy?'

'I think that's a little simplistic but it'll do as a working hypothesis for now.'

Stephen caught himself blushing like a schoolboy having his mistakes corrected in front of the class. He took refuge in prising open the buckle of his briefcase and hauling his papers onto his lap.

'I like your beard, by the way.' Helen tipped her head as if studying him. 'It makes you look so much older – sorry, that sounded rude; distinguished, I meant.'

'One of his nubile medical students certainly seems to think so.' Peter was grinning through a haze of pipe smoke.

The heat in Stephen's cheeks increased.

'It was a bit scratchy to kiss, though.' Helen ran her fingertips over her lips. 'But I'm sure she's willing to make the sacrifice. Oh, Stephen, I've embarrassed you; since when did you become so sensitive?'

He tried to smile with what he hoped could be interpreted as chivalrous discretion. When he finally realised it had become fixed, he cleared his throat.

'Well, assuming that the underlying cause of the dis-ease is firmly rooted and nothing can be done to change the events that led to its acquisition – the past being something we can distance ourselves from at best – then what would you regard as the primary clinical manifestations that might indicate a greater or lesser movement towards acceptance?'

Helen raised her eyebrows. He thought he saw her mouth the word *bravo*. He picked up his pen in readiness.

'I'm pretty sure it depends on whether or not one knows the exact point about which the person is grieving. Or if they are aware of it themselves.'

'Let's take it that they are.'

'I use the word *grieving* intentionally because inadequacy is based on the actual or imagined loss of something, someone, or state – such as happiness, security, or love …'

Was that directed at him? Her lips were slightly upturned as if to harbour a secret smile, and he wondered if she remembered everything that'd passed between them as clearly as he did.

'… the problems arise because the person either won't, or can't, accept their limitations to control reality.'

'And that's interesting in itself.' Peter was poking the stem of his pipe at his wife's upper arm. 'Reality is actually more a state of emotion than anything else so when you get difficult feelings resulting from something as nebulous as our relation to our existence then it only takes a slight tremor for it all to come tumbling down like a worm-eaten hovel.' He sucked on his pipe once more. 'Back to you, professor.'

Helen hit him lightly on the chest. Stephen's lungs deflated a little as if he'd been the recipient of the love-tap.

'As much as I hate to admit it, Peter – on this occasion at least – is right. A person disturbed in this way may not have their reason or intellect seriously impaired and, to all intents and purposes, appear to be functioning perfectly normally – able to hold rational conversations for example, or follow quite complex thought processes. But at heart they are responding to the world as a child does when they're unable to adapt to their environment; or more usually the frustration they experience when they can't change their environment to suit themselves. However, on top of that, as rational adults they have an awareness of their lack of inner harmony. So there are warring elements on the inside as well as the outside. It's as if … as if … they are trying to fight to retain an eroding beach-head, but with an army that's already in the process of mutinying.'

Stephen thought Helen couldn't have summed up Edith's state of mind more accurately if she'd psychoanalysed the woman. A profound respect piled on top of his other feelings for her.

Although the concepts were ones he worked with every day, hearing them said by someone using a different language, and making different connections, was illuminating – particularly as Helen had exposure to those blighted by long-term shell-shock whereas his experience was confined to the initial acute stages. He scribbled a few quick notes.

'I've just remembered the case McDougall quoted which illustrates that very nicely.' Helen took a sip of her whisky. 'In 1901 a highly respected and competent village schoolmaster got drunk and committed an act of sodomy resulting in him, twelve years later, murdering his wife and children while they slept then setting fire to a neighbouring village and shooting the inhabitants – killing nine and seriously wounding eleven. The question you have to ask is not why he did it, but why it took him so long.'

'In your experience does every deep-seated trauma manifest itself – sooner or later – in violence?'

'Not necessarily. Sometimes. It isn't even a consistent approach in the same person.'

Helen bit at the skin at the side of her thumbnail for a moment.

'I think that sums it up, actually: unpredictability. I've known some get very aggressive but the next minute they are all sweetness and light; over-affectionate, clinging, inappropriately demonstrative, penitent, needy. And then there was one who had to have his entire family sit on him whenever there was a bugle playing on the wireless to stop him breaking every stick of furniture in the house.'

'How much of this do they remember afterwards?'

'Interesting you should ask that.'

She bit at her thumb again.

'The memory seems to be the key mental process affected by long-term shell-shock. Obviously they are fixated on things they remember too vividly and dwell on them as if they are current experiences, but other events they transmogrify into representing their inner turmoil.'

Stephen managed to make himself look away as Helen readjusted her kimono where it had been threatening to slip apart over her crossed knees.

'Sometimes the memory itself is severely affected often resulting in slips of the tongue, slips of the pen, the mislaying of important objects, forgetting significant facts – one man forgot to turn up at his wedding; all are indications that the memory is doing its best to destroy any equanimity the mind is desperately trying to hang on to. Ring any bells with your Edith Potter?'

Stephen nodded. 'But I'm at the stage with her where I can't tell the difference between self-protective memory lapses which will be broken down as a defence mechanism when she becomes more aware of her subconscious reactions to her condition, and repression. One could be considered to be almost healthy given her past trauma, the other …'

'I think you've got yourself a very tricky one. Whenever I talk to her, she seems on one level to be adopting a persona that is working for her in terms of being relatively able to cope. But at the same time it's as if there's a part of her that is desperate to be forced to open up in some way. There aren't any easy answers I'm afraid, Stephen. But I could do a lot worse than quote you a little of Jung's wisdom on the subject.'

Peter groaned. 'Not again? She bores everyone with this at the drop of a hat; you could say it's her party piece.'

'Shut up.'

There was no affection in her tone. She leaned forward, her elbows on her knees, her eyes sparking with intensity. Stephen felt the hairs on the back of his neck stand up.

'*No one could express any better, or any more directly, what we never cease to maintain, however lacking in science it may seem at first – namely, the real therapeutic action of kindness.*'

CHAPTER THIRTY-FIVE

Edith woke up. This surprised her as she didn't think she'd been asleep. Something was banging in her head. No, it was downstairs. At the door. The tip of her nose was icy. She raised her head off the pillow and looked at the window. Bubbles of condensation distorted the view. There was no denying that, after a little delay, autumn had well and truly started; it was her favourite time of year with its crisp crinkly leaves, and freshly dug vegetables from the garden. Except she remembered that her London flat hadn't had one. Perhaps she meant her granny's way back in Cambridge. The knocking continued.

She swung her legs free from the blankets and reached for the candlewick dressing gown they'd finally got around to providing. Her hands were unaccountably grubby; grey smudges on the fingertips. She would wash them thoroughly, and then see who it was. Perhaps it was time for her breakfast. She had a hollow sensation in her stomach so it could be; but then she was always hungry these days.

When she got to the door, it was Helen. She was carrying a steaming bowl of porridge and something wrapped in a tea towel that smelt like toast.

'Good morning, Edith. Did you sleep well? I won't stay so you can eat this up before it gets cold. I didn't bother with the tea this time because I know you won't drink it; there's plenty of water in the tap.'

She walked in and placed the tray on the table.

'I've a message for you. Dr Maynard isn't likely to come this weekend.'

Edith thought she felt relieved. Or disappointed. Or maybe both.

'What day is it?'

'Thursday.'

'Where have the other days gone?'

'Time does have a habit of slipping past, doesn't it? I remember when I was lucky enough to be able to take a holiday and afterwards I'd always wonder why it always felt as if it never happened. Our way of switching off and getting a complete rest I suppose. Anyway, Stephen telephoned Peter first thing to warn him – really to get a little sympathy would be my guess. It seems he went for a long walk yesterday evening and nearly drowned in a downpour – men, they do exaggerate – and has a bit of a sniffle. His own diagnosis is probably galloping influenza.'

Helen's smile was like that of an indulgent mother. Edith felt a flash of irritation; why was it that men were always allowed their foibles whereas women were immediately labelled neurotic or hysteric, or worse. She suspected that right now they'd have her down as bitter and frustrated and jealous. And they'd be right.

'So what will you do with yourself today?'

'Nothing I expect. As usual.'

'You could come up to the Hall and play chess again. Or some of the men have a card school going – bridge, I think.'

'And have the hours drag even more?'

'Edith, you are down in the dumps this morning. Maybe we're partially at fault for not organising any specific activities but you've always displayed such an independence of spirit that we didn't want to crowd you. Look, why don't you come to tea with Peter and me this afternoon?'

'Will any of the other freaks be there?'

She noted with satisfaction Helen's moue of disapproval. But then she saw how the younger woman lifted her hand towards her scar, and experienced a pang of shame. It was something she hadn't felt for a long time. Being made to feel as if Helen was offering her company as some sort of therapy had provoked her into acting like a spiteful child and now she was suffering the consequences.

'Thank you very much for your kind invitation. I will be delighted to accept. Just don't expect me to dress for the occasion.'

'And that's another thing; I don't want you to take this the wrong way but I'm going into Lewes in a bit to pick up some barely worn clothes from a wealthy supporter of ours; her son was killed at Ypres. We could go through them if you like and see if there's something suitable.'

Edith tried not to recall what her grandmother said about *charity cases* and worked on an it'll-be-fun-being-girls-together expression instead.

'Is there anything I can get you whilst I'm there?'

The only things missing in her life couldn't be bought over the counter, but having some distractions might make her notice their absence less. 'Can I have some paper and pencils? Instead of waiting for Dr Maynard to give me my books I thought I might try my hand at writing one myself. I've enough material here,' she tapped the side of her head, 'to produce another *War and Peace*.'

She knew there was something else the promise-breaker was going to procure but couldn't remember what. Helen beamed at her.

'That's an excellent idea. Why didn't I think of that? Hold on though, I've an even better one … Why don't you come to Lewes with me? We can have tea there instead, and get you one of those loose-leaf journals along with anything else that tickles your fancy. The Asylum Board grants us an allowance to cover your board and lodgings, only as you eat next to nothing the majority of it is still sitting waiting for a rainy day.'

'Dr Maynard will already have spent it then.'

'No, he … Oh, I see, his deluge. Very good.'

'Could I have a garden? I've always wanted one.'

She didn't know how long that thought had been planted in her head; unless it was since about half an hour ago.

'Another brainwave. Arnold Gage – you'll have seen him around, he sees the grounds as his private park to look after – loves having new challenges and I'm sure he'd be happy to dig some flowerbeds around the cottage. In fact the arrangement should suit you both very well because he'd only need showing once what you want and then you'd be able to get on with your writing project in peace and quiet; Arnold isn't one of those who likes to chatter away whilst he's working.'

Edith couldn't tell if that was supposed to be a joke or not; Helen had been smiling since she'd issued the invite to tea so her facial expression wasn't a clue. The frog-man who clipped the hedges had a mouth of the slash kind and the right side of his jaw was missing. Had no lips to form words even if he wanted to. Edith decided it was her own desire to put every cruelty down to another of life's bitter ironies that had made her find Helen's comment amusing. She mentally apologised for tarring the good doctor with the same brush.

'We've some deliveries arriving in about an hour and I was planning on hitching a lift into town. Start out for the Hall when you hear the church clock begin striking ten and we won't have to keep him hanging around. See you in a bit. And eat all your breakfast because you'll need your strength if we're to embark on a mammoth shopping expedition.'

Helen clasped Edith's hand briefly before she left. Edith went to wash again as the porridge congealed in the bowl.

CHAPTER THIRTY-SIX

Helen had to catch hold of Edith's arm to stop her from walking out in front of a motorcar. The activity all around was disorientating. She stood for a moment with her back pressed against a wall to gather her thoughts and calm her senses. It had been a long time since she'd been exposed to a busy street and it seemed as if everyone had chosen today to be out and about. She felt Helen's steadying presence beside her and took some deep breaths. She could do this. Yes, she could. It was only overload, not panic. As long as she remembered that she could cope.

They were outside a pawn shop. There was an untidy pile of spectacles in the window. Perhaps a pair would bring her life back into focus. Edith made the suggestion and in another five minutes she was adjusting wire frames to sit more comfortably behind her ears. She looked down at her hands. They were something she wished she couldn't see clearly. She didn't know how they'd got into that state. The knuckles were cracked, and the skin red and flaking.

'I'll need some gardening gloves.'

'I think we can stretch to those, Edith. And to something a little more. Come on, the chemist is just on this corner; let's see if we can't make you feel feminine again.'

A bell rang over the door as they entered. The shop had floor to ceiling shelves on one wall stacked with jars and bottles in a variety of hues; a counter partially covered with advertising displays for stomach powders, skin cream, toothpaste, and muscle embrocation.

A woman in a white coat approached Helen who had opened a pot of cream and was rubbing some into the side of her thumb.

'Does this have lanolin in it?'

The assistant smirked. 'Only the finest ingredients go into that one: rose water, glycerine, and almond oil.'

'Then I'll take two pots. And a pair of lightweight cotton gloves. Some talcum powder – preferably lily of the valley – a complexion soap, a bottle of that pink shampoo over there, some emery boards and nail scissors.' She looked across at Edith and smiled. 'And a bottle of 4711 eau de cologne. I'll take the laudanum from our usual order as I'm here but the rest of it can wait until you deliver again next week.'

The woman produced a heavy-duty brown paper bag then proceeded to wander from one shelf to another collecting the items. Edith waited until she had gone into the dispensary and then walked over to stand beside Helen.

'Don't you think you'll end up smelling like a cheap florist with all that lot?'

'They're not for me: they're for you. If you rub the cream onto your hands lavishly and put on the cotton gloves overnight the cracks should soon heal. The rest is just for the fun of it.'

Edith wasn't ungrateful for the thought but she did wonder what she'd have to sacrifice in terms of plants. Helen touched her on the forearm.

'And they're my treat – mine and Peter's. I don't see why you should have to be deprived of some of the fripperies of life just because you've ended up in a place full of men. After all, they get their hair oil and astringent to titivate themselves with so it isn't fair you should have to go without. Except I couldn't include these things on the requisitions list or they'll think I'm stocking up my bathroom cabinet. It's not that your presence at Beddingham Hall is a secret, however we don't advertise the fact. It's our choice that you're with us – and one I'm very glad we made – but I think the less the bureaucrats in Whitehall know about our bending of the rules, the better. Or they might insist that we take more than the odd woman, and that could play havoc with some of the men's new-found equilibrium.'

'One odd woman's certainly enough for anyone to contend with.'

Helen's smile dimmed. 'Edith, you know I didn't mean that. You're going to have to make an effort to appreciate that no one sees or judges you in the way you do yourself if you want people to be friendly.'

'I don't want people to be anything.'

'Yes, you do. We're all social beings, whether we like it or not, and it's a much more pleasant experience to accept the fact than fight it.'

The assistant returned from the back room with a slim green bottle in one hand and a large leather-bound ledger in the other.

'You'll have to be signing the drugs' register if you're to be taking this now.' She offered the book and pen to Helen then popped the bottle into the bag.

'We've something new in, if you're interested. It's a pan-stick make-up. All the movie stars in Hollywood are using it now. It doesn't run under the lights, nor wash off in water neither. The box says it has an extra thick formulation and covers even the reddest of scars and blemishes a treat.'

Edith felt a pang of compassion as Helen's hand fluttered on its way up to her forehead. So this was what it was like to watch someone wear their vulnerabilities in the open. Her words surprised her as she heard herself saying: 'We'll take what we've asked for, thank you. Keep the bag for us and we'll pay for it when we return. Come on, Mrs Hargreaves, or the best plants will be gone.'

She received a squeeze of her hand in reply, and the two of them set the bell jangling once more as they walked out into the street.

*

'We've a little time before the fish van is due to take us back. I know it'll be smelly but beggars must. I could always ask that woman to add a vial of smelling salts.' Helen shifted the string bag she was carrying into the other hand. 'Who'd have thought a few plants could be so heavy? I think we're way overdue for our refreshment and there's a teashop at the bottom of the hill. Why don't you take these things and meet me there? I'll pick up the stuff from the chemist, pop into the stationers for that journal I promised, and then nip along to the fishmonger to tell him where we'll be. Then we'll have nothing else to do but relax until it's time for us to be picked up.'

Edith accepted the proffered bags and walked in the opposite direction. As she crossed the bridge over the railway line, she stuck close to the flint wall. She didn't like heights at the best of times and the smell of smoke and soot always reminded her of the fire and brimstone sermons of Sunday School; but making sure she didn't squash any of her precious plants gave her something else to think about other than how far she had to fall. Nevertheless she was grateful when she saw the tearoom sign up ahead. A dodge of a young man pushing a hand- truck piled high with crates, another of an elderly couple dithering in the doorway, and she was, at last, inside.

The place was of the dainty sort with tables covered in white cloths, and doilies. Wooden beams spanned the low ceiling. Edith chose the table in the bay window and settled herself down with her back to the door. There was nothing she hated more when waiting than not being able to resist the impulse to look up every time someone entered the room. It betrayed an impatient nature – and a desperation of being alone.

A pudgy young girl in a starched white apron came over. 'What can I get you?'

'I'll order when my companion gets here.' It felt absurdly good to be in a position to say that. 'But do you have a piece of paper and something to write with?'

The girl tore the top sheet off her pad and placed it, and her pencil, on the table.

'I'll get another from the till. Let me know when you're ready. The card's there by the sugar bowl; we've a nut sundae dripping with chocolate sauce on special.'

She walked away and left behind the memory of her cheeky grin.

Edith picked up the pencil. She wanted to write down the flower colours she'd chosen so she wouldn't forget them. It also had the advantage of making her look busy. She had almost finished listing the contents of the largest of the bags and had taken her glasses off to rest her eyes when heavy breathing at her elbow made her look up. The sudden change in focus made her sight blurry. At first, all she saw was a blob of blue. Then she noticed the bright buttons and belt buckle. The skin on her back grew clammy.

'Miss Potter. I was thinking it was you when I cycled past so then I turned around and came back again. Uphill this time. Mrs Billings always says as I should be taking more exercise – what with me being a bit partial to her fruitcake, and a spot of cream on the side if truth be told – and now if the chickens haven't come home to roost and I'm puffing and panting like one of Giblet Gibson's old bulls. Will you be minding if I be taking the weight off?'

Edith couldn't speak. He knew her. And she knew him. From the same source as she'd known which plants to select. In the time it took to lick her lips she became another person entirely. One she had every reason to wish she wasn't. Coming to Lewes with Helen had been a very bad idea; for once she could truly empathise with the men's compulsion to remain at Beddingham Hall. If she put her glasses back on, maybe he would vanish and take her new-found uncertainty with him … It was no good, it just made him loom even larger.

'Have you come to arrest me?'

He wheezed a laugh. 'Stone the crows, no. What would be giving you that idea?'

He took off his helmet and placed it on the table before sitting down.

'There's me thinking I'm paying my respects to one of my fellow villagers – every one of which I feel it is my bounden duty to ascertain how life is treating them whether they are in Fletching or not – and now I find all I have done is to be scaring you from here to next week and back.'

The sadness of his expression relaxed her a little. But the jumble in her head only increased; snatches of pictures like washed-out sketches flitted through her mind – only now they weren't of the London flat but a dreary cottage and chalky lanes. An impression of senses really, nothing that could constitute joined-up memories.

'It is very nice to see you.'

He smiled again. 'Now I know you're not really meaning that because of the shock of me coming up on you like I did. But it does my sore heart good to see you looking so hale and hearty. Nothing like the last time.'

'In the village?'

'No, in the … the place where they were looking after you. I paid you a visit whenever I was over here on court business. I expect you're not remembering.'

'No.'

'Well, don't be fretting yourself about that. Mrs Billings says I would be forgetting my own name if it wasn't written right here for me to look at in the mirror. Arse about face, of course.' He tapped his epaulet. 'But now I know you're ready to join us again, is there anything I can do for you, in my official capacity, like?'

Edith wanted to tell him he could go away; she could feel all the other patrons staring. But he looked so earnest and eager. Helen's words about her needing to make more overtures of friendliness came back to her.

'I won't be returning to live in Fletching quite yet, so maybe you could keep an eye on my cottage for me.'

'I'm happy to report that's already being taken care of. Wilf Drayton's made it his business to be seeing that everything's in order as far as that is concerned. Checking the windows and locks, that sort of thing.' He pulled at his whiskers. 'I've even seen with my own eyes that he's put a fence 'round those roses of yours to keep his geese off.' He laughed. 'Happen that's why I'm getting more complaints than ever about the racket they're making; they'll be giving him what for over keeping them from eating what they like best in all the world.'

'Now I think of it, there is something. With my … abrupt departure, I will have left my post office book, my watch, and some other things I wouldn't want to get into the wrong hands.'

'There you go, fretting yourself over nothing again. I did a thorough search of the premises the day after you left, and everything of any value is in safe custody. Anyways, I told you, old Wilf and his geese are keeping watch so that no one untoward goes anywhere near your cottage. In fact the whole village is on the alert regarding a strange face – on account of the Taro Fair just passing. I'll be minding you won't be knowing that last year a young lad was feared to be snatched away by Gypsies.'

'Was he? How terrible.' Had he always talked as much as this?

'Only we found the poor little tyke, him having been messing around at the old chalk quarry where his parents should've told him he had no business being. Slipped in and smashed his head, we reckon. Sad business, but not breaking the law. Excepting try telling the likes of Sneezer Crowhurst and Giblets Gibson that; I was having to be apprehending them stalking the common with bailing hooks, meat cleavers and whatnot. Still, that's what they gave me this uniform for, and nothing you have to be concerning yourself with. Where is it you're staying? A nice restful spot, I hope.'

'Very. The perfect place for recuperation.'

'Glad to hear it.' He stood up. 'I'll be moving along now as I have to be discharging the errands I came for, then cycle back in time for supper. Mrs Billings is a stickler for having the meal on the table just when she said she would, and she expects me to be sitting with my knife and fork in hand ready.' He sighed. 'To this day I'll never understand why she had the notion to marry a village constable who's lucky if he can have a cup of tea without getting called out over something and nothing.' He put his helmet on and flicked the chinstrap in place. 'But I'm right proud down to my boots that she did. Now don't you be telling her that when you see her or I'll never be hearing the end of it.'

He tapped the side of his nose with his finger, threw a nearly-wink, and walked out of the tearoom leaving a booming 'afternoon all' hanging in the air behind him.

CHAPTER THIRTY-SEVEN

He watched the constable leave. His figure was framed in the triangular side window like a shaft within an arrowhead. A poisoned one at that. He'd always known it would come to this. That she would betray him. That's why he'd holed up in that shabby room in Uckfield. Watching. Waiting. Close, but never too close to startle; always within reach for the moment when it would become necessary to burst forth into the world again. He'd been twiddling his thumbs through all those long months in the loony bin. Had tracked her progress to Beddingham Hall – the skills he'd learned in his former life had never been put to better use. Joined the band of volunteers with a reason to hang around the accursed place. Although the temptation to reveal himself had almost overwhelmed him once or twice, in the end good sense and judgement had prevailed. Why take the risk unless – or until – the option for a quiet life was denied him?

Patience was something he had a lot of. Time may no longer be. From this moment forward, every second needed to count. He'd no longer haunt like a spectre in the shadows. Make his presence felt. Check the state of affairs. Shore things up if need be. Protect his interests.

A dark trail of exhaust fumes followed the blue van as it sped away to join the traffic crossing the River Ouse.

CHAPTER THIRTY-EIGHT

Arnold dribbled water into the last hole. At first, Edith had been content to observe him from inside the cottage but then the desire to get involved and feel the gentle autumn sun on her back had proved irresistible. Now she was on her knees, the remaining plant wrapped in damp newspaper lying on the grass between them. Their fingers touched as they reached for it at the same time. Arnold withdrew his hand as if he'd been stung, and grunted. Edith was anxious she'd transgressed some boundary – perhaps the man didn't like physical contact? – but he was only scrabbling in his pocket for his notebook. He scribbled a few words then showed her the dirt-streaked page.

Your privilege, missus. Make garden complete …

His thoughtfulness was strangely moving.

'Thank you, Arnold. But I think we should do it together. How about I hold it at the right height while you bed it in? That way we can both share in the sense of achievement.'

Arnold took back the notepad.

Finished?

'Far from it; if you think the earth will be fertile enough, I'd like to have some roses. I hope – in the nicest possible way – not to be still here once they are fully established but you'll be able to enjoy them.'

Not going anywhere!

The note thrust under her nose made her chuckle. A soft breeze sprang up and the wilted stem of the newly planted snapdragon bent further as if already overshadowed by luxuriant foliage.

Moss or damascene?

'Do you know about roses? Yesterday I suddenly remembered that my father was quite a celebrated amateur grower.'

So much wish I could forget.

'Oh, Arnold, I'm sorry. I'll tell you what, we can choose them together and you can write and tell me what they're like in full bloom. And I'll reply with the news of the ones in my garden in Fletching. Maybe you could come and see them for yourself one day.'

For a moment, his face had screwed up so much he looked as though he was going to cry but then a muscle over his left cheekbone twitched and Edith realised he was attempting a smile. It was the most heart-warming thing she'd witnessed for a long time. She pulled at the blades of grass protruding over the edge of the dug bed so as not to embarrass him by staring.

'My father and I went to the first National Rose Show in London when I was eighteen. The Reverend Hole Reynolds organised it and, after that, came down to spend an occasional weekend with us in Cambridge. Over six feet tall and with a commanding presence, he was very striking, if a little odd.'

Fit in here then.

Edith laughed. 'Most certainly. He was the squire of Caunton in Nottinghamshire and I used to imagine him swirling around his manor house grounds in a sweeping black cloak issuing commands to the rose bushes to grow.'

The gong sounded up at the Hall.

'I mustn't keep you from your tea, Arnold; you've earned every drop of it. We're done here anyway.'

Coming?

'No, thank you. I think I'll go for a walk; it's a beautiful day and such a shame to spend any more of it indoors. I'll see you later … for a game of chess, perhaps?'

He gathered up his dibber, hand-fork and watering can, before turning away with another tortured smile pulling his face even further askew. Edith watched him stroll away.

*

She leaned on the top rung of the fence surrounding the far hay meadow. Sheep were dotted like puffs of cotton wool on the horizon, and in the field to her right, the dairy cattle were chewing the cud. It was peaceful this far away from the Hall with no intrusions in the form of delivery vans arriving or leaving or the occasional – and more distressing – anguished screams from a resident in the grips of a nightmare. Her mind drifted back to another time and another world. The memories were fresh and surprising, creeping up on her whenever she stopped trying to force them … Her cottage had been close to a pond, with ducks and geese – hadn't the policeman said they belonged to her neighbour? She wondered if he kept them to fatten up for the Christmas table … There'd been a common where Gypsies camped; she remembered the smell of the cooking fires and the spicy tang of their unkempt horses. The annual Taro Fair where children paid pennies to throw hoops and the adults tossed wooden balls at coconuts. Edith wrapped her arms across her chest as the wind kicked off the Downs bringing with it a chill from the sea five miles to the south. If she closed her eyes she could taste the salt in the air.

When she opened them again the mood of gentle reverie vanished. She'd remembered much more unpleasant things. The children had tormented her by throwing stones at her windows; the villagers were dismissive and rude; her father had been attacked and murdered by an unknown assailant in that hovel of a cottage; her daily life was a grind of mediocrity. She recalled the grocer with his sinister deformity and sneering remarks, and the policeman – PC Billings – who'd been as sweet as pie to her in the teashop, had pretended to humour her whenever she'd been given cause to complain about one of the many injustices meted out to her. Those bloody geese had destroyed her garden and Wilf Drayton was anything but a kindly soul, probably only looking after the cottage for what he thought he could get. Robbing her blind at this very minute for all she knew. Fletching was a horrible place. She'd hated it. She didn't want to go back. Besides, she liked it here. She felt safe. Here she had friends – Helen and Arnold, and the shell-shocked chess player if he'd allow her to get to know him a little more. Paying for her keep long-term wasn't a problem because she could sell the cottage and hand the money over to the Hargreaves. Hadn't Helen said that the authorities didn't even know she was in residence? She could have a pleasant existence here, perhaps offer to become involved in the running of the place; she had her problems but she wasn't stupid and could easily work on a plan to grow the furniture restoration business.

Except there was one big fly in the ointment to making this daydream a reality. Dr Maynard. What if he really was as good a psychoanalyst as he thought and was able to cure her? With their lofty ideals, the Hargreaves would never let her stay, taking the place of someone they thought in genuine need. She had to find a way to stop him wanting to continue her treatment. Edith began to stride towards the Hall. There were two possibilities she could think of – three, in fact, but the last carried the danger of him committing her back to the asylum. So, the options were to appeal to Helen and get her to agree to make her a permanent resident in return for the intellectual rigour she could instil in the whole set-up, or engineer it so that Stephen Maynard would find he was persona non grata at Beddingham Hall and the doors firmly bolted against him. Of course in that eventuality her case might be passed over to some other doctor – Helen perhaps, which would be nice – but it would be a simple matter to ensure that she never quite achieved a full recovery under the care of someone less ego-driven to prove their worth.

*

Helen was in the upstairs office when Edith finally found her. She didn't think she'd seen Helen looking so lovely with one hand tangled in her fiery hair as she studied a pile of paperwork on the desk.

'Can't you manage without me for even a minute?' Helen glanced up. 'Oh, I'm sorry, I thought it was Peter interrupting me again over something he's perfectly capable of dealing with.'

From the irritation in her voice it was clear not everything in the marital garden was rosy. Edith felt a distinct shiver of pleasure: it would make her proposal all the more rewarding for them both. Helen was evidently in need of an equal she could confide her troubles to; how terribly isolated she must feel surrounded by the needy who wanted something from her all the time. Only someone who knew what it felt like to be pulled in all directions could truly appreciate that.

'Has something happened?' Helen replaced the sheet of paper she'd been holding with another. 'You're looking a tad flushed. Is everything all right?'

'Perfectly. Only things have changed. Are changing for me. My memory is coming back.'

'That's a good sign and nothing to get agitated about. Edith, can you stand still for a moment? You're making me dizzy.'

She hadn't realised she'd been pacing around in circles. She stopped and lowered herself into a chair. But her muscles were fizzing too much and she walked over to the other side of the desk. Helen didn't seem to notice as she opened a buff file and began poring over the contents.

'Stephen has a bit of a reputation as a miracle worker, but don't you dare breathe a word I said that or he'll become impossible.'

'Oh, I wouldn't give him that much credit. It was seeing one of the villagers in the teashop in Lewes that did it; the policeman, I told you about him.'

'Mmm ...'

Edith returned to the chair and tried to focus on her mission. 'Can I help you with some of that? I acted as my father's unpaid secretary for years.'

'It's very kind of you to offer but much of the correspondence is confidential.'

'I can be trusted.'

'That's not the issue: it would be inappropriate.'

'How would it be if I went over the accounts for the work we did at Firle Place then? When we were last there I had some ideas about how we could shave costs and plough the savings into getting some second-hand machinery that would make the work more efficient.'

'Only that would sort of defeat the object of why we do it at all, wouldn't it? The men need to loosen their rusty motor skills and to feel valued for the unique contribution each of them can make. I'm sorry, Edith, I really don't mean to be rude but can we have this discussion another time? I've a mountain of this to get through.'

Edith had never known Helen to be so dismissive; she wanted to do something childish to catch her attention but settled for a petulant sigh. Helen ignored her and ripped open an envelope before starting to read the contents. Perhaps if she said more about her memory coming back, implied there was something ugly in the woodshed on the cusp of returning, intrigue with the imitation of a secret: she'd never known anyone in the business of healing damaged minds who couldn't resist the prick of professional curiosity.

'I lied to you when I said everything was fine, the truth is I'm finding it hard to adjust to my new-found powers of recall. Because there are gaps …'

'You must cultivate a little more patience, Edith.'

The irritation was back in Helen's voice, but at least she did stop reading and look up. It was a start.

'You've been suffering from what is known as traumatic amnesia; we often find events of the past will come back of their own accord when triggered by something in the present.'

Edith stood up and started pacing again. The excitement she'd experienced on the walk over had turned into something darker. She didn't need a fully functioning memory to know she'd always hated being patronised. Hadn't she typed that diagnosis dozens of times when writing up her father's case notes? It came to her that in different circumstances – very different circumstances – she could be the one sitting there being the lofty doctor preoccupied with a host of pathetic cripples who were never going to get any better, and a rackety private life. She'd been a fool to think Helen regarded her as anything approaching an equal.

'Honestly. I don't believe it. I've never known anyone so convinced the whole world revolves around them.'

Edith swivelled her neck to look over her shoulder. She'd thought the remark addressed to her, but Helen had gone back to reading the letter. Then Dr Hargreaves smiled. A tender smile that crinkled the corners of her eyes; and shut Edith out completely.

'It's from Dr Maynard. Feeling very sorry for himself, apparently. Has hardly been out of bed all week and hasn't seen a soul. Been living off dried fruit and water – a likely story; I bet when we see him again he won't be a shadow of his former self – but he does sound very dispirited. I think we'd better make a big fuss of him when he next comes to see us.'

Edith got her delayed satisfaction when she slammed the office door behind her. But she now knew exactly what she needed to instigate to put her alternative plan into action.

CHAPTER THIRTY-NINE

Stephen felt as though he'd been absent from Beddingham Hall for more than a fortnight. And it wasn't only because the season seemed to have turned irrevocably down here away from the insulating properties of a London smog. The fledgling garden made Edith's cottage look completely different. More like a home. More as if she belonged. He hoped it was an external manifestation of her acceptance that she probably would be living here for some time to come.

He knocked on the door. There was no answer. He stepped back to look up at the bedroom window; the curtains were open. A wind whipped up. He shivered and pulled at the collar of his coat. A figure stepped around from the side of the cottage and made Stephen jump. Not because the man had any gross deformity but for the simple reason that he hadn't heard him approach. The stranger had rather a fine face, actually, marred only by a shilling-sized indentation on his right temple surrounded by a starburst scar.

'I'm afraid you've had a wasted journey, squire. She's not in. In fact she spends most of her time visiting at the Hall these days. I'd put in an appearance up there if I were you; she'll be having tea and crumpets around now.'

'Have you moved into one of the vacant cottages down this end? I'm glad Miss Potter has finally got a neighbour to act as a companion, particularly as once the cold weather really starts I doubt she'll be wanting to traipse the slope quite so often.'

'No, I'm not a resident. You'll have seen my blue van parked up on the driveway. I come and help out as often as I can, put something back you know. Only I'd rather you didn't mention that you've seen me today – I was supposed to be lending a hand mucking out the stables but I sort of bunked off. I'd hate the Hargreaves to think I'm not dedicated to the good work they do here; I'd just had too many noxious smells up my nose for one day and found myself in possession of a strategic prior appointment, that's all.'

His manner was so delightfully conspiratorial that it made Stephen smile.

'Of course. Consider us bumping into each other like this never happened.'

The man took Stephen's hand, shook it with a surprisingly firm grip, and strolled off, whistling.

Stephen decided not to go and seek out Edith; he didn't want her to feel as if she was a child playing truant. Presumably she knew it was Sunday and would come down when she was ready. If not, it could mean she didn't want to see him – maybe was irritated by him not turning up last week – that, in itself, would be a good sign; show she was allowing her emotions full rein. In any event, the fact that Edith had stopped condemning herself to solitary confinement was a turning point. A light, but penetrating, drizzle began to fall. Stephen wondered if it was sensible to subject himself to getting wet so soon after his recent touch of influenza. Maybe he should take refuge in her cottage. If he watched for her out of the window then he could nip outside again and she need never know he'd invaded her privacy. He certainly wasn't going to volunteer the information and give her a valid reason to accuse him of not recognising boundaries.

The front room was as clean and tidy as ever. But, as with the establishment of a garden, it was showing signs that she was beginning to inhabit the place rather than merely existing in it. A bowl of apples sat in the centre of the table, an open book beside it. He went over and read the spine. It was a volume of John Donne's poetry he'd included in the selection he'd brought from her cottage. Peter must've given them to her at long last; Stephen slapped his forehead when he remembered that was something he'd promised to arrange. Perhaps Edith was punishing him for not doing so with her absence. An apology for his oversight wouldn't go amiss.

Something on the seat of the high-backed chair caught his attention. A small pile of paper, the sort found in cheap foolscap journals bound together with metal fasteners. After a brief stint of toying with his conscience – that privacy thing again – he picked them up and squinted at the faint pencil writing covering the top sheet. It appeared to be a dry, but lucid, account of Dr Potter's early work in the field of neurasthenia. She'd bracketed some names and dates – presumably as markers to insert the case history details at a later date – the rest being an observation of his approach and theories. It was interesting, but nothing he hadn't read in the academic papers the man had produced before he'd become a recluse. What was illuminating though was why she had chosen to document his life and not her own. Did she feel hers not worthy? Or was this her attempt to exorcise his ghost so that she could finally see herself as someone in her own right and not merely the daughter of Dr Potter. Stephen shuddered. The daughter Dr Potter hadn't been able to forgive for the tragic death of his wife.

He turned it over to reveal the sheet underneath. More of her neat handwriting except this time it was partially obliterated by a phrase printed in large block capitals with such force the pencil lines were thick and black: *Where vice is, vengeance follows.* The next page was the same, the words stretching diagonally from corner to corner reading: *How all occasions do inform against me; And spur my dull revenge!* He thought that came from *Hamlet*, he'd played the part once in a medical school production; had he pulled a copy of Shakespeare off Edith's shelves along with the poetry? Two unadulterated sheets summarising her father's work followed. Then: *Vengeance is mine; I will repay.* The final page was blank except for: *Blood is thicker than water, and more satisfying to spill* written with the deliberation of the other messages.

The door latch clicked behind him.

'Edith, I'm sorry … it began to rain.'

'Dr Maynard. I was hoping I hadn't missed you. I'm afraid I got a little carried away talking to Helen. She's a fascinating woman, isn't she? But of course you know that better than I. You've shaved your beard off. A great improvement. I didn't like to say anything but it gave you the air of a confidence trickster. Have you recovered from your cold? Speaking of which, I'd better get these wet things off or I'll catch a death. I'd tell you to make yourself at home but you've already done so. I won't be a minute.'

Stephen was astonished to see that she'd already removed her cardigan and that underneath she was wearing a light blue short-sleeved blouse; she'd never willingly showed him the scars on her arms before. And her talkativeness; it wasn't the garrulous spouting of nonsense associated with over-stimulation or hysteria but honest to goodness communication. She was coming downstairs again already. It seemed as if now she'd taken the plunge into other people's company she couldn't get enough of it. He found he was still clutching the pages; he placed them on the table and turned away so that he wouldn't be tempted to open with an interrogation. The last thing he needed was her to close up on him again.

'So, have you been seeing a lot of the Hargreaves lately?'

'Her, not him. I find that if you strip away the easy banter and the apparent interest in whatever topic I throw at him to see if he ever has anything original to contribute rather than simply reflecting back my opinions, then he is rather limited. Whereas Helen is quite delightful.'

It was as if a completely different woman was standing in front of him. Edith was articulate, insightful, certainly perceptive about Peter's annoying habit of playing the amateur psychoanalyst in every social situation, positively glowing about her emotional attachment to Helen, and exhibiting no signs of whatever dark impulse had compelled her to deface her work.

'How do you find them when they are together?'

He felt a blush warming his cheeks but prevented it from deepening by reminding himself that her ability to analyse a relationship being played out in front of her could give him some valuable evidence of her emotional literacy.

But it seemed she wasn't so easily fooled.

'Now, now, Dr Maynard. Listening to tales told out of school isn't nearly as satisfying as hearing them firsthand. It you're so very interested in the state of their marriage, why don't you ask her yourself? I'm sure she'd tell you.'

Stephen did flush heavily now. He could feel her grin etching into his shoulder blades.

'I hope you don't mind.' He cleared his throat. 'But I took a glimpse at what you've written whilst I was waiting. Is this all you've done or do you have another chapter somewhere?'

Edith walked over to stand beside him. She pulled a pair of glasses from her skirt pocket and put them on. 'Before you say it, I do know they make me look like a caricature of a spinster. But then I am one, except now I can see.'

'Helen's doing?'

'Indirectly. I don't know why you didn't suggest something of the sort a long time ago; it might've saved a lot of misunderstandings.'

'Like you not recognising me with my beard?'

'I doubt they would've made any difference to that – but we'll never know now, will we? As for my fledgling memoir, this looks like the beginning. In the capacity of a literary critic, do you think I'm likely to do the great Dr Potter's reputation justice if I continue in this vein?'

Stephen didn't want to be drawn. 'As you've brought him up I think it'd be good to focus our session today on your relationship with him; when we've finished perhaps you'll be in a position to judge what you've written for yourself. Shall we assume our usual positions and make a start?'

Edith settled herself in the armchair. 'Amongst all his other accomplishments, he was quite an expert on roses.'

'Did you talk together about horticulture often? It's obviously an interest you had in common.'

'He'd had a formal garden planted at the back of the Cambridge house – the soil and climate suited the rarer cultivars perfectly – but Granny didn't like the regimentation of the bushes. And there'd always be a row when she cut the blooms. She considered flowers' only purpose to adorn the sideboard or hall table whereas he wanted them perpetually kissed by the dew and sunshine. I took his side of course.'

'Would you say that typified how things were between you, a feeling of being as one against the world?'

'Undoubtedly. I always felt he was making an extra effort to include me in his life in order to make up for my being deprived of a mother. But it didn't take me long to realise that he wasn't a man blessed with much imagination and consequently not able to indulge in games of make-believe or create the silly nonsenses that would appeal to a young girl. As it happens, it didn't matter because I was more than happy to sit at his knee solving the sort of mathematical puzzles that fascinated him.'

'A chip off the old block.'

'I did my best to make him proud of me.'

'I'm sure you did, it's one of the major preoccupations of every child as regards winning their parents' love and approval.'

'I thought I'd made it clear there was never any question of my having to fight for either.'

'Sorry if you think I misinterpreted or am labouring the point – but it is important. Freud believes our entire development depends on how well the early seeds were sown and nurtured. And our memories and impressions of that process can easily become distorted over time. After all, none of us wants to think badly about, or harbour grudges against, those who were only doing their best given the circumstances of their own upbringing. It's a never-ending circle, you see, Edith.'

'The sins of the fathers ...'

'That isn't quite what I meant, except I suppose the premise is the same.'

Stephen could sense how much control she was exerting not to let her irritation show.

'In fact that reminds me, I have this for you …'

She pulled what appeared to be a piece of paper from under the waistband of her skirt. Had their conversation sparked a need to show him something she'd written but self-censored?

'As you can see, the envelope has your name on it.'

He took it from her and made to slide his finger under the sealed flap.

'I wouldn't open it now if I were you. I suspect it's a missive best read in private. Helen dropped it as I was helping her with the tea things. A Freudian slip of a billet-doux perhaps? I decided I'd save her conscience the trouble and elect to play postman.'

Stephen's fingers reached up to pluck at his beard before he remembered it was no longer there.

'I see you're itching to find out what could only be penned whilst her husband was away on farm business. What is it they say? Out of sight, out of mind.'

He forced his hand to slip the envelope into his open briefcase. He had to tackle the existence of those poisonous phrases. But his concentration was faltering, his mind focusing its energies on why Helen would feel the need to write to him at all when she knew he'd pop up to the Hall before leaving. Had she wanted to prepare him beforehand? Confess her … tell him something she found easier to put into words on paper? The briefcase pressed heavily against his leg. On reflection, perhaps the best approach with Edith – given that she did look a little tired – would be to say a little about the topic in general terms and let her come to her own conclusions about its relevance to those journal pages. Yes, that was infinitely the better way. Besides, there was the added advantage that she might not erect immediate defences against the notion if she thought he'd chosen to talk about it because of Helen's note. She had been the one to bring up Freudian slips after all.

Stephen cleared his throat prior to adopting his favoured tone when posing a theoretical problem a split second before the end of a lecture. 'Have you ever heard of automatic writing, Edith? That the phenomenon exists is backed up by an abundance of case studies – even though I've never come across it professionally myself. Essentially, it is writing that's produced without the author being aware of the content. The circumstances of how it is automatic varies. Some subjects write in a trance or sleep-like condition; some are awake and alert, aware their hand is moving but unaware of what they are writing. Others are reported as having their hand totally anesthetised during the process and, if it has been screened from view, believe it to have been motionless. Some are aware of the strokes contained in each word as it is being written, but have no idea of the word itself or what sentences it will form a part of; there appears to be no intention, planning, forethought, or concept of what is about to be written. In all cases, it's as if the conscious patterns in the brain have been bypassed or switched off.'

'Fascinating. Now why would someone want to do that, do you think?'

'And that's the question I'd like to leave you with, Edith. Mull it over while you're tending your garden perhaps. You can let me know what you come up with at our next session. Except that won't be until the Sunday after Guy Fawkes because I'm taking myself off for my annual busman's holiday in the Lake District – I work the first week in the rehabilitation centre up there and get the next fortnight to tramp the Fells.'

'It really makes no difference to me when you plan to see me again. Please do get going, Dr Maynard, you're making me fidgety just watching your eyes flick to the escape route of the door every few seconds. Enjoy your break if it won't be too much of a wrench to be absent from Beddingham Hall. Although I trust you're about to be the recipient of a delightful send-off that will keep us at the forefront of your mind …'

CHAPTER FORTY

Stephen read the note standing on the doorstep. Then he virtually ran up to the Hall, slipping and sliding on the wet grass as he veered from the path for the shortest route.

*

Stephen felt as though a train had hit him when he saw Peter Hargreaves sitting on the sofa. He'd knocked and entered the flat in the space of one breath. Hadn't Edith said he was away? Or had he taken everyone by surprise – including Helen – by returning early?

'Greetings, old son. I see you've done something about that fungus crawling over your face at last. Helen will approve. You look as though a bottle of pea-shuck wine is called for. One of my best, if I say so myself. I'm sure the vibrancy of the bouquet will be wasted on you but a lip-smack or two of appreciation wouldn't go amiss.'

The oblivion of alcohol had never held more appeal. Stephen accepted the tumbler Peter offered him and drained it in one draught.

'Well, you certainly needed that. Another?'

Stephen held his glass out – his hand steadier than he would've thought possible. He took a mouthful.

'Better leave you the bottle then if it's going to one of those sessions.'

Peter placed it on the floor by Stephen's feet and returned to his chair.

'So, are you going to tell me what's eating you?'

'Can't.'

'Can't or won't?'

'Both.'

'Okay, have it your way … Raining a lot for the time of year, don't you think? But at least it's good for the allotment.'

Stephen searched for something to say. But he couldn't find anything that didn't lead back to his feelings for Helen. He finished his wine, and then poured himself some more.

'Hey, go easy, it's potent stuff.'

'How do you set about making it?'

It was the best he could do. And it was safe. His senses were growing foggy already so he thought he could just about bear having to listen to the answer.

'If I told you, then I'd have to kill you; the entire process is a closely-guarded family secret.'

'I thought you told me you picked it up in France.'

'I didn't say from whose family, did I?'

Peter was looking insufferably smug for having dug the trap.

'What caused them to consider you worthy of the knowledge then; were you knocking up the daughter?'

He was gratified to see Peter blanch. *Deuce.*

'I was married to Ellie by then, as well you know. If you can't make civil conversation then I suggest you keep filling your mouth with wine and shut up.'

'Is it civil to bring up France?'

Stephen was beginning to enjoy himself; there was a lot to be said for this needling lark.

'I'm going to find Helen, and leave you to stew in your own neuroses.'

'No point. She's down at one of the cottages for the evening. Didn't I tell you?'

'All you did was waltz in here as though you owned the bloody place, and help yourself to my booze.'

'What's yours is mine; isn't that the way between old friends? By the way, Helen told me there's some food I'm welcome to put my hands on. Not that I'm hungry but it was uncommonly thoughtful of her, don't you think?'

'I know what you're trying to do, Stephen, and I'm not playing. Here, hand me what's left in the bottle. If you're going to be in this mood, then I think I'll join you.'

'Good idea, dear chap; it's all rather pleasant on this side of sobriety.'

'I'd have thought you'd have forgotten what it's like to be otherwise.'

'Meaning?'

'You drink too much.'

'Ha. That's rich coming from a man who always has a bottle on hand for every occasion.'

'I only make it, Stephen, not store it in my liver.'

'And what did you do in France then? Refuse the *pastis* and confine yourself to holy water?'

'I've asked you before not to blaspheme. And you know very well what I was doing there; let's not go over all that again.'

'Yes, let's. You were simply patching men up to send them back to The Front, weren't you?'

'I suppose that's one way of looking at it.'

'Is there any other? What was the routine: sew a poor sod's arm back on then stick a gun in his hand and exhort him to resume fighting for King and Country and never darken your door again? I wonder you can sleep at night.'

'That's bloody offensive, and you know it.'

'Pretending you were trying to save lives is offensive. The whole charade was nothing more than a brief intervention in the butchery.'

'I did my duty, Stephen. And the soldiers knew they were doing theirs; not one of them cried to be excused.'

'I'm not surprised. They'd have all been warned that you'd only have them court-martialled.'

'And I would've done. They were there to fight, and every gap in the line could've got their fellow soldiers killed because they were too cowardly to go back and stand beside them.'

'Did you?'

'What?'

'Have someone court-martialled?'

'An artillery gunner who shot his toes off.'

'I bet he was young, wasn't he?'

'Not the youngest.'

'Had he even started shaving?'

'Stop it, Stephen. He was guilty of gross cowardice in the face of the enemy.'

'So, firing squad for him, was it? How does that work then? Because there'd still have been a gap in the line.'

'He had to be made an example of, to stop others doing the same. War is a brutal and inhumane business. And yes, I can sleep at night as it happens. You'd have done exactly the same in my position.'

'No, I wouldn't.'

'Have it your own way.'

Peter got up and fetched another bottle from the sideboard. He re-filled Stephen's tumbler without asking, then topped up his own. Stephen took delight in watching the great connoisseur pour the pinkish wine on top of the remains of the old. Sacrilege. He laughed quietly but couldn't be bothered to point it out. Even in his befuddled state, he knew the skirmishing had moved way beyond that stage. And the bottomless pit of resentment that lay behind his part in it. Obviously he envied Peter being over there with Helen and all the heightened emotions brought about by the close proximity to death at their disposal, but that was too shallow and self-serving to be at the core of Stephen's bitterness. It was the sheer, bloody, sausage-machine of war itself that really grated. It hadn't crossed his mind to register as a conchie but he had, instead, done all he could to draw limits to the carnage. He'd taken a post examining shell-shock victims with the remit of passing as many as possible as fit to resume active service. So far, so Peter Hargreaves' war. But the difference was that he'd signed so few off his sick list that he'd been summoned in front of the Board of Medical Directors to be read the riot act. Not that it'd made any difference. He just became more adept at coaching the men in how to exaggerate their symptoms – except they didn't really have to try very hard; most were on the edge of insanity already but the official line was that if they could walk and understand orders and knew which was the business end of a gun, then they were on a troop ship almost before the ink was dry on their papers.

The skin on the inside of Stephen's mouth shrivelled under the acidity of the wine. But he needed more. Bottles more if he was ever going to forgive and forget. Because the poor bastards who hadn't the wits to follow his instructions were very probably the same ones who abandoned all survival instincts and got themselves wounded and on the slab under Peter's knife. Then he did his patching and sending back up the line in the name of duty routine, and that was their fate signed, sealed, and delivered. The irony of course being that it was the truly shell-shocked ones – the ones who couldn't remember their own name but could still pass muster – who were unable to grasp the concept of how to beat the system. And so they died. Or ended up here in Beddingham Hall. It had all been such a callous, futile, pointless, empty fucking waste of what could've been ordinary and decent lives well lived.

He felt tears bead on his lashes and wiped them away with the back of his hand. He saw Peter staring but didn't care. He was so close to the descent of blissful anaesthesia that he no longer felt the need to defend himself. He closed his eyes.

*

Ten minutes later (or it could've been three hours) he woke up to find Helen in the room with them. He watched Peter stand up and greet her with a kiss.

'He'd reached the maudlin self-pity stage before he passed out. He's all yours. I'm going to bed.'

'I'll join you in a bit; I just need a little time to unwind. Are you okay?'

'I've had enough of him, that's all. His incessant need to compete for the moral high ground. But we'll be back to being friends again tomorrow. I wouldn't bother trying to get him into the spare room, just throw a blanket over him.'

He kissed her again, and then left.

Stephen was pleasantly surprised to realise he was still drunk. But the room wasn't spinning. He heaved himself into a sitting position and picked up the bottle Peter had thoughtfully placed within his reach. He waved it.

'Want one?'

Helen fished a glass out of the sideboard and came over to join him. 'Shove up.'

He poured them both some wine.

'What's all this in aid of, did you have a bruising encounter with Edith?'

'I'm fine – well I was before I started drinking this stuff.' He swallowed another mouthful and pulled a theatrical face. 'God, I'm tired. And more than a little confused. Damn and blast him for being here. Why did he have to be?'

'Ah, your fight was one of the serious kind.'

'Why did you say those things?'

'What things, Stephen? Has my husband been telling tales out of school? Take it all with a pinch of salt; you know how much he likes to goad a willing victim.'

'I was going to wait in the empty cottage like you suggested.'

'You're babbling.'

'In your note. You may have had second thoughts but I got it all the same.'

'If you were one of your own patients you'd see this is an alcohol-induced fantasy. I never wrote you a note.'

'Then how did I know where you'd be?'

'I told Edith I'd be babysitting one of the new residents and she probably mentioned it to you.'

Stephen's fuzzy brain belatedly latched on to the truth: Edith Potter had discovered the power of the written word to deceive. She had played him for a fool and he was just stupid – or desperate – enough to be taken in.

'You look as though you're about to throw up.'

'I told you, I'm fit to drop.'

'But it's more than that, isn't it?'

She placed her hand on his knee. Stephen felt the fire in every cell of his body.

'This case is testing everything I have, kitten. And I've a horrible feeling I may not be up to it.'

Helen smiled. 'It's years since I heard you call me that.'

'Sorry.'

'No, I like it.' She turned her body slightly towards him. 'But another thing I remember is how you always judge yourself so harshly; you're a very good psychoanalyst, Stephen, one of the best. Hang in there and prove it.' She kissed him on the cheek. 'Nice and smooth. Much better. Now I'm off to get you that bedding.' She stood up.

'Helen ...'

'No, Stephen, please.'

'But you don't know what I'm going to say.'

'Yes, I do. The same as always when you have too much to drink. You want to know why I chose Peter over you.'

Stephen flushed at his predictability. He was sobering up fast. She sat on the couch again – but this time a little further away.

'Peter is a thoughtful, intelligent man. And a driven and dedicated doctor.'

'That doesn't sound like the best recommendation I've ever heard.'

'You can never truly explain why you love someone, Stephen, what you see in them. We both know that, at its most basic, it's a projection of the values and attributes we feel are missing in ourselves. The things you think you need to make you complete. And I don't feel up to exposing my failings to your scrutiny at the moment.'

'I think you're pretty near perfect.'

He hadn't meant to say that. Sodding alcohol.

She laughed. 'Oh, Stephen, and that's what I love in you. The world is always so black and white in your book, isn't it? Goodies and baddies like in the cowboy reels. Well, I'm certainly not going to shatter your illusions. I'll be back in a minute.'

Stephen felt himself drifting off again but this time with a warm glow inside him that had nothing to do with the wine. He hoped there would be one snatch of this particular drunken conversation he wouldn't forget in the morning.

PART IV

BEDDINGHAM HALL

November 1927

Experiences in general involve the presence of objects to the mind. We cannot perceive without perceiving something, we cannot suppose without supposing something to be the case, and even apparently objectless emotions are found in analysis to be directed upon something before the mind.

CHAPTER FORTY-ONE

Edith stood back from the window. The glass was streak free at last. She'd been awoken by dreams that were confusing in their content but riven with guilt and fear. They'd left her feeling suffocated. As soon as the light was creeping over the rim of the Downs she'd gone up to the house and removed some vinegar from the kitchen, and an old newspaper from the pile by the front door. For what felt like hours she'd rubbed away at the flyspecks and filthy corners of each pane, going around the four again and again because dirt was bound to have settled in the interim. The acetic acid had etched into the torn skin on her knuckles but that had somehow made the whole exercise more satisfying. And now one component of the room could pass as clean. There was little she could do about the floor without a mop and bucket but she'd put on the gloves Helen had bought her and wash down the furniture and surfaces using her face flannel.

By the time she'd polished the apples and replaced them in the bowl, the sun was trying to break through the fog obscuring her view of the slope up to the Hall. It must've started coagulating the minute her back was turned. She felt as she imagined a ship's captain would when a sea mist descended without warning. It disconcerted her to be so cut adrift. Perhaps if she re-cleaned the windows then things would become clear again.

Her world was feeling a little more ordered by the time her breakfast arrived. Except it only lasted as long as it took for Helen to place the tray on the table and tell her that Dr Maynard had cut short his holiday, had arrived at the Hall first thing, and was going to stay the rest of the week. The note idea had failed spectacularly: she should've realised they were all in it together and would've conspired to arrive at a suitable punishment. Her suspicions were confirmed when Helen had given her a funny look before she'd left. In the past it would have upset her but she now knew that what she'd mistaken for friendship had only been a cynical ploy to get her to open up. Most probably suggested by Dr Maynard. The two deserved each other.

A hangover from her dreams had left her convinced she could smell pipe smoke, although it could have been the memory of pipe smoke – something made it impossible to distinguish what was thought, and what sensation. The burning tobacco had mixed with the vinegar to resemble fried onions. Not unpleasant, but it had no business being here at all; if she softened the block of laundry soap in water and slid it over the cushions she might be able to get rid of it.

*

He knocked on the door as she was burnishing the mantelshelf. She peeled off the cotton gloves, pausing to examine where the fingertips had nearly worn through before hiding them in the fruit bowl. When she let him in he virtually bounded over to fetch his chair.

'It's a wonderful day for a walk over the fields, Edith. Just think, I'd have been battling with some landlady's rubbery over-cooked fried egg about now if I'd remained up north as originally intended.'

'I take it you and your adulteress came up with a suitable ruse for your impromptu return?'

'I want you to know that's there's nothing – and never has been – anything like that between Mrs Hargreaves and myself. We're just good friends.'

'But you knew who I meant, didn't you?'

It was a lot more satisfying to see him flush without that ridiculous beard for him to hide behind. He was staring at his shoes now, all his puppy-dog eagerness long gone.

'I want you to know that I don't hold any rancour about the note – although it was cruel of you to pretend it was from her. Can you tell me why you did it?'

'No. Unless it was some of that automatic writing you were so persuasively lecturing me about.'

'That was after you instigated the charade. I'm not reprimanding you, Edith; I just want to understand what was in your head at the time, that's all.'

A late-season fly buzzed against the windowpane. The distraction soothed her a little. She wanted to open the door and let it out. The room was beginning to feel awfully small.

'I can see this is difficult so we'll leave it for now; we've plenty of time ahead of us. I suspect you'll get pretty sick of the sight of me by Sunday.'

Edith wanted to say that she wouldn't have to wait nearly that long – within the hour would do it – but instead walked across the room to stand beside the armchair.

'I'd like to grow some roses. As you're going to be hanging around, do you think you'd be able to make a trip to Fletching and bring back the Reverend Hole Reynolds' book on the subject? I remembered I had it when discussing the possibilities with Arnold. It has a green cloth cover with a gilt floral design embossed on the front with a large red letter R in the centre. It's on one of the top shelves if my memory serves me correctly.'

Good. The precision of the details should be enough to convince him that everything in her mind was under control.

'There's bound to be someone going over that way, so I'll see what I can do about cadging a lift. I'm here now so let's start the session proper, shall we? Can you tell me something about your feelings towards your father?'

'And perhaps you could pop into the Police House and ask for my watch? It's most inconvenient to have to keep relying on the church clock in the village. I don't always hear the chimes.'

'Do you get the impression that time is going quickly or slowly for you?'

'Oh, relatively, I'd say.' Edith busied herself with plumping up the still-damp cushions to hide her smile of victory. 'For example, it must be nearly lunchtime because I'm starving.'

'Didn't you have your breakfast?'

'Yes, except that was hours ago.'

'It's good that you've got your appetite back but I wonder why you're hungry again so quickly. It's only ten o'clock.'

'Physical activity.'

'I noticed you've been cleaning. The place is spotless.'

'Hardly that. Look over there. See that cobweb? I'll just fetch something to flick it down.'

'Why don't you leave it for now?'

'No, I can't. I won't be a second.'

*

He was writing more notes when she came back from returning the towel to the bathroom. She sat again, being careful not to allow her eyes to stray from the now soothingly clean corner.

'Your father ...'

'Is dead and buried, Dr Maynard. I really can't understand your obsession with the past; surely it's my future you're here to do something about? I'd like a bright one if it's all right with you. Despite the fog.'

'It's a beautiful day, Edith, I told you. Why don't you put your glasses on?'

She sighed as a mother would to a persistently inquisitive child. She took them from her skirt pocket, hooked the wires behind her ears and turned to look out of the window. The fog was now thick and sulphurous.

'Ah, that's better. Lovely sunshine.'

'If you're ready, I think it would be a useful exercise if you talked a little about your father's decline. After that we can work back to what you remember about your early years with him.'

'Sort of warm up on the irrelevancies?'

'That's a good way of putting it.'

She stared at the hearth for a while. Were they specks of soot? Why hadn't she noticed them before? But of course she hadn't had her glasses on then. Maybe she'd better go over the whole place again when he left. Now … what to tell him?

'It was the bouts of extreme melancholy I noticed first. *Dark dungeon days* he'd call them. Then his use of language became affected. He developed a pattern of using certain words in a strange context. Like … oh, yes, he'd appear with a pruning knife in his hand and say *I'm just going to transmogrify the roses.* In anyone else that might've been them trying to be clever but he was the great Dr Gerald Potter and prided himself on being accurate and precise in every single thing he uttered. That deteriorated into calling things by the wrong names. A mirror would become a *puddle*, his collars *rope.* I remember him once asking for me to bring him a *walking stick* and when I handed him one from the umbrella stand he'd said *you cloth-eared, half-brained imbecile, how do you expect me to write with that?* He'd wanted a pen of course; and it wasn't one of his good mood days. But there was always a sort of warped logic in his confusion and I got quite good at guessing because I just thought about whether the noun he'd used was hard, soft, flat, shiny, edible, or whatever, and then narrow it down from there.'

She paused for a moment to lick her lips. She'd kill right now for a cup of tea. Should she suggest that they go up to the house to get one? But then the fog would get into her lungs and make her wheeze. No, better finish this and then she could have a mouthful of water from the tap.

'Would you say you liked your father?'

'What a strange thing to say. You're not supposed to like your parents: respect, honour and obey – revere even – but like?'

'Can you remember him ever doing … or saying … anything that might've sparked off this antagonism?'

'You really must stop trying to put words into my mouth, Dr Maynard, because I never said any such thing.'

'But I believe there is something in your subconscious trying to tell you that there was, and it's emerging via the automatic writing.

We understand better what we're able to articulate – which is why I always tell you everything I can about the process we're going through together …'

Edith preferred her interpretation: that he loved the sound of his own pompous voice. Her gaze had wandered again; the streaks on the glass were like backlit rainbows reminding her of the flanks of bacon beside the slicer in Treadwell's shop. The fog must be lifting at last. But Dr Maynard hadn't stopped talking.

'… then again it occurs with children who invent an imaginary friend who can act out things such as breaking rules, manipulating adults, or committing acts of cruelty. In adulthood, such projections can populate the daydreams of the lonely or deeply dissatisfied. All constructs of the mind serve a purpose … except if carried too far the temporary relief from harsh reality can become a permanent flight. Has anything I've said rung a bell with you, Edith?'

So loud and clear her hands began twitching in her lap like voles trying not to betray themselves to a circling hawk. She turned back to face him, willing the muscles in her face to behave themselves.

'With so much time spent in hospital and my sickbed, you won't be surprised to learn I amused myself by inventing an older sister I called Rebecca – no, no, that's wrong, my memory's playing tricks again; she was named Wendy …'

Much easier to remember, with shades of *Peter Pan* to flesh her out a little.

' … She had long blonde ringlets, whereas mine were cut short after the fire, and chattered non-stop to make up for my moody silences. Wendy was always daring me to do things I knew were naughty such as throwing my jelly on the floor for the nurses to slip on or hiding my pills under the blanket so they thought I'd taken them.'

He looked so ridiculously pleased with her that Edith almost felt sorry for him.

'Were you always clear on the fact that she didn't exist?'

'But she did, Dr Maynard, in my head and that made her real to me.'

'Of course, of course.'

'She smelt of violets. So I always knew when she was about to pay me a visit because the sickly scent would be there a minute or two before she arrived.'

'Was she consistently badly behaved?'

'She could be kind when she wanted to be, when I was in too much pain to sleep, for example. Then she'd spin me tales about beautiful princesses or magical ponies that could fly off to a desert island with white sand and a turquoise sea. Do you mind if I get a drink of water? I'll be back in a moment.'

It wasn't only her mouth that was drying up. Besides, it would give her a chance to wash her hands again; she'd been resting them on the arms of the chair in an effort to appear relaxed and who knew what germs she might have picked up.

Edith returned from the bathroom carrying a tooth-glass full of water. She'd decided not to drink from the tap to give the drugs time to settle. Or had that been in the other place? All this making things up was confusing her. She had to put a stop to it.

'Wendy did do something very bad once … She put arsenic in Dr Potter's evening cocoa. Rat poison. He was sick as a dog right off, and then confined to bed for a week. When Granny found the empty box on the shed floor she blamed me of course, but it wasn't because I wasn't allowed in there and didn't even know we had any.'

'Edith, think back to what I said earlier about the role of imaginary friends … If Wendy poisoned your father then it was your unconscious desire to cause him a degree of harm that could've ended in death.'

'Except that wouldn't count as murder if it wasn't deliberate.' She took a sip of water. Her throat closed around the coldness as it slipped down.

'In psychoanalysis deliberation isn't everything: intent is.' He leaned towards her, his elbows on his knees. 'We've covered more than enough for now. I don't want to over-tax you but it would help if you could spend a little time seeing if you can work out what might be behind that automatic writing you produced because I'd like to use it as a platform for our next session. Don't worry about the words at this stage; it's the drive to write them that interests me.'

'Is that what you want me to do this afternoon?'

'That, and to draw me a picture.'

'Are we back at school now?'

'Not exactly, but visual memory seems to inhabit a different part of the brain from the verbal one and the exercise might release some clues as to what it is that's blocking you.'

He reached into his briefcase.

'I brought some coloured pencils and a sketchpad down from the Hall. Some of the men are quite accomplished artists.'

So it wasn't only her he patronised. But with the materials she'd be able to make a proper plan for her garden; ensure the roses were planted to best contrast their form and colour.

'Will you be going to Fletching to get my book?'

'As soon as I can, Edith.'

'And my watch.'

'I won't forget. But it can't be for a day or two because I've promised the Hargreaves I'll pay them back for their hospitality by taking over a few of their sessions with the men. I'm seeing Arnold in an hour.'

'It's a good job you're so used to being the one doing all the talking then. Are you going now? I'm tired and would like to go for a lie down.'

'Of course. Don't forget the picture.'

'I'm not a child. I can remember a straightforward request when I'm given one.'

'Sorry. I didn't mean to imply otherwise. I'll see you tomorrow at the usual time.'

'Leave the door open, will you? The space seems to have become cluttered with so many people in it.'

He looked as though he was about to say something but settled for packing away his papers, smiling in an overly cheery manner, and leaving her alone at last.

CHAPTER FORTY-TWO

She'd just had her lunch up at the Hall of soup, bread, stew and mashed potatoes, and still she was hungry. Helen had been too busy to make any of her false overtures, and Edith had managed to avoid Arnold's attentions by sitting at the end of the long table frequented by the men who usually had it to themselves because they spat more food than they consumed. Although her stomach felt empty, her mind was very full. Like a cupboard with one too many things crammed on its shelves – if the door flew open they would all come tumbling out. Best turn the lock and pocket the key then.

Back in her cottage, the smell had returned. Not fried onions this time but the cloying sweetness of honey. Perhaps Wilfred Drayton's bees had flown over from Fletching and had taken up residence in the roof space. It was thoughtful of them to keep her company. Edith prised the lid off the tin of coloured pencils. They were the sort you could dip in water to make the pigment soft and smudgy. She went to the bathroom and returned with her tooth-glass half full. But she drank it before she remembered what it was for. She refilled it, placing her hand over the top to stop herself from making the same mistake twice.

When was it she'd last sat down to draw a picture? When she was a child, obviously, it was a far too arty unscientific thing for her to ever contemplate doing as an adult. Except she had liked to reproduce circuit diagrams for her telegraphic equipment. Variable condensers, transformers, valves, tuning inducers; yellow-orange for the copper wire. She drew one out now. Her hands were a bit shaky so the lines weren't as straight as she'd like but it was pleasingly symmetrical none the less. She wondered if that was what the inside of her head looked like – with a few snapped connections perhaps. She thought she remembered perching at the dining room table and drawing a picture of a house. Her chubby fingers had curled around the stick of chalk – or had it been a paintbrush? No, it couldn't have been because she'd never have been allowed anywhere near the rosewood furniture with that. Had she had more than one colour to choose from? Had Father brought them back from the hospital after making one of his madmen do the same as Dr Maynard had requested of her? They only came to the house occasionally in those early days. Not many of them, and never the same faces twice – she'd got very good at spying from behind the living room curtains. Father would meet them at the front door himself, and from the top of the stairs she'd watch him usher them into his study with a hand on their backs as if he were propelling them.

A propeller. She turned over to a clean sheet and outlined an aeroplane. Two wings on either side, and a jaunty rudder on the tail. The perspective was all wrong but it was a long time since she'd seen one. She turned to the last sheet on the pad. Did he really expect her to fill it? Her imagination would be a desiccated husk by then. She selected the bright red pencil, dipped the tip into the water until it glowed like Christmas, and made a dot in the bottom right-hand corner of the page. Then she flipped over the preceding one and circled a bigger blob. Seized by compulsion, she drew random shapes on every one of the pages – never more than half an inch in size and always the same distance from the edges. Sometimes she over-wetted the pencil and had to wait for the strokes to dry before she moved onto the page in front. She tried blowing on the damp paper once or twice resulting in any unabsorbed red fanning out unpredictably. She didn't like that much but these imperfections would no doubt become lost in the greater scheme of things. Besides, it wasn't as if she had any design in mind.

Finally she got to the ruined sheets with the wonky aeroplane and aesthetically pleasing, but scientifically inaccurate, circuit diagram.

These she ripped from the pad, screwed into tight balls, and stuffed into her skirt pocket. Her fingers were cramped, the fringes of her lips sore where she'd been sticking her tongue out and licking them. Had she developed the habit of doing that to aid concentration when at the Ministry? If so it was no wonder they'd always looked at her as if she were a little odd. She got up and went to the lavatory. Putting off the moment of revelation rekindled the exquisite anticipation she'd felt when about to see moving pictures for the first time. The painted slides had depicted a horse jumping over a fence. Or had it been a fairground scene with a carousel? That would've had horses, too, albeit carved wooden ones. It was interesting how her memory could recall elements or patterns but be wavery on the specific details. Hadn't Dr Maynard said something of that sort? He might've done but she hadn't really been listening.

She scrubbed at her fingers with the nailbrush. The laundry soap started as a thick yellow mucus on the bristles but burst into a creamy lather under the friction. The principles of physics in action: first the inertia, then the application of energy – she could feel the heat from the movement on her skin – lastly the impelling force of momentum so she couldn't have stopped even if she'd wanted to. Not that she did. She wanted her fingers so clean that the pages would remain unmarked, apart from the strokes of red. It was important. Perhaps she should pop upstairs and fetch the cotton gloves. She'd put them somewhere. In a drawer maybe? Or under her pillow? But if she did that then would the moment be held in abeyance just that little bit too long and consequently tip over into apathy, boredom, or indifference? She thought she did have a habit of doing that.

Deciding against hunting for the gloves, Edith walked back into the front room. The sun had burned off the last vestiges of the fog and was shining weakly through the window. The streaks were still on the glass but she'd have to leave them for now; using the newspaper and vinegar again would only necessitate more hand scrubbing. And if too much time passed then the shadows of the trees would reach her before she'd finished and she'd lose the opportunity to create the effect she'd wanted when the fancy had originally taken hold.

Turning her back to the light, she gathered up all but the final sheet of the pad in her left hand. Steadying the cardboard back cover with her other, she flicked over to the next page. The red dot grew into a blob. She allowed the corner of the next sheet to spring loose. Now, a red halo. Next, a furry line. She continued the process slowly and methodically, going back over the points where two or more of the pages stuck together. It was gratifying the way she'd managed to keep the red marks in exactly the same places so that the preceding one was immediately replaced as if by a conjurer's sleight of hand. But there was no movement. And it failed to induce a sense of wonder; it was all too obviously a mechanical process.

She sat back down at the table. Maybe she'd been too ambitious. Maybe the sunlight was an extravagant touch too far. The red marks were still distinct with the pad laid flat. If she positioned her forearm across it on the diagonal, she could pull the remaining triangle back with her other hand creating a tension that would cause the stiffish paper to spring free from her fingers. She tried the first few pages. The dot grew like a sponge expanding in water. She closed her eyes so as not to spoil the surprise and practised flicking through them all in a fluid, even way. Once more for luck.

Her fingertips now had the measure of the paper thickness and she knew that this next time would be as perfect as she could ever get. After this, the muscles in her hand would grow clumsy with tiredness and all her efforts would end in a damp squib. She let the pad sit quietly for a moment as she pushed her glasses back up the bridge of her nose and concertinaed the sleeves of her cardigan to her elbows.

The movement was slick. The moving pictures transparent in meaning. A red fire burned in the hearth of the page corners. Flames leapt, fizzled, and leapt again. Random strokes of heat threatened to envelop her. The skin on her fingertips shrunk back as if singed. She could smell herself roasting. Taste the smoke. Her throat closed. Her lungs fought to expand.

But as she relived the nightmare of her torment, another story broke free. Played out in reverse. She saw leaking blood. Severed gobs of her flesh. Cauterised wounds. Back, back, back to the beginning. The red dot of a gaping hole. Birth.

CHAPTER FORTY-THREE

Edith had been lying on her bed for what seemed like hours when her nostrils prickled with the scent of something spicy. She got up and stuffed her feet into the too-small slippers – the other pair unaccountably absent. The stairs felt steep but manageable. At the bottom, she thought perhaps the fog had started to seep in under the door until she realised it was smoke; blue veins of it curling up from the armchair. She could see the back of his head and the pipe slanting out to the side. There was no need to wonder who it was; after all, she'd been dreaming about him all last night, and having been controlled by the vagaries of her mind for so long she had no doubts about its power to bring about wish-fulfilment.

'Oh, Edward, you're back.'

'The truth of the matter is that I never actually left. I've been keeping an eye on you – looking after our best interests, you might say – and I felt the time was right to put in an appearance in the flesh.'

Edith dragged one of the hard-backed chairs around to where Dr Maynard usually positioned it. As soon as she sat, she could appreciate why he always chose this spot; the light from the window was directly on Edward's face, pulling out his features and making it as easy to read as an illustrated book. If she had her glasses. If she hadn't left them upstairs. That was why she'd been mistaken about the fog.

'Are you here to pay me a visit or have you come to take me away?'

'We both know I'm never going to be doing the latter, Edith. Only now even here doesn't seem a safe place for you to be. I had assumed you'd be able to keep yourself to yourself tucked away in this godforsaken place. But it seems I couldn't trust you after all.'

'Why do you say that?

'I was willing to let the first betrayal ride – seeing as nothing came of it – but two becomes the beginning of a pattern I can't possibly ignore.'

'I haven't. I didn't. I never would. Why are you being like this?'

'Life in the real world isn't like it is in your head; us normal people can't go conveniently forgetting the facts of what has taken place quite so easily.' Edward puffed at his pipe. 'I watched you in Uckfield from my hotel window. I was taking a break from staring at the four walls when I espied my erstwhile co-conspirator outside the portals of the local constabulary. I rubbed my eyes – really I did – in case my mind was proving to be as defective as yours turned out to be, after which you'd vanished. Edward, my boy, I thought to myself, you're manufacturing problems for yourself where none exist. Only much later there you were again, staggering your way to the bus stop as if you'd undergone a most bruising encounter. Did your friends in blue believe you, Edith? Did they write down every word you said in their little notebooks? Did you volunteer to meet them at the scene of the crime? You'll have to enlighten me on that portion of the narrative because, by then, I'd removed myself from any place of possible detection.'

'But I'd gone to find you. That's why I was in town in the first place. The hotel said you'd never been registered.'

'I suspect they did so to get rid of you; there's a wild air of instability about those who've just confessed to the police.'

'I hadn't. And I was fine … Or maybe not … I can't remember … It was a long time ago … I've been ill.'

'Only you've been making a remarkable recovery. Well enough to renew your acquaintance with your favourite policeman over a cosy cuppa. What did you tell him, Edith? What poisoned secrets did you spill into his shell-like?'

Edward was sitting back smiling in his lopsided way at her. The pipe had gone out and he was cradling the bowl in his hand as he let his arm flop down beside the chair. Edith was so full of emotion that she couldn't separate one feeling from another long enough to be able to put a name to them all. She thought there might be love there somewhere; obligation; excitement; and something so dark and dirty it could've been guilt. But not surprise.

'He talked to me. About the village. About a dead boy they found. I dreamed about him afterwards.'

'The policeman?'

'Alfie Thresher.'

The name had crept into her head from nowhere.

'And, pray, just what was it your somnambulant mind threw up? Justifications? A wholly fantastical version of the truth?'

'That he wasn't found in the quarry at all but in the graveyard. That you were there, we both were …'

The fog was back again, so thick she couldn't perceive anything, and could barely breathe. It was filling her lungs and squeezing her heart … Then it cleared to reveal everything that had previously been hidden. She knew. Beyond a shadow of a doubt, she knew what Edward was talking about. Why he'd come. Why he was sitting in her chair regarding her with an expression of bleak disappointment.

'It wasn't a dream, was it? That is exactly what happened.'

'Ah, but how can you know that when your recall is so unreliable? The memory is a funny old thing – I'm sure you and your head-shrink jabber about that incessantly. In-between you telling him things that you really would have been better off keeping to yourself.'

'He's the one. I don't say anything.'

'Now, now, that is a blatant untruth, my dear Ede, and unworthy of your brand of subtle trickery. You read my messages, I assume?'

She was confused for a moment until he indicated the table behind him with a waft of his hand.

'The automatic writing? I thought I did that. He told me I did.'

'Surely you've worked out by now that the good doctor only finds that which he is intent on seeking. The man's one walking, talking, self-fulfilling prophecy. Whereas his patient is wilfully blind to the truth. Because I've never importuned you to do one single thing for me, Edith. Never. The tartan slipper – and those are a particularly ugly example of the breed, most unbecoming – has always been on the other foot. The nasty web of deceit we find ourselves flailing around in now is solely the result of me putting myself out for you.'

'To protect me. To stop the boy stealing the journal, I know.'

'Whatever else we may disagree on, can we at least establish that there is only one person in this room in possession of faultless recollection? Yes? Good. So you have no choice but to believe me when I tell you that at no time on that particular evening did I refer to a book.'

'You said you dropped it when you ran after him …'

'I mentioned he had something of yours, nothing else. How could you know the particulars unless it was you who caught him at it?'

'I found it on the study floor. Afterwards.'

'And if you saw him, caught him, chased him … Then the inevitable conclusion is that it was also you who put the child to death.'

'It was an accident … he fell and hit his head. It was an accident.'

'Almost the exact same words, only this time said with much more emotion behind them. I was amazed at how cold and calm you were that night; at your rational best explaining things away, working out a plan of how to dispose of the body and cover your tracks. I didn't know you had it in you, Edith. It was chilling to witness.'

But none of that could be right; he was twisting the things that hadn't been back with her long enough for her own mind to have distorted. Except could she really truly swear – on a stack of Bibles if need be – that she hadn't?

'You like it here, Edith, don't you? Making friends, settling down, feeling unburdened. And you'd like that to continue. I'd like that to continue for you. There's no earthly reason why it shouldn't if you behave yourself. Keep quiet. Don't say any more. Let on to nobody that the black heart of a murderess beats in your breast. You'll need to be especially careful if he hypnotises you; Dr Myers tried that on me once or twice but I was on to his game of winning trust to winkle out secrets. It's possible to resist, but you have to really want to. And I'll help you do that, Edith. I'll give you something to fill every portion of your consciousness so that your thoughts will be mere static in the ether; never quite making sense, the threads breaking apart under the pressure of forced connections. Would you like me to tell you what it is? Would you like me to help you one last time, my dear Ede?'

Her legs were itching so much it felt like the flames were licking at the marrow of her bones again. The fog had filled the room from floor to ceiling, her visitor a patch of still darkness in swirling grey.

'Yes, please, Edward.'

The shape shifted. And then he was right in front of her face, his straight arms on either side of her ears as he leaned on the back of the chair. She felt her body tilt until her feet were hanging. His breath smelt of rotting leaves.

'Then it's this … you let slip one more fact about that night – real or imagined – and I will make you fucking regret the day you were born.'

CHAPTER FORTY-FOUR

She had been awake all night. Pacing, pacing, pacing. Edith's legs hurt and her head felt dizzy but she couldn't stop. At some time she'd shattered her glasses by treading on them wearing outdoor shoes. There was nothing wrong with her eyes anyway; she could see everything she needed to, the rest was just noise.

Now she was on her knees in the front flowerbed. It had been taking too long with the small fork, so she'd started pulling up the plants and deepening the resulting hole with her fingers. Their tips were sore, one nail bleeding where she'd caught it on a shard of flint but she'd almost finished. Only three more sheets to go. She tore the one with the smudgy red halo into dozens of irregular pieces and planted them where the sun would never shine.

He came up on her like a sneak thief intent on stealing her solitude. She completed her business then straightened up. Dr Maynard was carrying a tray with her porridge and two enamel mugs of tea.

'Edith, your beautiful garden. What happened?'

'Moles.'

She walked into the cottage. He followed and placed the tray on the table.

'Would you please leave me alone with my breakfast? I don't like to be watched while I'm eating. In fact, there are a lot of things I'd prefer not to be observed doing. It's bad enough that I feel under a microscope with all your questions. Like an insect about to be dissected.'

He gave a short laugh devoid of meaning, then retreated outside.

It was so very easy to make him swallow anything she felt like feeding him. Unlike this porridge. She heaved up a gob with the spoon. He'd left his briefcase beside the chair. The idea wasn't even fully formed before she began to act on it by undoing the buckles on the two front pockets and sliding in as many spoonfuls as each would hold. The thick goo pressed itself into the rounded corners – thank heavens Helen didn't believe in using too much milk or some would ooze through the stitching. Then she pulled the leather flaps down and refastened them. Edith tossed the spoon back into the, now empty, bowl. It clattered for about as long as her satisfaction lasted. She wanted more. And he deserved to be punished for all the unsettling thoughts he'd put in her head. If Wendy had really existed, she'd have been proud of what she decided to do next.

Edith picked up one of the mugs and took it through into the bathroom. Resting it next to her toothbrush, she set about gouging a crescent moon from the block of laundry soap with the longest of her soil-packed fingernails. When it was clear she couldn't make it any bigger, she flicked it with her thumb into the tea. She pared off some more. Only they were refusing to sink. She plopped her finger down on each one and held it under the surface to dissolve. Then she created a mini-whirlpool by swirling the liquid around until there was nothing when it settled except a faint scum. That would suffice for post-breakfast hand washing.

Once back in the front room, she sat in the armchair and waited. It was up to Dr Maynard to decide when to return. He was the mind reader, after all. He crept in like a cat when she'd almost finished her tea. His would be lukewarm by now. Well, that was his problem for leaving it unattended for so long. He pulled across the hard-backed chair and opened his briefcase. Not even a twitch of his nose. The man's sense of smell must be faulty; damp leather could not be mistaken for anything other than what it was. As a child she'd always known when Granny had put her shoes by the range to dry. But perhaps he'd been a mollycoddled little boy and never allowed out in the wet. Whereas it should've been her who'd been sheltered from harsh conditions after what she'd been through.

Holding the comfort-blanket of his notes he leaned over to the table and picked up his tea. He took a large mouthful as if he was parched. He wouldn't be doing that again in a hurry. The corners of his mouth turned down. It was amusing to watch a psychoanalyst's reactions and speculate what he was thinking; it was no wonder Dr Maynard seemed to get so much satisfaction from trying to out-guess her.

'This tastes very strange.'

'That'll be the water. All the lime from the chalk. I'm surprised you haven't noticed it before.'

He took another sip. Stupid man.

'No, there's definitely something different about it.'

'Perhaps you took the wrong mug. The one intended for me. The one with the drugs in it.'

'They've never administered anything to you here, Edith. That was in the other place, remember?'

'Lewes County Lunatic Asylum. I recall the details of that particular institution very well. You would do too if you'd been locked up there against your will. Why don't you try it some time? Live a little of life as a mad person; I can assure you that the world looks very different through these eyes.'

'Different from what?'

'Normality. Oh, I forgot. I can't possibly know what that is, can I, having been like this since I first became conscious of being anyone at all. They say awareness of self occurs around the age of three don't they?'

'Approximately ... Sorry, can I use your bathroom to get some water?'

'I used to try rinsing my mouth out as well but it never quite got rid of it all. Have a go though; it can't do you any harm.'

She listened to the sound of him gargling vigorously. If he started to foam at the mouth then maybe he would think he was having a fugue. She'd like to see how he'd cope with being on the receiving end for a change. He returned and sat down.

'I've not experienced you in this mood before, Edith. Can you give me a little insight into what's behind it?'

She looked at him for a while, pretending to think. Then she held one hand up and started to count on her fingers.

'Let me see … well … firstly, a company of moles laboured long and hard through the night and decimated my garden. Arnold will be beside himself with fury.' She laughed. 'Maybe that will add dementia praecox to his other, more obvious, disabilities. You see, I can apply labels to people just as easily as you. Anyway, where was I? … The nipping of my horticultural aspirations in the bud. Secondly, both the porridge and the tea were dreadful this morning; perhaps you'd have a quiet word with Helen for me – I know I can trust you to be discreet – I'd hate to be the one to hurt her feelings. What next … oh, yes … I've been plagued all morning by flies buzzing in my head. And last – but I'm sure you'll agree – by no means least, due to you forcing me to contemplate the tragic decline and traumatic death of my father, I haven't had a wink of sleep. Do you think that's enough to keep you going for a while, Doctor?'

She smiled with a malicious sweetness she could almost taste.

'If it's any consolation it is common for patients …'

'Residents.'

'… when they first embark on an intensive bout of therapy to feel an acute dissatisfaction with everything around them, often accompanied by auditory and visual hallucinations. The patterns of your mind are in transition which will throw everything up in the air for a while. They'll settle again once we can get at the nub of what is really disturbing you. Did you get around to doing some drawings for me?'

'No.'

'What about any childhood memories; did any resurface after our session yesterday?'

'No.'

'And now? Are there any that are currently fuelling your sense of frustration?'

She stared him in the eyes until he looked away.

'Perhaps you had a chance to consider the meaning of the automatic writing?'

'Why?'

'Because I asked you to. I know you're feeling very resistant to me at the moment but if you don't co-operate then I can't see there's any possibility of us making progress.'

'That's fine by me.'

'You don't mean that. Surely you want to be able to return to Fletching and see your roses again? I haven't forgotten about the book, by the way, I'll get over and fetch it as soon as I can. Will you tell me why you didn't want to look at what you wrote? Was it the mania of the act or the words themselves upsetting you?'

'How could I know when I didn't read them? If you were more observant and less inclined to leap to conclusions then you'd notice I'm not wearing my glasses. I've lost them.'

'Then allow me to read them to you.'

She watched him retrieve the pile of journal papers from beside the fruit bowl on the table. Maybe the movement would help the soap work its way through his system. She was looking forward to him experiencing his very own unstoppable compulsion. But he was sitting back in front of her again with no signs of any internal shiftings.

'I'd like you to tell me what comes into your head – in words or images – when I finish each phrase.'

She'd enjoyed playing that game; the opportunities for unpredictability gave her so much scope.

'*Where vice is, vengeance follows ...*'

'I suspect that's what Peter Hargreaves would feel if he caught you at it with his wife.'

A hit scored with her first arrow. Her mind must be sharper this morning than she'd given it credit for.

'*How all occasions do inform against me: And spur my dull revenge ...*'

'Ditto.'

Edith folded her hands in her lap.

'*Vengeance is mine; I will repay …*'

The flies in her head began buzzing louder. As she listened to them, something floated free. The smell of pipe tobacco … A visitor sitting in this chair … Surely she could remember who it was; she hadn't had many and none, other than Dr Maynard, from her life before this place. Because that's where he'd come from: the distant past. The flies were telling her that. They'd pretended to be Wilf Drayton's bees for a while but they couldn't fool her again.

'Have you no response to that one? Okay, how about the last: *Blood is thicker than water, and more satisfying to spill …*'

Her hands began crawling. She thought if she looked hard enough she'd be able to see the maggots under the skin. Edward. He told her he'd left messages. She hadn't been lying about not reading them. Edith shook her head to throw the flies off course. She wished she could ask Dr Maynard to read her his notes of their conversations because then she'd be free of doubt, be able to reassure Edward when he came back that nothing had changed. How she regretted giving in to the notion to adulterate the tea; if he had to rush off then she'd have to wait until tomorrow to find out – unless, of course, that was when he intended fulfilling the errand she'd badgered him about. Clear evidence of compounding behaviour that he'd no doubt call self-sabotage. Was it too late to retrace her steps? If she gave him a little of what he wanted then perhaps he'd return the favour. What was it he kept probing for? Childhood memories of her father. He thought it was one of those that had provoked what he mistakenly believed to be her automatic writing. What could she tell him that spoke of a subconscious desire for revenge and death? She didn't have much time left to come up with something, the soap wouldn't wait forever.

'After the fire. A long while after, when I was free of hospital and was living with Granny and Father in Cambridge … something he said shook me violently. There's no point in asking me what it was because I really can't remember but I can recall how it made me shrivel inside. They say that moments like that never leave you, don't they? Lie in wait to trap you again with their power. I suspect you've been right all along and something happened in Fletching to make me hate myself as much as I did then. Something that left me wanting nothing more than to give up on living.'

'That's the best articulation of the motivation for a flight into catatonia I've ever heard.'

And it probably was because he was writing it down. When he finished, his face was all concern.

'In one of our hypnosis sessions you talked about the longing to escape what you felt to be intolerable circumstances. Give me a moment and I'll find the passage in my notes …'

She'd managed to lose the smile by the time he looked across at her again. Whatever he was about to recite wouldn't be enough to reassure her totally but she couldn't imagine there'd been any other occasions when she'd have had cause to mention either Edward or her involvement in the death of the boy.

'Here it is. You'd been talking about your grandmother's canary.'

This wasn't anything near what she'd wanted. She should have taken his fixation with her childhood into account and consequently steered him with a firmer hand on the tiller. It would mean more precious time wasted before she could reach the shores she'd been navigating towards.

'*In time, as I knew it would, the bird stopped plucking at itself and the feathers grew back until it was beautiful and bright and happy. Then, one day, after it had performed all its tricks and was flying back to land on my shoulder, I opened the window and it flew out and over the trees. I found it dead the next morning. I was heartbroken and bitter with myself for what I had done but, late at night, when I was in bed and outlining the map of my scars like I always did when I couldn't sleep, I was happy. I was glad I'd done it. I was pleased it was dead. And I wished it was me.* Edith, this feels to me like an early fantasy about taking your own life. Not necessarily a desire to put the thought into action but more a taste of the posthumous power it would give you in terms of the hurt and anger you could inflict. Revenge, do you see? A paying back of scores in the most devastating way possible. Could this have been in response to your father's wounding words, do you think?'

She could scream with the frustration of it all. What had that poet said about being trapped in webs of deceit? She'd had enough of this. Wanted to be left alone. Needed to have her thoughts clear enough to concentrate on finding another way to get the message across to Edward that she'd never breathed a word about his existence to anyone. Except ... might she have told Helen in a pathetic attempt at female solidarity? She couldn't remember. If she had then it was another good reason to ensure their friendship remained broken.

'A voice spoke to me in my dream last night. It told me to poison your tea ... Are you all right? You've gone very pale. Maybe you'd like a sip of mine. It's only cold dregs though. But I didn't put anything in it. Rest assured that if either the voice or me decide I must to do away with myself then it won't be via poison. Very unreliable. Messy.'

She picked up the mug from the floor and held it out to him. He shrank back in his chair as if she was offering him acid. Not that she blamed him. By tonight the soap would've worked its way through to his bowels and he really would have a most uncomfortable time of it. He was stuffing his papers back into his briefcase. Was now the time to tell him about the porridge? Best not ... let that come as a nice surprise.

'Edith, I want you to know that – whatever happens as a consequence – I don't hold you responsible for this. When you acted you were literally not in your right mind. I'm sorry; I'm going to have to go ...'

He exited the room in an indecent scrabble. Edith's soft smile spread into a grin. Then she pressed her neck into the enveloping armchair and laughed. Until she cried.

CHAPTER FORTY-FIVE

Stephen pulled the chain for what he hoped would be the last time. He'd been on and off the toilet for the past two hours – the discomfort not made any easier by the Hargreaves' lavatory being on the floor below. He felt he knew every one of the turret's stone steps, his heels bruised from where he'd clattered down them in his desperation.

He ate a piece of dry toast standing at the kitchen sink. Through the window, the Downs rolled away into the distance. He could be walking the Lake District Fells now with a lunch packed by an attentive landlady instead of nursing gripey guts caused by the misplaced aggression of a woman who was acting more and more like a textbook schizophrenic. Stephen pulled himself up on his tendency to be too quick to hide his doubts behind the security of clinical labels – she was merely deeply distressed and disturbed. He coughed as a crumb caught at the back of his throat. Merely? Swinging the other way to underestimation was just as bad. The sort of balanced assessment of her condition he'd expect from his students was that she was experiencing the anger that always erupted after a plateau of denial; the treatment for which was to weather her storms in the most self-protective but non-defensive way possible until she could be moved on to wanting to display more constructive behaviour.

But how? All their recent interactions boiled down to her wielding what little power she had by playing the classic consulting room game of turning a triangle into a circle. The way it went was that the patient manoeuvred the therapist into occupying one of three roles in turn whilst slipping neatly behind into the position most recently vacated. Thus began a damaging dance in which each became the other's rescuer, persecutor, and victim … ad infinitum until they both were all three things at the same time. It was a disabling strategy easy to dissect in theory, but incredibly difficult to avoid unless one of the parties steadfastly refused to play. And he was the only one capable of doing so. Except he hadn't been quick-footed enough to sidestep being the victim of her cruelty over the note she'd pretended was from Helen. Let alone her latest malevolence – whether she had really put something in his tea or simply slipped him the possibility via her glibly fabricated tale of Wendy attempting to poison her father didn't matter. Either way she was doing her best to induce paranoia: the woman was imaginative, as well as sadistic.

He settled himself on the couch in the living room, Jung's *The Psychology of Dementia Praecox* open on his lap. He was making notes when Peter came in.

'You shouldn't spend all your time cooped up inside, it's not healthy. I could do with a hand digging up the potatoes in the allotment. Not that you'd get to the end of the row without collapsing with exhaustion.'

Another person intent on fitting him up for a part playing the weak and helpless. But the trouble with Peter was that his accomplished gamesmanship was even more difficult than Edith's to walk away from. They'd been colluding for too long. And Peter knew precisely which triggers to squeeze. It was all about competition. Underneath the façade of civilised behaviour they were cavemen fighting to prove their superior strength, jostling to be the one to win the respect of their tribe. The tribe of one. Helen. It would be as amusing as watching small boys in a pissing competition if it weren't so painful.

Peter threw himself into the armchair. 'Not that I'm complaining about you being here, but do you think you could dabble a little more in the art of conversation? I've spent the last three hours attempting to make columns of figures balance and could do with a bit of livening up.'

'Haven't you got sessions with patients this afternoon?'

'Residents. How many times do I have to tell you that?' Peter bent down and unlaced his shoes. 'If I get mud on the rug, Helen'll kill me. No, they've both cried off. There's some sort of a bug going around. Can't avoid it, even in the best run residential establishments. Arnold pigeonholed me on the way in wanting to know if Edith's been laid low. Seems she was to come up to the Hall to plan the rest of her garden.'

Stephen marked his place in the book with a piece of paper. 'I doubt if they'll be in a position to do that for a while yet. She's going through a stage of being pretty anti-social.'

'How's the therapy going in general?'

'Satisfactorily … what you'd expect given her recent history … predictable in its unpredictability.' The weight of his desire to be accurate felt like a physical presence. 'I've never encountered a case so riddled with complexities and contradictions before; it's making me doubt everything I thought I knew about the workings of the mind. Peter …'

'Mmm?'

'Do you think that self-deception can ever be truly said to be total?'

'In your case: completely and utterly.'

'If that is your idea of intelligent discourse then I'll finish this in my room.'

Stephen stood up and Jung toppled to the floor.

'Don't go getting the hump; I can't help it, you know. There's something about the impenetrability of your sincerity that always brings out the worst in me. I'm an arse. Helen tells me that all the time.'

This was the most fulsome apology he was ever going to get from Peter Hargreaves. He sank back down into the cushions.

'I obviously can't talk about the specifics but would appreciate testing my thinking. Forget about repression, dissociation and all the rest, and just suppose a perfectly sane person believed something everyone else would laugh out of court. Is it conceivable that they can maintain their world picture without ever having a chink of doubt?'

'That's an interesting one. But it depends on whether we are talking about actively lying to yourself or telling the truth as you perceive it. A subtle but profound distinction. I suspect the Old Testament prophets were a ragbag of the two. Using them as an example, the question you have to ask is: what's in it for them to lie? Power, prestige, riches on earth, a crowd of supplicants to do their bidding … but not access to the Kingdom of God.'

'Would they know that though?'

'Of course. However, if they thought the lie was a truth then the outcome would be the same but the reason why different.'

'That hardly seems fair. That someone who is essentially being honest by their own definition receives the same punishment as those who deliberately mislead.'

'Always batting for the underdog, aren't you, Stephen? When will you realise that it's sometimes the outcomes themselves that matter; they stand alone to be judged without the noisy accompaniment of motivation, intention, and integrity.'

'It must be comforting to know everything's so cut and dried.'

'It's not actually. Because, of course, it means that I'm as condemned as the next man.'

'Fate?'

'The will of God.'

'That's another thing we'll never see eye to eye on. It doesn't help me much with my theorising on the pervasiveness of self-deception either.'

'Okay, let's bring it down to our earthly existence.' Peter started the business of lighting his pipe. 'This is just like the old days, isn't it? I really missed you in the intervening years, Stephen. We really shouldn't have fallen out as we did.'

'Did we? I thought we just went our different ways and lost contact.'

'Perfect.' Peter clapped his hands. 'I can always rely on you to come up with the goods.'

'What do you mean?'

'I pull your strings and you twitch, right on cue.'

Stephen's hand reached up to pluck at his non-existent beard. He pulled at his bottom lip instead.

'A classic example of lying to self, old son. You and I both know that we came as close to exchanging blows over Helen as two respectable, educated, intelligent, physically cowardly men ever can. But that isn't the point. And believe me, I meant it about the joys of clashing wits with you again, even if I did have an ulterior motive for saying it.'

He puffed up a veil of aromatic smoke.

'Now, only you know how thoroughly you believe what you've just said, but the fact is that your voice contained an edge of sharpness, and the words you chose were thoroughly precise. Both of which mean your self-deception isn't as complete as you might think – or may want it to be – because I can only hit a nerve and therefore provoke a reaction if some part of you recognises the truth of my version of events. Down the other end of continuum, it wouldn't have hurt if your self-deception was complete because you would've simply dismissed it as a flaw in my memory. It would be a falsehood maintained by me – deliberately or inadvertently, it's irrelevant which – and you wouldn't have felt the prick of it one little bit.'

Stephen fought hard to squash his wounded pride at being so easily played. 'So far, so obvious. But you only know that because you can refer to an external event, a conflict where one would expect there to be different sides to the story. But what about if the conflict is internal only; it exists nowhere but in the mind with few manifestations of its presence? Then the validation, observation, and correction can only come from the self-deceived themselves which, if it is complete, will result in stalemate.'

'Are we talking about Edith Potter now?'

'Let's say more the theoretical possibility that a mind can shift itself without the stimulus of even being aware that it needs to.'

'I know it's a little early, but I seem to remember that a little lubrication always used to benefit our discussions. Can I get you one?' Peter got up and walked to the sideboard.

'Not for me, thanks. My digestion's not behaving itself.'

'You coming down with the bug too?'

'No. Except I suppose I might be; the reaction was rather quick.'

'To what? Helen's splendid breakfast? I did notice you tucking into it as though you were going to take the pattern off the plate.'

'It doesn't matter. I will have that drink after all; maybe it might help settle something.'

'As it's you, I'll crack open the brandy. The real stuff; gift from a grateful resident, or a resident's grateful mother to be accurate. Here you are, get that down your neck.'

Stephen's nostrils prickled with anticipation. Maybe he did drink too much but this one was medicinal and didn't count.

Peter returned to his chair. 'I suppose an observer could only pick up any clues that something was or wasn't going on if they knew the person well enough to be able to judge the differences between their mind being in repose, as it were, and in the process of actively changing or denying. Almost impossible to do without a benchmark, I'd say. Assuming that the person we're hypothesising about was a patient in need of psychiatric care and attention then their mind would already be playing tricks, and any shifts would be likely to be lost in the chaos of temporary, or permanent, insanity.'

'That's precisely what I'm struggling with.' Stephen sipped his brandy. 'It's like being presented with a kaleidoscope but not knowing where the mirror is: which is the real pattern, and which the reflection. To be able to get the right perspective is crucial if I'm not to spend time being misled into treating the symptoms and missing the cause of the dis-ease itself.'

'Got you.' Peter stabbed the air with the end of his pipe. 'Something else that's pertinent here is that, whether you want to or not, you can't help being a factor in how the pattern is arranged in the first place. Edith Potter will inevitably react differently to you, and even she might never know if her persona as your patient is an exposure of the truth or a cover-up. I'll tell you what, why don't we pool our knowledge on her a little bit.'

'I'm not about to breach patient confidentiality.'

'Wouldn't expect anything less of you, old son. No, what I mean is let's share what we think her character traits are, what you like and dislike about her, how she came across to me on our first meeting, and my impressions of her subsequently. Try to get some of those kaleidoscope patterns of yours to coalesce into a recognisable picture. This composite Edith can then be your touchstone against which you can measure the progress of any of her internal power struggles. Here, chuck me over that pad and a pencil and I'll be scribe.'

Stephen did so, then swirled the brandy around in the glass. 'She's intelligent. Honest when she wants to be – except the whole problem is that I don't know when that is.'

'No analysing your responses. Just throw out your thoughts and gut-level feelings about her.'

'She is genuinely interested in learning about psychology in general and hers in particular. There's an independence about her; she's prepared to challenge me and won't always accept what I say just because I've said it. I admire that. It shows courage.'

'Funnily enough, that's the first thing I was going to say about her.'

'She has a thorough grounding in scientific principles but can still appreciate the aesthetics of things; beauty without form or purpose.'

'She did admire my painting when we had her up for tea and some of Helen's chocolate cake.'

'Now who's being self-delusional? A capacity to recognise her need for help even when it pains her to ask for it. She's pretty forgiving of my blunders or linguistic faux pas; is trusting enough to allow herself to be led without fully understanding the path we're going down … She is analytical, logical, quick to grasp and accept conclusions – if they are backed up by empirical evidence.'

'Okay, but you forgot her wit. The woman has a wry sense of humour and isn't afraid to make the occasional joke at her own expense. She acknowledges when another's expertise on a subject is greater than her own – to whit: accepting Arnold's advice about fertilising her garden. She has convictions greater than herself … probably including a religious faith going by the amount of time she said she spent on church activities back in her village; I know that won't rate highly in your book but it matters a great deal to me that someone believes in something.'

'Granted.' Stephen finished his drink. 'Except there are other frames of reference besides Christianity.'

'Let's not get into squabbling over her soul like two dogs with a bone. Quite a healthy list we've got here. Now we've gone and got ourselves a living breathing saint, let's dish the dirt a little. What don't you like or admire about the woman?'

Stephen took a deep breath. It didn't sit well criticising a patient's character or temperament, even to himself. But Peter was right; it was a three-dimensional picture they were endeavouring to build up, and it was essential not to hold anything back.

'She can be stubborn, manipulative, childish, prone to ridiculous levels of frustration. Sometimes she uses silence as a weapon; at others she takes great delight in testing and taunting me. I think she has a wide streak of cruelty somewhere in her make up. She can be verbally vicious, intolerant of others' weaknesses, sarcastic, and devastatingly patronising.'

'I've seen her ridicule some of the residents to their faces, and she has a nasty habit of laughing at them behind their backs. She tried playing Helen and me off against each other when she was refused a bottle of bleach.'

'Did you know she thinks you've been drugging her tea all this time?'

'Really? I'll put down suspicious and paranoid then.'

'When I went to Fletching I found out she was caught slaughtering ducks and geese with an axe; and I've thought she was going to cause me actual physical harm once or twice. All in all, a formidable enemy.'

'But possibly a good friend.'

'Her neighbour, Wilfred Drayton, and Old Sophie the Gypsy seemed to think so. She reads poetry, I forgot that one.'

'There's one more thing I'd like to add. Helen likes her. Very, very much. And her judgement carries a lot of weight with me.'

'Me, too.'

They smiled at each other.

'Thanks, Peter, this has been a tremendous help. I had quite a session with her this morning and came away almost hating her. Not a healthy emotion for a psychoanalyst to harbour towards his patient. Mind if I take myself off to have a bath?'

'Be my guest. It's steak and kidney pudding tonight, my favourite, so don't stay wallowing in there too long or there'll be none left.'

Stephen picked up the Jung book and placed it, along with his notes, where he'd been sitting on the couch. Peter tapped his pipe in the ashtray.

'Tell me one more thing before you embark on titivating yourself. What is it that's stopped you giving up on her? I know the depth of your professional pride but even that wouldn't be enough to keep you going in the face of all this. So, what has Edith Potter got that keeps you coming back for more?'

Stephen didn't have to think about that one. 'She looks at me sometimes and I see a spark of energy from deep inside that she's managed to keep alive against all odds. The easy thing to say is that I come back because she needs me. But, in reality, I come back because she reinforces my belief in the indomitability of the human spirit.'

He patted Peter's shoulder on his way out. Although he wasn't about to tell him so, he'd missed him, too.

CHAPTER FORTY-SIX

The bug, or borax, or whatever it was, hadn't had any long-lasting effects, and Stephen had been blessed with a good night's sleep. Maybe his body had needed the exhaustion to force his mind to rest. The upcoming session with Edith was going to be a tough one. He had yet to determine if she recalled her revelation under hypnosis about her father's murderous resentment; except forcing the recollection would bring problems of its own. In an attempt to clarify his approach, he'd creased the spine of Helen's new copy of McDougall's *An Outline of Abnormal Psychology* at the breakfast table (much to Peter's annoyance) and made copious notes from the relevant passages. His trepidation had subsided a little when Helen had cleared away his plate and squeezed his hand in a sweetly reminiscent gesture of when they'd been about to sit a medical exam. All in all, he was now as up to the ordeal as he'd ever be. Although the question remained: was Edith? He was about to find out.

*

Her breakfast tray was on the cottage doorstep, the remains of the porridge clinging to the sides of the bowl. Stephen clutched his briefcase to his chest; he'd found her little gift when he'd been searching for a sharp pencil. At first he'd been irritated as he'd scraped at the mess with his penknife but eventually found he could extrapolate some learning from the fact that the childish act had been tempered with some of Edith's neat orderliness; she may not be behaving rationally but her rational mind was still in evidence. It gave him some hope of her at least listening to his arguments.

He knocked, waited for half a minute, then let himself in. She was sitting in the armchair. Dressed in a skirt, blouse, and cardigan in preference to the curtain-frock which he now recognised she wore whenever she thought she should be back in the asylum. Her hair had been combed through and she looked better rested than yesterday. But even from the other side of the room, he could see the muscles in her neck and shoulders quivering. He felt a pang of pity; she was trying so hard to maintain control over something she didn't understand. He would help her peel away the layers. After dragging over the chair, he sat in front of her a little closer than usual so she couldn't pretend to ignore his presence. Her expression was vacant.

'Edith, I've only another few days before I have to return to London so I'm going to start accelerating things a bit. You're ready for it.'

'Whatever you like, after all I'm only your laboratory rat to be poked and squeezed as you see fit. It would all be your fault if I turn around and bite you.'

Was this an admission of gamesmanship? If so, it was a good indication of her objective state of mind; he had to try to get her to maintain it.

'Why are you telling yourself that; is that how you want it to be?'

'It's as good a position as any, and more comfortable than most because I know where I stand, what you expect from me.'

'Do you like regarding yourself as a victim?'

'Of what … Life? My father? Your utterly pointless questions?'

Her lips twitched into a half-smile.

'Granny always said *I smell burning martyr* whenever I reluctantly did something around the house. A peculiarly vicious turn of phrase to use to a child whose mother perished in a house fire, don't you think?'

'Does remembering anything about either woman make you angry?'

Silence.

'It would be perfectly reasonable if it did. The one was wrenched away from you in tragic circumstances just at the period in your life when you needed her most and, from what I can gather, your grandmother seemed unnecessarily strict towards a little girl who'd undergone such a terrible loss. Do you think I've got that right?'

Again, silence. But now the muscular tremor had travelled down her arms; he could see them vibrating under the thin wool of her cardigan.

'And if I were to take that assumption even further, I'd say that your father and his mother colluded in making you feel unwanted, unloved, a nuisance … in short, nothing but a burden.'

He had to provoke her into releasing some of the tension threatening to consume her. And it was best if the resulting vitriol wasn't directed at him. It wasn't just self-protection; if he was going to be able to help her achieve some sort of breakthrough then she had to see him as being on her side. But given her recent antagonism he had a lot of ground to reclaim in that respect. He needed a different approach.

'We can come back to your family later. For now, I want to explore how your subconscious has attempted to compensate for such a crushing blow to your self-esteem. Because we all need to feel good about ourselves, Edith – I don't mean in a vain or deluded way but so that the very core of our being believes we deserve to take up the space we occupy on this earth.'

The tremors had travelled to her feet and ankles. He could hear the soft shuffle of her slippers on the floorboards.

'You think you're so clever, don't you, with your neat explanations for everything. The only thing I've ever regarded myself as is a freak. How are you going to incorporate that into your little theory?'

Accepting a challenge was not the same as willingly stepping into one of her games. And he had got her to engage her intellect; even a heated argument would be preferable to stubborn resistance.

'Freakishness is nothing more than a deviation from what is culturally considered to be normal. On the slaughter-fields of France the men here wouldn't have drawn a second glance but in 1927 England they have to take refuge in Beddingham Hall because the environment around them has changed, and they've changed too much to be tolerated – both for how they look and the carnage they represent. Normality is relative, Edith. The devastating injuries you sustained in the fire have made it impossible for you to experience an ordinary family life – as a child or adult – and it's my contention that you are locked in the sadness and anger of acceptance. Of letting go of the dream of the woman you might have been.'

'Do you see me crying? Where are the tears, Doctor?'

'We express our deepest emotions in different ways – sometimes quite bizarrely to people looking in on them – but they're nonetheless real, and potent, for that. To continue … for some time you've been experiencing the unwelcome side-effects of your subconscious mind's adoption of a secondary persona. Such a defensive strategy against pain is ultimately ineffective because it exacerbates inner conflict; throws up clashes of wills; brings to the fore the perils of disintegration. The Greek dramatists always had it that the double represents the messenger of death, with the truth that two can never live as peaceably as one; the catharsis for the audience invariably centred on who would triumph in the end, the original or the doppelganger. Modern psychology isn't so very different in its understanding, we just use different language.'

'With you as my very own Greek god fallen to earth full of pride, arrogance, and stubbornness …'

'Why are you so determined to undermine everything I say?'

'Because you're stupid.'

'Okay, let's agree on that for the moment. But, given your own fierce intellect, doesn't that make you feel even a little sorry for me?'

'I don't see why I should. If you raise yourself onto a pedestal where your failings will become glaringly obvious then you are only compounding your inadequacies and I feel no reason to pity you for not being able to recognise your limitations.'

'I don't know everything about my personality, nobody ever can; but what I do know I, on the whole, like. And there's a reason for that. It's not because I think I'm a wonderful and infallible specimen of humanity – far from it – I've merely done what everybody does and built up a story to prop up and maintain my image of myself. Our memories make us who we are; not due to the things that happened in themselves, but because we weave them into an elaborate – and self-aggrandising – fiction where we are the hero of a world that revolves around us. Memories are the stories we tell ourselves to make sense of our lives. Everybody else's opinion of us is just a product of how they see themselves. Their judgement doesn't, in effect, matter so long as our own definition is whole and consistent. That's not to say that people can't change – they do, and should, as they blossom and mature – but the fundamental essence of who we are is self-reverential. We create it, Edith. To sustain, encourage, fortify, inspire, enthuse and motivate us to become the best example of ourselves we can possibly be.'

He'd been watching her carefully as he'd been talking; twice her gaze had been pulled to him as if against her will, but her face had remained impassive throughout.

'I had a dream last night. In colour. And it hasn't gone away even now …'

Stephen wanted to clap his hands with vindication; she'd reacted exactly as he'd hoped and drawn the attention back to herself. It was an act of will, not coercion, and meant that at least a part of her wanted to open up to him. Which part though? The clue would be in whatever fabrication she was about to come out with.

'I was in a room – this one, I think – it was full of spiders and paper. Spiders and paper. They'd built webs, the pieces of white flowing from them like streamers. I was standing at the bottom of the stairs. They were talking to each other; I couldn't hear them but I knew because they all marched across from web to web and opened the window. Then they all scurried outside. I couldn't move because if I walked into the threads and one of them touched my eyes then they'd be sealed forever. A gust of wind moaned down the chimney. Fingers of soot were picking their way through the air. They left little black smudges, and before long I could see where every web was and I could walk through without getting trapped.'

'What happened to the pieces of paper?'

'Nothing. They were still hanging. But instead of catching flies, words were sticking to them. Words that had been floating around but were invisible until they touched the paper.'

'What did they say?'

'Things about me. Things I wouldn't have listened to if they'd been spoken but had to look at as I sidled past. I got to the empty centre of the room. It was as if I was woven into a delicate cage. I knew I could sweep the sooty threads away with my arms if I wanted but then the words would stick to me and I'd have to carry them around wherever I went. Then I looked up. A fat spider was dropping from the ceiling. It spun itself to eye-level. It had your face. But covered with hair, so only the eyes and mouth showed. It began to smile, showing rows of tiny pointed teeth. I knew it wanted to bite me. To suck my blood so it could swell to grow as big as the cottage, and then there would be nothing left of me but a pile of skin and bone. I told it to drop a little further so I could put it in my pocket. It began to sway in the breeze from the open window as it twizzled down. A gust caught its bloated body and it released too much silk. It was inches from the floor, and I lifted my foot and stamped on it. Hard. It screamed. I felt it pop and squelch under my shoe. And I was happy. I was alone.'

She glanced across at him but couldn't hold the gaze and her eyes flicked towards a space on the floor just beyond her feet. The muscles of her face grew slack. A tremor rippled through her.

'There's blood on the floor. A pool of it. Even if I close my eyes …'

She did so.

'… I can smell it. Like pennies that have been too long in a drawer. Like the change Treadwell gave me. I had to wash the memories off those coins when I got home.'

Her voice had dropped, the edges frayed with something approximating fear.

'But they never really went away. I could taste them when they were in my purse. Then I'd have to take them one by one and bury them in the garden. Not to grow; to rot and decay. Except I knew they never would. They'd travel through the soil and find their way back to scatter themselves on my bedroom floor or under the sideboard. They knew they belonged to me, you see, and I knew I could never get rid of them.'

Her distress was genuine. The blood on the floor was real – or she thought it was. Stephen had to exert every ounce of his willpower to stop from looking for himself. It occurred to him that maybe the dream had been real, too, and that she'd only invented the final *coup de grâce* about the spider having his face. The internal confrontation he'd been edging her towards had begun.

CHAPTER FORTY-SEVEN

'I'm screaming … Am I screaming? … I'm screaming …'

The terror in her voice startled him. The skin on her face was slick with sweat. She was clawing at her hands as if she wanted to tear them to sinew. He had to intervene – but too soon and he'd miss the chance to expose what it was causing her so much distress.

'I can't hear anything. There is no sound other than inside your head. But is it you screaming, or is the voice? Because it's screamed before, hasn't it? Did you hear it that day in Fletching when the old Gypsy was with you?'

She moved her head from side to side. 'Yes … no … it's not the same … Just a noise …'

'Give it a name, Edith; personalise it and it will be able to speak for itself.'

'Edward …'

'Good. Let me talk to Edward, Edith, let me talk to him and he'll leave you.'

'No, he won't. He never does.'

'Do you want him to?'

'No, I need him. Without him I'm nothing. He comforts me.'

'Is it really comfort you feel or torment?'

'Both. They are the same thing. He knows they are the same thing.'

'Can you tell me what is going on in your head right now?'

'There's a sort of whooshing. It stings …'

Stephen watched as she turned to stare behind her.

'What is it, Edith? What's there?'

'Fire.'

'Edith. Face me again. Describe what Edward is showing you.'

'Blues flames turning yellow at the edges. Hungry flames. Licking their lips.'

Stephen leaned forward to hold her wrists. His papers tumbled to the floor. 'Look into my eyes, Edith. Do you see the fire reflected there?'

She did what he asked, but didn't answer.

'Because, if you don't, then it's not real. Can you feel the heat on your back?'

'No.'

'What you are experiencing is the deep-seated memories you've ascribed to Edward so that they don't have to be yours.'

Her whole body was convulsing. He could feel the electricity sparking up his arms. Her flesh was scorching. He had the absurd notion that if he didn't wrench his hands away then they would be burned to a crisp. He closed his fingers tightly around her thin wrists. Her pulse was strong and fast. She was in the throes of flight anxiety. He made a show of breathing loudly and rhythmically. Blowing his cheeks out and releasing the air in slow exhalations.

'Breath with me, Edith … That's it … in and out … the air in your lungs will be enough to put out the flames … but you have to take it in deeply, and let it out steadily … That's better. Good girl … that's a good, brave, girl …'

He hadn't meant to start talking to her as if she were a child but it seemed to be doing the trick. The jerking of her muscles had quelled to soft vibrations like that of a tuning fork, and her features were no longer contorted in panic. He held onto her for a little while longer until he felt thin threads of her attention come back.

'Edward doesn't want to hurt you, Edith; he's just trying to express feelings on your behalf. He's being kind really by wanting to protect you from them. But he doesn't realise that you can't shut yourself off from him, as he can from you. If you can remember that then you'll find him his presence less upsetting.'

Stephen gently withdrew his hands and sat back in his chair. His stomach was beginning to churn. He wanted to be able to put it down to catching her agitation but he knew that it was really because he had just transgressed a line he shouldn't even have been nudging his toes against; he had an image of a tightrope walker taking a step into the void. He hadn't intended to stray into treating Edward as if he actually existed. No psychoanalyst should ever overtly reinforce a patient's fantasies. Not exorcising a delusion too soon before it could be put to therapeutic use was one thing, but to actively encourage it was a mistake only first-year students made. It was stupidity bordering on incompetence. Professional malpractice, even. He wanted to punch the wall in his fury with himself. How could he now stop from tumbling into a morass of confused reality of his own making – and dragging Edith down with him? Maybe by climbing a little way into it.

'Edith, I want you to imagine Edward as a baby in your lap. He is whimpering and squirming … You stroke his hair … He grows calmer … Quieter … more still … You whisper something to him. Words that you know will soothe and heal … What do you say, Edith?'

'Hush little baby don't you cry …' Her voice was soft, lilting, but she wasn't quite singing.

'Good, Edith, good. What is he doing now?'

'Smiling.'

'I want you to wait until you see his grin grow as wide as it possibly can, and then I want you to lay your hand gently over his mouth … I want you to feel his hot breath as he lets go of all the anger he had balled up inside him …'

He watched as her right hand moved to hover somewhere in front of her left breast. 'Now I want you to open your fingers so all the hurt and pain he was feeling can slip between them and melt away.'

She was responding exactly as she would've done in an induced trance; her fingers were splayed, her thighs slightly tense as if she did have a weight resting on them. He wondered if he shouldn't have tried something like this a little earlier. But he doubted if she'd have been ready for it, ready to externalise Edward so completely she could hallucinate him into her arms. But Stephen wasn't going to repeat his elementary mistake.

'Edward isn't really in this room with us. Edward doesn't exist. But all your terrifying memories do. They are real. And they are what he represents. They are what you are cradling, and soothing, and staring in the face with courage.'

Edith opened her eyes. Her gaze was steady, clear of challenge. This wasn't the end by a long way, but he did think they'd turned a corner. He got the impression she did, too. He was so struck by the apparent success of his approach that he had an idea. It was not without risk but he thought it worth a try.

'I'd like to hypnotise you; we've done it many times before, remember? But this won't be very deep; it'll feel like that moment of complete peace before you drop off to sleep. Nothing more. You'll be aware of absolutely everything around you at all times. If you feel uncomfortable or out of control at any point then just open your eyes – it'll be no different to waking up from a nap. All I want to do is to get behind the barrier of your fear of him and help you to comprehend Edward for what he is. Will you agree to letting me do that?'

'If it'll make him go away and never come back.'

'I would be misleading you if I promised that would happen … but if you tell me all about him then his power over you will wane until the reasons for his influence are something you are able to understand and manage.'

'I can't … he said that if I spoke about any of the things that passed between us … betrayed him in any way … then he'll see to it that I perish along with him.'

'Then I won't ask you to. Once I get you into a relaxed state, I'll simply ask about you in relation to him; speak to your rational mind and leave your subconscious well alone. That is one promise I can make with no fear of it ending up broken.'

She nodded. He gave her a moment to see if she'd reacted without thinking and would think better of it, then he moved his chair to sit beside her. 'Lean back … that's it; let the cushions support you. Close your eyes and breathe deeply. Imagine you are inhaling a sweet scent that carries with it all the promises of summer.'

In Edith's willingness to co-operate her muscles relaxed almost immediately; her face lost its hunted look.

'Are you cold at all? Would you like me to fetch a blanket from your bed?'

'No thank you, Dr Maynard. I'm perfectly fine.'

A nice even tone of voice without the cadence of suppressed emotions; it was a good start.

'You are strolling through a meadow filled with flowers. The colours are soft dots of pigment, soothing to your sight. There are butterflies; the gentle hum of bees accompanies the swishing of the grass. You let your hand trail through the feathery fronds …'

Edith's fingers were making tiny caressing movements on the chair arms. Even if he gained nothing from this she would feel the benefits of total absorption.

'I'd like you to find a patch of grass that looks so inviting you want to lie down in it … To feel the sun on your face and the warmth of the earth ooze up into your calves and spine.'

Her body unwound a degree or so further.

'Now I'm going to begin asking some questions. Do you feel ready? Safe enough to continue … Edith, do you trust me?'

'Yes, of course. Because you and I both know the consequences if you break your word, and you'd never forgive yourself if that happened.'

A small smile was playing on her lips. It hadn't been a threat but proof that she had judged the situation accurately.

'If you want me to stop then just open your eyes. We're going to have a normal conversation that you'll remember every detail of, except this way you won't experience the compulsion to have to fight what you want to say to me. I'll be taking notes – but not to confront you with as in the past, only for my own records.'

'To compensate for your lousy memory.'

He laughed. 'Got it in one. So, tell me, Edith, how did you feel when Edward first came into your life?'

'Surprised … shocked … excited. As if I'd always expected him but didn't dare hope.'

'When was this?'

'A long time ago. I was young then. But we were parted.'

'And what about more recently when he returned, where were you then?'

'Outside my cottage in Fletching.'

'Can you remember what had happened to you just before the encounter?'

'I'd been to the doctor to check I wasn't going mad like my father. He pronounced I wasn't but then spoiled the relief by coming up with one of those facile diagnoses that you medical men have at your fingertips.'

'Ah, yes, sorry about that. It's a disease of the profession brought about by our inability to leave a vacuum of knowledge unfilled. What did he say?'

He saw her eyelids flicker and realised, with a start, she thought he'd transgressed into forbidden territory.

'I don't mean Edward. The doctor. Can you recall coming away from the consultation feeling upset?'

'Anybody would. He told me that my memory lapses and insomnia boiled down to under-stimulation. That I was suffering from common-or-garden loneliness. The patronising bastard.'

Stephen's pencil skidded over the page. He couldn't remember ever having heard her use language that wasn't precise and proper. She must've felt extremely provoked and angry. Already the patterns were fitting his hypothesis perfectly.

'Was it pleasant to be with Edward again?'

'Very. We had tea.'

'Who did most of the talking?'

'He did. We had a lot to catch up on.'

'I suspect you steered the conversation though. So what did you ask him?'

'Where he'd been, why he'd come back … if he was married.'

He caught the hint of a flush on her cheeks.

'Think very carefully about this one: did he ever volunteer any information – and you don't have to tell me what it was – that wasn't in response to some prompt from you?'

'I know what you're getting at. But he wasn't a figment of my imagination; he was there – I could see him, touch him, smell his pipe tobacco.'

'Except those things aren't in conflict, Edith. Our minds control our senses by filtering what we acknowledge or ignore. I'd like to try a little experiment to demonstrate the truth of this: What can you feel under your fingertips right at this moment?'

'The armchair.'

'Okay. Without moving your hand and resting just as lightly, concentrate on the pressure of your skin on the cloth. What now?'

'The weave … a slight greasiness … a bump under my right thumb where the horsehair stuffing has bunched.'

'Excellent. You see? Those sensations had been available to you the instant you sat down but your brain didn't regard them worthy of notice until your mind forced it to pay attention. It's the only way we can cope or our circuits would be permanently overloaded. So sometimes we don't feel what is there and, equally, sometimes our senses genuinely perceive what isn't externally present but is a hallucination of the mind. The latter is essentially the *trick* behind hypnotism: I can get you to relax because the image we conjure up together – my words, your senses – transports you to a less threatening environment.'

'Except the logic breaks down because he said some things I certainly wouldn't want to make myself hear.'

'No one has ever said the psyche is anything but complex. I'll admit I've been known to fantasise the odd lover's tiff with the sole aim of experiencing a sweet resolution.'

Her look of lofty scepticism had been replaced with a smirk. If she was going to goad him again about Helen then so be it; he'd consider it a small price to pay if he'd got his point home. But Edith surprised him by letting it pass; she was probably thinking too much about herself to bite. Stephen pushed up the cuff of his jacket and timed the silence. The hands had ticked away a full two minutes before he heard her clear her throat. Whatever she said next would determine whether he'd made any real progress or if she was just tolerating his explorations.

'So you're saying I made him up?'

'Not exactly. My contention is that he is a projection. Let me put it this way … When we go to the cinema the images are there in front of us and if it's a good story that has some resonance for us then we utterly believe the scenes are being played out before our eyes there and then. But the actors are in Hollywood and not in the picture house. And the characters they're impersonating don't exist in any temporal reality but it makes no difference.'

'*That willing suspension of disbelief.*'

'What?'

'Samuel Taylor Coleridge. You really should read more to augment your scientific training, Dr Maynard; you'll find poets have summed up the human condition in far more imaginative ways than you'll ever be able to.'

'*Touché*. But you admit that means I could be on the right lines then?'

'During the picnic, Edward talked for hours about his time in the Bolivian Rain Forests.'

'And I found a heap of *National Geographic* magazines in your cottage, some with notes marking articles on South American expeditions – in fact I brought them over with me because I thought they must've meant something to you. Am I correct in assuming you studied them before you met up with him?'

'He brought things, beer and some rugs.'

'Could you not have taken them along yourself?'

'We swapped memories of the first picnic we had together.'

'Two differencing perspectives from the same mind.'

'He knew people I'd never met.'

'You might have done only to relegate the encounters to your subconscious, or they were products of distant daydreams. Did he ever say he'd met anyone you knew?'

'My father.'

'I'm afraid he doesn't count if, as I believe, your mind constructed Edward as an alternative personality to absorb and deflect paternal rejection.'

'Some of the shell-shocked officers he was treating …'

'Ditto. Neighbours; anyone in the village; PC Billings? Did you see him conversing with strangers in the street or on the bus? Was there ever another person, even one in your peripheral vision, when you were together?'

The silence lasted four minutes this time. He was hitting her hard with uncomfortable realities but she was contemplating them. And she hadn't signalled she no longer wished to participate.

'He tormented me. Issued threats.' Her voice was tinged with hurt, not irritation at her interrogator.

'Can anything wound or torture us more than our own minds via remembered humiliations, suppressed memories, replays of regrets and recriminations?'

'What you're saying is that everything I thought he did was really me … I was the one who … who …'

Edith's eyes shot open. She wasn't looking at anything in the room, her unfocused gaze stretching back beyond the reach of his interpretation. For a split second he saw naked terror reflected in them, but then her mind's protective barriers shuttered down on the source. A blink … and she was back with him again. Now he'd got her to consider the unsettling truth about Edward, it was vital he reinforce her sense of self with some of the corporeal reality of her past. A woman would probably be less threatening; there was only one he could think of.

'Would you like to have a visitor, Edith? Apart from me, I mean. How would it be if I telephoned the constable in Fletching and see if he can arrange for Old Sophie to come over for luncheon?

You could perhaps ask her if she has any old-fashioned remedies to get rid of those moles.'

'I've no idea what you're talking about.'

Edith looked confused and he thought maybe she was going to deny any associations from her past. Then she laughed. 'Oh, the moles; I'd completely forgotten I'd told you about them.' Her expression changed to one of wariness.

'Will you be joining us to take notes of the experiment?'

'Of course not. But you needn't fret I'll be at a loose end because I can occupy myself fulfilling my promise to Peter to help dig over the allotments, and after that I'll clear all my outstanding debts by going over to fetch your rose book. Shall I get up to the Hall now and make that telephone call?'

Edith didn't look excited at the prospect, but neither was she objecting to his proposal. Stephen packed his briefcase with a fizzing excitement tickling in his belly. If his intuition was right then the reputed habit Dr Potter had acquired for almost pathologically documenting every thought process might not have been confined to his clinical work and could well have spilled over into his private life. Somewhere within the walls of that cottage in Fletching might lurk written evidence of his dreadful desire to be rid of his child. If so, he could use it to confront Edith's conscious mind with something more than a repressed memory and thereby force it to begin the process of healing.

CHAPTER FORTY-EIGHT

The black car looked like a beetle scurrying over the Downland chalk as it crested the rise. He didn't have long. From his vantage point, he could see both the cottage and the stable block. One would offer sanctuary, the other a reckoning that could end up amounting to the beginning of the end.

Except when he saw the car draw up to the Hall's main entrance and the figure in a blue uniform get out, he knew that the death dance had already begun. Hiding would only delay, not prevent, exposure. And running away was the act of a coward. The time before he'd had no choice but to disappear, but now he did. He could end this. Remove the doubt. Take control – of the timescale, if not the outcome. What was left of his freedom could be spent in fear and loathing or climax with a supreme act of self-sacrifice. Martyrdom even.

Edward shivered before turning back towards his fate.

CHAPTER FORTY-NINE

Stephen jumped off the back of the cart. The journey had been longer – and bumpier – than he had anticipated. He wondered if Edith was having a pleasant time. PC Billings had been remarkably efficient and rung back before suppertime yesterday with the offer of driving the Gypsy over himself in his brother-in-law's car. His only qualification being that it'd have to be for tea rather than luncheon because of the Lewes Crown Court's Friday sittings. Which had foiled Stephen's plan of the luxury of a ride all the way to Fletching, and he'd had to cadge a lift in one of the clothes collection vans, completing the final leg with the Uckfield seed merchant. But he had benefitted by having the perfect excuse to cut short his allotment digging. As it was, he had an aching back – not helped, of course, by being jostled by sacks of grain – and the palms of his hands were criss-crossed with emergent blisters. Physical activity, even when performed in the clean crisp air of a perfect autumnal morning, wasn't all it was cracked up to be.

As the policeman had told him it would, the cottage key was hanging on a piece of string inside the letterbox. Stephen was glad he hadn't had to ask the geese-keeping neighbour for it. Although his visit was far from being clandestine, he hadn't wanted someone looking over his shoulder to ask awkward questions as to why he was prying into all the places a senile old man might've secreted something of an intensely private nature. Not that there was any guarantee that anything of that sort had ever, or still, existed, but he wasn't going to leave this place until he'd conducted a thorough search PC Billings would've been proud of. Except he was never going to know: his may not be the actions of a trespasser but neither did they feel exactly on the right side of the law.

Someone had been paying attention to keeping the garden in good order but the inside had that mildew odour of closed-up houses. Stephen stepped back over the threshold, shut the front door once more and pocketed the key. A jar of eucalyptus balm was called for to block off his nostrils, and some food wouldn't go amiss; he didn't know why he hadn't asked Helen to pack him something: yes he did, she'd have queried what was going to take him so long he couldn't stop at a pub catering for the rambling brigade.

The walk up the lane was delightful. No wonder Dr Potter had chosen to retire here. In the distance, Stephen could hear the cries of seagulls following a plough. He'd been born and brought up a city boy but could see the attraction of living in a place like this – provided he didn't have to work the land of course. November in the lea of the Downs had none of the bleak dreariness you found in London. The scent of wood fires rather than the acrid stench of coal smoke probably had something to do with it. Although he suspected that, even for him, the romance would vanish once winter began to bite; he wondered if the villagers found themselves completely housebound when it snowed. Stephen's heart squeezed for Edith trapped indoors with the man who had given her life but, who they both knew on some level or other, had wished it taken away again. It came to him that he'd never got to the bottom of what had compelled Edith to face the truth in the days, hours, or minutes, before her fugue; it hadn't felt important because his real work had been to erect a platform of reality to keep her from descending back into a catatonic state. It was a frustrating twist that at this moment the only two people who could shed any light on what happened were over at Beddingham Hall.

A pub was up ahead just beyond the expanse of the common. On the corner opposite sat a forge, the rhythmic ring of a hammer hitting an anvil counterpointing his steps. So far – apart from the thin blue wisps rising from chimneys – he'd almost got the impression the place was deserted. The grocery shop was at the bottom of a hill curving up and away towards a copse of bare-branched trees.

The bell over the door tinkled. A voice drifted down from somewhere near the ceiling.

'A very good afternoon and what can I be doing you for?'

Stephen's eyes took a while to adjust to the gloom but when they did it was as though he'd walked into a theatrical stage-set. He hadn't known emporiums like this really existed. Anything and everything seemed to be for sale, short of a kitchen sink. He dodged a pile of lethal-looking animal traps seemingly laid there to catch strangers unawares. The grocer descended a ladder on his left, his arms full of boxes of Green's Egg Custard Mix.

'Never get that shelf stacked if I keep getting interruptions – not that I'm complaining mind, or my till would be empty.' He clicked his false teeth as he dropped his goods on the counter. 'Are you seeing what you're wanting or do you require me to fulfil an order?'

Stephen guessed the man dreamed of the day someone would answer that they needed the latter. 'A jar of vapour rub please.'

'No call for stocking that in these parts. Got a touch of the sniffles have you? Mrs Gibson, the butcher's wife, makes up a powerful tonic I could be selling you a bottle of.'

The thought of what went into such a concoction wasn't appealing.

'Some peppermint oil instead perhaps?'

'That I can accommodate. Only you're missing giving your body a treat by not taking the tonic.'

Stephen waited until the grocer returned to the counter with a small brown bottle. He pointed to an open zinc tin of loose biscuits. 'I'll have a dozen of these, thank you.' He watched them being counted out. 'It's a nice village you have here.'

'You wouldn't be thinking the same when Baker's Lane is ankle-deep in mud. Take my word for it; you're seeing us at the fag-end of the year and it don't get much better after this. But I'll be giving you it's a fair-to-middling day.'

He started to wrap the biscuits into a small parcel, holding the brown paper down with his stumps while reaching with the other hand for the string. Stephen breathed in the scents of cloves and washing soap and wondered what Edith had made of it all. Would she have found the quaintness amusing after the London department stores, or would she have discovered that traditional values often went hand in hand with old-fashioned small-mindedness?

'Anything else I can be helping you with?'

'A piece of strong cheddar and a small loaf.'

'Have to be getting along to Crowhurst's bakery if it's bread you're wanting. Only I reckon he won't have much left at this time of day – never been one to slave over a hot oven when it's destined for the ducks, is our Sneezer. Box of crackers do you?'

The anticipation of a freshly-baked cob had begun to make Stephen's mouth water but he thought it probably better to make all his purchases in one place if he was to avoid drawing too much attention to himself; he didn't relish any inquisitive knocks on the door of Edith's cottage.

'That'll be fine. A bottle of lemonade as well.'

He leafed idly through a stack of magazines on the end of the counter as the grocer shuffled about getting everything together. He was back to catch Stephen thumbing an edition of *National Geographic*.

'That kind of thing to your liking is it? If so may I take the liberty of recommending the December '26? Plenty of fuzzy-wuzzies not wearing very much in that one … if you get my drift.'

Stephen couldn't stop a blush from searing his cheeks. What an odious little man to reduce cultural exploration to cheap titillation. Poor Edith must've had to endure a fair degree of sniggering if she'd had to pick up her subscription from here rather than having it delivered by the postman. Except, Stephen suspected, even then her elevated interests would still have been gossiped about.

'Got a lot of them, I have,' the grocer called out from behind his cheese cutter, 'all out of date, but that hardly matters none. Constable Billings took it into his head to be telling the post office that her as ordered them was wanting them cancelled, but not before there was all those you see there sitting on her mat. He thought rather than them go to waste I might get a few pennies for the pictures.'

Stephen threw himself into the opening. 'Not Edith Potter by any chance? I knew a little of her father, and met her once or twice.'

'The very same. Strange bird she was, shut up in the loony bin now. Lucky thing she never got hitched.'

He returned to the counter and started folding a sheet of greaseproof around the cheese.

'What?'

'Because what with the old man being daft as a brush and her soft in the noggin, she'd have raised bigger village idiots than we has already.'

Stephen picked up his purchases and tossed a half-a-crown on the counter. Why was it that people had to be so bloody spitefully condemning of the unfortunate? He'd like to arrange for the residents of Beddingham Hall to descend on this place and let them see for themselves why they were better off out of so-called decent society.

'Is there a bus service to Uckfield from here?'

'Five-thirty from the stop opposite Tilgate Wood. Miss it and you'll have the choice of a long tramp or getting cooty bites from dossing at the Barley Mow. I'd be opting to wear out my shoe leather if I were you.'

Edith's words about having to wash the taint of distaste off the coins came into his head as he took his change. He knew exactly how she felt.

*

Stephen walked back down the cottage stairs. The smell in Dr Potter's bedroom had penetrated even the peppermint-soaked handkerchief he'd tied as a mask over his nose and mouth. The door had been locked but he'd found the key resting on the top of the frame. As well as the ingrained stench of an incontinent old man, he'd had to combat a queasiness from having to look under the mattress that had cradled a dead body two years previously. The pockets of the suits hanging in the wardrobe had been empty. He could push his fingers to the end of the shoes without encountering anything. Short of prising up the floorboards, there was nowhere else for him to try. He'd ignored Edith's room on the basis that not only would Dr Potter not have hidden anything there, it would be a breach of privacy too far to peek into her underwear drawer or rifle through any of her less intimate belongings.

The study was dusty and stuffy, the floor covered with balls of fluff. Stephen walked across to the desk and pulled open the drawer. It was empty. He stood motionless for a moment in an effort to replace his frustration with something approaching a plan of campaign. Things weren't suddenly going to leap out and bite him just because he wanted them to. If he thought about it logically, whatever it was would've had to have been hidden very well and a long time ago – very possibly before Edith had moved to Fletching.

What else, apart from the ancient desk, was there that might be decades old? A battered armchair was pushed against the wall, the stuffing so lumpy it looked to be a treasured favourite. Stephen went over and tipped it upside down to rest on its wooden arms. Then he took his pocketknife and slit open the back and seat. If Edith wanted it kept then he would pay for one of the craftsmen at Beddingham Hall to do the re-upholstery; there was no doubt it needed work to make it comfortable again even without his butchery. Plunging his hands into the interior, he yanked out every last tangled knot of horsehair until there was nothing remaining of its substance but a frame and rusted springs. Could he have got it wrong and there wasn't anything to be discovered in the cottage?

He perched on the edge of the disembowelled chair and tried to think. What if Edith hadn't known her father's attitude to her all along and it had been the finding of it committed to paper that had propelled her into the fugue? One thing he was certain of: she'd never have allowed herself to destroy something that she might want to stand up one day and wave in the face of his glorious reputation. So, assuming that she'd come across this thing unexpectedly, and the truth contained within it was as devastating as he believed it to be, then she wouldn't have wanted anyone else to stumble across it and would have re-hidden it straight away without giving it too much thought. Any temporary hiding place must've therefore been one she could easily come back to when her mind had settled on a more permanent burial of the secret. The pre-psychotic Edith Potter would've taken comfort in the rationality of such an approach.

Stephen stood up and, starting at the short wall by the window, pulled each book off its shelf, opened it to make sure it hadn't been hollowed out, shook it for loose sheets, and then checked in the gap it had left. Ten shelves: hundreds of books. He took down the one on roses and laid it on the floor in case he forgot that part of the quest in the excitement of vindication or despair of defeat. Then he resumed his systematic examination of the rest until his arms were sore and his back screaming. Eventually there was only a collection of bound scientific papers in several volumes left before he'd have to start the process on the more daunting larger bookcases.

Resting his fingers on top of *Index and Introductory Remarks on Notable Royal Society Lectures*, he tipped it towards him before sliding the book free. There, pressed against the back wall was a small Victorian pocket journal covered in green leather and tooled with gold swags and curls. He lifted it out and carried it over to the desk where he pulled a pen and paper from his pocket before sitting in the cane-seated captain's chair.

The corners of the book were dented and it smelt damp but it appeared to have survived the decades relatively unharmed. The first page that had been written on appeared to be a list of dates with some initials or shorthand references beside them. All in a hand he recognised as Dr Potter's from an annotated article Stephen had studied some years ago. He thought the cryptic notations might be something to do with his early career at the National Hospital for the Relief of Paralysis, Epilepsy and Allied Diseases. If this was a lost record of pioneering treatments or procedures then it would be of inestimable value to the profession, but it hardly constituted the confession of a man half-crazed with grief.

But the pages of excited scrawl that followed told a different story. Even with his experience of reading hastily written medical notes they weren't easy to decipher. Then, one after another, words began to lace together into meaning. With a sickening lurch of his stomach, Stephen knew he had found what he was looking for. What Edith would never have wanted to see.

For the next three hours, as the afternoon light faded into dusk, Stephen transcribed page after page of Dr Potter's journal. Now that he had some idea of the narrative he went back to the original page and translated the shorthand notes against the list of dates. Sweat soaked his crotch and trickled down his spine.

When he could no longer see without lighting a lamp and revealing his presence he picked up his notes and the journal and left. He'd never been so glad to get out of anywhere in all his life.

NOTES FROM DR GERALD POTTER'S JOURNAL

[Transcribed by Dr Stephen Maynard, Nov 1927]

[Third Page]

1893

Can there be any man alive who has been granted such a great opportunity? Nor had such responsibility placed on his shoulders? Please God, I will not fail. Neither will I shirk my duty to Science, to my profession, and to my country. To that end I will faithfully record here in my journal my findings for this, the most profound experiment any man can ever conduct.

It is my contention that human instincts involve more than ~~creatin~~ certain motor aptitudes. For the Alienist, the study of the sexual instinct is of the first importance ... greatest of all mental forces, the ~~disarrangement~~ derangement or disharmony of which is the leading feature, and perhaps the principal ætiological factor, in mental disorder and lunacy.

I will prove the falsity of the sense-stimulus theory of sexual impulse.

[What follows is illegible. Appears to be meaningless scrawl.]

I will ~~undoubtedly~~ attempt to disprove:

- that instinctive action is merely compound reflex action
- pleasure and pain are the prime movers of all human and bestial behaviour.

Within the next few years I will have shown that what we now think of as immutable is, in fact, as subject to the new laws of Science as everything else.

I am hardly able to sleep at nights knowing what rests on my actions and observations. All surgical intervention has now been completed.

★★★★★★★★★★★★★★★★★★★★★★★★★★★★★

NOTES FROM DR GERALD POTTER'S JOURNAL

[Twentieth Page]

[The writing from this point on is less frenetic; the thought processes seem to follow a more logical pattern and it is altogether much easier to read.]

I have committed the following thoughts to paper after an interval of 24 months following the cessation of the experiment. It did not prove practical to continue after the child attained the age of 10 years, primarily due to the increasing demands placed on me by the faculty in which I was working. Deprived of the facility of continuous observation, the impossibility of ensuring the purity of the environment for purposes of empirical scientific study became clear. However I am firmly of the opinion that I have amassed sufficient evidence to take my findings before The Psychological Society. I am convinced that it will be on the basis of their reaction to my findings that I will be offered the first directorship of the proposed Cambridge Psychological Laboratory.

Points to note when writing the paper for submission:

- A clear difference exists between the sexes from early infancy – manner, habits of mind, and in illness – becoming more marked before the onset of puberty.
- Although there are some cases of infantile masturbation, there is much positive evidence that the sexual instinct first awakens in the majority of mankind about the eight or ninth year.
- Dr Marie has recorded the case of an insane Egyptian eunuch whose penis and scrotum were removed in infancy yet he had frequent and intense sexual desire with ejaculation of mucus. Although the body had a feminine appearance, the prostate was normal and the vesiculæ seminales not atrophied.

[The journal from hereon in has not been transcribed.]

★★★★★★★★★★★★★★★★★★★★★★★★★★★★★

★★★★★★★★★★★★★★★★★★★★★★★★★★★★

NOTES FROM DR GERALD POTTER'S JOURNAL

[Preface]

[List as written with my guess as to the meaning underneath. Will need verification.]

5/4/1893 prelim obs. Ep +der caut. Ex tis dam. C – bladder + urth funct. R exam.

[Preliminary observations. Epidermis and dermis cauterised. Extensive tissue damage. Catheter (inserted?) bladder and urethra functioning. Rectal examination.]

12/4/1893 1st op. Gl c: pros damg. V.d: V. s. 1 + mal. Cong?

[Glands – Cowper's; prostate damaged. Vasa defentia. Vesiculæ seminales – one malformed. Congenital?]

7/5/1893 2nd op. N.P: F.p. Glan T od. Rep muc mem. Ing canal emty.
Anorchism?
Monorchid?
Cryptorchid?

[Not present (or non- ?) Frænum preputi; glandulæ Tysonii, ororiferæ. Mucous membrane repaired (?) Inguinal canal empty.]

19 – 11 – 70 3rd op. Repair corp cev. Cut trab struct. Rem. exc. Tis. Fibrous septum. Raphe into labia.

[Repair corpora cavernosa. Cut trabecular structure. Remove (excess? Extraneous?) tissue.]

23/5/1893 obs. Scar tis. form. Dec. in pain morp red.

[Observations: scar tissue formed(ing). Decrease in pain; morphine reduced.]

★★★★★★★★★★★★★★★★★★★★★★★★★★★★

CHAPTER FIFTY

The blankets lay heavily on her scars and made them itch. Edith supposed she should feel relieved for some sort of sensation; the rest of her felt dead. How long had she been in bed? She'd crawled into it the minute they'd left and had hardly moved since. That made it two nights and one very long day. When Helen had brought the first of the unwanted meals, she'd pronounced rest the best thing to shake off whatever was ailing Edith, although it felt as though she hadn't closed her eyes once in all the hours following. Helen had been wrong anyway; a bottle of whisky would probably have done her more good.

It had been the shock of course. Seeing the policeman and the Gypsy together like that. As if she'd needed any reminding of what had happened. She'd been reliving every detail ever since Edward had brought it all back. How much easier it had been when she'd been drugged and couldn't remember anything. They'd talked at her about births and christenings and the September Taro Fair, and how the gyppo had stayed in Fletching because her horse was getting too old to climb icy hills. She could only throw in a remark about how Wilf Drayton's geese hated the snow, or ask if either of them wanted another sandwich. Even then she'd thought it amazing the way her mouth could engage in pleasantries whilst everything behind it was numb and void.

This time she hadn't thought PC Billings had come to arrest her. This time it was herself she didn't trust. Not to blurt out the lies Dr Maynard had put in her head. She was merely guilty of a lesser crime. Not murder. She accepted she was ultimately responsible for the death, but it had been Edward's doing. He'd been the one … Only it had been an accident so why was she now adding lies of her own; was her mind finally disintegrating, twisting reality of its own accord without waiting to have them whispered like poison into her ear?

She wondered if that young man who'd come to the Ministry that day and cut his throat had felt as she did now, crushed by a hopelessness that flattened everything into a grey cloud filled with nothingness. Had he believed, as she had once done, that the afterlife was a continuation of earthly existence? Because, if so, he had condemned himself to everlasting misery. But surely the alternative would be to elect to commit suicide in a moment of supreme happiness and what sort of a person would want to do that?

Defeat. Despair. Despondency. Depression. Why did they all have to begin with D? Like dank, dark, dreary. All those things contained in this moment, wrapped in these four walls. So entrenched that it would be like this tomorrow, and the day after, and fill every imaginable stretch of time.

When they'd left, Old Sophie had patted her on the cheek and said *this, too, will pass*. But it wouldn't. It couldn't. Not completely. If she ever did survive this then she'd be left with scars of bleakness as permanent as those on her skin. Every failure, humiliation, and withering sadness she'd ever encountered had scoured her like a retreating glacier but this would be worse because it was her sense of self that was being eroded.

The trial by fire had been easier; the drowning in madness, more comforting.

The minutes of her life were slipping by. Untouched. Untainted. Pure in their transience. How many more did she have left to call her own? If she were dead there'd be none to mourn as unfulfilled; but lying here, staring blankly up at the ceiling, she felt the breath of each one passing. Diminishing her. Her fingers clawed at the mattress. She could catch them if she tried. If she wanted to enough. It was all a question of desire. Or of need.

Perhaps they amounted to the same thing.

CHAPTER FIFTY-ONE

The night air was biting. A clear sky pinpricked with stars meant there'd be a heavy frost; all the talk in the bar had been about the expectation of snow. Stephen hadn't bothered to wear a coat over his jacket; somehow it felt fitting that he should be chilled to the bone. Light from the un-curtained windows of the ground floor chequered the terrace. He heard the heavy front door of the Hall open and close. He hoped to God it wasn't Peter, he didn't think he could cope with his brand of teasing quite yet. He was still slightly drunk for one thing and his tongue couldn't be relied on not to run away with him. But it wasn't.

'Since when did you take up smoking, Stephen?'

Helen had wrapped a travelling rug over a jumper that was baggy enough to be her husband's. She looked sweetly vulnerable in the moonlight.

'I haven't. I just needed this one. You could say to calm my nerves.'

'That's not the only self-medication you've been indulging in by the smell of gin. Did you spill more on yourself than made it down your throat? Why drink that stuff anyway? You know it makes you maudlin.'

'It seemed a good idea at the time. Whisky doesn't cut such a neat path to oblivion for me these days. A clear case, my dear doctor, of over-familiarity breeding sobriety.'

He laughed softly at the joke to stop the tears from springing to his eyes. Helen was right: gin always had been his emotional ruin.

'Why didn't you come back when we expected you? Or any time over the past fortnight come to that.'

'Were you worried about me?'

'Don't flatter yourself – I really don't like you very much when you're like this, Stephen; self-pity is a remarkably unattractive quality when it's shared. Snap out of it.'

'Sorry. And sorry I didn't let you know.'

'You don't have to, you're not a resident, but it was unforgivably selfish and thoughtless to stand Edith up. Luckily for you she was feeling a bit under the weather and, in any event, would probably have refused to undergo any sessions; when I took down her meals – which remained untouched I might add – she hadn't stirred out of bed. Neither did she feel like speaking much but then I haven't been her favourite person of late; think her nose was out-of-joint because I declined to reinforce her belief that she was more important and special than the other residents. So … did you get a better offer?'

The cogs in Stephen's brain whirred for a moment until he realised what Helen meant. A gin-soaked flush crawled over his skin.

'I couldn't get a lift back from Uckfield that evening so I took a room at the Chequers Hotel. Then decided to cry off work, sick, and stay there.'

'Where the residents' bar never closed.'

'Can't you throw a hangdog even a small bone of compassion? I was suffering from a terrible shock.'

'Okay, so you've wheedled an apology out of me …'

She laid her hand on his forearm. The thrill was only mildly muted by the alcohol in his veins. He dropped the cigarette that was beginning to burn his fingers and fished in his pocket for the half-empty packet.

'Want to talk about it? They can be getting on with the cocoa round without me. Sometimes I think I'm nothing but a glorified housekeeper instead of a medical practitioner as it is.'

'Why don't you get a woman from the village to take on the chores?'

'Can't afford to. The money we get is nearly all used up subsidising the farm. Besides, bustling around like Mrs Mop gives me the opportunity to winkle out any residents who've slumped into depression, on the pretext of needing to give their rooms a good going over.' She sighed. 'But I doubt our efforts at frugality will be enough to keep us going for much longer ... That isn't a flask you're scrabbling around for is it? Because I could do with a drink right now myself.'

'I wish it was – didn't think to take precautions against my skinful wearing off before morning. Have one of these though?'

He held out the cigarettes. They both took one. He bent his head to within kissing range as he lit Helen's. But she appeared to be a world away as she sucked down a lungful of smoke.

'We've a team of inspectors from the MOD coming down next month and I know they're expecting to see more evidence of attempts at rehabilitation – no matter how often we tell them it'd be counterproductive. Peter's going into Lewes tomorrow to see if he can get anyone to take on the more able residents for a few hours a week. If any agree – and why shouldn't they because it'll be free labour – then I'll be spending all my time counselling and supporting them through the trauma of being back in society again. So perhaps we will have to get someone in then, and maybe the farm will have to go. Peter will be heartbroken.'

'At losing playing his starring role as Son of the Soil?'

She squinted at him as she pulled on her cigarette. 'Why do you always hold such uncharitable opinions about him? Peter will be devastated at seeing his noble experiment undermined by petty bureaucrats who've no idea of what we're trying to do here.'

'And you?'

'Oh, I'll be angry. And probably take it out on him. Then we'll both be miserable.'

She walked to one side, bent down, and examined a spider's web spanning the bare branches of a bush.

'Still, I suppose we've had a good run at it and even good things have to come to an end.'

Stephen didn't know whether she was referring to Beddingham Hall or the disintegration of her marriage. And he didn't want to ask. The thought of it being either made him feel queasy: the first on behalf of Edith, the second for himself. 'Seeing as we're on the subject of things that are worrying us, I'd like to take the plunge and ask your advice.'

She straightened up and stepped a pace closer. 'Is this why you plied me with a cigarette? So I'd stay out here because we both know Peter thinks a woman smoking is irredeemably ugly.'

'You always look beautiful to me.' He'd tried to throw the line away but it hung in the air like the spider's sticky thread. 'It's to do with Edith of course. Obviously I can't tell you what's at the root of her problems except to say I don't think it's dissimilar to the trauma you say the men will have to go through when they have to face the brunt of society's rejection again. Hers is compounded, however, by a deep and abiding rejection of herself. With due cause, I may add. That I can help her overcome – or come to terms with at least. My quandary is whether to reveal to her something that she doesn't consciously know at present, but could destroy her equilibrium if she does.'

'Then what is the point in telling her?'

'There is a chance the truth may emerge from her subconscious at a later date.'

'Do you think that likely?'

'No … I don't think so … I don't know. She has dissociated it from the moment she was old enough to have any awareness of her self, and her conscious mind is actively repressing that a secret may even exist at all.'

'If she does come across the truth …'

'That will never happen. I'm convinced that no one else can possibly know about it.'

'Okay, so if it does resurface of its own accord then; how do you think she will deal with it?'

'She'll weave an alternative story with plausible facts and motivations that will satisfy her rational mind completely.'

'Then why can't you work on helping her to do that?'

He dropped the neglected cigarette on the stone slab at his feet and pulverised it under his heel. 'Withholding from a patient is a clinical judgement whereas to replace self-deception with an actual deception is negligent, unprofessional, and unethical.'

Helen was looking at him, her head tipped to one side so her scar appeared silver in the moonlight. 'So the view from your moral high ground is that you're damned if you do, and damned if you don't?'

Could he sprint up the turret stairs and liberate a bottle of something from under Peter's nose? The pleasant numbness he'd been experiencing at the beginning of this encounter had evaporated to leave his mind, nerves, and skin, as prickly as hell.

'Do you realise that whenever we've ever discussed your treatment of any patient it's always revolved around your fear of failure and not their welfare at all?'

'That's not fair.' He sounded like a wailing schoolboy. His fingers fastened around the cigarette packet in his pocket.

'Fair or not, it's accurate. Peter and I were only talking about it the other day.'

'So now I'm the subject of idle gossip? Thank you very much.'

'I don't feel inclined to coax you out of yet another bout of self-pity, Stephen, so grow up. It was nothing of the sort and well you know it. We are your oldest friends – possibly your only ones given your inability to accept anything you deem to be criticism; you really should learn to stop being so over-sensitive.'

'Self-absorbed, defensive, blinkered … is there anything else you want to add to the litany of my character assassination while you're at it?'

He hit her with a challenging stare but, in the end, couldn't hold her gaze.

'I'm probably the only person in the world who can say this to you … Believe me, it doesn't give me any pleasure and I don't want to hurt you. I care about you. Very deeply. And I hate to see you punishing yourself so much …'

Stephen lit another cigarette, dragging down as much smoke as he could with his first puff.

'You appear to have no comprehension of what it's like to take a risk and get it wrong. Most of us mortals do it all the time, and are better people for facing up to the consequences. Oh, it's painful and humiliating at the time but it makes us appreciate other people's frailties, as well as our own. All the doubts you revel in expressing over clinical choices aren't really doubts at all: they're intellectual arguments to rationalise after the fact. The things we live to regret aren't the things we do, they're the things we don't do. Because we'll never know how they would've turned out … Do you remember the night of the medical school dance?'

How could he forget? He turned away so she wouldn't be able to read his face.

'We were in the rose garden. You were looking very handsome in that borrowed dinner suit, and I had on that terrible frothy creation that Susan ran up for me from a pattern book of her mother's. God, I must've looked a sight.'

'I thought you so lovely it took my breath away.'

Hardly louder than a whisper but her chuckle said she'd caught it all the same.

'I know you did. Your eyes shone with it. And that's the point: in that moment I knew you loved me more than anything else in the world. You'd even have changed your career path for me. I was certain of it then, and I'm certain of it now.'

He nodded. He didn't trust himself to speak again. Although he could no longer keep his back to her. Helen had closed her eyes, a soft smile making her look every bit as young as they'd been then.

'I stood there on the terrace, the music from the orchestra floating past whilst I plucked the petals from that rose you'd picked for me. I was doing *he loves me, he loves me not* and waiting for you to ask me to marry you.'

He felt as though she'd punched him in the stomach. His breathing turned shallow.

'You were? … I didn't realise … I thought … I assumed … you and Peter were always going off on those bicycle rides together … I didn't think I stood a chance … I couldn't have borne it if you'd turned me down … or worse, if you'd patted me on the cheek and laughed … I had no idea … it was beyond my wildest dreams that you might've wanted me to …'

His voice cracked. He stared at the smoke from the cigarette's glowing tip as it spiralled up in the still air. 'What might you have said, do you think?'

'That's one of those things we'll never know now. The moment has gone. The people we were then have gone. Don't you see, Stephen? Because you didn't possess the guts to taste failure all you are left with is the hollowness of an unanswered question.'

He could hear the *pop* of ping-pong balls on bats through the open window of the Hall's games' room. Not for the first time in his life he envied the men who wore their wounds on the outside.

'Tell me this then: if you loved me, why did you accept Peter?'

'I loved the two of you equally. But only he asked. He took the risk that you could barely look in the face. I know he gets under your skin – he even annoys me sometimes with his irony and cynical teasing – but that's because you're both men who believe deeply in things. However the difference between you is that he's prepared to fail in his quest to fulfil his dreams – like with this place – whereas you play things too safe. You always want the answer before you ask the question; to have worked out all the possible solutions before you address a problem; only to act when you feel yourself to be in the right.'

'You make me sound like an unmitigated prig and a boor. I do know my failings. I'm not perfect.'

'No, but you want to be. You feel you should be. You won't take the chance of finding out that you're even more fallible than you think you are. There's a supreme arrogance in that, Stephen.'

She shivered and pulled the rug more tightly around her shoulders.

'I have to go in. A couple of the men need injections to help them sleep. Are you coming? Peter will open some blackberry wine as a nightcap if you ask him nicely.'

'No, thanks. I think I'll take a walk.'

'Suit yourself. But don't brood or sulk. And be nice to me over the breakfast table.

I said everything I have because I love you as my oldest and dearest friend, please don't punish me for my honesty. Soon, if the Department has its way, it may be the only ideal I have left.'

PART V

BEDDINGHAM HALL

December 1927

In spite of the mental assertion that we are not going to perform a certain action, the idea of that action, owing to other conditions, acquires and maintains a dominance in consciousness which ultimately leads to its realisation.

CHAPTER FIFTY-TWO

Edith slipped on the bulky overcoat. Helen had sorted out an array of winter garments for her the minute the weather had started turning bitter but she'd left them bundled in the bottom of the wardrobe. She'd welcomed the hair-shirt scourge of wearing her thin cardigan over her blouse or the curtain-frock around the cold cottage, but now she had to venture outside and didn't relish the thought of dying slowly from double pneumonia. In the mournful hours of the night she'd realised atonement was the only way she'd ever be granted any rest from the chattering in her head. Words were the key: those who said too much were always made to suffer but sharing her secret shame would bring its own rewards. She had to seek him out before cowardice got the better of it.

*

The atmosphere up at the Hall was surprisingly festive. Edith had forgotten that last weekend had been Advent Sunday and it would be Christmas in a few weeks. A small group had commandeered the table in the window and were making cards and presents. One, with a billiard-ball smooth head and a fist-shaped dent in the back of his skull, was constructing a theatre in a shoebox. She hovered for a moment at his elbow, pulled by the memory of the intricate illustration she'd devoured in a Gamages' catalogue as a child and longed to find wrapped as a present under the tree. Every year was a disappointment of course; Granny ignored all her hints and never would have granted her something so nakedly pleasurable anyway. The man wiped his gluey fingers on his trousers before moving to one side.

'We're not exactly ready for curtain up as yet; still I reckon you'd be the perfect audience for a dress rehearsal, so you get in here and tell me what you think.'

Edith felt a little shy at the invitation but the model-maker's sense of pride and her curiosity were irresistible. She bent forward, scarcely daring to breathe in case she dislodged anything not securely stuck down. A portion of the lid had been wedged into the far end for a stage, and protruding from the sides of the box at precisely calculated angles so they fell into view one after another, was a series of painted scenic flats. Fastened with drawing pins pushed into the tabletop, cloth backdrops – probably cut from old sheets – were stretched flat. One was a woodland scene complete with impressionistic oak trees in green and brown, purple dots representing a carpet of shaded bluebells. The tiny head of an antlered deer poked its way onto one edge as if waiting for permission to run across. Another was a seascape whipped into shades of grey and sparkling white by a storm. The third had a pencil sketch in the centre of a fairytale castle perched atop a hill, conical-capped turrets pointing like fingers into a cluster of roughly outlined clouds. They were perfect examples of artistic imagination tempered by a draughtsman's attention to perspective and perception.

She sighed as she drew herself upright again. The world of Beddingham Hall came back into focus, rendered less threatening by a dusting of make-believe. Edith turned to deliver her verdict to the man shifting from foot to foot in anticipation. He was one of the ones with port-wine shiny skin stretched drum-tight over his face; slits for eyes – no lashes or eyebrows – and a mouth only defined by it being a hole. Months ago, the sight of him would've triggered a shiver of revulsion but now … now, she merely noted his appearance in relation to the others. It was like a hierarchy of deformities. She mentally slotted herself into the upper ranks of the echelon.

'This is outstandingly beautiful. You're very talented.'

'I was a set designer at the Lyceum before my call-up. Never get to work on the real thing again of course but my eye for detail is as sharp as it ever was. It's a gift for my Dora and Christopher; do you think they'll like it?'

'They'll treasure it for the rest of their lives, if for no other reason than it's clear the amount of love that went into the making of it.'

'Thank you, you're very kind. I don't want to be rude but I'd better get on if I'm going to get all the bits and pieces finished in time.'

He gave her a bow in lieu of a smile and set about cutting around the pencil outline of a cardboard dragon with tabs under its tail and front paw so it could stand up and be pushed around with ease by chubby fingers. Edith felt a pang for the children he would never see grow up and whose memories of him would probably fade in tandem with the patterns of bricks he'd inked on the theatre's external walls.

Shuffling her arms out of the coat sleeves, she moved away and sat in the winged chair beside the fireplace. The blazing log spat an ember at her feet. A chessboard was laid out within reach on a low stool. As she didn't know how long she'd have to wait, she cast furtive glances for anyone at a loose end who might be willing to help her pass the time with a game. But then the door opened and he came in. It had been such a long time since she'd seen him and in the intervening period he looked to have shrunk in size and confidence. Catching sight of her, he appeared to struggle against an internal resistance before making up his mind to walk over. When he got closer she thought she could taste the layers of his disappointment and disapproval. Except how could that be when he didn't yet know? Perhaps not everyone was as blinkered in self-absorption as her and he'd guessed. How much worse would he feel when she told him? But he couldn't hate her as much as she hated herself for what she'd done.

He pulled across a chair and sat opposite her. Edith cleared her throat.

'I'm so very sorry about the plants, Arnold. I know you were as keen as I was to create something special.'

He tried to articulate something but then pulled a notebook from his pocket and laid it on his knee. He scribbled quickly before holding the page out for her to read.

My fault. Sent to work. Big garden at Firle.

He wrote some more.

Rabbits. Pest. Should've guarded until properly rooted.

'No, it wasn't rabbits. It was me.' She couldn't have him assuming responsibility. 'I pulled them up. And I shouldn't have done. It was a very ungrateful thing to do after all the time and trouble you took to make a garden for me. My only excuse is that I wasn't quite myself. But it was still a childishly spiteful act.'

Arnold gestured for his pad back.

Water under bridge. Enjoyed time together.

'Can you forgive me?'

This time his mouth worked. Edith watched, fascinated, as the muscles in his cheeks quivered.

'No … cause.'

His voice was rusty and the sound was like that made by an ill-practised ventriloquist but the light in his eyes conveyed all the meaning she needed. He didn't blame her, even after he knew the truth. It was clear he'd felt bad about the fate of the garden, however not distressed at the death of the plants. Schooled by her father to believe that attainment was everything, she'd never considered that the doing of something might be an achievement in itself. Exactly like the set designer who was taking such pride in crafting his theatre even though he'd never get to witness the joy and excitement it elicited. She took a moment to look around the room at those she'd shunned in her arrogance and ignorance. These men – who she'd pitied as shadows of their former selves with nothing to look forward to but an early death to end their misery – were stoic in the true sense of the word: no expectations, only the satisfaction of experience. Happiness, peace, contentment were words too small to contain the rewards of a life lived in such a way. Once upon a time, she'd thought she might have been able to be like them – hoped she could – but for the conspiracy of those hell-bent on making things otherwise. A line of them with a flaming torch of destruction passed from one to the other like a relay team. Her father. Edward. Dr Maynard. The branding iron was in his possession now and if he handed it back to Edward then it wouldn't be a case of third time lucky.

Arnold plucked two pawns from the chessboard and held them behind his back. All she had to do was to choose sides. The game could be relied on to play itself out after that.

CHAPTER FIFTY-THREE

Light from the cottage windows beckoned through the gathering gloom. It had been a month since he'd walked down the chalk path to face whatever awaited him. The past two weeks plucking up courage to return had been amongst the worst he could ever remember having to endure. Whilst not engaged in seeing his clinic patients or delivering badly prepared lectures to bunches of eager-faced students, he'd been wallowing in a succession of brandy bottles.

Stephen knocked tentatively on the door. He never expected to feel an affinity with the despicable Gerald Potter but the words he'd read in the journal punched into his head: *I am hardly able to sleep at nights knowing what rests on my actions and observations …* He rapped harder with his knuckles and called out Edith's name. There was no answer. Helen had said she'd been under the weather the last time he'd been at Beddingham Hall; maybe a chill had developed into a chest cold and she was bed-ridden. He should have ascertained her state of health first – another omission – but he hadn't wanted to subject himself to Peter's knowing glances at his own debauched pallor. He was ashamed to admit how much he hoped she was incapacitated, before belatedly remembering he was still a doctor and should check on her welfare.

The room was warmer than he expected. Paraffin stoves were placed in front of the fireplace and table, purple flames dancing in the grilles. The air was laced with fumes. Would they be enough to overcome an invalid? But the Hargreaves wouldn't have supplied them if they hadn't considered it safe. Placing his briefcase beside the armchair, Stephen took off his outdoor things and hung them on the back of the door before shutting it with a bang to alert

Edith to the fact she had a visitor. He called out her name once more then climbed the stairs. The door at the top was flung wide, the room empty, the bed made. Had she been taken so poorly she was in the infirmary? But then why would Helen be wasting fuel they could ill-afford on an empty cottage? Were the stoves in preparation for Edith's imminent return? The thought plunged him into another agony of indecision: to go or stay? To flee back to London on the pretext of allowing his patient to make a full recovery, or to wait and see which of them was really too weak to face an encounter?

Back down in the living room, Stephen paced around to try to bring an end to his dithering. Pausing to warm his icy fingers he spotted a folded piece of paper on the table behind the top of the heater. He picked it up. A note written in the same hand he'd come across unexpectedly once before. A poem, rather; he thought he recognised the language of John Donne:

And since thou so desirously
Did'st long to die, that long before thou could'st,
And long since thou no more couldst die,
Thou in thy scatter'd mystic body wouldst
In Abel die, and ever since
In thine; let their blood come
To beg for us, a discreet patience
Of death, or of worse life: for Oh, to some
Not to be Martyrs, is a martyrdom.

He read it again, slower this time, the words bouncing in front of his eyes as the paper magnified the tremor in his hands. Then he noticed it. A trail of dots staining the floorboards red. He felt sick as his eyes followed them to the bathroom tucked away under the stairs.

Stephen lunged forward, knocking over the stove. Hungry yellow flames spat up from the slick of spilt paraffin. Christ! What to do, what to do? Whirling back around, he snatched open the front door before lifting up the heater and throwing it outside. He expected to hear the whoosh of an explosion but the rush of air must've extinguished the flame. However the fire in the centre of the room was still burning. The pounding in his ears made it feel as if the walls were pressing in on him; there was a frozen waste where his stomach should've been; tears of panic coursed down his cheeks. He needed a wet towel. He ran to the bathroom. The door was locked. A large pool of red was creeping out from underneath.

'No! Please, God, no!'

With the strength of a madman he battered his shoulder again and again against the thick planks. His upper arm was numb before the catch gave way with a screech and splinter of wood. He dived inside, desperately wanting to close his eyes to the sight of Edith Potter with slashed wrists gaping as she oozed life at his feet. But the tiny space was empty. He grabbed a towel from the rail, soaked it under the basin taps, and dashed back to smother the flames.

He was on his hands and knees dabbing at the last remaining traces of unconsumed paraffin when he heard the front door open.

'Dr Maynard! What are you doing? And why is one of my precious heaters smashed up on the grass?'

'Edith ... You're okay ... I thought ... I thought ...'

'Not very clearly, evidently.'

Stephen felt disorientated by the waves of hysteria and nausea colliding in his chest. His trousers from the knees down were sodden – as was the entire front of his jacket – and the reek of paraffin was making his head spin. He hauled himself up using the table as support.

'Excuse me; I won't be a moment ...'

He staggered out into the cold drizzle and threw up violently until there was nothing left for him to give.

*

'I was feeling cooped up and went for a walk.'

'With the threat of an imminent storm?'

'The weather was acceptable enough when I left.'

She had donated the armchair and he was sitting wrapped in his overcoat and a blanket from her bed; his trousers and jacket steaming in front of the remaining stove. The room was beginning to resemble the inside of a London bus during a downpour.

'Did you forget it was Sunday? We have a standing arrangement for Sundays.'

'Of course I didn't; I'm not stupid. How was I to know you were going to bother to turn up seeing as you neglected so many others? I'm still waiting for an apology for the discourtesy of not even a word to release me from hanging around like a wallflower.'

She was being prickly and combative, her voice laced with a tone of contempt. He supposed he had it coming to him; she was right about his breaching the contract between them, and it must've been a shock to arrive back to witness the aftermath of him almost setting fire to her home. But not nearly such a shock as he'd had when he'd thought she'd killed herself.

'I am truly sorry about that, but I did make it clear that I'm seeing you in my own time and that there will be occasions when work with my other patients makes my absence unavoidable.'

It would do her no harm to realise that the entire world didn't revolve around Edith Potter. Besides, now wasn't time for the truth of why he'd acted like such a coward; in the mood she was in he wouldn't put it past her to take refuge in physically attacking him. She'd done it before when her anger hadn't been anywhere so near the surface. He tried to remind himself that she was playing the victim/rescuer/persecutor game again and that he mustn't allow his own raw emotions to suck him into the triangle.

'Tell me about the blood on the floor, Edith; did you cut yourself, have a nosebleed?'

'What? … Oh, the red ink. That's down to you, that is. Those watercolour pencils you gave me that time reawakened my interest in art. I've been taking drawing lessons from a very talented man up at the Hall. He wanted me to produce some pen and ink sketches but the nib kept getting blocked so I made a number of trips to wash it under the tap. Then decided to water down the bottle only to bang into the bathroom doorknob and drop it. At that point I decided some fresh air was called for … And you assumed … Got it into your head …'

She began choking on her laughter. Then let it out in great peals that bounced off the walls. As if he didn't feel humiliated enough sitting there without his trousers on. The look she gave him through her tears of mirth was triumphant. And vicious.

'Well then, show me. Let's see some of your artistic endeavours.'

'I threw them away. Tore them up in little pieces and cast them to the wind. They weren't good enough.'

Or had they been too revealing of her inner turmoil? He'd always believed that visual representations would be the key to circumventing her repression except now he knew the tenor of the horrors that might have resurfaced during the process. But he wouldn't push her until he felt ready to deal with the consequences; he was still more than a little shaky and, much as he didn't like to admit it, her antagonism was going way beyond making him irritated.

'Why the poem; did that have anything to do with the pictures you were working on?'

'It must be very tedious to have to try to force a connection between everything. Having nothing else better to do last weekend – for reasons you are very well aware of – I decided to see if I could sharpen my recall. You do remember I have problems with my memory, don't you?'

Stephen knew to show he wasn't immune to her goading would be a mistake so he bent forward to fiddle with the buckles on his briefcase. But as he pulled out the notepad, the blanket slipped from his knees and he ended up scrabbling to preserve his modesty like a maiden aunt mortified at revealing her bloomers. He was beginning to feel as if he hadn't any self-control left. She must be having the time of her life at his expense.

'So I flicked through the book of John Donne sonnets you so thoughtfully brought me from Fletching searching for one I might have memorised when I was going through one of the more romantic phases of my life – believe it or not I did have some. *Death Be Not Proud* had always been a particular favourite but when I sat down to write it out that other one flowed from my pen. More of that automatic writing from deep in my subconscious, no doubt. For which I owe you for planting the seed. Do you think it worth analysing for significance and portent?'

She'd finally done it. Laid the responsibility for everything – from his over-reaction, the accident with the stove, and each of the factors that had led him to draw his erroneous conclusion – firmly at his own door. Slammed shut with a hefty dose of mockery. She was grinning at him now with …

Stephen leapt to his feet, his concern over cutting a ridiculous figure eclipsed by the feeling that at any moment he might erupt with fury. He covered the distance to the bathroom in three strides.

'Just as I thought. No glass. You smashed the bottle, Edith, remember? So where's the glass?'

'I cleared it up.'

'No you didn't. You told me you went straight out for a walk.'

'Maybe I implied that but it was after I picked up the shards.'

'The wastepaper basket in here is empty so what did you do, put the pieces in your pocket and scatter them in the fields?'

'Precisely.'

'You're a liar.'

He stepped back into the living room, his whole body shaking.

'You heartless bitch; was it Helen who told you about Olive?'

'Another of your unrequited love affairs?'

'I bet she did. You set this up. You knew I was terrified of another patient committing suicide whilst under my care and you wanted me convinced I'd pushed you into taking your own life. How could you be so cruel? What have I ever done to make you hate me so much except try to help?'

She had been looking down at her feet but now she stared straight into his eyes, the inhuman coldness of her gaze evaporating his outrage. Then her mind disengaged and there was nothing. Edith was gone. This could be the beginning of her edging back into a catatonic stupor. He had to do something quickly. But what? Could he leave her even for a minute? Why hadn't the Hargreaves thought of installing an alarm in the cottages; or he of arming himself with a sedative? That's what he'd do, go and find Helen. With any luck she'd be starting the drugs round about now.

Stephen snatched up his trousers, blew out the stove flame, wrapped the blanket around Edith, briefly checked her pulse and breathing, then ran out into the rain.

CHAPTER FIFTY-FOUR

His feet slid from under him as he took a shortcut across the grassy slope. When he reached the Hall, six of the more able-bodied men were negotiating their way through the entrance with a large Norway Spruce. Stephen pushed past roughly and one of the troupe ended up face first in the needled branches. Obscenities tracked him up the stairs. Helen was emerging from a consulting room.

'Do you have the dispensary key on you?'

She nodded. He grabbed her arm.

'Hurry. Edith needs something to knock her out. Right out. Comatose. Insensible. Now!'

Something of his urgency got through Helen's surprise and she ran with him down the corridor. She opened the door to the dispensary without breaking stride.

'Okay, I'll trust your clinical judgement on this one, Stephen, but I decide what to give her, right?' Helen unlocked the drugs cupboard and pulled out a number of vials and a hypodermic syringe. 'Vital signs?'

'Thready pulse. Rapid, shallow breathing. Clammy skin. The sort of pallor you'd expect from shock ...'

'What have you done to her?'

'Nothing. Except maybe take that risk you were so keen on ...'

It wasn't fair to blame Helen but he'd heaped so much of it on himself on the mad dash over that he couldn't take any coming from another quarter.

'... She did it to herself – or rather, he did. Look, I'll explain at a more appropriate moment.'

'Point taken. Has she eaten today?'

'You're in a better position to know something like that.'

Helen had picked out two vials and appeared to be weighing them up in either hand.

'She was at the Hall all morning ...'

'So she didn't go out for a walk?'

'... playing chess with Arnold which means she'd have had a pretty good luncheon. This one then.' She pocketed the drug. 'What are you afraid of, self harm?'

'No, not at this stage: that'll she'll become catatonic.'

'Did she have a fugue?'

'Not in the classic sense – no foaming at the mouth, drumming heels ...'

'And the moment I administer this she'll be in no state to. Let's hope there were no seizures in the meantime. But if needs be I'll get an ambulance out and the hospital can take it from there. Assuming everything's okay, I'll sit with her while it takes effect.'

They were on the terrace now.

'Go and tell Peter what I'm up to and get him to lend you some dry clothes; I don't fancy having to play nursemaid when you collapse in a fever.'

Helen ran down the slope and turned when she reached the sure footing of the path.

'And a large slug of brandy. Doctor's orders. Tell him I'll batter his brains out if he raises so much as one eyebrow.'

Her voice had barely reached him through the wind funnelling off the Downs. The rain was coming off Stephen in rivulets before he dragged his heavy legs into the shelter of Beddingham Hall.

*

Two hours later, he let himself into the cottage. Helen was slumped in the armchair, her exhaustion making her look vulnerable and ethereally beautiful.

'Edith's all tucked up and out like a light. She's fine, Stephen, no damage done.'

Stephen gave an account of the near-disaster with the stove and how Edith had walked in on him dousing the flames. He left out everything else.

'Well, that explains everything then – her stunned withdrawal, the scorch marks on the floor, the ruined towel, and the irreparable heater.'

'I was stupidly clumsy, and then I panicked. I'll pay for a new one of course.'

'Don't be daft. These things happen. I'm only glad it was you knocked it over and not Edith. I should have considered that possibility when I offered them to her, but not having had the experience of children to alert me to the dangers.'

Her expression was so sad Stephen wanted to take her in his arms and soothe it away.

'Are you going back to London tonight or would you like to stay for supper? Your room's made up and you could always catch the Lewes milk-train if you need to be at the clinic early.'

The way she made it sound as if he belonged up at the Hall, with her, made his blood tingle.

'I won't thanks. Only I will stay. Here with Edith.'

'A bedside vigil is all very laudable but totally unnecessary. After what I've given her she will have no awareness of your presence, and probably no memory of anything that happened from the moment she finished her last chess match with Arnold. When she comes to, some time tomorrow afternoon, she'll have slept through the effects of the shock and be no worse off than if she'd simply come down to her empty cottage. Edith Potter is upstairs dead to the world, Stephen; you don't have to sit around playing the martyr because of something that could have happened, but didn't.'

How could she possibly know that in trying to get him of the hook she'd just reminded him of everything he'd prefer to forget? It was more than a little tempting to ask her to stick one of her magic needles in his arm. He peeled off Peter's oilskin cape.

'Here, take this. It's cats and dogs outside. Ask one of the farmhands to wake me when they round up the cows for milking, will you? I won't say goodbye in the morning, but all being well, I'll see you next Sunday.'

'Have you forgotten that'll be Christmas Day? There'll be no trains. Why don't you come down on the Friday night and stay over to celebrate with us – if you haven't any other plans? We have a bit of a carol concert but after that it's nothing but eating, drinking, and making merry. You can let me know what you decide. I don't want you fretting about Edith whilst you're away from us though; she'll soon be back to normal.'

He almost winced at Helen's use of such a layman's casual prognosis. But she'd performed a clinical intervention and therefore the patient was now under dual care: next weekend he'd reveal everything about Edith Potter. The thought of having Helen to hold his hand through the minefield was all the reassurance about the future he needed. He bent down, pecked her on the cheek, and then walked up the stairs to Edith's bedroom before he said – or did – anything he'd regret in the cold light of a less traumatic day.

*

He'd found some candles, and the room was bathed in the soft tranquillity of a shrine. The storm had blown itself out a long while back to be replaced by a temperature he could see dropping, degree by degree, in the huffiness of his breath; there'd be snow on the ground before dawn. The armchair fitted neatly between the wall and the bed, and with both their overcoats topped by a spare eiderdown he'd found in the top of the wardrobe draped over him, Stephen was able to remain immobile without freezing solid. The flask of gin he'd liberated from Peter's sideboard helped.

For hour after hour, he watched the rise and fall of Edith's chest. Her breathing was steady with only an occasional cat-dream muscle tremor in her limbs to remind him that she wasn't catatonic. Their relative positions were so reminiscent of the asylum that he wondered what he had to show for the past year of his life. He'd thought professional recognition and the adulation of his students would bring him happiness. The whole package of everything he'd ever wanted had been so close: respect; veneration; a secure financial future; a shelf of published books; invitations to speak at the psychological institutes in Vienna and America; an end to self-doubt; satisfaction. But he had none of those things – not permanently or irrevocably or in any sense that mattered. If he was summoned to the Pearly Gates now, in the lonely death-watch of a new day, and St Peter asked him to account for himself then he could do so in one word: failure. He scrabbled on his lap for the flask. The raw spirit burned his throat and brought tears to his eyes. Helen was right about gin lubricating his maudlin streak. Except if he couldn't indulge in both when he was in all-but solitary confinement, then when could he?

'Have you ever mused on why I drink so much, Edith? To seek refuge in the bottle? Quite simple really, and not unlike what you're experiencing with your veins full of sedative: a numbing of the pain. The ache – physical, and in the soul, and in the psyche; a longing, a pull, a tug into despair. To escape the incessant need to probe the wound.'

He took another swig from the flask, the skin on his fingertips sticking momentarily to the cold metal.

'It's shaped me into the man you see sitting before you and I hate the thought that I'm sadder, wiser, more cautious, scared, diminished … all because of this one trick of fate. I've turned into a not very nice person, Edith; I'm vengeful and bitter, and want she who has caused me such pain to suffer for it. Once upon a time I was so self-contained but now my happiness depends on things over which I have no control or on the whim of someone else to want to change things. And she's made it very clear to me since our re-acquaintance that she doesn't.'

Why hadn't he thought to steal a packet of cigarettes along with the gin? He expected that if he went up to the Hall he'd probably find something to smoke left about in the recreation room. Only he'd made a promise to himself that, other than a call of nature, he'd maintain his vigil until it was time for the train. Not that it would make any difference to Edith. But he owed her the sacrifice. Besides, they say to shrive oneself is good for the soul and he'd never said any of this – drunk or sober – to a single person; the fact she couldn't hear him or comprehend a single word in the depths of her unconsciousness made no difference to the lightening of his burden. Or, rather, it did. The flask was three-quarters empty now and his focus was dancing around the candle flames. He wasn't about to close his eyes in sleep though; the gin-fuelled energy surging through him would see to that.

'Do you know something I've never understood about you, Edith? Why you took flight in catatonia … wasn't that a bit like being dead? I suppose there are two types of people when it comes to pain: those who run away, and those who embrace it. The latter not because they are brave or masochistic or need to prove to themselves they can fight the dragon, but because it makes them feel alive. Right plumb centre of that camp is where I'd put myself. Can you understand that over and above all the anguish is the fear that if I fell out of love with her tomorrow then all the emotion in me would be extinguished forever? I'll never be happy again. Ah ha, you might well say that I'm not happy now – which is true and just goes to show that you really have been paying attention – but sadness, grief, desperation are all preferable to an unbroken bleak expanse of nothingness. The fact I can feel anything at all is fundamentally what distinguishes me from this bed or the cottage or the ice crystals hitting the window. And, when I weigh everything in the balance, that is a good thing.'

The warmth of the gin and his growing conviction that he'd hit on a profound philosophy stirred Stephen to a decision he wouldn't have contemplated in any other circumstances. If he let it out then the purgatory of waiting a whole week until he could unburden himself to Helen was one thing he didn't have to endure. Raising himself on stiff joints, he untucked the bedclothes around Edith's feet before stumbling over to light new candles from the stubs of the old. He secured them in their holders then moved two to the side of the cabinet to spill their brightness fully on Edith's face. The third he picked up and stood where he could both reach Edith's foot and scrutinise her features at the same time. If she displayed she could feel any sensation by a response even as small as a rapid movement of her eyeballs under their lids then he'd know she was in a state analogous to a hypnotic trance and he wouldn't take the risk. A touch unsteady – from the alcohol and the numbness in his calf muscles – he lifted Edith's right ankle, counted to five, and then brought the flame to lick the skin of her sole at the same time as pin-pointing all his attention on discerning any reaction. None. He performed the action a second time just to make sure.

Stephen placed the candle beside the others, re-covered Edith's feet, then returned to the armchair. He reached into the inside pocket of Peter's jacket for the slim bundle of papers he'd transferred from his own sodden one. Ever since he'd written them, the notes never left his person; he slept with them under his pillow. They were the only remaining evidence that the journal had ever existed – it had never been published, he was certain of that: the world of psychology would have thought very differently about Dr Gerald Potter if it had. And Stephen had destroyed the original on a pyre in Fletching churchyard on the eve of his discovery.

He drained the flask of gin. No matter that his sight had become too blurry to read, he knew every word by heart from all the times he'd gone over them during those terrible weeks holed up in Uckfield. He could recite them chapter and verse at the drop of a hat – not that he was ever going to. When he eventually told Helen, he'd keep it to the bare bones and spare her – and him – from having to listen to the details. Stephen laid the notes on the bed to breach the space between him and Edith. He coughed and cleared his throat.

'I got it wrong. I thought your father resented you for the fact that your mother sacrificed her life for yours. And your games about a childhood imaginary friend, automatic writing, and hearing voices led me down the path of multiple personalities. It didn't cross my mind – not once – that there might be an alternative explanation. But I know now. I know why you hated him so much and I know what he did to you.'

He could stop at this point. Shut his mouth on the rest. Except he couldn't. The alcohol had made him loquacious; besides, it would take the willpower of a saint to deny himself the redemption of confession and he was no Thomas Becket. Stephen closed his eyes and the room spun briefly.

'When you were so badly burned … Oh, Jesus, Edith, I'm sorry. I didn't realise until now what you must've felt walking in to find me putting out a blaze. No wonder you acted the way you did, went into shock. I'll make it up to you, I promise; if you do by any chance have any recall I can replace the memory with a more pleasant one under hypnosis. A highly unethical practice but you won't tell anyone, will you?'

He giggled. The tension in his chest relaxed a notch. But he'd started crying. The tears fell onto his clasped hands.

'After the fire, only your father and the surgeon he instructed knew the extent of your injuries. And your father kept it from you. If it weren't for his journal I might've thought he did that out of kindness. To prevent you feeling incomplete over what you had lost. But in it he revealed himself to be a monster.'

The gin rebelled in his stomach and a bitter thread of bile rose to his throat.

'He experimented on you, his own child. He wanted to see what would happen if you were presented to the world as one thing, but inside you were another. You were to be his contribution to the great Nature versus Nurture debate. That is the root of your psychosis. That is why your mind first split, and then concealed. That is why you suffered as intensely as you did: you were being controlled by a knowledge you'd have done anything to keep secret from your conscious self.'

His tongue felt fat and clumsy and stuck to the roof of his mouth. There were only so many words with which to say it. He had to get them out. He squeezed her hand under the blankets as he worked hard to squash the revulsion he still felt at Dr Potter's words: *Abnormality or conformity? Can you turn what is humanly unacceptable into normality? We will see …*

'You were born Edward Potter. The fire that so nearly took your life, took your masculinity, and with it your identity. Your father did the rest.'

*

The room was quieter than he would've thought possible. Once he felt he could stand without falling over, Stephen took his notes and the remaining lit candle over to the tiny hearth. With his back to the bed, he held the wad of paper by one corner as flames first charred silver and grey, then turned the truth into nothingness.

CHAPTER FIFTY-FIVE

At the smell of smoke, Edith's eyes sprang open and she turned her head to watch him.

CHAPTER FIFTY-SIX

Edith caught the dribbles of water sliding down her newly bare neck and wrapped the towel around her head. Helen had taken her into Lewes to get her hair cut and the image that had stared back from the salon mirror had been startling. The whole visit had been a great success. They'd purchased some block mascara, rouge, and a tube of soft-pink lipstick. Helen had chatted away the entire trip making her feel both special and ordinary at the same time; in a circle of attention but not the centre of it.

As a consequence, Edith hadn't once felt Helen's company to be hard work during the entire day. Not like when she'd been angling for Helen to grant a mother's approval and pride in her accomplishments, or when she'd played the role herself for the hapless vicar's wife all that time ago in Fletching. She could now see that's what she'd been doing with both women; what the difference was between those still-born relationships and uncomplicated friendship free of the burdens of control or need.

She hadn't been able to make much conversation herself but Helen didn't seem to mind as she bustled about buying up the things on her list for the Christmas party. There'd been rolls of red and green crêpe paper to decorate the table edges, some glittery snowflakes to hang from the rafters, a few small presents to put in the bran tub. Everything else had been taken care of. The mistletoe was to be cut from the gnarled apple trees flanking the terrace at the back of the Hall, and Arnold had been charged to gather as much holly and ivy as could be loaded onto a hand barrow.

All these preparations Edith felt a part of, but strangely outside. She hadn't celebrated Christmas in over a decade – there had never been any point with her father for whom one day was exactly the same as the next and she'd been disinclined to endure the sadness of going through the rituals of the festive season alone. So this was to be a first in many ways. A fresh start. Perhaps the true spirit of Christmas with its promise of new life and salvation. She was looking forward to it.

Against her own rules, Helen had given Edith a mirror. Not a large one that could splinter and cut but in the lid of a compact, its surface fuzzy with a coating of powder. Edith would try her hand at applying the mascara while her hair dried. She thought she'd need a number of goes to get it right because she could only see the reflection of one eye at a time and the result might end up with her looking like a clown. Ditto with the rouge, of course, but she hadn't been so sure about using that anyway and had only agreed to its purchase to make Helen happy.

Edith left the bathroom and walked over to the table. The gifts she'd got for the Hargreaves were sitting in the centre of the sheet of hand-decorated paper the theatre designer had given her. Two identical packets of pen nibs. She'd been wrong-footed when Helen had said they needed to split up as she had to buy Edith's present. The thought of being given anything hadn't occurred to her and, panicked by the obligation to reciprocate, she'd plunged into the first shop she'd come to on Lewes High Street. The stationers. She was embarrassed by her choice the minute they'd come back and Helen had thrust a tissue-covered square in her hands and insisted Edith open it immediately; she'd said it wouldn't wait until Christmas itself as it was for wearing tonight. It was draped over the end of Edith's bed now. A beautiful satin coffee-coloured chemise edged in lace, the straps slender ribbons embroidered with tiny cream daises. She hadn't tried it on yet. Didn't dare in case she creased the fabric or got it dirty. The temptation to wash her hands again was almost overwhelming but she reminded herself that her knuckles were already as red as Rudolph's nose, and wrapped up the inadequate gifts to her benefactors instead.

*

With her hair dry and brushed until she could feel it as slick as a helmet under her palms, Edith glanced at her watch. There were still some hours to go. She could fill in the time by reading – her eyesight wasn't as bad as it had been and would stand looking at the rose book if she ignored the small print Latin names in italics. But her heart wasn't in her garden at the moment; it represented her far future and that had come increasingly difficult to picture. The roses would wait for when she was ready to give choosing the care and attention it warranted. If she learned nothing else from her stay at Beddingham Hall, she'd take away the imperative to put your energies into the minutes and hours immediately before you because something could so easily happen to snatch the rest away forever. Just as she'd lost all those in the asylum, and many, many more since then. Already, for that one thing alone, she was an older and wiser woman.

For the first time since she'd been inside St Margaret's church in Fletching, Edith got down on her knees to pray. With her palms together like a Sunday School child, and her elbows resting on the edge of the bed, she gave thanks before cataloguing her faults and misdemeanours and beseeching forgiveness. One by one, she felt the burdens she'd been carrying fall away. She stood up cleansed and renewed, and determined to remain that way. She'd turn over the new leaf by doing something for others with no expectation of return – hidden or otherwise. Slipping the curtain-frock over her head, Edith left the bedroom with the intention of accepting any task Helen might choose to give her without complaint, even if it meant peeling every potato for this evening's dinner.

CHAPTER FIFTY-SEVEN

'We have had a high old time of it recently, haven't we, Ede? I don't know about you but I'm quite exhausted from leading the merry dance.'

Edward was sitting in the armchair tamping down the tobacco in his pipe.

'Where have you been hiding yourself all day? Chatting up at the Hall over tea and crumpets with the frog-faced man? Helen? I must say that of the two of them I prefer her. She reminds me of the rubber planter's wife in La Paz – different colouring, of course, the sun would've flayed off her Celtic skin in a second. Oops, sorry, insensitive of me to bring up a topic we are so touchy about.'

'Why have you come back? What do you want?'

'I never left, remember; we are two parts of a whole. A circle complete and entire of itself. And I wanted us to talk. A little heart-to-heart is long overdue, don't you think?'

'I'm not sure I've got anything to say …'

'Which is why it's so good there are two of us because I've more than enough words bottled up inside me to last a lifetime. After all, I wasn't really allowed to stray onto the things that really mattered on the picnic, was I? You were very naughty then, sidetracking me away from my history and onto stories you invented for the two of us to share. But I'll forgive you for overlooking my needs – mainly due to the fact that from now on everything is going to be rebalanced … in my favour. You owe me, Ede. You owe us. It's not really as if you issued an invitation, I had to crawl through the chinks in your armour; jolly hard work it was too. However, I've got a taste for the limelight now and I'm never going back. Are you ready for us to saunter arm in arm down memory lane?'

'I don't remember anything.'

'Oh, I think you do. Everything is as clear as a bell in my mind which means the same can be said of yours. Pretence … what does the Good Doctor call it? Repression, that's it … doesn't suit you. It makes you a lesser person, which of course, without me you are. Shall we start at the beginning and trip up through the years, pushing aside all the stumbling blocks as we go?'

'I don't want to.'

'Yes, we do. Now, let's see … the first life you so ruthlessly disposed of was mine.'

'It was none of my doing; if you believe everything in that filthy journal then I didn't exist.'

'Please don't tell me you're doubting God's Honest Truth? Because that's what our father was for the both of us. The heavens cracked, bolts of lightning flew, and with a wave of His magic wand – or rather a scalpel and a fair degree of imagination – there you were. And there I wasn't. You have no idea how long I cried for the loss of my little pee-pee. Or perhaps you do because you must have started into being the moment the flames gobbled up my privates. A judicious nip and tuck or two, and, voilà. Welcome, Edith: goodbye, forever, Edward. But God wasn't as omniscient as He thought and overlooked the fact I might not want to leave. You've always known: you've always known everything.'

'How could I have done? I was less than three years old.'

'It's going to get very tiresome if I have to keep correcting you the entire time … I was less than three years old, you had only just been created. A gleam in our father's eye, as the saying goes. But as I've so amply demonstrated over the past year or so, I do enjoy a little gamesmanship; you'll never outwit me but I guarantee we'll have fun while you try. And, truly, I have nothing else better to do. Tell me, I'm curious, what was it like growing up as Edith Potter?'

'I was as happy as could be expected with no mother and all the physical frailties that went with the accident.'

'Can we agree on one thing and not be mealy-mouthed about what went on? If we have to refer to it again – and I'd really prefer if we didn't – can we use the term *butchery*?'

'Father and Granny were strict but I got a good education, a thorough grounding in the science disciplines ...'

'Displaced attention to make up for the absence of love, no doubt. God Turned Satan regarded you as an experiment – isn't that what the Good Doctor babbled out amongst the gin fumes? The old woman who was unfortunate enough to give birth to such a travesty of humanity cursed him for being the fruit of her loins. She forgot and called you by my name sometimes, didn't she? And taught you to treat him with the contempt he deserved.'

'You're wrong: I revered Father, respected him. He took me to Institute meetings; spent hours drilling me on the fundamentals of mathematics; had me read books by some of the heroes of his own youth – Newton, William Herschel, Leonhard Euler. All in all, he responded to me as if I were his ...'

'Son. Well, well, that's slip up number one. You sensed something was awry way back then, didn't you? Don't deny it. And when he'd proved his point, he cut you adrift. Isn't that the way it went?'

'He was a busy and eminent man. He had no time for a child's inane prattle. In time, I learned only to engage in conversation when I had something worthwhile to say.'

'The silence between you was your choice? I don't think so. It's a good job I was beginning to emerge from the fog of oblivion about then or there'd be no one left alive to point out the errors of your ways. Why did you murder him, by the way? Was it something he said?'

'That's an appalling accusation. He was smothered in his bed by an itinerant whilst I was fetching his medicines from Uckfield.'

'All right, I'll admit it, you have a point there. I was the one made the thought manifest – I must say I rather take to your description of me as a soul with no fixed abode, most apposite. But, of course, that means I have no bodily presence of my own, so you were not, by any stretch of the imagination, absent at the moment of consummation. We spent a fair bit of time in that cottage together, didn't we? I grew rather fond of the place. Began to quite like your company; you weren't always so miserable and dreary. I admired your desire to surround us by frivolous things – the boy's blue knitted jacket was a very nice touch. That you selected it especially made me feel most indulged. Except I don't want you to go running away with the thought that the good ideas were only ever yours. Putting the notion of a picnic in our head was entirely my own stroke of genius. You invented the first one to inject a little romance into an unlovable young woman's life; I created the opportunity for the reprise in order to reduce the sting of that quack's facile condemnation.'

'He said all my physical symptoms could be put down to loneliness.'

'Just goes to show how wrong you can be. Little did he know that Edith Potter was never alone. Not for one single second in all her appropriated life. It did the trick though, didn't it? Made you realise how much you need me.'

'We were going to go away, travel abroad …'

'And we would have done too. I meant every word of that. I have never told a falsehood to you, Ede. How could I when that would mean lying to myself and there's only so much self-denial a being can stomach without leading himself so far astray he begins to doubt his own existence. And then where would we be, eh?'

'I wouldn't be here or have been locked in a loony bin; I'd have my mind back.'

'None of those things can you lay at my door.'

'You drove me to it.'

'Did what I had to for our own protection. Imagine what would have happened if someone else had read that journal other than ourselves and Dr Maybe-Maybenot. Didn't you get fed up with his pansy dithering around the subject? Between us we'd laid it all out for him in those séance sessions of his, if only he'd had the wits to see it. Couldn't have given him more clues if we'd tried. The boy, of course, was unfortunate. Don't feel badly about it because you had no choice but to do what you did; the little snot-nose would've sold a glittering prize like that to the highest bidder – even if he didn't comprehend the content. And it being written by such a pillar of the medical establishment, it's clear it would've been snapped up by the wrong hands sooner or later. I think we should be grateful we heard the gory details the other night and not read them splashed over the newspapers. Because then they'd have labelled you a freak instead of a madwoman. Perhaps had another go at shooting all that electricity through our head to split our mutually beneficial partnership asunder ...'

'Aren't those things exactly what will happen now?'

'Far from it. I made a promise to you, Ede, and you should know by now that my word is as good as my bond. We're going away together. I sorted out everything we need earlier. We're travelling light. And we're leaving now. Although, on second thoughts, do us both a favour and change out of that hideous frock, will you? I would hate for the way you look now to be the lasting impression.'

*

Edith, dressed in an inappropriately thin silk shirt and moss-green tweed skirt Helen had slipped into her wardrobe to wear at the Hall's Christmas party, carried the straight-backed chair so often occupied by Stephen Maynard out onto the snow-covered grass. It was Edward who was responsible for the coil of rope.

Printed in Great Britain
by Amazon

32149886R00209